WestBow Press books may be ordered through booksellers or by contacting:

WestBow Press
A Division of Thomas Nelson & Zondervan
1663 Liberty Drive
Bloomington, IN 47403
www.westbowpress.com
1 (866) 928-1240

Scripture taken from the King James Version of the Bible.

Designed by: Caitlin Blackmore & WestBow Press

ISBN: 978-1-5127-6477-2 (sc)
ISBN: 978-1-5127-6478-9 (hc)
ISBN: 978-1-5127-6476-5 (e)

Library of Congress Control Number: 2016919454

Print information available on the last page.

WestBow Press rev. date: 1/30/2017

To: Carolyn,

THE HOUSE OF
BLOOD AND TEARS

Lenore Eidse

Lenore Eidse

A. van Tongeren

Carolyn,
Thank you so much
for coming out tonight!
Enjoy the read!
Joanne van Tongeren :)

WESTBOW
PRESS®
A DIVISION OF THOMAS NELSON
& ZONDERVAN

Dedicated to the memory of Anje's mother,
Hillie H. Stutvoet Minnes

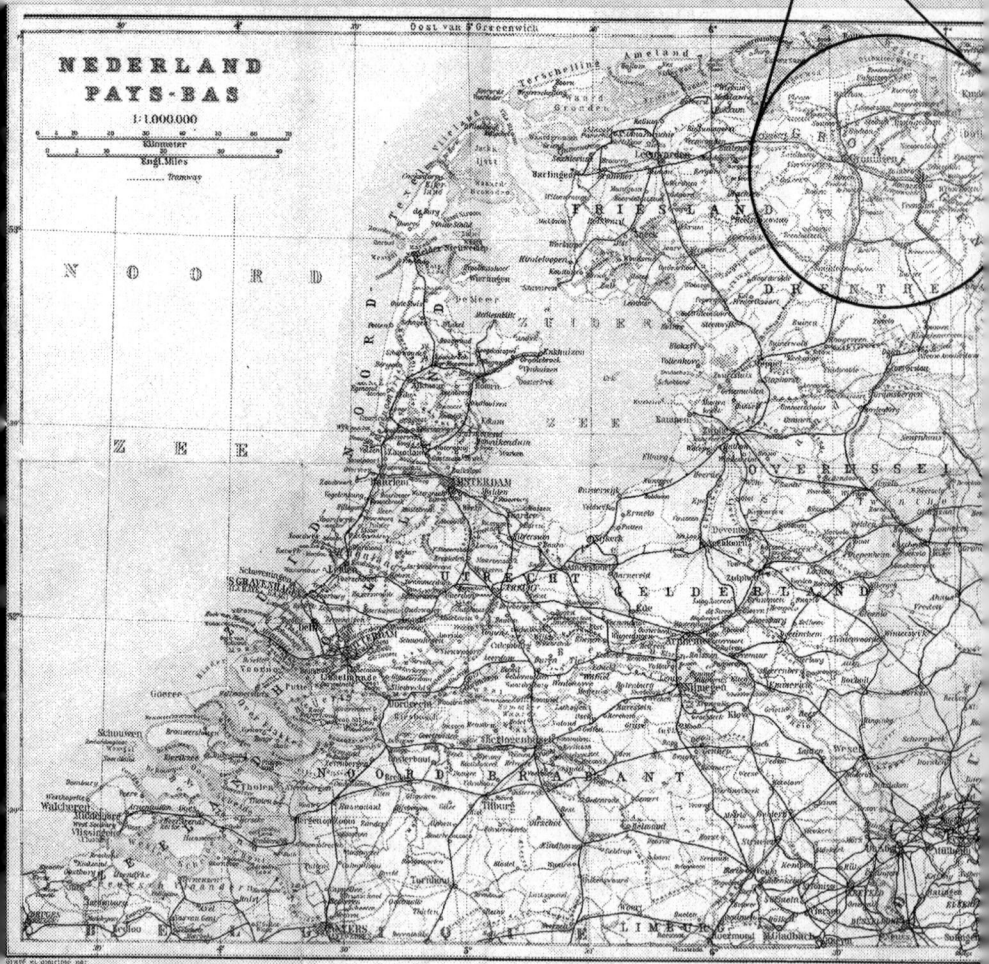

Groningen, Holland

NEDERLAND
PAYS-BAS
1:1.000.000

GRONINGEN

1:18.000

0 100 200 300 400
Meter

1 Archiefgebouw   C3
2 Militaire Hoofdwacht   C3
3 Muziekschool   B3
4 Nederlandsche Bank   C4
5 Telephoonkantoor   C3
6 Universiteits Bibliotheek C3
7 Goudkantoor   C3
8 Korenbeurs   B4

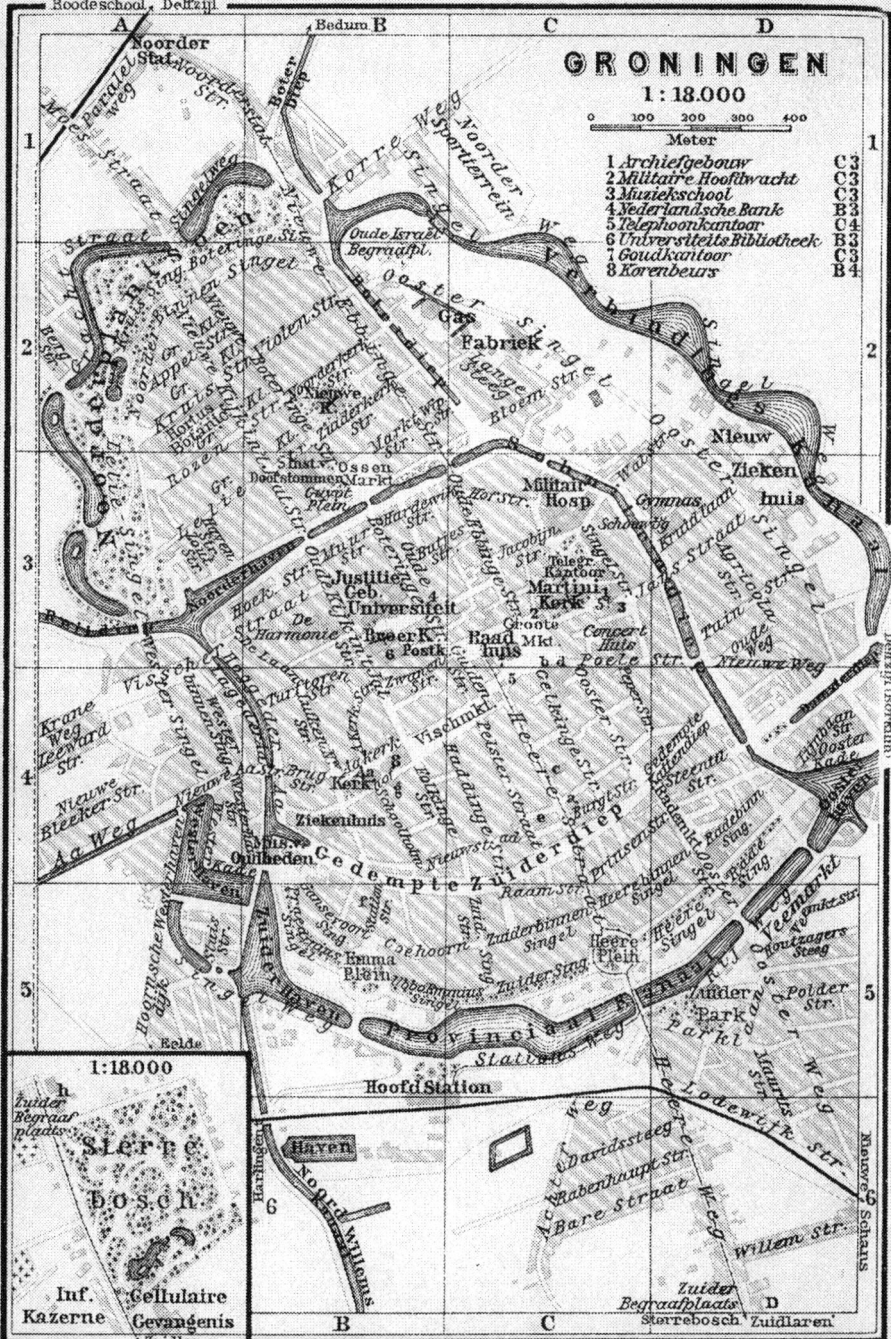

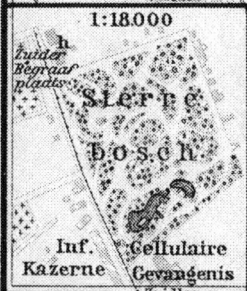

Roodeschool, Delfzijl

A   Bedum   B   C   D

Noorder Stat.

Noorderstraat
Mozerstraat
Singelweg
Noorddiepstraat
Boteringe Singel
Bote Dwp
Korre Weg
Noorder Sporterrein
Spoorwegsingel
Noorder Singel
Oosterhamrikkade
Weg
Wester Singel

Oude Israel. Begraafpl.

Gas Fabriek

Nieuw Zieken huis

Oostersingel

Lange Haag Str.
Bloem str.

Inst. v. Ossen
Doofstommen Markt
Groote Plein
Guyot Plein
Nieuwe Ebbinge Str.
Kruisstraat
Hortus Botanicus
Appel Singel
Voorde Ebbinge Str.
Rozen
Kleine

Militair Hosp.
Horst Str.
Jacobijn Str.
Telegr. Kantoor
Martini Kerk
Gymnas.
Schoolholm
Jodenstraat
Agricola Singel

Justitie Geb.
Universiteit
Beer K.
6 Postk.
Raad huis
De Harmonie
Groote Markt
Concert Zaal
Poele Str.
Oude Weg
Nieuwe Weg

Krane Weg
Leonard Str.
Visschersdijk
Turftoren
Brug Str.
Viscmkt.
Heere Str.
Gelkingestr.
Oosterstr.
Steenti Str.
Hinderstr.
Ooster Kade

Nieuwe Bleeker Str.
Aa Weg
Nieuwe Kerk
Radesingel
Heere
Zuiderdiep

Gedempte Zuiderdiep
Mus. v. Oudheden
Ziekenhuis
Raamstr.
Zuiderbinnen Singel
Heerebinnen Singel
Radebin. Sing.
Veemarkt
Houtzagers Steeg

Emma Plein
Coehoorn
Zuider Sing.
Heere Plein
Heere Singel
Zuider Park
Polder Str.
Maurits Weg
Lodewijk Str.

Eelde
Provinciale Weg
Stations Weg

Hoofd Station

Harlingen
Haven
Noord Willems

a. Davidsteeg
Rabenhaupt Str.
Bare straat
Willem str.

Zuider Begraafplaats
Sterrebosch Zuidlaren

B   C   D

1:18.000

Zuider Begraafplaats
Sterre Bosch
Inf. Kazerne
Cellulaire Gevangenis
Zuidlaren

Delfzijl (Borkum)
Nieuwe Schans

Geogr. Anst. v. Wagner & Debes, Leipzig

"Courage is the first of human qualities, because it is the quality that guarantees all others."

— SIR WINSTON CHURCHILL

CONTENTS

FOREWORD

*T*he House of Blood and Tears is a historical novel based on the real-life story and experiences of Anje, a young and precocious yet very brave Dutch girl, during World War II and beyond.

Blood and tears? A young girl's life should not be tainted with blood and tears! And yet that was the case for so many European people who were the victims of the Nazi expansionist movement and atrocities. Blood? What else, when so many were inhumanely killed? Tears? What other reaction might there be when Anje's family was torn apart because of divided political loyalties?

In writing Anje's story and that of the Dutch people, Lenore Eidse has done a remarkable job in tracing the life of the young girl, Anje Minnes, from the idyllic country setting of the peaceful Netherlands prior to World War II through the terrors of that terrible war. Anje's involvement during that time was courageous; she helped the down-trodden and persecuted Jews to safety by supplying them with food, clothing, and forged documents. Her youth was her protection from the enemy; her skills were her value to the Resistance; and her tenacity was undaunting.

In years she was a child, but in strategy and tactics she was brilliant; her gifts did not go unnoticed and were utilized by those who had become the protectors of the homeland. Nothing fazed her, it seemed. On the outside, we see the young, carefree schoolgirl, yet on the inside, ideas, plans, and strategies were percolating in her brain—schemes far beyond her years.

It is a tribute to the author that she was able to draw the memories that were suppressed for over seventy years from the recesses of Anje's brain, and it reveals the trust the subject had in the author.

Corrie ten Boom and Anne Frank are names that we link with World War II in Holland. Anje and Hillie Minnes's exploits rank with the best, among the unsung heroes who were instrumental in saving many lives during the terrible atrocities committed during World War II. The documentation of their feats is vital in understanding the average and yet brave people who lived and made a difference.

Enjoy this book, a document of courage and fortitude, of good eventually prevailing over evil.

Hardy Enns
Educator and Volunteer Teacher in Lithuania, 1996–2007
April 11, 2016

PREFACE

As I was sitting and listening to Anje van Tongeren speak about her life at a Women's Aglow meeting, I was touched by her honesty and sincerity. Her experience of working for the Dutch Underground at the age of twelve was in itself incredible, but her stories also showed her ingenuity and intelligence. Who would think of hollowing out a fancy cake and placing phony ID cards inside to be carried right under the noses of the German police and delivered to another city? Anje did, and this was only the beginning of her journey. One day, as we were having tea at her place, I asked if she had ever thought of putting her story into print, and she said, "Yes, but I have no one to write it."

"I'll write it," I said boldly. I had no idea what I was getting myself into! And with this verbal agreement, we began, on December 28, 2008. At first we used a tape recorder, and when I found that too cumbersome, I resorted to longhand, which had served me so well during the years I had worked as a newspaper reporter. I began to interview Anje as she sat in her big, leather easy chair in her living room, where she was surrounded with her books. Books had always been her passion, and this was obvious. She had ordered a book every time she saw something that intrigued her—biographies, stories of World War II, the Holocaust, the Resistance, and stories of people who had survived the trauma of that war. The resources I needed to begin were sitting right there at our feet.

We began to pull more and more things from the "closet," and I discovered that her memory was amazing for an eighty year old. Thousands of hours of conversation just generated more questions and answers. I found her charming, and I was delighted that she had an answer for everything I asked. My primary thought was, "Why did you start working for the Underground? Lots of people chose not to."

There was a faraway look in her blue eyes when she said, "It was necessary. Somebody had to do it. We were proud of our country, and we just started helping the Jews in small ways. They were our friends. They needed groceries or someone to get a prescription for them, and that's how it all began." After many more sessions, one day she said, "Now I have told you all our family secrets."

When I asked, "Do you really want to put everything in this story?"

"Yes," she replied. "It's the truth."

In the story of the bombing of a certain Dutch city, my research showed that fewer than two thousand people died. She disagreed. Her account put the number at closer to twenty thousand. "Why the difference?" I asked? "Oh, our enemies were the ones who released those low numbers to make themselves look good, but we were there. We knew how many people died."

When we spoke about the Jewish question, she said, "I have something to show you." She got up, went into another room, and returned with a tiny box that she handed to me. Nestled inside were two gold wedding rings. "These rings belonged to a Jewish couple," she told me. "They brought them to my uncle and asked him to keep them until the war was over." She treasured all of her keepsakes of the past. With this discovery, another chapter was opened: "The Wolff Family." "Only one member of that family survived; his name was Ernst. He was a few years older than me."

"Is he still alive?" She didn't know, but we decided to find out. Joanne van Tongeren, Anje's daughter, found a Jair Wolff on Facebook, and when I corresponded with him, he confirmed that Ernst Wolff was his father and said that he lived in Israel. Another piece of the puzzle fell into place. The rest of that story is told by Anje in the Afterword.

Just as we prepared to send this manuscript to the publisher, Anje's daughter Freda received a reply to a query about Anje's mother, Hillie, which she had made a year earlier with the International Tracking Service. We have included those documents for validation and interest. So little was known of Hillie's life after she left Holland, and it was the same for the many who were incarcerated. They just disappeared.

It was impossible to tell Anje's story without including the war, for she lived in spite of it. It was also impossible to tell her story without including the Underground, for her life revolved around this activity. And it was impossible to tell her story without involving the Holocaust, for it claimed her friends and relatives.

Anje says, "Remembrance Day, November 11, is still the most difficult day of the year, for I remember every day. For me it is not the remembrance of it that is difficult, but rather the forgiving and forgetting of it. The official ceremony with the lone trumpet sound and two minutes of silence just causes me to revisualize all the terror, insanity, and painful experiences. I don't want to remember; I would like to forget."

There is still much that has not been told, but those things remain untapped in the memory of a woman who does not desire to remember anymore. Her own personal war is the essence of this story.

ACKNOWLEDGMENTS

How does one go about thanking everyone who had a part in a book's coming to fruition? So many people lent their support in so many different ways. It is always great to be encouraged, and maybe prodded, along the way. My first thoughts and thanks go to my dear friend and sister-in-law, Margaret Penner. Right from the very beginning, she said, "Yes, this is a good idea. Do it." Margaret is an avid reader, as am I, and we have often shared with each other the content of an exciting book we were reading. We still do.

Kathie Wiebe, my dear friend of forty years, was the person I sometimes called twice a day to get the meaning of a German word, the correct spelling of it, or the proper usage in a sentence. I think her thesaurus and dictionary were used almost as much as mine! Her constant encouragement and vision for this story kept me pressing on.

Sandra Birdsell, my beautiful, talented sister, you were so patient with me. As she is a published author of numerous books herself, I was almost jealous when she wrote *The Russlander*. It is a historical and accurate depiction of times in Russia we had heard recounted by our mother. Others agreed on its merits. A Giller nomination and the Governor General's award were her prizes. Her advice for me has been valuable, and her precious time spent critiquing my work is appreciated more than I can say.

Author Alma Barkman edited an early version of this story and was quick to point out that there was too much history in it. You can tell I did not heed her advice. I couldn't resist; the history kept pulling at me, for it tells us how we got to where we are. I love your stories, Alma; they are beautiful, just not historical.

My cousin and friend Hardy Enns, retired educator, spent numerous hours reading and critiquing this manuscript and came up with the question, "How many thousands of hours did you spend on research?" Five and a half years. Thanks, Hardy.

To Anje's daughters, Freda and Joanne, you have been supportive in every way, providing photos and helping me to tell your mom's story. I hope you like it.

Pastor Rudy Fidel and wife Gina, what a blessing you are! Always ready and eager to help in any way to encourage and promote Anje's story, they believe, as do I, that the commission of this work was none other than by divine inspiration. This is true. I could not have done this work myself. The Fidel's have a great love for the Jewish people, which I share. This story needs to be told again and again.

Thank you to my lovely daughters, Annette and Desiree, who encouraged me, critiqued my work, and often asked, "How is it going, Mom?" My sons, Darrell and Grant, encouraged me also. My husband, Ralph, gave me his support in many ways. I needed countless hours and days of quiet time so I could research and write, and he provided that.

My beautiful granddaughter, Caitlin, assisted me with computer and art work. Being a very talented artist and photographer, she created the cover design and formatted this book, in addition to fulfilling her role as a busy new mother.

I owe a large debt of gratitude to Arina Vandenbrink for her assistance in translating numerous articles from the Dutch language into English. Sometimes a literal translation does not flow well in our English language. She translated many pages from the text of the book *Groningen 1939–1945*. I doubt I could have written this story without that background information of the war in Holland, and specifically Groningen, Anje's birthplace. Thank you, Arina—you were invaluable.

The library of Anje van Tongeren was immense. When I sat in her living room, all I saw was books; she was surrounded with books, many of which related to the subjects contained in this story. It was as though they sitting there waiting to be perused and used. I was off to a running start with my research.

Long before I undertook the writing of this book, Eugene Derksen, of Derksen Printers in Steinbach, asked me to write feature news stories for his newspaper and mentored me along the way. I eventually became the editor of a small country newspaper, writing the news and feature stories. As a result, my newspaper won first prize in the Canadian Weekly Newspaper Competition for the best feature news. Eugene was a great encouragement to me in my writing career.

My thanks to Lee Scalia for assistance in helping me find information I needed at various times and for providing photos that validated the story.

The Rural Municipality of Morris commissioned me to write one hundred years of history for their centennial project. Two years later, *Furrows in the Valley* was published, and I discovered how much I love history and doing research. I was not able to write until later when my husband and I sold our transportation business, which allowed me time for my own projects. *The House of Blood and Tears* is my first historical nonfiction work written in novel style.

Thanks to my sister Sandra for choosing the title.

INTRODUCTION

Anje, a remarkable woman now well into her eighties and living in Winnipeg, sits comfortably while dozing in her rocking chair. She is jolted into consciousness as she hears yet another airplane overhead. *Alert! Find a safe shelter!* She pauses for a moment, realizing there is no alert, no screaming sirens. She has been dreaming again, dreaming of the day when the Messerschmitts and the Mustangs were battling overhead as she walked home from school. She sighs and settles back into the comfort of her chair as the memories roll past as on a movie screen.

World War II was raging, and the people of the Netherlands had been drawn into it by the devouring force of Adolf Hitler's army, an army that was driven to make Europe

Hitler's Third Reich, his kingdom. Nothing would stand in the way of achieving his goals, and in the process he would destroy the Jews of Europe. What could possibly be a hindrance to his plans or a barrier to his dreams? The people—the young and the old, the rich and the poor, the brave and even the fearful—the stalwart Dutch people who dared to resist. They stood in his way. People like Anje and her mother, Hillie, who knew the meaning of the motto of the Netherlands, "I will maintain," and willingly offered their services to the Underground.

Did all of these things really happen to me? Anje thought as she sat in her rocking chair almost seven decades later. Was I actually invisible when the Storm Troopers were patrolling the streets? How did I manage to elude a raid that was in progress? Didn't they see me? All those messages I delivered for the Underground on my way to school—why was I never caught? No one imagined I was dreaming up techniques and strategies for the Underground intelligence when I was only twelve. I guess that's why the Nazis didn't suspect me. Now it is hard for me to believe the Underground really needed me at that age; I was so young. The four Nazi Security Service officers, in their desperate last stance, surely intended my destruction on Liberation Day, April 13, 1945. But whoever shot them before they killed me was invisible too!

They called me "the Thinker." I guess they were right; I was always thinking—thinking about how to outsmart the Nazis, thinking about what to do next. Even now, I am still thinking …

THE HOUSE OF
BLOOD AND TEARS

Anje at the age of two with her mother Hillie.

GRONINGEN HOLLAND
1945

She was hurrying across Rabenhauptstraat towards the Café, crouching low to avoid flying bullets. Her curiosity had gotten the better of her again. She should have stayed inside where she was safe, but she wanted a better view of what was going on. Safe? She knew no one was safe from the monstrous war machines that were rolling down her street, but she could not resist this urge that was always in her belly to run toward the action. This was something her mother had constantly cautioned about, cautions that so far had failed. She spied a foreign army tank coming across the bridge on the canal, and it began firing at the Nazi soldiers, who were returning fire from a gun on wheels. The sound of the tank gun was so loud and the flying bullets so close, she decided the street was a dangerous place to be. A movement caught her attention out of the corner of her eye as she ran. Four Nazi officers stood tall in the street. Their legs were slightly apart, with rifles raised in a stance for firing. The identification breastplate that hung from a shiny, heavy chain around each man's neck was boldly inscribed with "*Sicherheitspolizei.*" They were members of the Nazi party's security police, and she was in their gun sight. They were ready to shoot. Her heart was pounding with fear as she realized that she was their target. She closed her eyes and thought; *this is my last day on earth*, when she heard the "Bang!" of rifles firing.

SAND DUNES AND HEATHER
1938

The sky was red at night, and dawn broke on Sunday to a sunny sky with frothy wisps of clouds as Anje peered out the bedroom window. As she looked at the sky, her heart soared as she remembered. *We are going to Sand Dunes and Heather today. Yippee!*

She was prepared to have fun that day with the whole group who were travelling together to the beach. She ran downstairs, and carefully began packing her bathing suit, towels, and sunglasses into the saddlebags on her bicycle.

Anje was an only child, the nine-year-old daughter of Jan and Hillie Minnes. Her father was a sports fan who worked as an accountant. He was tall and dark, and he always wore nice clothes. His friends were also avid sports fans, and he had met

Mother at one of those events. She was very popular, outgoing and friendly. He was attracted to her vibrant personality but was also very attached to his siblings and parents, and he frequently spent time with them in Utrecht, a village nearby. Hillie didn't mind; she had a big heart and arms that were always open to helping anyone who was in need. She treated Jan like someone very special, and he thrived on her doting on him. Her dark brown hair was blowing in the wind as they cycled, and her vivid hazel eyes twinkled with the joy of this special day of fun.

Anje had one other special person in her life, and that was her Uncle Hans. Hans was not really her uncle—he was her father's best friend—but he treated Anje as though she were his own daughter.

"Come on, Sunshine," he called to her. "Is everything ready?" He came over to check her bicycle and see if everything was in order. Uncle Hans's blue eyes always twinkled when he spoke to her, and she loved that nickname he had given her. It was a sign of affection.

As they set out together for the eight-kilometer ride, the rays of the sun warmed Anje's body this July day while her bicycle tires bounced along the streets of Groningen. The route took them past the waterway, and Anje noticed that some of the pavement they rode on was smooth, other streets were fitted with bricks of different hues, and some were old cobblestones that belied their age. As she crossed an aged stone bridge over the canal, she saw the arch cast an image into the water that created a perfect circle, and several ducks glided by, creating small ripples in the water behind them. *Such a beautiful sight!* she thought.

As she pedaled through the commercial zone, heavily laden barges were docked nearby as men loaded goods for transport, and in the distance, she could see the white canvas sails of a sailboat billowing from the pressure of the wind, moving it swiftly along the canal. Occasionally, the deep bellow of a horn on one of the barges broke the silence, amid the cries of seagulls flapping their wings as they swooped over the water, their beaks breaking the surface as they hunted for tasty fish. Tall reeds, which had been used by Dutch architects since the seventeenth century as a natural roof covering, grew in abundance along the banks of the canal. Some homes with these thatched roofs still stood. The older architecture was adorned with decorated cornices, shaped gables, and ornate red bricks, all embellished with white latticework trimmings. As Anje gazed, she thought the trimmings look just like icing on a gingerbread house.

Sunday was the family's favorite day for excursions, and Anje felt the eagerness of the cyclists who had come from across the city for their own rendezvous. Everyone had a look of expectation on his or her face. The Minnes family formed a large group as they mingled with aunts, uncles, cousins, and friends riding along in the countryside. Mother's brother, Uncle Martijn, and his wife, Frieda, rode alongside his sister, Aunt Dolly, and her husband, Albert. Their children, Sophie and Willie, were cousins and great friends of Anje's, and they were delighted to ride along beside her; they were determined to keep pace with the adults, even though their bikes were smaller. Mother's friend Sonjia loved teasing and cracking jokes with Uncle Hans and the others; she was fun to be with. Hans was a typical Groninger, with blond hair, blue eyes, and average build. His kindness and friendly personality made him popular. There was anticipation in the air, the anticipation of a good time. As they cycled past the small wooden sign that announced the tiny village of Appelscha, they knew that Sand Dunes and Heather was just ahead.

From right to left; Anje's father Jan, Anje, and her mother Hillie on one of their frequent bicycle excursions in Groningen on the weekend. Two ladies at left are unidentified.

Huge ash trees and decorative shrubs edged the site along with the natural growth of poplars, which were native to the area. A yellow sign showed the route to walking trails and bicycle paths that wound through the woods. The beach was pristine, with large rolling sand dunes and an occasional outcrop of grasses. A large swimming pool had been built on this site for the times the sea wasn't calm enough for the younger swimmers, and it was surrounded by sand. Anje was immediately attracted to the voices of the children who had built impressive sand castles on the beach and others who were eagerly shouting as they splashed one another while playing tag in the pool. As she watched, one of the better swimmers executed a swan dive from the highest perch on the diving board at the deep end, making a big splash as he entered the water.

A small refreshment stand with its red-and-white-striped awning beckoned the customers who were sitting at small, round, wrought-iron tables on the stone patio, enjoying their ice cream and sipping cold beverages. The shade of a small, colorful canopy above each table sheltered them from the sun on this warm day, and the clatter of glasses and chatter of people filled the air with happy sounds of activity.

With a rumble and a roar, Erich arrived at Sand Dunes and Heather at the wheel of his blue sedan. Erich was a handsome guy; with his dark, curly hair and dark eyes, he was a favorite with the girls, which was obvious with his two female passengers. Now that he had a car, his popularity would be increasing as every girl wanted to be escorted in a nice car. When Anje heard the sound of his car, she scurried over to the place where she knew her dad and Uncle Hans would be standing. The men gathered wherever there was a new car, and some of their eyes were twinkling like lights on a Christmas tree, Anje thought as she watched.

Hans was the first one to grab the door handle and jump in. As he did, one of the men walked around the car, kicked the tires, and ran his hand over the shiny body. "I hear that you can now have a radio installed," he said as he leaned inside to look at the dashboard. "You thinking about getting one?" he asked Erich inquisitively.

"Naw," Erich proclaimed as he tilted his head, but if he would have had buttons on his britches, he would have burst them right then! He beamed with pride at his new car. "I just wanted wheels. I don't care about sound."

"But we came here to swim," one of the girls protested weakly.

"Yo! Hans! Come on!" Erich shouted as he leaped out of the vehicle and began running toward the pool. "I'll race you to the diving board."

"Wait a minute!" Hans replied hastily. "I have to get my bathing suit on first!"

But Erich had come prepared, wearing his swimsuit under his clothes, and he wasn't waiting for anybody. He jogged on ahead, shed his clothes by the pool's edge, jumped on the diving board, and hit the water headfirst, creating a big splash. A few people nearby cheered and clapped as his head emerged from the water. His hair was plastered to his head, and water was dripping from the top downward as he held his nostrils closed, his other hand wiping his eyes. "Whew! That was colder than I thought it would be," he complained as he exhaled.

"Yes," Hans laughed, "you are the guy who doesn't think before he leaps."

Hans walked toward the pool, where Anje was waiting, and slid over the edge of the pool into the cool water. "Come on. Jump in, sunshine girl," he called. "I'll flip you so you can do a somersault into the water." The others watched as she flew through the air into the pool and he flipped her off his shoulders. She had taken swimming lessons at school and could hold her own in the water.

"Good girl, Anje!" He smiled as he fluffed her blonde hair with his towel and wiped the water from her face. "Now go and have some more fun with your friends."

Between the enjoyment of the water and the sand, the other adults in the group took pleasure in relaxing at the refreshment stand, drinking coffee or lemonade while discussing the latest news.

"It looks as though Germany is determined to have war," Edgar remarked while sipping his coffee. He had his Panama hat pulled down low to shield his eyes from the sun. It was obvious that Edgar wasn't there to swim or to supervise; his wife was busy watching the children. He just wanted to discuss the latest news and see whether he could spark a little controversy among the group. Edgar was one of Jan's friends, but not a close one. Jan didn't care much for Edgar's philosophy; he would frequently attempt to get a person to express his opinion, while Jan was often reluctant to commit himself. Anje watched with interest when she noticed her father's change in attitude.

"Why do you say that?" Erich asked.

"Well," Edgar said, "first Hitler marched into Rhineland with his troops, and now he has pushed into Austria."

"That's not a fair statement, Edgar. Rhineland belonged to Germany in the first place. It was taken away from them by the Treaty of Versailles, and now they are claiming it back!" Jan exclaimed. "And in Austria, they held a vote on whether they wanted their government run by the Germans, and over 90 percent of the people voted yes. That was just Anschluss. How can you say that was a warlike move?"

"Oh, yes!" another man interjected drily. "This is just the beginning. Hitler needed the Austrian iron-ore mine in Erzberg and the 748 million Reichsmark in their federal reserves to make war. Those were the real motives of annexing Austria. Let's remember that."

Edgar raised his hand to push his hat back off his forehead as he tilted back on his chair legs. "You know, a couple of years ago, there were pictures in the paper of that huge parade and ceremony the Germans had in Berlin celebrating the new power of the Luftwaffe and their 2,500 aircraft. When I saw that I thought, This man, Hitler,—he is planning for war."

"Oh, I doubt that the Netherlands would ever get drawn into a war," Jan commented.

Just then, Erich, who had been standing in the background, leaned toward the table, his brow furrowed with concern. "I have a cousin in Germany, and he tells me they are building airplanes in a factory near him. They have doubled the size of the plant and are hiring laborers from all over Europe by promoting this slogan: 'Come work in Germany. There is room for all.' Besides that, there is an ammunition factory being built in Frankfurt, and they are also advertising for workers."

"That's not all," another one commented. "The Germans have already built a huge ball-bearing manufacturing plant at Schweinfurt, and now they're enlarging it."

"What does that prove?" Jan asked.

"Ball bearings are needed for the construction of machinery. It could be war machines."

"Hmph!" was the unbelieving sound that came from Jan.

"Yes," Hans interjected, "and if you are thinking about going to work in Germany and you want to be favored there, then you must be sure you are of Aryan descent because that's what Hitler is propagating. Did you hear the long, passionate speech he gave recently in which he kept pounding the idea of the superior Nordic race? That's the tall, muscular, blonde, blue-eyed, Adonis-like male. That leaves you out, Erich. You wouldn't make it there!"

Erich replied with a grin and a feigned punch to Hans's shoulder; and then he ducked in response to the expected retaliation. "Well, I'm not worried," he said with a laugh. "The girls in the Netherlands like me. I think I'll stay here!"

Just then his female companion approached in time to respond, "Oh, they do? Well, I heard you say girls," emphasizing the s. I'm glad you are so popular," she said as she flicked her beach towel toward his bare body.

Edgar exclaimed with triumph, "You know, I think I won this discussion today." He smiled as he sipped his hot coffee. With that he got up from his chair, pushed his beige Panama forward on his head, and walked over to the booth to get another cup of coffee.

To which the other replied, "Your ideas make about as much sense as you drinking hot coffee on a sultry summer day."

"I don't think Netherlands has anything to worry about anyway," Erich quipped. "We are neutral."

Hans cocked his head slightly and said, "I hope you're right, Erich," and Jan silently nodded in agreement.

Anje listened and observed. She wasn't familiar with this topic of adult conversation, but she could sense the tension in the air and wondered if this was something to worry about. *Then again*, she thought, *if Erich and Father are not worried, why should I worry?*

JAN'S FOLLY

Jan felt apprehensive as he was called into his boss's office. Mr. Boeker was a good employer. He had given Jan a raise and had promoted him to head accountant of his large firm that manufactured bicycles. Everyone in Holland owned a bicycle; it was big business. Jan's problem was that he loved money. Perhaps it was not just money he loved but the things it could buy. He wore the latest, and not the cheapest clothes. He liked fine cigars and loved attending all the sporting events in Holland, sometimes gambling on the outcome. It was nothing serious, but it all added up. He would have liked having a son with whom he could share all of these sporting adventures, but that was not to be for him. He had to find his pleasures in other ways: he liked being the life of the party and being noticed by attractive women. Some of his brothers thought he had been spoiled by his mother, as he was the youngest in the family. Yes, he was used to being treated well and given whatever he wanted—what was wrong with that? But his mother had passed away, and now he had a problem to solve. He knew his paycheck wouldn't cover all the things he wanted, and he was adept at hiding his "loans" in the books. He did feel a little nervous when the auditors were there, but they had come before and not found anything, so what was he nervous about? What did Mr. Boeker want now?

He couldn't adequately explain his actions to the satisfaction of his boss, and when he realized he had been found out, he was annoyed—and yes, he was guilty. Could he pay the money back? When he heard the sum, he froze in his boots. How could he handle that? Was it really that much? He berated himself. He was a numbers man. How could an accountant not be aware of how much he had taken? Where would he get that much money? Finally, Mr. Boeker agreed not to report him to the authorities if he would repay the debt. After all, Jan thought, shouldn't his boss be a little lenient? He had worked for him for almost ten years. But how would he explain all this to Hillie? They had bought a very nice house, Hillie did not have to work outside the home, he thought he had been a good husband—these things were in his favor. But Hillie was a very honest person, and her father was a policeman. He knew she would be upset about this situation.

As he entered the house, he realized he was home early. She would not be expecting him yet.

"What's wrong?" Hillie asked, seeing he was in some distress.

He sat down dejectedly on the couch with his head in his hands as the words rolled out of his mouth.

"I lost my job today," he moaned.

"What happened?" she queried as she came to sit down beside him.

When he told her the truth of the whole sad tale, she asked, "Well, how much is it?"

"Ten thousand guilders," he replied morosely as he raised his head to look at her, continuing to rub his hand over his forehead.

"Ten thousand guilders!" she exclaimed fiercely. "Who on earth is going to lend us that kind of money when you don't have a job?"

"Well, I have been thinking about that," he replied. "You will have to go and get money from my brother, Paul," he said. "He has more than enough."

Hillie knew this man in front of her all right. He could spend the money and be the "big man," but he could not solve problems or deal with anything unpleasant. She recalled when she was at home giving birth to Anje, he had left for a number of days because he couldn't stand the trauma. It would be up to her to solve this. She realized she would have to go back to her old job at the distribution center so they would have some stability in their lives; but for now, she would have to go and see Paul.

Hillie covered her head with her blue and gray woolen shawl, tying it under her chin as she walked along Amersfoort Straat toward the train station. She knew there really was no other solution, and her mind was focused on what she would say to Paul. She was more than a little uneasy about speaking with her brother-in-law about a loan of this proportion. She didn't care that much for him. After his wife died, he seemed rather brusque, somewhat distant and unapproachable. This was not going to be easy. She wished Jan hadn't asked her to do this.

The journey from Groningen to Utrecht was a few hours by rail, with many stops in between, and as she neared her destination, the queasy feeling in the pit of her stomach loomed larger. She rehearsed everything in her mind many times over. What approach should she take? As the train whistled and the brakes screeched to a stop, she knew this was her destination; she must disembark. She climbed down the steel steps of the train onto the platform as steam poured from beneath its belly; the people scattered in all directions as she began to walk brusquely toward the western part of the city.

The last time she had been at this home was for the funeral of his wife, Angelina. She turned to walk down Helmerstrad, looking carefully to check the house numbers; she was looking for #63.

Yes, this was the one. She hesitated as she peered up at the tall, brick dwelling, four stories high. She walked up the stone steps to the front door, reached out, and pressed her finger on the doorbell. When it opened, Paul appeared, and a look of surprise crossed his face. He greeted her with a warm handshake. Was that actually friendliness she could see in his eyes? Perhaps she had been mistaken about Paul. This may be easier than she thought.

As he escorted her into the spacious front room, she removed her woolen shawl and guided herself rather uneasily onto the soft cushions of the couch. She could feel her heartbeat throbbing in her throat. She was nervous, but she resisted twisting the ends of her shawl; she knew that would appear weak. Paul retreated to the other room, returning with two fancy cut glasses, one in each hand.

He offered her a glass of Advocaat, brandy and eggnog, and she accepted graciously, hoping the drink would relax her. She wrapped both hands around the round crystal goblet as she began to tell Paul the whole story of Jan's folly, their present demise, and their request for money. Paul listened carefully while moving closer to her on the couch.

As he looked deeply into her eyes, he asked in a low voice, "And how do you expect to repay me for this loan?"

She agonized inwardly, knowing this was a reasonable question for which she had no answer.

"Well?" he said as he awaited a reply.

She began slowly and uneasily, "Well, I really don't know."

He spoke quickly and passionately, almost interrupting her. "What is it that you could offer me that I don't have? As you know, my wife passed away just a few years ago, and I miss her dearly." The expression of those words slid out of his mouth in a way that made her realize that they had a different meaning than what he had actually spoken.

He grabbed her wrist firmly and thrust his lips so closely to her ear that she could feel his breath on her cheek as he spoke.

"You want something from me, and I want something

from you." The fierceness in his dark eyes disclosed that there was no mistaking his intentions; he was not to be put off.

What should she tell him? What should she do? What would Jan suggest in this situation? She didn't know. She felt like trash. She paused momentarily, inhaled, and spoke haltingly, "Would you please excuse me? I would like use your bathroom first." She arose from her sitting place, smoothing her dress with her hands as she stood up.

Paul seemed to recover his graces instantly. "Of course," he replied, and he escorted her down a hallway toward an elegant bathroom. He nodded his head slightly, stretched his arm toward the open bathroom door, and retreated.

Hillie grasped the brass handle and closed the oak door, firmly twisting the key in the lock. As she proceeded toward the sink to wash her face, she realized how much her knees were shaking. She looked in the mirror at her image. *Do I look like a woman who would do what he is suggesting?* she thought. Of all things, she had not anticipated this. She was angry—angry at Jan for forcing her to solve his problem. He knew his brother better than she did. What would Jan expect her to do? How would she get out of this house without being compromised?

As time passed, Paul began calling her name, apologizing for his actions and suggesting it was time for coffee and a nice friendly talk. Surely she didn't think he would cause her harm, for then he would have to answer to Jan. She did not want to have a physical confrontation with Paul. This was not the way to solve this problem, she reasoned. This continued for what seemed like hours. Finally she heard a curse word, and from the sounds she heard, she thought perhaps he had abandoned the vigil. Hours proceeded into nightfall while she sat on the floor with her back against the door, her arms wrapped around her raised knees. She berated herself for failing her assignment. She put her head down on her knees, and in this mode, she briefly fell asleep.

She awakened with a start when she heard sounds in the house. Listening intently, her ear to the door, she looked at her watch; it was six o'clock in the morning. Questions rolled around in her mind: Would he go to work? Would a maid come? Would she be brave enough to open the door? At one point it became very quiet, and she waited and listened until she dared open the door silently. She slowly stuck her head out to peek, and she peered down the hall in both directions. It looked safe.

Cautiously, step by step, she tiptoed toward the front door. When the floor creaked under the weight of her body, she paused, just as something touched her leg. She jumped and quickly put her hand over her mouth. She had almost screamed! As she looked down at her leg, she heaved a sigh of relief. Thank God! A big, fat, gray cat peered up at her, his fluffy tail waving back and forth while he purred loudly, his yellow eyes saying, *What are you doing here?*

She eased the front door of the house open to see if the coast was clear, wondering if any surprises awaited her outside. There was nothing to fear; she proceeded to walk confidently down the street toward the train station.

Her journey home was much different than her arrival the day before, which had held the anticipation of a favor; today as the wind blew against her, she felt the resistance of the elements, and she wondered what Jan would say. She felt like a failure. They really needed this money for the predicament they were in. Now what would they do?

As she arrived home, she was relieved to discover that Anje had gone to school on her own, but Jan was home. What would he think, considering she had been away for the whole night? She pulled off her shawl as she entered the room, her eyes cast downward. Where would she begin? Jan gazed at her inquisitively, as her appearance indicated something was amiss. As Hillie poured out the story of the events of the preceding day and reiterated how this had been a terrible idea, he interrupted her to ask, "Are we getting the money?"

She looked at him incredulously and said in a clipped tone, "You will have to ask him yourself." She removed her shoes, wearily climbed the stairs, and slammed the door behind her.

THE TRANSITION

Anje was reading a book from her favorite series when she heard Mother calling. She put the book down, climbed down from her tall bed, and went into the kitchen.

Mother was making cookies. Good, this was one of her favorite treats; she would be taking cookies to school. "Come here for a moment, Anje. I'd like to talk to you."

She entered the room and looked inquisitively at Mother.

"What kind of cookies are you making?" Anje asked as she peered inside the mixing bowl.

"Your favorite, Anje, the ones with coconut in them," Mother replied.

"Mmm," Anje said with a smile on her face. She could taste them already.

"Anje," Mother said as she put her arm around her shoulder, "you know there will be some changes around here. We will be moving soon. We have someone who wants to buy our house, and you know Opa Minnes has not been well ever since Oma died, and he needs someone to look after him. We are moving into his place."

Anje's thoughts whirled as she flounced into her room and began throwing things around. She cast her stuffed toy doll into the corner. She kicked her chair. She was angry. She didn't like Opa Minnes; he was a grumpy old man. Why did she have to give up her nice house for him? Why couldn't they find someone else to look after him? She had heard Mother and Father talking quietly in the evenings, discussing things, and she knew the real reason they had to move was because Father had stolen some money and now they had to pay it back. They had to sell their home to get that much money. "There! That's the real truth," she muttered furiously to herself. Wherever they were moving to, she was sure she would not like it. She liked it here. She would have to go to a different school and make new friends. Why, oh why, did this have to happen to her?

Her bedroom had doors that opened to the outside, and she opened them fully and stepped out. She inhaled the clean, fresh air of the day. Children were playing in the field just beyond her house, and as she watched them laugh and play, she thought, *they look happy, but I am not happy!* It had been such a nice day to begin, and now as she looked up at the sky, the clouds seemed to be rolling in, like the thick blanket of gloom that was rolling into her heart.

Rabenhauptstraat

Their home was on the second floor above a café in a group of four attached houses, with a bakery in the middle. This dwelling was 78A Rabenhauptstraat. There was nothing distinct about their home; the houses all looked the same, with stucco on the front with red brick trim, and a small alcove by the front step.

Anje soon discovered that she would not be bored here, for they had many interesting neighbors. Ba Timms owned two businesses right on the corner of Rabenhauptstraat and Achterfweg. His small café was operated by his sons, and Ba's liquor store was managed by his daughter Annie. The Timms family included twins, Treeny and Ricki, who were the same age as Anje. Ba was a very hardworking man, but everyone knew that Thursday was his day off, and his time was spent drinking in his liquor store. Anje often heard his boisterous voice all the way down the street.

Directly across the street from her home was a large white two story school house. It was easily identified by the rows of large windows across the front. But when she inquired about school, she was told that she was not able to attend there. Beside the large school playground were two homes and a store that sold wool, fabric, and notions. Kitty-corner across from Opa Minnes's home, Jan and Evelyn Mekel operated a cigar and candy store, and at the end of the block was the Henricks' busy drugstore. It was not a quiet place, for just a few blocks away the railroad tracks crossed Achterfweg, and trains could be heard rolling over the tracks on their journey to destinations in the Netherlands and beyond. This territory was Anje's new home in Groningen.

Anje age 9, in her navy and white dress, standing near her home on Rabenhauptstraat. The Elementary School is the white building in the background.

She may have been unhappy about moving, but she soon discovered that within these dwellings were many children with whom she became good friends. Mother and Father had felt sorry for her and decided to buy her a gift that would help her make friends. It was a type of scooter, called the Flying Dutchman, and she soon became the most popular kid on the street. The contraption, as Father called it, had four rubber wheels, a platform to stand on, and a large handle, and when it was pumped up and down, the whole thing moved forward. Neighbors became familiar with the sight of this scooter traveling with two or three children aboard who were squealing with delight!

Anje also became friends with the children of Samuel and Esther Troostwijck, a Jewish couple who lived on

Achterfweg with their two lively sons, Max, thirteen, and
Bennie, twelve. Their cousin named Max Lev loved to join
their group playing games on the street. Anje was a tomboy
and loved playing with the boys. They were rough and tough
and didn't cry as soon as they fell down or hurt themselves.
But when she met Janny Mekel, she knew they were kindred
spirits. Janny was just two months younger than Anje, and
they soon became fast friends and partners in adventure.
They were often joined by Anna Marie Bakker on their
walk to school every day.

Anje lived with roller skates on her feet; she wanted to go
everywhere fast! The Henricks' son Fritz loved roller skating,
and when they were clamping on their roller skates, he was
always right there. They were a large group of children, and
their activities included Anti-I-Over and hide and seek.
On one occasion when Anje was playing this game, no one
could find her even though they walked right past her a few
times. She just sat motionless behind a bush. Then she had to
climb through a barbed wire fence to make it to home base
before she was found, and even though blood was flowing
down her leg from being snagged by the fence, she didn't
care. She was home free before anyone saw her. It was just
a game, but Anje was seriously competitive.

When Anje came home from school, she entered the
house on the main floor; and because they lived above the
bakery, she always had to climb steep, narrow stairs to enter
their dwelling. The entrance contained a storage space beside
the stairs where she parked her bicycle as soon as she arrived.

She headed for the kitchen and called, "Mother, are you here?" It was always the same greeting, and then she smiled. *Of course Mother is here. She is always here!* The only bright spots in the small kitchen were the paisley curtains that substituted for cupboard doors, and nearby stood the simple two-burner gas stove used for cooking. She could tell from the aromas in the house what Mother was cooking. It was usually something she really liked. She lifted the lid on the pot and saw a tasty stew bubbling that would be their supper; went into the back room, which was their common room; and set down her pile of school books. She loved to do her homework here, for it was at the center of everything.

The front room was used only at Christmas or on other special occasions, but it housed the coal stove that heated the main floor of the house. On chilly days, Mother would make a fire in the stove, and Anje would sit there in the comfort of her surroundings. When the fire died down, she would place her wool socks against the stove to warm her feet. Groningen was beside the North Sea, and the weather was often windy and rainy; on those cool, wet days the stove was a most welcome companion. A warm stove and a good book—these were her favorite things.

Every Sunday night, the Mekel, Minnes and Troost-wijck families gathered together to visit, the parents congregating in one home, and the children in the neighboring house. The favorite pastime of the children was cooking edible treats, and that generated a lot of excitement. Only a few ingredients were available, but that didn't stop them, they loved mixing a batch of what they called "truffles," the main ingredient being oatmeal. The recipe was never the same. Friendly arguments took place over whose turn it was to stir, add ingredients, and lick the spoon! Janny was good at keeping them all in order. Everyone wanted more sugar, but this was a scarce commodity. Every little speck of food was consumed amidst laughter and teasing. They couldn't know that in the future, seven of that Sunday night group would die.

Anje with bow in her hair, and her friend Janny playing with the chickens.

Anje didn't enjoy being in Opa's home. Their quarters were tight, and he used a cane, always to his advantage. He used it not just to aid his walking but to bang on the floor when he wanted something, and Hillie was sure he used it to try and trip Anje occasionally. She was watchful around him. She prepared nice meals, but his short comments were complaints, not compliments. The times when Jan was home, his father was prone to contradict everything Jan said. Hillie could not imagine what it had been like in the Minnes' home when Jan was young. She heard that Jan's mother had ruled the home; perhaps that was the reason his father was so cranky? Whenever they had a war of words, Jan would leave and not come home for a number of days. Mother paid no attention to these outbursts but gave Opa tender loving care every day, even though he seemed to be ungrateful. She just smiled at him and carried on about her tasks.

Opa's bedroom was a "bed in the wall," in the common room. There was a cupboard with double doors, and when the doors were opened, it revealed a high feather bed, at the foot of which stood a large ceramic chamber pot.

Opa used a small wheelchair, and although he could shuffle about the house fairly well on his own, the stairs were his main hindrance. His baggy black pants were held up by wide suspenders, and he wore armbands over his large cotton shirt that was covered with a wrinkled, navy-striped vest. These were evidence of a time when his body had been robust and strong, but now it was emaciated from the effects of a stroke that had left him weak—though not at a shortage of words. His sharp retorts were aimed at anyone who came within the range of his voice, and his gravelly voice could often be heard admonishing Anje for some small infraction of his rules.

His frame was rather stooped, and the sparse white hair on top of his head always seemed to be in disarray. Perhaps that was from getting in and out of bed so many times a day, Hillie thought. She could tell Anje was amused by watching Opa's huge white handlebar moustache that curved downward and then upward, and it wiggled about when he talked or ate. She agreed with Anje—when he ate pea soup and dribbles of soup hung from his moustache, they did look like worms hanging out of a bird's nest. Then sometimes he sneezed, and pea soup flew all over the table. She could tell from the expression on Anje's face how displeased that she was with him and the mess he made.

"Anje, we have to be tolerant of him. He is an old man," she reassured her daughter.

⁂

Hillie and Jan went for a short walk early one evening while Anje was fast asleep and Opa was resting.

"Do you think this is the best place for Father?" she asked Jan. "The stairs are hard for him to climb, and there is barely enough room for his wheelchair."

"So far, none of my brothers or sisters have offered to take him, even though they have much more room. And you know," he added, "this is his home."

"Oh, yes, I know," Hillie commented. "It's just that he never seems to be very happy."

Hillie knew this was unfamiliar territory for Jan. She came from a very stable, happy family, and Jan did not seem to understand the difference. Jan's position was that if a person was well cared for, that was all that counted. What did "happy" have to do with that, anyway?

As they unlocked the door and walked into the house, they proceeded up the stairs as Hillie remarked, "I'm going to check on your father, and then we'll have a cup of tea."

She trotted up the second stairs to the bedroom, and the sight before her eyes alarmed her.

"Jan, come here!" she called. As Jan reached the top of the stairs, in the dim light he saw his father dressed in his wrinkled nightshirt, hair disheveled, standing on the chair Anje used to crawl into her high bed. One knee was perched on her bed, and when he saw them his face expressed alarm at their presence. Anje was fast asleep. Hillie firmly grasped Opa's arm, quietly helping him to climb down and then leading him down the stairs into his own bed.

Hillie turned on the gas to heat water to brew some tea, but her mind was in a turmoil. "What was he up to?" she muttered to herself. Her hands were shaking, and the tea cup clattered in the saucer as she placed it on the table before Jan.

Jan looked up, placing his hand on hers. "He was just a little confused; he probably got up to go to the bathroom and was still a bit groggy. Don't worry; he's really too old for anything else," he consoled.

Hillie sipped her tea thoughtfully while resolving to be more watchful.

Although Anje was shy and very quiet, a spirit of adventure rolled around inside of her. Whenever she left the house, she and Janny went off on some exploit. This day, they went to the park, where they discovered that park maintenance workers had cut down some large, old trees and were in the process of making them into five-foot lengths that were more manageable. There was a slope on this location, and the girls were soon rolling the logs with their feet, trying to race each other. Suddenly, the slope got steeper, and Anje was unable to control the speed of the log and fell off. Ouch! Something had happened to her arm, and it was in a lot of pain. When they went home to see Mother, she took Anje to the hospital, and the arm was put in a cast. Phooey! She was not impressed with this. For six weeks she couldn't ride her bicycle or properly roller skate—the momentum wasn't the same with just one working arm. Finally the cast was cut off, and the girls resumed their games. On Saturday it was such a nice day, they headed for their favorite swimming hole. A small stream fed water into that swimming hole, and a concrete slab had been put there so the soil wouldn't erode, but when they ran down the slippery concrete surface to the swimming hole, Anje fell and broke the same arm again. For the rest of her summer holidays, she was not without a plaster cast. This definitely was not her favorite summer.

Hillie lamented to her friend Sonjia as they were sitting at the table having a cup of tea, "Every week that girl comes home with her white socks and shoes green with algae, as she has tried to jump over another slough. Even though she never succeeds, she just keeps trying."

Sonjia's words were comforting, "Hillie, be patient. She will soon outgrow those antics."

Summer was over, fall had arrived, and school was in session. Anje was always looking forward to October 28, her birthday, and this was the day! When Opa heard it was her birthday, he reached into his pocket and took out a small, worn, leather change purse.

"You can go to the store and get some candy for yourself," he said. She reached out her hand to receive the coins. His hand shook as, one by one, he dropped the pennies into her open palm. It was six cents. "Buy some toffee, and bring it back to me," he said.

She looked at all the choices in the store, yummy things she loved, but Opa had told her to buy toffee, and so she did. She hurried home and placed the little brown bag into his hand. He took out one piece of toffee and handed it to her, and then he closed the bag and ambled off to his favorite chair.

"And a happy birthday to you too," she muttered under her breath.

Her thoughts scrolled back to her ninth birthday, which had been her favorite. Uncle Hans had told her he had a big surprise for her. She recalled how they had hurried down the stairs to the street and walked to the store to buy her birthday present.

"This is your birthday present, sunshine girl," he had said, his eyes twinkling with pride as he pointed to a shiny black bicycle that stood on the floor of the store. She felt like jumping, hugging him, and shouting all at the same time. Instead, she went to the bicycle, ran her hands over it, checked out the silvery headlamp, and the leather saddlebags hanging on the side—it had everything she needed. And now it was all hers! She would be able to go anywhere she wanted. That idea enthralled her.

Mother had bought her a lovely birthday cake and Uncle Hans had given her a bicycle, but Father hadn't come home for her birthday, or the next day, or the next. She lay in bed, staring at the dark boards of the cove ceiling and thinking about all the things that had happened on her special day. The school always had a special party for the birthday person.

She had to bring the cake, and the teacher served it to all her classmates. It was the custom for each student.

Why was Father never at home? Oh, she knew that Father had been so disappointed she wasn't a boy, but he had worked many years at the bicycle factory and yet never bought her a bicycle. Today, Uncle Hans had brought her a wonderful bicycle, and he was just Father's friend. How could this be important to him and not be important to Father? Where was Father, anyway, when he wasn't at home? She did not know that her father preferred his siblings over his own family and frequently spent his leisure time with them in Utrecht.

From left to right: Aunt Lulu, Hillie, baby Anje being held by unknown person; on one of Aunt Lulu's visits to Groningen.

GROTE MARKT,
THE GRAND PLACE

Yoo hoo! I'm here!" Lulu exclaimed as she reached out to hug Hillie at the doorstep. Aunt Lulu was married to Jan's brother Roland. She had doted on Anje since the day she was born, buying clothes for her, showering her with attention and special treats, and taking her on excursions. Lulu's dark eyes were always sparkling with excitement. She asked the bicycle taxi driver to wait until she returned. "Come on, we'll take the taxi to Grote Markt. We will do all our walking once we get there," she exclaimed as they made their way down to the taxi and climbed in.

There was a hub of activity at the Grote Markt (Grand

Place), which was located in the center of the city. They strolled around the perimeter of the huge paved square among the impressive buildings, and peeked in the windows of all the unique shops. Among the many opulent buildings, the outline of two large churches built in the 1400s soared above the street—the Martini and the A *kerk* (church). The Martini Tower, built of gray sandstone in Gothic design, rose ninety-seven meters above the ground. Tall, cathedral-style stone arches graced every level; and Hillie, Anje and Lulu looked up to the fourth gallery just as the sixty-two bells in the carillon chimed the time on the half hour.

Grote Markt Oostzijde in 1906.

"Oh!" Aunt Lulu called out. "See, Anje? It's one thirty already. Look up! Do you see that? The steeple on the Martini Tower looks like it has a crown on top, and it looks just like the Imperial Crown of India!"

Hillie smiled. "Lulu, you have such a good imagination. Do you want to go inside the church? We can, you know!"

When they entered the sanctuary of the church, Lulu was struck by the beauty of the huge, colorful frescoes from the thirteenth century that covered the cavernous ceiling. As they looked up, they couldn't imagine how many hours it had taken the artist to complete that magnificent work.

"I am sorry you can't hear the wonderful sounds from the organ," Anje exclaimed. "This is the largest baroque organ in northwestern Europe, and it produces such a wonderful sound. My school class often attends the concerts here." She loved classical music and looked forward to those evenings when the class was treated to concerts by famous artists in the church.

Anje thought the most interesting sight in the square was the Hoofdwacht Building, the main guardhouse, which had been built in front of the Martini Tower in typical Dutch style. Outside, the pillory was still visible where wrongdoers had been punished publicly with their heads and hands in stocks.

"What do you think they did to deserve that?" Lulu asked.

"This is how thieves were punished," Hillie responded.

Anje could not imagine what a humiliating experience it would be to sit all day in public, for everyone to see, knowing you had stolen something. She thought the people passing by would shame them, and surely this would be enough penalty so they would never want to steal again.

They continued walking past the north and east sides of the Grote Markt where most of the wealthy families built their homes. In European style, most owners lived above their businesses, and since space was at a premium, they built upward. By early 1900, many of these mansions were converted into shops and offices, though the fine rich façades were kept.

The three stood in front of Scholtenshuis and admired the stunning dwelling that had been built by the wealthy industrialist Willem Albert Scholten at the end of the nineteenth century. Though his business ventures took him around the world, he chose to live in Groningen in order to build a large family home in Grote Markt. He had his eye on a number of spots, but since no property was for sale, he had to exercise a great deal of patience. Eventually, the owners died one by one, and he bought their properties. This allowed him to build this magnificent home on the east side of the square, overlooking the Grand Place and facing the Groningen town hall. He always wanted to know which direction the wind was blowing, so he installed a weather vane in front of city hall! The Scholten House became the social hub of Groningen—the site of symphonies, dinner parties, and private celebrations, which were held in the Great Room. This private palace contained twenty-eight rooms with fifteen-foot ceilings on the main floor and arched windows eight feet high. Anje admired the exquisite satin draperies in the front windows; they looked rich.

The architectural design on the exterior was equally beautiful. The six front steps were marble, and one entered under a canopy that was held in place by four pillars with wide, embossed copper flanges at the base, and the ornamental trim around the arched door gave one the impression of entering a palace.

"I would certainly love to live in a house like this!" Lulu exclaimed as they walked past. The lace curtains that hung in the windows of the first floor hindered their view of the interior, but they could see the rich golden tassels that hung from the satin swags above them.

"Have you even been in this house, Hillie?" Lulu asked.

"Oh, no," she replied quickly. "Only the rich are invited here."

"Ah, yes," Lulu replied with a faraway look in her eyes. "Only the rich."

On the east side of the square were many opportunities to purchase something delightful in the Koffiehuis, the chocolate shop, or the Apotheek (drugstore). As they continued walking past the chocolate shop, Anje asked casually, "Do you think we can go inside?"

Lulu laughed as she hugged Anje's neck. "My dear, of course we can go inside. We might even find something to buy." Anje selected a bar made from dark chocolate, her favorite. She ate it slowly and thought she should really save half of it; then again, it was a very warm day. If it was going to melt, it may as well melt in her stomach!

Bright yellow awnings shaded them from the sun as they passed the Panserhuis and Electrolux shops, and they marveled at the artistic neon signs blazing advertising for Perez, Orangeboom Beer, Pilsener beer, and cigars. As they walked past Hotel Ninteman, Meeyers Koek (bakery), and Kinder Paradise, they found a wool shop and café. Lulu loved the variety of stores and what they had to offer, and they decided to stop and have a cup of tea.

"Aunt Lulu," Anje commented, "you will have to come

back on the weekend, on the market days. It is even more interesting."

Sunday was the Jewish market day, and the Grote Markt bustled with activity; on Saturday, the regular market day, it took on the flavor and appearance of a small fair. Canopied stalls were hauled in by horses and assembled by business owners. There was no limit to the imagination when there was an opportunity to make a few guilders! A variety of goods were available—new and used bicycle parts, screws, nuts, and bolts. Customers examined the fresh chickens that hung from the rail inside the awning as clothing flapped in the wind on hangers in the next stall. One man set up many varieties of sausage on his two-wheeled pushcart, and the next spot was occupied by an enterprising couple who brought a small stove and prepared cooked fish for their patrons.

The fish market was open only on specific days, and Hillie was a frequent customer. The fishermen sold fresh fish from the sea—turbot, herring, eel, haddock—and all were in demand. Vendors called out in their auctioneer-style voices to those who passed by, "Get your fish for supper now! Two for twenty-five cents, three for thirty, and one for mother-in-law!"

For ten days in May, people came to the Grote Markt from all over the city to enjoy the biggest fair of the year. It didn't matter that hints of war were all around them; this was the time for celebration! The square was full of vendors, customers, jugglers, and music; there was an activity for everyone. Anje and her mother loved coming to the fair; it was their time for fun. They were like two children as they tried their hand at games of chance and their prowess in the shooting gallery. When the sounds of the barrel organ attracted them to the carousel, Hillie climbed on a black horse and Anje a white one, and they hung onto the brass rail with one hand and ate their delicious ice cream cones with the other. Anje was just finishing the last licks of her crispy cone when a barker called out to those who passed by, "Come and try your hand at knocking down pins! Everyone wins! Yes, everyone wins!"

"Let's try that!" Anje exclaimed excitedly.

So Hillie bought three balls, and on her third try, she knocked down all of the pins.

"You did it!" the people shouted as the balls clattered to the bottom of the chute.

"What do you want for a prize, Anje?" Mother asked.

"Take that little blue flowered box," Anje exclaimed. "I can keep my things in there." So the pretty fabric-covered box became her personal treasure—that would one day have a story to tell.

Summer became fall, and this brought the anticipation of every Dutch child to the fore—the opportunity of gliding upon the ice on the canals with their skates. In October it was rarely cold enough for the canals to freeze over, but the children often tested the surface to see if it would hold their weight. Anje loved it when ice appeared on the canal for it gave her a shortcut to school, even though it was risky. She never told Mother when she was testing the thickness of the ice; she knew Mother would never approve of her taking chances. One Friday as she hurried across the canal, she thought she should try another strategy for crossing the ice, for she could hear the ice cracking all around her. She thought if she distributed her weight more evenly, it would be safer. So she went back to the bank, took a good run, and dove onto the ice headfirst with her arms above her head, just the way a diver does. The ice was very smooth, so she slid a long way across. Oh! Not quite the result she wanted. She decided on the way home that she would just run across the ice, maybe a little faster. Perhaps the cracking wouldn't catch up with her. She never gave it a second thought. After school, she and Janny decided that if it was still cold the next day, they would glide along the ice with their skates.

On Saturday, a cold sharp wind was blowing across the North Sea, and it stung when it hit Anje's face, but she didn't care because the weather had created ice that was as smooth as glass. The water had frozen so quickly that it was not pocked or pebbled; it was almost like a mirror. It would be a shame, she thought, to mar that perfect image with their blades, but the young folk congregated near the canals in this weather, and when they discovered that the surface was solid enough to skate on, one by one they appeared on the banks with their skates slung over their shoulders. Anje and Janny wore their warmest woolen hats and mittens, but the bitter wind penetrated their jackets, and their bodies were cold. Max and Bennie never failed to come up with a good idea. They appeared with their arms full of old newspapers, which they wrapped around their bodies. Layer after layer they wrapped them, thick enough to stay warm but not so thick that they couldn't close the zippers on their jackets. They shared them with everyone. Anje and Janny hurriedly tied up the leather laces that held the wooden skates on their shoes, as their fingers were getting stiff from the cold. Anje and some of the others had brought their hockey sticks along, but today, there weren't enough players to make teams, so they were content to play tag on the canal.

Max and Bennie were good skaters, and aggressive hockey players, but they were also mischievous, constantly teasing the girls and challenging them to race. The girls were not daunted; they certainly were not going to be beaten by the boys! On the long walk home, Max and Bennie sauntered behind the girls all the way to Rabenhauptstraat, poking fun, teasing, and challenging them. When Janny rolled her eyes and asked Anje how they could get rid of them, Anje replied, "They're our neighbors and our friends; they are just being boys."

CHRISTMAS CELEBRATIONS

The cold gray days of November were just a fore-runner to the greatest celebration of the year. Children were on their best behavior; after all, Christmas was coming! Gift giving was a very old tradition that was cherished by all. Members of the family focused their energy on creating little gifts for their loved ones. Mother was busy with her crochet needle, fashioning a small doily and trimming the edge of a dainty handkerchief with a bit of frilly lace. The click of Oma's knitting needles was constant, as she sat in her rocking chair with a ball of dark blue wool in her lap. Anje didn't know what Oma was making, but she watched as Oma cast on and cast off stitches, and it looked as though a pair of mittens was taking shape.

Anje was eagerly waiting for Saint Nicholas Day on December 5. Tradition was, on that night, Saint Nicholas came from Spain on his white horse, along with his helper Black Peter, bringing gifts for the family. Fourteen days prior to that, Anje set out her shoe beside the stove at night, placing in it small gifts such as a juicy apple, a carrot, cookies, and candies for Saint Nicholas or his horse. In return, she hoped to receive taai-taai, or sweet marzipan that had been carefully molded into the shape of animals; an apple or orange; or a note telling her how good she had been! She wasn't so certain she would get a note, for she had disobeyed Mother many times. In the morning, she eagerly jumped out of bed to go and see what was in her shoe. It was a sad morning if someone found a piece of coal, for then they knew they had not been good. Anje was always a bit fearful she would get a piece of coal in her shoe because she knew she had not always been good, but only once did Saint Nicholas admonish her in this way.

Anje loved to be involved when Mother was baking Christmas goodies. But her involvement was usually just being the taste tester; Mother was the baker. But the beating of the dough on the sides of the bowl meant that Mother was preparing rolletjes, sweet pancakes that were rolled up, to be filled later with a sweet filling. This was one of Anje's favorites for their Christmas celebration.

"Mmm, this is good," she remarked as she licked the traces of powdered sugar from her lips. She loved being the taste tester. "I wish we could have them every day!"

"Well, that would spoil it," Mother said with a smile as she removed her apron and prepared to put the baking away, "for then it wouldn't be a treat!"

On the eve of December 5, the doorbell continued to ring at the Minnes' home as neighbors, relatives, and friends gathered to celebrate the holiday. Warm hugs and greetings passed from one to the other as they removed their coats and hats. Uncle Martijn and his wife, Frieda, and Mother's sister Dolly and her husband, Albert, and their children were among the guests. Anje had been eagerly waiting for the arrival of her cousins, Sophie and Willie, because she had plans for them.

Anje was the hostess as she and her cousins sat at the table in the back room, sipping a cup of hot milk flavored with tasty cubes of anise. As Aunt Dolly climbed the stairs into the kitchen, she handed Mother a package of doughnuts she had brought as a gift.

"Hillie," she whispered quietly, "these are for you!" Hillie thanked her and smiled, and then she opened the bag and prepared to serve them to her guests. As Anje watched, she thought, *Mother, you always give everything away. What about us?*

Other gifts were being exchanged. Anje saw Uncle Hans gave Father a cigar, and in return he received a straight pen. Sophie had written a poem for Anje, and Uncle Hans appeared and whispered quietly to her, "Anje, I have something for you for Christmas, but it will come later. Okay?"

She nodded in reply.

Christmas celebrations were a long affair, as guests would go from one house to the next, bringing greetings, treats, and Advocaat. It often lasted until morning. Father left around midnight, saying he had many places to go, and Anje knew they wouldn't see him until the next day. This was nothing new to her. Her father often left and came home whenever he felt like it; at least this was the way it seemed to her. Sometimes she felt a little pang of jealousy when she saw the happy home life of her friends.

Morning didn't come soon enough for the children who waited this night. Anje lay in bed wondering, *When St. Nicholas arrives during the night, what will he place in my shoe?*

She looked in her shoe every morning, and what was this? It was a little chamber pot with a lid made of dark chocolate, and when she lifted the lid, she was surprised to see inside a little, round, brown chocolate ball! She grinned as she took out all those pieces of chocolate, so delicately made, and popped them in her mouth one by one. St. Nicholas treats were so good!

The next morning, she could barely contain her excitement as Uncle Hans appeared at their door with an evergreen tree he had just purchased down the street. "What do you think, Anje? Will it do?" She nodded and smiled as he hauled it up the stairs and through the door into the front room. She ran into the back room to find the box that contained the ornaments, some very old and fragile, and her favorite, an oblong silver ornament that looked like a teardrop that sparkled as it gently rotated in the light. One by one, she removed the decorations from the box, and Mother and Hans hung them on the branches. They all stood back to observe the beauty of the tree and smell the sweet fragrance of pine as it wafted through the house.

"I will come back with your present," Hans said eagerly.

Anje was mystified. What could it be that Uncle Hans could not bring to their Christmas celebration? She could not help but love Uncle Hans. He was a kind, gentle, generous person. He never failed to bring her a treat whenever he came over—perhaps a toy, a book, or some candy. He was the loving father figure in her life. Hans never married. He lived at home with his parents since his mother was a paraplegic. After his father died, since he had no siblings, the duty of his mother's care fell solely upon him. Their home was only a block away from Hans's workplace, and he would go home at noon, sling her over his shoulder like a sack of potatoes, take her to the bathroom, give her lunch, and return to work. This was his daily routine. The Minnes family frequently visited in their home. Anje enjoyed visiting with his mother, Eva, for she had a cheerful, positive personality. She adored rings and wore one on every finger. Eva gestured with her hands as she spoke, and when the light caught those gems, they sparkled, just like her personality.

What was Uncle Hans going to bring her? She had already received the best present ever when he gave her a bicycle for her birthday. Now she could hear him returning, and he was carrying a cardboard box under his arm.

"You must close your eyes," he prompted, as she heard him opening the flaps on the box. What were those strange sounds she was hearing?

"Okay, you can open them!" he declared as he smiled.

To her utter amazement, Hans placed a white puppy in her lap. He was wiggly and friendly, he kept wagging his tail and trying to lick her face, and the quiet little girl who refused all kisses was being lavishly showered with puppy kisses. No one knew how lonely it was being an only child. Now she would have a companion that was all her own. She would have to show Janny. Janny was a wonderful friend, but she didn't sleep on Anje's bed or follow at her side everywhere she went. This puppy was soft, loving, and cuddly, and it was exactly what Anje needed. She picked him up, looked full into his face, and said, "I think I will call him Jamada."

The Christmas Eve tradition of attending church at midnight was honored by all, whether they were religious or not. As Hillie, Jan, and Anje walked home from Mass, exactly at midnight the air was filled with the reverberating sound of church bells ringing. One by one they began pealing forth their song, "Peace on earth, good will towards men." At that same moment, the deep voice of foghorns blasted across the canals, and every ship and barge, docked or running, rang its bells as they announced the day of Christ's birth.

On December 25, Mother lit the white candles and clamped their metal holders on the tree; and as she did, the flickering flames brought a festive glow to the room. This was a day to share with others, and Anje was elated as the ringing of the doorbell announced the arrival of Dolly and Albert along with Sophie and Willie. The room was filled with an air of celebration as the children shouted and played their card games. Shouts of, "I won!" filled the room, and the words, "I'll win next time" were exchanged back and forth as they kept the game lively. The air was blue with smoke from the cigarettes hanging from the lips of the men, who were serious card players. Anje perked up her ears once or twice when she heard comments about the rumors of war. About half of the men believed them, and the other half scoffed. Each man had a glass of gin beside him and a full bottle not far away; the sandwiches and sweets were a welcome addition to the table. The ladies observed the proceedings as they visited and sipped the golden custard-like beverage Advocaat, which was their Christmas treat. They all knew that January was just around the corner.

January was always a long, bleak month with gray skies and cold weather, and this year was no exception. The days seemed endless as Opa became weaker and weaker. He remained in bed, and as Mother sat at his bedside feeding him, he looked up at her with weary eyes, his brow furrowed, and whispered in a hoarse voice, "You have been very good to me. You have treated me better than my own children did. Thank you." A few days later he died.

His body never left their home. The funeral director came and washed the body, dressing it in a long, white paper gown and placing it in a black wooden coffin with a glass dome lid. The front room was always reserved for special occasions, usually Christmas, but now it was prepared for a funeral. Everything in the front room was covered with a black cloth, and a black rug was placed on the floor. The coffin was placed in the middle of the room. It was a somber sight.

Anje had never seen a dead person before, and she didn't know quite what to think about it. When she looked at the stiffness of her grandfather's white face and his bony fingers, she almost expected him to shake his finger at her the way he had so often done before. His skin looked so parched and wrinkled. She watched closely—was his chest rising and falling? *No. He really is dead,* she thought. *What is death anyway? Where does a person go when he dies? Just into the grave?* That didn't seem right. She knew Opa would go into the grave, but where was the part of him that was missing? It wasn't just his breath that was missing; his life was gone. She carefully observed the family members as they came and went, watching to see how they would behave as they came to pay their respects. One of Opa's daughters approached Hillie muttering urgently under her breath, "I want you to take that ring off his finger," gesturing toward his gold wedding ring.

Mother paused for a moment, looked at her coolly, and replied, "If you want it, you will have to take it off yourself." With that comment, the daughter flounced out of the room, agitated.

Anje was aghast. What was the meaning of that? Didn't that ring belong to Opa? Couldn't he take it with him wherever he was going? Why did his daughter think she should have it? She smiled when she thought of Mother's answer. That was such a good answer to such a foolish request.

On January 16, 1940, when the funeral was held, all eleven children and their spouses crowded into the small room. Anje had never seen so many people in their house at one time. The undertaker removed the glass cover from the coffin, and each one approached the body to say good-bye. Anje puzzled over this: *Opa isn't here. He's dead. Who are you talking to? He can't hear you.* When they were done paying their respects, the undertaker placed a wooden cover over the coffin, and his sons attempted to carry it down the stairs. The curve in the narrow stairs posed a problem. They tilted the coffin this way and that, finally having to bring it almost upright in order to pass through. Anje watched with more than a little angst, fearful the body would fall out. Finally, the men were able to maneuver it down the stairs to the waiting hearse.

Anje watched from her upstairs window as the black funeral wagon, pulled by a team of dappled gray horses, moved down the street followed by the buggies that carried the relatives of the deceased. She heard the clip clop of the horses' hooves on the pavement and watched as the rear of the hearse bounced down the street, the black tassels in the windows swinging back and forth, with ebony ribbons blowing in the breeze.

A SUMMER HOLIDAY

It was the end of the school year and a great celebration was planned, as the Groningen school students traveled to an area known as Sand Dunes and Heather. There, they splashed in the water, played games, and created happy memories. Anje was excited when the train pulled into the station, for when they disembarked, they formed ranks and marched proudly in a parade into the Grote Markt. They had no idea that before long the square at Grote Markt would be occupied with the sounds of marching bands and parades of enemy soldiers.

Anje's blond hair was fluttering in the wind as she hurried through the door, depositing her bicycle at the bottom of the stairs. She flew up the stairs, eager to show Mother the report card she was so proud of. Mother always had time for Anje. She carefully perused the report card, discussing the subjects individually and praising her daughter for the high marks she had obtained. Her father sat comfortably in his big chair smoking a cigar and reading the paper, not engaging in the conversation around him.

Mother encouraged Jan to look at Anje's report card, but when she handed it to him, he scanned it briefly and then said drily, "She could have done better." He tossed the report on the table, got up from his chair, and walked away.

All the air went out of Anje's balloon; the fun of the day disappeared in the distance, and it felt like her heart sank into her stomach. It didn't matter what she accomplished, her father would never praise her. She had disappointed him the day she was born. There was one thing she couldn't do—she couldn't be a boy.

Her mother showed her wisdom in many ways; she knew what her daughter needed. She announced the surprise reward that was waiting for her. Anje and her cousin Sophie would be going on a little holiday to Utrecht for a few days to visit Aunt Lulu and Uncle Roland.

Anje was thrilled, and Sophie was delighted; they were going on a vacation without their parents! As they sat on the wooden seat in the compartment of the train, they watched the scenery pass by the window. An old stone water tower stood beside the canal, and sheep grazed lazily on the green grass on top of the dike as bright yellow buttercups danced beside them in the breeze. The large vanes on the rustic old windmill beside the canal were turning, as they had for centuries, pumping the water from the land and channeling it back to the sea. Where one city ended, another village began, and before they knew it, their train was slowing down as it pulled into the station at Utrecht. Their eyes scanned the crowd to find Aunt Lulu, who would be meeting them at the train station.

Lulu was easy to find because she always had a hat on her head. Sure enough, moving through the crowd with a navy straw cloche firmly hugging her head was Aunt Lulu. The white handkerchief firmly held in her hand was waving like a flag—they couldn't miss her.

"Hullo! Girls, welcome! I hope you are going to have a good time," she said, hugging them as they proceeded to walk toward a taxi that was waiting to take them to her home.

"I have some very interesting things planned for you girls the next few days," she said animatedly. "We are going to visit the zoo; then I have a dressmaker who will be making some new clothes for you, Anje. She will be coming over to measure you. Tomorrow we are going to show you something very interesting—Uncle Roland's and Uncle Paul's plant where they manufacture hardware."

She was right. The following day as they motored to the factory, they were amazed to see the immense structure that housed this manufacturing process, which included a foundry. The plant was very noisy and very hot. Huge pieces of equipment were operating at the same time, making it almost impossible to hear her speak.

All kinds of hardware were being mass produced—nuts, bolts, nails, and screws—items that were in high demand. As they walked through the plant, they stopped at the spot where they could see the red hot, liquid steel being poured from a huge cauldron into something that looked like a large ladle. The ladle was tipped over by a machine, and the red hot molten steel rolled over the edge of the ladle and poured into molds that were moving past on a conveyor belt. At this location they were making nails, which were being passed through a cooling process; and as the girls moved along they could see nails being spewed out by the thousands, clattering into a huge bin that, when full, was wheeled away into another area. It was an amazing sight.

"Wasn't that fascinating?" Aunt Lulu said as she moved toward the bicycle taxi that was waiting. "Tomorrow we are going to the zoo, so you must have a good sleep tonight, girls."

As Anje lay in the cozy feather bed that night, thoughts continued to flood her mind. *These are Father's relatives, and they are rich. No wonder Father likes to spend time with them. This is a very different lifestyle than we have in Groningen,* she thought. She could see that his brothers had many privileges, but they worked hard. Father wanted to be rich, but he didn't want to work hard. He liked to walk around in nice clothes all day and concentrate on sports. She couldn't understand why he was so different from the rest of his family. She couldn't answer that, so she fell lazily into dreamland, thinking about tomorrow and their visit to the zoo.

The cacophony of sounds were typical for a zoo—sights and sounds and smells you didn't find anywhere else, Anje thought. She admired the strength of the elephants, the boldness of the stripes on the zebras, and the cheekiness of the monkeys as they hastily tried to grab the hands of the visitors as they offered treats. But her favorite was the big-eyed ostrich as he tried to pick at someone's hat as it appeared within striking distance. Aunt Lulu insisted that she wanted a picture to show Mother, and so they climbed on a great furry beast for a donkey ride. Anje was not impressed with this disobedient animal—it had a mind of its own—but

Aunt Lulu wanted a picture. So when she called, "Smile, girls! Smile!" they smiled, and she snapped a photo.

Being in Aunt Lulu's company was enjoyable; her big, dark eyes were always sparkling with excitement behind the round gold spectacles that sat on her nose. She was never without her little dog. His tail wagged furiously when he wanted to be picked up, and when she scooped him up, he was just a bundle of fluff in her arms.

"Okay, Anje, your dresses are done," Lulu said happily, as she began packing them in a bag for her to take home. "There is just one that is not finished, so I will bring it next time I come to visit you."

The girls were back on the train heading toward home, sucking on the delightful sweets Lulu had sent for their journey home. This had been a good holiday! When they returned to Groningen, sad news awaited them. Uncle Hans's mother Eva had passed away suddenly in her sleep.

It was a somber day for the family, as they trudged slowly toward the cemetery for Eva's burial. This was the first time Anje stood beside an open grave; it was an experience like no other. The hole in the ground seemed cavernous and final. As Mother comforted Hans, she reminded him how Eva had feared the rumblings of war. Since she was not able to get up and run to safety, she didn't know how she would get into a bomb shelter if they were attacked. Now all those fears were unfounded; the problems would never have to be solved. Her body was now being placed in the ground permanently. The coffin was opened one last time for the loved ones to get a final glimpse. Anje thought she looked lovely. It appeared as though she could just sit up and speak, but she could not. Her life had fled away. Where to? Anje did not know; this was one of the mysteries of life. As the last words were spoken by the minister, "The Lord giveth, and the Lord taketh away; blessed be the name of the Lord," the mourners left the cemetery feeling a sense of relief for Eva. Her battle was over. They did not know that their battle was about to begin.

"WE ARE AT WAR!"
MAY 10, 1940

War started in Groningen Holland, on May 10, 1940. Sporadic showers pelted down from the gray skies, and spurts of sunshine broke through the dense clouds this Friday morning as Hillie began to prepare breakfast in their small kitchen. She was spreading butter on a slice of bread laid out on the table as Jan reached for the knob on the radio. With a twist of the dial, the hum and crackle of the radio transmission began. Hillie lifted her apron to wipe her hands, and she paused as she heard the words coming through the speaker.

"This is the BBC News in London. We bring to you an urgent report. Germany has invaded the Netherlands. Though no official declaration of war has been made, the

Luftwaffe has launched a large-scale airborne attack, greater than has ever been experienced in the history of war." As the voice continued, Hillie and Jan looked at each other in shock. Hillie then looked at Anje sitting quietly on her chair listening to the broadcast. She wondered how much she understood of this chilling news.

The news broadcaster continued,

"Waves of Heinkel bombers filled the sky last night, releasing over four thousand parachutists and airborne troops into the Netherlands. German seaplanes landed on the Waal River in Rotterdam, dropping a company of soldiers who seized the bridges before the Dutch military could blow them. Outside the border town of Nieuwenschans, thousands of camouflaged Nazi soldiers were dropped from the air at three o' clock in the morning. They swarmed an armored artillery train and charged the Dutch border under cover of darkness. The Germans fired grenades at the small bunkers located at the border, but the Dutch military quickly responded by raising the railway bridge to deter the train from moving ahead. The border guards were overpowered by the Nazi soldiers, and the enemy lowered the bridge, enabling the train load of Nazi soldiers to penetrate into the Netherlands. We were not prepared for the voracious force of the German Army descending on our little country, for they came as thieves in the night. God save our land."

Hillie and Jan were still trying to assimilate what they had just heard. "The Netherlands has not been at war since the days of Napoleon," Jan said passionately. "We have been neutral for many years; we cannot defend our little country from a major assault from a nation as large as Germany." Anje had a surprised look on her face, and Hillie knew why. In all the discussions of war, Jan was always neutral and passive. What had changed? *I guess he never thought this would really happen,* Hillie said to herself.

She looked across the table at her eleven-year-old daughter, whose short, blond hair fell into bangs just above her clear, blue eyes, which were fixed on her mother's face. She had been nibbling innocently on her toast engrossed in her own thoughts.

"You will not be going to school today, my dear," Hillie announced nonchalantly. "I want you to stay home with me."

Anje looked up from the table, a look of surprise on her face. Her mother never encouraged her to stay home from school; this newscast must be more serious than she thought.

Jan's brow was furrowed after hearing the newscast. His dark eyes narrowed, and a troubled look flashed across his face. He rose abruptly from the table, and the wooden chair screeched as he pushed it across the floor. He grabbed his felt cap and jacket and stomped down the stairs while muttering something about needing to see some of his friends. His bicycle clattered as he removed it from its storage at the bottom of the stairs. The door slammed, and he was gone.

Hillie paused to think. *How could the Netherlands be caught off guard like this?* Her brain scrolled through the past as she remembered listening to the radio broadcast of King George VI of Great Britain, on September 3, 1939, saying, "We are at war." She recalled some of the other phrases, "It is unthinkable to think we would refuse this challenge.... Stand calm, firm, and united.... There will be dark days ahead.... Keep resolutely faithful to the cause." *Very wise words,* she thought. *I think we should heed that advice.*

Mrs. Lootens peered cautiously through the lace curtains

on her window above the bakery and was dazed by the sight of columns of uniformed soldiers marching aggressively on the cobblestone streets. When she walked to the market to buy groceries, soldiers in sage green uniforms were controlling traffic at busy intersections of the city while others were escorting tenants from large buildings with the intent of occupying them.

"Is this really happening in Groningen?" she said aloud.

Her nineteen-year-old son was standing nearby, watching the activities from another window. His mother gazed at him intently and placed her arms protectively around his shoulders. They are not getting my son, she thought fiercely. Her heart's cry was the same as that of many mothers and wives; they would have to hide their men from the clutches of the enemy.

Hans wheeled his bicycle down the street in Groningen to his first stop—he needed to pick up some forms from the printing shop on Wijnhaven before he went to his office. But he became aware of thousands of German troops swarming into the city of Groningen just as people were enjoying their noon meal. Waves of gray appeared everywhere simultaneously as German soldiers in their field gray uniforms began cascading over the dike, the barrels of their powerful rifles glistening from the moisture of the light rain. As he turned the corner, the street was blocked with contingents of soldiers marching with heads erect, the brims of their steel helmets shielding to the eyebrows. The studs in the soles of their jackboots made a metallic thud on the old stone streets as they stomped ahead. It was a sound of military force. A shiver went up his spine as German voices called out commands as they marched. A stark realization came over all who watched—they had been invaded! It was then Jan realized that the Netherlands was at war and that life in Groningen would never be the same.

That same day, colored leaflets fluttered down from the sky as people gazed upward in astonishment, looking at the rain of paper and wondering about the reason for it. Hans was walking down the street as he left the printing office when he saw leaflets falling from the planes above. He looked up, shielding his eyes with his hands. *What kind of propaganda are they feeding us now?* he wondered. He quickly extinguished his cigarette and reached down to pick up the piece of paper that lay at his feet. His lips pursed and his eyebrows arched as he read the message. It was stern, direct, and threatening.

Warning!

People of the Netherlands
DO NOT ENTER THE WAR!
Citizens caught in acts of sabotage
Or resistance will receive the death penalty.
Let this be a warning to you.

Hans and Erich sat together in the small coffee house discussing the military action of the past few days over a cup of coffee. Erich exhaled smoke in a small stream from his pursed lips and asked, "Can you really believe this?" He turned his head to look about the room that was full of local people sitting on the stools at their small tables speaking in subdued tones, all the while looking furtively over their shoulders. The atmosphere was usually jovial and loose, with customers greeting newcomers in the door with a smile and a wave. But the easy banter and loud laughter were gone, replaced with caution and fear. It seemed that in just a few days, everything had changed.

Hans never complained, but today the mood was different. "I was stopped twice today on my way over here by soldiers demanding to see my identification papers. And you know what else I heard through my office? Every Dutch citizen over the age of fifteen is to be fingerprinted and photographed. New identification cards will be issued. As if the existing documents aren't good enough!" he exclaimed with disgust. "But more than that, in the records we're keeping at the local registrar office, we will have to record the religious affiliation as well, and I think that's to single out the Jews. You've heard about the pogrom of the Jews in Poland and in Germany, haven't you, Erich?"

"Yes," Erich replied cautiously, "I've heard about that."

"Don't you have some Jewish blood in you?" Hans queried softly. He moved closer to his friend so that their discussion could not be overheard.

"My grandmother on my father's side was Jewish, but she married a Gentile, and so did my father. We don't follow the Jewish laws or faith, so I wouldn't call myself a Jew."

Then he smiled as he said, "My grandmother insisted that I be circumcised at birth, and to please her, my father complied. Hans, that is the extent of my Jewishness."

Hans gazed intently upon his companion. He was a good friend, fun to be with, and always optimistic, but an uncomfortable feeling began to rise inside. "I hope, Erich, that you will be very careful," he expressed with concern as he lifted his cup to his lips.

Erich smiled as he ran his fingers through his dark, curly hair. "You worry too much, my friend. I think we'll have much greater problems to solve than this. I have to be on my way now, but we'll keep in touch." He reached out with his arm, slapped his friend on the back with his cap, and exited through the front door of the shop.

Hans looked at his retreating form, pausing a while to gather his thoughts. What ramifications could this bring? How would this affect him at his job? What could the average person do in such a situation? A lot of thinking and planning was needed. Just then he realized he was doodling on his cigarette package, and it was time to go.

Anje thought colored paper raining from the sky was fun, if one looked on the sunny side. She just lifted up her arms to the sky to see how many she could catch! Of course, she knew the message was bad—and the day would come when she would find out how bad—but she thought it would be interesting to see how she could cope with that. She was just a young girl; she liked being quiet. She learned a lot that way, and sometimes people didn't even realize she was there and said things they wouldn't otherwise say. Yes, she was a listener, and because of that she became a thinker, because she had to think about the meaning of what she was hearing. If people thought she was odd because she was too quiet—well, she liked it that way.

Father didn't come home for almost a week after that

"rainy" day. Besides working, Mother was busy trying to figure out how this war would affect their lives. Mother and Sonjia had a big discussion about it while she was upstairs studying, but she heard every word. Something upstairs was unique. There was a small trap door in the floor with a round ring handle. When she pulled on the handle, the hinge lifted the trap door, which opened into the kitchen, and she could hear everything being said. Sonjia was a nice person, but Anje could tell from her comments that she was afraid.

"Hillie," she said, "they say all food is going to be rationed."

"I am sure there will be ways to solve that, Sonjia. I heard that we will be getting coupons for buying food," Hillie replied.

Sonjia sighed. She never won an argument with Hillie.

Anje had great confidence in her mother. Anje had been very sick when she was just six years old, and Mother nursed her back to health. She had missed six months of school, but Mother got the books and tutored her so she could catch up with her friends. Mother always had a wise answer for every problem, so Anje was sure that whatever lay ahead, she and her mother would manage just fine.

The radio became their source of accurate information, with BBC News keeping them informed. Queen Wilhelmina and her family had been rescued a few days before the Nazis arrived, and King George and Queen Elizabeth welcomed them to Buckingham Palace until they could find their own accommodations. They were lucky. Not everyone could sail away on a ship if there was trouble, but the queen was going to rule Holland from England. Anje didn't know how that was possible, but that's what she heard.

THE OCCUPATION

The sky was bright and clear as Anje walked down Grote Markt Straat past the university complex, which was usually bustling with activity. Students from all over the Netherlands went there to receive their education, as Groningen was known as a university city. However, in order to continue studies, the Germans now required students to sign a pledge of loyalty to the Third Reich and refrain from any action against the German empire. As a result, the buildings were empty, and the silence was evidence of the unyielding spirit of the Dutch to their oppressors. Students were forced to go underground to avoid being sent to Germany to do forced labor.

Anje was approaching a group of students she overheard discussing their dilemma.

"What do you think of this?" one twenty-year-old asked of his friend.

"I think it stinks," the other replied as he walked away.

"Are you going to sign?" another one asked.

"Never!" was the reply.

"I am in my second year of science. I'm studying to become a doctor," a tall fellow with glasses complained.

"What are our alternatives?" a female student questioned, her gloved hand raised in query.

"We will have to put our education on hold until this war is over. That's our alternative."

When Anje returned home, she questioned Mother about this problem.

That's right, Anje," Mother replied, "and there will be more things that will have to be adjusted. We won't know until we are faced with them, and then we will solve them."

Mother's calm, gentle reasoning put her fears at rest.

On May 12, 1940, Hillie was pedaling through the Grote Markt on her way home when she noticed the bustling activity of automobiles in the area. This was unusual; it was common to see bicycles everywhere but not motor cars. She was curious, so she passed by the massive buildings slowly at first and got a view of the first German autos parked in front of the Scholten House. Just then, a sleek black car sporting a Nazi flag on its standard pulled up and the doors opened; the German Vice Consul had arrived with his entourage. A new flag was being raised upon the building, the striking symbol of Hitler's regime—a black Hakenkreuz (broken cross) in a white circle on a blood red background.

This swastika would become a symbol of terror and death in Europe and beyond. Now this opulent building, which had been the hub of high society in Groningen, would be the feared Schutzstaffel headquarters that would become known to the locals as the House of Blood and Tears. The occupation had begun.

Hillie noticed that the old windmill shone a tranquil reflection on the canal, as it had for hundreds of years, its arms waving in the wind, as thousands of brilliantly colored tulips nodded their heads in a kaleidoscope of color. War didn't affect the beauty of the landscape. She was among the cyclists who traveled along the cobbled streets to their destinations while wooden barges glided lazily along the waterways as they had for centuries, transporting goods from place to place. On the surface, things appeared much the same, but in reality, many things had changed.

Hillie knew the motto of the Netherlands: "I will maintain." The Dutch had fought for every inch of space that was above water, diligently working to build and sustain their land, and they were not receptive to the occupation of a foreign power. Hans had helped to calm her fears about food, for he knew their government had stockpiled a six-year supply of food from their abundant agricultural resources in the event of a famine or other disaster. They would be able to weather a lengthy storm. But the Germans had a mind to pick this ripe plum—not just the food, but the other resources as well. The Reich began to pilfer five million marks every month from the Dutch treasury for occupation costs. The first two years of the occupation were bearable, but when the Nazis discovered that the people would not bow to their demands, the mighty power of the German Army was released.

The staccato sounds of fighter planes battling above, the whine of aircraft engines, the thunderous roar and vibration of the earth as the bombs fell—Anje had become accustomed to all of this. This was an air war, and her eyes were always trained on the sky, which resulted in running for cover to avoid stray bullets or falling debris. She watched the Heinkel bombers discharging tons of bombs from their bellies as she huddled behind a five-foot wall of sandbags stacked against the store's display windows. This would protect her from flying debris, but there was no shelter from above. She put her hands over her ears to block out the horrendous sounds of destruction. When the bombs exploded, buildings were destroyed in a moment—only concrete rubble remained. When the dust settled, steel girders were draped limply like pieces of tin, the façades of the buildings resembling the remnants of an eerie ghost town.

Hans was cycling past the square when he noticed a small group of people standing silently on the street watching as four soldiers—one with a ladder, another with tools, and two to supervise—were busily engaged with the assignment of replacing street signs in prominent places with German names.

Hans sat at their kitchen table and described the scene to Hillie:

One soldier climbed up the ladder, and the people were straining their necks to see what was going on.

"What do you think they are doing?" one asked the other quietly.

"You don't know?" the other replied. "He is going to replace the sign for Prins Hendrik Straat with a better name," he said sarcastically.

"What do you think they will replace it with?" the first one queried as he adjusted his cap to keep the sun from his eyes as he looked upward.

"We will know in just a minute," he responded.

The officer reached forth his gloved hand to pass the metal sign to the other soldier so it could be screwed into place. By now a small group had gathered to watch the procedure. The sign read, "Heinrich Himmler Weg." The observers looked at each other; one raised his eyebrows and turned away in disgust.

"Heinrich Himmler Weg," he said acidly and then decided the rest of his words would remain unspoken. What did this man have to do with their city except to destroy it?

They were muttering their displeasure to one another under their breath when they noticed a short Dutch man with a gray tweed coat and felt hat observing their every move with great interest, and one by one they silently began to move away from the scene.

"But that wasn't all," Hans continued. "Our interest was piqued by the sound of music that appeared to be moving in our direction, and as it turned the corner, we watched a military band come into view."

Parades in the streets were frequent. The musical instruments glittered in the sunshine as immaculately dressed soldiers in full uniform paraded with heads erect, white gloved hands swinging, marching the goose step in strict precision as their breeches billowed above the tall leather boots. They resembled proud peacocks with their magnificent tail feathers fanned out, as they passionately sang their German songs with robust voices.

> *"When the S.S. and the S.A.*
> *March up in formation.*
> *Taratata!*
> *Firm is the stride.*
> *Firm is the pace,*
> *Left two three four, everyone wants to join*
> *And so one marches today through every little town*
> *And every German girl dreams of this today*
> *Because the black S.S. and the brown S.A.*
> *Have what pleases everyone today*
> *And it's the most beautiful thing in the world."*

Men, women, and children—everyone was required to stand at attention with eyes forward during this performance. One man who turned his head to look in a shop window felt the stinging bite of a leather whip across his face, administered by the officer on the street.

Though the German music was entertaining, the people looked upon it with disdain; they did not desire to enjoy the music of the oppressor. Church people were offended by the playing of the German national anthem in their land as the melody was taken from an old Austrian hymn called "Glorious Things of Thee are Spoken." Accepted as the

German national anthem in 1922, the first stanza was the one that Hitler extolled, for this verse declared, "Deutschland, Deutschland, ueber alles. Ueber alles in der Welt," which means, *"Germany, Germany, above all, above everything in the world."* Supremacy was Hitler's greatest desire, and his passion was fueled by the ovation of the masses.

This oppression was a heavy yoke on the Dutch citizens, who detested the confinement of all the rules they were required to follow. "Independent! We are an independent people," Hans said almost to himself. "We don't need anyone to tell us where we can go, who we can see, and when to go home. These curfews are ridiculous." He needed a piece of paper called an Ausweis if he was going to be on the street after 6:00 p.m. in winter and 10:00 p.m. in summer. Street patrols diligently enforced these rules.

Sonjia arrived at the Minnes' place as agreed. She and Hillie were going to go shopping for some things for the house. Anje pulled on her blue sweater, as she had decided to go along. As they walked up the two steps into the store, a small bell tinkled to announce their arrival. Classen's store had been such an interesting place with a wide array of goods, until now. There were many empty spaces on the shelves. Anje looked at the large spool of string that hung from the ceiling above the counter to wrap parcels. The large roll of brown wrapping paper was empty. Sonjia had come prepared with a cloth bag from home, and she began examining the bolts of cloth in the fabric section as they prepared to make window coverings for the blackout.

"Oh, this looks so ugly," Sonjia declared as she fingered the black fabric that lay before them.

"I know," Hillie replied earnestly, "but we have to do it. I'm going to hang my curtains over top of that so at least it will look pretty on the inside. We might as well enjoy the view, as long as it keeps the light out."

"No lights on. Don't give the enemy a target," Sonjia mimicked the instructions that the Air Protection Service had dispensed. "And those black bulbs we have to use produce such a faint glow that I am sure by the end of the war we will all have bad eyes," she complained.

Anje smiled. Sonjia had a way of being dramatic about everything.

"Well," Hillie interjected, "we may have bad eyes, but at least we'll be alive!"

"The other night the police were banging loudly on our door because there was a tiny crack of light coming from our window," Sonjia said with a sighed. "I know we have to be careful. Our neighbors were punished for that same thing by having their electricity cut off for two weeks, so we were lucky."

Anje knew the rules; Mother had instilled them in her— black window coverings down, and only a small light could be used. She liked her little kicker light. It was small, had a strong battery, and was very useful for reading in bed.

The only lights visible at night were the searchlights scanning the skies for enemy aircraft; but from the sky, the city was safely hidden in the blackness of the night. Anje looked through her bedroom window up into the dark sky; it was raining now. *It will be a quiet night,* she thought. *Nobody flies in this kind of weather. I will have a good sleep.*

Food became scarce. There was never enough, and Anje's stomach was constantly reminding her that it was time to eat. Mother spent many hours at the grocery store as the lineups became longer and longer; the supply rarely reached the end of the line. She often came home empty-handed. People began to hoard food as rationing and food stamps were implemented. First it was coffee and tea; and then it was bread, flour, textiles, and meat (which by then was mostly horse meat); followed by milk and potatoes; and soon it was everything. Imported produce such as oranges and bananas were no longer available; after a time the people could no longer remember the taste of these foods. It was considered a treasure if one was able to obtain eggs from a farmer, but great caution had to be exercised for it was illegal to buy food directly from the farm. Since there was no yeast available, the bread was gray and doughy; it was cut into small squares after it was baked. Milk had been skimmed off so it became a bluish watery substance with little nutritional value. Nothing was for sale without vouchers; ration cards became as valuable as gold, for without them one couldn't eat. Substitutes for coffee or tea were made from roasted barley or even worse. Ersatz coffee came in the form of a brown pill that did not even resemble coffee. Products that came directly from Dutch soil were scarce, for the Germans systematically looted the country as long trains laden with food daily crossed the eastern border into Germany. Eggs were 1.60 guilders each, butter was 50 guilders per pound, wheat was 60 guilders per bushel, and milk was 1.25 guilders per liter. Bacon was 25 guilders per pound. (For reference, 2.642 guilders is equal to one US dollar.)

One day, Anje was happy as she pedaled to the farm. The sky was full of the promise of sunshine, as every few minutes it appeared from behind the clouds. She was humming as her tires bumped along the rough road along the canal; she moved in and out among the traffic, enjoying her journey. She was going to have a treat today, and the thought of it warmed her insides.

"Anje," Mother had said as she put some coins into her hand, "today you can go to the farm and buy some milk for us. Make sure nobody sees you."

What a pleasure it would be to have a glass of milk! But she smiled a little at Mother's words, "Make sure nobody sees you." *That would be quite impossible,* she thought, *unless I was invisible!* As she pedaled down the long drive into the farmyard, she was greeted by a large, friendly black dog that led her right to the barn. *Yes,* she thought, *that's where the farmer will be; the dog knows where his master is.* And she was right!

When she pulled on the handle of the barn door, she could smell a variety of odors—one of fresh manure, another of sweet hay, the other of the warmth of the bodies of the animals—but the best smell of all was the aroma of fresh milk. The farmer, dressed in dark blue overalls and a faded plaid shirt, was pouring freshly strained milk into the tall milk can. Hearing the door creak as someone entered, he turned to see this young girl watching him, a jar in her hand.

"Good morning," he said with a smile. "You are my first customer for today!" He set the milk pail down and reached out his hand for her jar.

She eagerly handed him her coins.

He pocketed the coins in the slit of his overalls and began to fill her jar as she watched the white liquid coming down through the funnel into her jar.

"There, it's full," he said as he handed the milk to her. She thought only a moment and then raised the jar to her lips and began to drink; it was still warm. She could feel the milk slide down her throat and into her tummy. Her body responded immediately to the nutrition. The scent that wafted to her nostrils was as good as the taste. No one would be able to rob her of this wonderful treat—she would enjoy it now! Life was so unpredictable that she didn't know when she would be able to come again.

The farmer wiped his brow with his red handkerchief and smiled as he began to fill the jar again. She carried it carefully to her bicycle, stashing it in the leather pouch to take home to Mother. The journey homeward was even better, for her tummy was warm and full of food. She looked toward the sky. It didn't matter if the sun wasn't shining; it was shining in her heart.

When spring arrived in March 1941, the mild winds blew across the land, warming the soil, and thoughts of planting a garden emerged. Mother was fortunate enough to secure a small plot of land eight kilometers from the city.

"Guess what I found today, Anje?" Mother said as she came in the door. "I found some seeds. But the only seed that was available was winter carrots and green beans." She smiled as she opened the small packet of seeds wrapped in brown paper. "But this is better than nothing."

They were both anxious to see what their garden would look like as they sowed their seeds into the soft, brown soil. When the green seedlings emerged, they weeded and protected them from the wind, watching with great interest as they grew. After the plants finished blooming, Anje watched the small beans form and grow until they were ready for picking. As they filled their bags to the brim with lovely, dark green beans, Anje thought, *I can taste them already!*

In order to mature, the carrots had to remain in the ground until late fall, where they became sweeter and juicier as each day went by. Whenever Anje and Mother pedaled to their garden, they saw people taking advantage of every square inch of ground they could find; green beans and pea vines grew along the shoulder of the road, and potato plants painstakingly cared for were thriving beside the railroad bed. It was an exciting day when they were able to pick these new green beans.

Anje heaved a bored sigh as she filled her dinner plate with beans again. *I know it is good for me,* she thought, *but I am tired of eating beans for breakfast, beans for dinner, and beans for supper.*

"I know what you're thinking," Mother commented, "but we are fortunate to have beans when so many people have nothing."

"Mother, do you know what I would really like? A nice piece of bread, and maybe some jam, too," she declared, her hand under her chin in a thoughtful pose.

"I know, Anje," Mother replied as she put her arm around her. "When the war is over, we will have bread and jam, and probably other good things too."

Each winter morning as she packed her school lunch, she put a large carrot in her bicycle pouch. At lunchtime, she enjoyed munching on the orange flesh on the outside and gnawing around the hard yellow core in the center. Each meal was like a project, and she entertained herself in her thoughts as she nibbled her way through lunch. Mother was right—this was better than nothing!

Sonjia slid off her bicycle, parked it, and rang the doorbell at the Minnes home.

"Come in, Sonjia," Anje called out when she opened the door.

Hillie was wiping her hands as she came into the vestibule. "What brings you over here today?"

"Oh," Sonjia complained as she hauled her bicycle into the house, "I need a new tire for my bicycle. I just can't patch it anymore. You know, Hillie," she continued, "with this war on, it's almost impossible to get a bicycle tire. They have one at Boonstra's, but they are asking four hundred guilders for it, and they told me I was very lucky to even find one. Well, I don't have four hundred guilders!" she exclaimed disgustedly.

Anje listened carefully. *It is amazing that Mother is*

able to make everything work out like she does, she thought. *Her salary at the center doesn't give us much, but somehow we manage.* We have never had to buy a tire yet; four hundred guilders is a fortune. She understood that the war caused rubber to be expensive.

"Let's have a cup of tea," Hillie said in consolation as she hurried to make a little fire in the stove. "I was fortunate; I was able to get some pressed wood. Well, actually, it's just compressed straw. You know how awful it is trying to get enough gas to make a meal—well, that is, if there is anything to cook."

"You know what Boonstra's told me?" Sonjia continued as she sipped her tea. "'You might have to make your own tire,' they said. The Germans have taken everything valuable for the use of the Wehrmacht," she rolled her eyes as she concluded her remarks.

"Well," Hillie replied as she stirred her tea with a spoon, "I saw someone riding a bicycle, and one wheel was taken from a baby carriage."

"I am not going to do that," Sonjia snorted.

"You know, Sonjia, we are living in times that we don't know what will be required of us in order to survive this war. Come on. I have some heavy string, and I'll help you to bind that tire securely to the rim. Does it hold air at all?"

"No, it doesn't, I drove over here on a flat tire." Sonjia lamented.

"Do you know what you can be happy about?" Hillie asked. "The enemy will not try to steal your bicycle. They're just looking for those with good tires."As she listened, Anje resolved, *I'm going to make very sure no one gets my bicycle, I have good tires, and a good bike, and I'm going to keep it!* *

"Just look at my jacket," Sonjia lamented. "I have mended the elbows and cuffs with so many patches I can't even tell what my original jacket looked like. The worst thing is, now I can't even find anything to make patches with, and look how this cuff is fraying again," she said as she pulled some strands of cloth from her sleeve.

"Anje is growing so much that I just sewed another frill on the bottom of her skirt, trying to make it last another year or two. Oma had a little bit of fabric tucked away in her chest, and we made good use of it," Hillie replied.

"Shoes are another story," Sonjia lamented. "I've had my shoes resoled so many times that there is nothing left of them. I don't think there will be enough old car tires in Holland to fix all of our shoes!"

"We can always go to clogs," Hillie continued. "The way Anje is growing, she may soon have to wear clogs if we can't find her a pair of shoes!"

Clogs! Anje thought. She had worn them a few times, but they were cumbersome, and she couldn't run in clogs. But her toes were beginning to push out the end of her leather shoes; she knew Mother was right. She had seen some leather strips in the store when she had been with Uncle Hans—maybe he could get her a pair of sandals made with that leather.

* Six million bicycles were confiscated during the war, and shipped to Germany.

"Yes, but clogs are hard to get used to, and you can't sneak up on anybody if you're wearing them," Sonjia replied.

"Ah, but there is another advantage, Sonjia. If you're ever in a fight, clogs can be a good weapon," Hillie said with an impish smile.

Anje thought about that statement. She thought she would rather run than fight. She was a very good runner on the track team at school, and she didn't like fighting.

Not everyone was loyal to the Netherlands. People could be bought. Food and favors were available to citizens who were loyal to the Third Reich.

"Mother, you will not believe what I saw today," Anje said. "I was visiting my friends Herman and Heinz, and I saw the swastika, the German flag, and pictures of Adolf Hitler hanging on the walls of their home. I was so surprised. Instead of going to the table to say grace over their food, they walked up to the picture of Hitler, stood erect, clicked their heels, raised their right hands, and said, 'Heil Hitler,' before eating their meal. It made me shudder. I think Hitler has become their God!"

Hillie lowered her head sadly, nodded, and turned away. She was pleased that her daughter had seen the truth and recognized the evils of the Nazi regime, but it was tragic to see Dutch people bow to the Führer.

At the beginning of the war, Jews who lived in the province of Groningen were free to practice their religion, and those who had fled Germany, Poland, Austria, and Russia were welcomed to the hospitable Netherlands. In this neutral, tolerant country, they were safe and would be able to live free from pogroms, they thought.

In January 1941, dense clouds formed in Groningen. The gray sky seemed to bring the ceiling down low, and the cold air condensed when someone spoke; they could "see their breath." Anje cycled past the square where long rows of people formed along the sidewalks outside Scholten House to register as Jews. This was required for anyone over the age of fifteen who had one grandparent with Jewish blood.

She stopped her bicycle out of curiosity, to see what was happening, and she listened to their conversations.

"What do you think this is really all about?" one woman asked another as they stood in line.

"They say we are going to be resettled," the woman replied as she rubbed her hands together to keep them warm.

"You don't have any gloves?" the first one queried.

"I left them at home," she responded as she put her hands in the pockets of her wool coat and nestled her head a little deeper into her fur collar.

"Whenever we're requested to come and register for something, always come prepared. I had a letter from my sister in Poland, and when they came to register, they were immediately put on a train to a camp. She sent me a letter to warn me of things to come. I am amazed that it got past the censors," she said sadly as she glanced about furtively.

"My daughter will only be fifteen next month, and I'm glad because she doesn't have to be registered today," the other commented slowly, her eyes staring into the distance. "I hope that will make a difference."

A German soldier strutted along the edge of the group wearing his greatcoat; his hands moved the bayonet on his gun menacingly towards the women. He turned his head sharply and shouted authoritatively, "Still! Quiet! There will be no talking!"

The people looked at one another silently, but their eyes spoke their thoughts; there was no doubt, fear was in the air.

"Mother," Anje asked pointedly, "Why do Jews have to be registered?" She had related her experience at the Grote Markt.

"It is what the government requires, Anje," Mother replied.

"But why?" Anje insisted.

"I really don't know that answer, my dear," she continued. "Jews in the Netherlands have always been free to practice their religion, do business, practice law, or anything they chose to do. But I don't know what Hitler plans for them."

As Anje observed her surroundings, she could see something happening. Signs began to appear in public places. She hopped off her bicycle, propped it on the stand, and walked closer to read the printing. It said,

JEWS FORBIDDEN!

Jews are not allowed to enter hotels, restaurants, parks, playgrounds, swimming pools, libraries, cinemas, museums, and concert halls. Pharmacists and physicians are forbidden to perform services to non-Jewish patients.

She could not wait to tell Mother what she had seen. Her legs could not pedal fast enough to take her home. The bicycle clattered as she hurriedly dropped it at the bottom of the stairs and ran up to the kitchen.

"Mother, what does this all mean?" Anje questioned between gasps of air. "We have many Jews who are our friends. Why are they being picked on? They are good citizens; they haven't done anything wrong. Why do the Germans hate them so much?"

"It isn't the Germans, Anje. It's the Nazis. This is what Hitler has taught them, to hate the Jewish people," Mother replied sadly.

"But it isn't right," she objected as she thought of the Troostwijcks and their sons Max and Bennie. "They're not bad people."

"No, they are not, but they are Jews. And you know our favorite doctor, Dr. Bernstein? He is also Jewish," Mother said.

"I hope nothing happens to them," Anje said cautiously.

"The Jew is the emblem of eternity. He whom neither slaughter nor torture could destroy; he whom neither fire nor sword, nor inquisition was able to wipe off the face of the earth; he who was first to produce the oracles of God; he who has been for so long a time the guardian of prophecy, and who has transmitted it to the rest of the world—his nation cannot be destroyed. The Jew is as everlasting as eternity itself."

~ LEO TOLSTOI

THE STRIKE!

The strike of February 1941 was one of the boldest initiatives fueled by the Resistance in Amsterdam, and the origin was a simple incident. Erich fervently described the details to Hans in the living room of Erich's small apartment on Amstel Canal.

"I didn't want to discuss this in public," Erich commented as they sipped cups of tea.

"My relatives in Amsterdam informed me of this attack, and I am afraid, Hans, that this is going to be coming here also, and we need to be prepared. Jewish artists in a cabaret had completed their performance when sounds of a riot could be heard in the street. Anti-Semite riots were initiated by the WA (a defense division), Ordnungs Polizei, Nationaal

Socialistische Beweging, and Nazi sympathizers, as they approached the Jewish Quarter. Reason flew out the window as people on the street were taunted and beaten with baseball bats. This was not enough. The Nazis entered Jewish homes in the late evening; my brother-in-law's was one of them. They came to his house and hauled the children out of their beds to watch as their mother was molested. My brother-in-law was tied to a chair with ropes, and two SS officers ransacked their home looking for anything of value. Now you know, most German soldiers would not rape a Jewess because they consider her unclean, not human, but they will beat the women and harass them. When his wife begged them not to take a certain piece of jewelry from her bureau in the bedroom, because it had belonged to her mother, they laughed and took it all. They left with her fur coat and many of my brother-in-law's best suits and coats, plus his engraved pocket watch and gold wristwatch. The children were not hurt, for the youngest was in his crib in another room, and his wife had pushed the eight-year-old boy under her bed. She did not want him to see what they would do to her."

Hans was overwhelmed at what he had just heard. He asked, "What are the police doing about this?"

"The police stood idly by, making no effort to protect the Jews from these violent gangs, and as a result the Joden-hoek formed fighting squads to protect themselves and non-Jewish neighbors. You know, there was a reason the Germans demanded the confiscation of all weapons from the Jews. Now our people have only rocks and chains to defend themselves. One old man walking down the street had to protect himself with his cane. That's how bad it is," Erich remarked.

"What happened as a result of this?" Hans asked.

"The German officers, the WA and the NSB, dramatized this episode for propaganda purposes in order to show how dangerous these Jewish terrorists were, and they succeeded in their efforts to demonize them," Erich replied.

On February 12, 1941, the Jodenhoek was cut off from the rest of the city. High wire fences were erected, encircled with numerous strands of sharp barbed wire to deter anyone from escaping. Machine gun nests were set up in the surrounding streets to gun down those who tried to leave the compound for any reason. "Judenviertel/Joodsche Wijk" (meaning "Jewish Quarter") signs were affixed to the wire fence. In order to maintain control, all Jewish homes were searched for weapons, and that same day a Jewish Council for Amsterdam was formed to rule the Jodenhoek in an attempt to restore peace to Amsterdam.

At the same time, the occupation government began sending thousands of Dutch workers to Germany as forced labor, which led to more protests. All unemployed workers were sent into the countryside to repair dikes, and these men began rioting over their starvation pay and miserable working conditions. Unrest was everywhere.

"Hillie," Hans called, as he pulled something out of his briefcase, "look what the Resistance has printed. They're calling for a nationwide strike in protest of the treatment of the Jews." Together they read the words printed on the small grayish pamphlet. The first line was a command.

"Protest Against the Unlawful Persecution of Jews!"

1.   *Organize a protest strike in all enterprises!!*

2.   *Fight unanimously against this terror!!*

3.   *Require immediate freedom for arrested Jews!!*

4.   *Require the dissolution of WA terror groups!!*

5.   *Organize self-defense in enterprises and neighborhood!!*

6.   *Show solidarity with severely hurt Jewish working people!!*

7.   *Protect Jewish children from Nazi violence by taking them into your families!!*

As Hillie's eyes scanned the paper, she was particularly attentive to the last point, which tugged at her heartstrings—"protect Jewish children." *Yes, children should always be protected,* she thought.

"Anje," Mother called, "did you see this paper? Let us think about how we could help Jewish children."

Anje was upstairs writing something in her notebook, but when Mother called, she came immediately. She would have to think about this. She was sure she would come up with an idea!

When Erich told them about the results of the strike, they were appalled. Two hundred people were arrested and marched into the Lloyd Hotel, where they were tormented and terrorized. By February 27, 1941, the strike was over, but the penalty was not. A mock trial was held on March

13, 1941, and the punishment was death by firing squad. Fifteen members of a resistance group and three strikers who were held responsible paid the penalty for this uprising with their lives.

Anje was quiet. This was the first time she had heard of something this violent. *Can people really be that cruel? What would they do if this happened in Groningen?* she asked herself. She didn't know.

These events had a huge impact on the Dutch population; no massive national resistance was shown after February 1941. The people decided it was safer to work underground.

V FOR VICTORY

This Saturday around noon, in January 1941, the doorbell rang at the Minnes home with clarity. Two short rings indicated it was their Jewish friend Samuel Troostwijck, who had come to listen to the Dutch news on Radio Orange with Mother and Anje. The three huddled around the small Bakelite radio in the back room listening intently, for the sound had to be kept very low in the event there were other listening ears.

Father was rarely at home. He was preoccupied with his sports interests, and his family felt as though they were not important to him. He appeared aloof and noncommittal when Mother tried to talk to him. *It's as though we live in different worlds. Why is that?* Anje asked herself. *Here is*

Samuel, just a neighbor, and we can have a friendly discussion about the news and events happening around us, and we cannot do that with my own father. Why? It puzzled her. When she asked Mother to explain this, she replied, "Anje, your father hates this war and is afraid of how it may affect his life, so he believes the safest thing is not to get involved."

The January 14 BBC radio broadcast was of great interest to them. Victor De Laveleye, a Belgian refugee in Britain, suggested a new way of striking back at their Nazi occupiers. Since *V* was the first letter of the word *victory*, he suggested that the people rally with the emblem of the letter *V*. His campaign was taken up by the BBC, which began to broadcast the Morse code for *V* (dot-dot-dot-dash) followed by the opening bars of Beethoven's Fifth Symphony, whose notes correspond to the Morse signal "fifth," which is also represented by the Roman numeral V. It captured the imagination of all. It was a message of hope!

Before long, teachers were calling their children to order by clapping the signal, and train engineers were making the sound with their whistles as they came down the tracks. Every time someone knocked on a door or rang a church bell, they were encouraged to use the rhythm of *victory!* Many newborn sons were named Victor in honor of this important time in history.

As a result, the letter *V* became known throughout Europe as an anti-Nazi sign. The Germans were bombarded continually with the message that the victory would not be theirs but the Netherlands'! The Dutch people rallied to this cry and took great pleasure in displaying the symbol everywhere. Joseph Goebbels, the German Minister of Propaganda, was tremendously annoyed at the success of the English propaganda idea and ordered it to be inscribed in white paint on every fence, wall, or flat surface. The letter *V* for *victory* was changed to indicate that it was for *Germany* on all fronts, and while Goebbels groaned at it, the people took every opportunity to deface his message.

All of this excitement tickled Anje's brain. First of all, she loved classical music, and Beethoven's Fifth Symphony was one of her favorites. Now that she knew it was being promoted as a sign of victory, she hummed it as she walked to school and when she lay in bed, and it thrilled her. An idea popped into her head that she would share with her friends on Saturday morning. She hoped it wouldn't rain, and she hummed that tune as she walked to the store to buy some hydrated lime to make whitewash. She found a pail and some gloves, added water, and followed Mother's advice to add a little salt to the mixture. She was in luck; Saturday was a dry summer morning. It was easy to find willing hands, as everyone wanted to help when they discovered the plan. With paint and brushes in hand, they changed the *V* to *W* for *Wilhelmina* in every location they could find and reach. They were exuberant to fulfill the mission of painting the message on fences, buildings, sidewalks, and every empty space. The letters *OZO* also appeared, representing the first letters of the words in the Dutch phrase for "Orange will overcome!"

Pictures of Prime Minister Winston Churchill dressed in his traditional top hat and scarf began to appear in the media abroad, standing boldly with a cane in his hand, cigar in his mouth, and two fingers raised in the "V for Victory" sign. The press extolled this message, and it was touted by BBC News. The people were being motivated and challenged to work toward and expect victory. The desire for it could not be quenched. The dream had taken root in the hearts of the people of Europe, and it would not be extinguished.

* * *

The BBC radio was the people's main source of information, for it was truthful, or they hoped it was. The Underground radio was forbidden, and no one would admit to owning a crystal set required to receive the signal. The news on the Nazi channel was basically propaganda, and few considered it honest or reliable.

However, the political scene was changing in the Netherlands as Anton Mussert came preaching new politics in 1941, which he thought would blend the Dutch with the Nazis seamlessly. At a political rally, he expounded, "The German tree has many branches, and we can be the strongest branch."

"What does this mean anyway?" Hans asked Erich when they heard that message on the radio.

"I can't imagine Mussert as anything but a yes-man," replied Erich as he chewed on the end of a wooden match.

"Oh, he must be important," Hans said loftily. "After all, Himmler installed him as chief of the Nazi Party. Let's wait and see what kind of a welcome the Underground gives him."

Netherlanders called him the "Little Führer," and as he appointed men to his cabinet, they were rapidly assassinated by the Underground. In the face of so much opposition, Mussert was forced to declare, "Between the NSB and the

Dutch people, lies a deep chasm which drives me to despair," which earned him the nickname Lord Despair.*

Most Dutch people were suspicious of a political party that was endorsed by the Führer when all other parties were abolished. Mayors and aldermen who refused to follow the new order were systematically replaced with NSBers. Eventually, the NSBers' total loyalty was to the Nazis, and members were basically spies for the Germans. They betrayed their own nation in order to advance themselves. As a result, members of the NSB were fiercely hated by the faithful Dutch people, who considered them traitors.

One of the tasks of the NSB was selling the German propaganda newspaper, *Volk und Vaderland*, on the street corners. The scorn of the Dutch was so great that young and old began to sing this ditty with conviction

> *"At the corner of the street,*
> *Stands an NSB'er*
> *It's no man, it's no woman,*
> *But a Pharisee(er).*
> *With a paper in his hand,*
> *Standing there he vends;*
> *And sells his Fatherland*
> *For six measly cents."*

Anje was young, but she was smart. She understood what was happening. She and her friends delighted to sing

* *Mussert* was the founder the Nationaal Socialistische Beweging, NSB movement, in 1933).

this little rhyme in the presence of the NSB vendors on the street corners.

Change was everywhere, even in Anje's school, and some of the changes were alarming. Her classmates suddenly began to disappear. Jetty von Danzich was the first person to go missing. She and Anje had been classmates since the first grade, and they were now in grade five. Since they sat right across the aisle from each other, they often exchanged glances and smiles throughout the day. Jetty had huddled over her desk diligently working on her assignments; occasionally she would slip her hand inside her pocket and nibble on a forbidden snack. Her passion was her studies; she wanted to do something important with her life, and as a result her classmates called her a bookworm. Now her desk was empty. It seemed unthinkable to Anje that Jetty was gone, yet no one knew her whereabouts. This was a mystery. *Can someone just disappear without anyone taking notice of it? Isn't anyone looking for her?* These thoughts bombarded Anje's mind as she looked across the aisle at the empty desk.

Sally Siemetz vanished a few days later. The teacher stood before the class, the pointing stick in her hand as she questioned her pupils. "Does anyone know where Sally is?" The heads all shook negatively. "Possibly she is sick and may return in a few days," the teacher suggested. She picked up the book on her desk said, "And now, class, we must get back to work." As the days passed and Sally did not reappear, the students knew she would not be coming back. *Where do they go to when they are gone? What about all the bad things we are hearing? Has Sally been taken away on one of those trains?*

Anje missed Hetty Hirs for she was a sparkly girl with wavy red hair and a smile that caused her to stand out in a crowd. She made friends easily and always had someone hovering around, listening to her talk! She was bubbly and full of energy, and she always had an answer or an opinion to express. Hetty composed a page in Anje's little "poezie album" (autograph book), painstakingly decorating it with colorful stickers and inscribing this verse in beautiful penmanship: "Never too little, never too much. In this life you will have your daily portion. Signed, Hetty Hirs, March 15, 1940." Hetty was saying, *I hope you will always have enough in life.* Now Anje was wondering, *Hetty, do you have enough in your life?*

There was one thing her friends had in common: they were all Jewish. Had they gone into hiding? Had they been sent to a concentration camp? No one knew. No one understood much about concentration camps. There were work camps, and the Jews were told they were being sent away for resettlement. No one actually knew what that meant; they just accepted it. Anje couldn't imagine her friends in a camp somewhere. *What do they do there? Are they with their parents?* She didn't know. It seemed as though people didn't want to talk about this subject openly. It was mysterious. One day the students were in school, and the next day they were gone. As Anje walked home that day, she thought, *I am so lucky to have Mother.* It gave her such a feeling of safety.

Just a few kilometers from Groningen, Rabbi Abraham Toncman served the Dutch-Israeli congregation in Pekela.

The rabbi puttered about his tiny office, stroking his beard and muttering prayers softly as he worked. He was troubled. He knew the events he saw around him spelled disaster for his people. Quite moved from the depths of his heart, he inscribed in the minute book of the church council on New Year's Eve, 1942, "And now we are a few left over from many; we are regarded as a flock (of sheep) led to the slaughter house, to be killed and destroyed, to misfortune and shame. May there come salvation and deliverance for the Jews! Soon, in our days! Amen!"

THE WOLFF FAMILY

The five kilometers from Groningen to Haren, where Hans lived, were an easy journey by bicycle, and the Minnes family visited frequently, as Jan and Hans's friendship was of long standing. More recently Jan had not visited as often, but they became well acquainted with the Wolff family since they lived next door to Hans.

Hans flipped through the documents slowly as he sat at the mahogany desk in his office thinking about the present situation. As a secretary in the administration for the local government, much information was stored there. Census and other population records were kept there, and he knew the statistics: his small country of Holland was almost bursting at the seams with twenty-five thousand Jewish refugees from

Germany and Austria who were fleeing Hitler's wrath. More
were arriving daily, and they could not be refused sanctuary.
The Wolff family had come to Haren from Aurich, Germany,
in 1937, and they had settled here quite comfortably. Hans
had helped the family to find jobs when they arrived. As he
looked at their documents, he saw that the father, Herman,
was born in 1893, and his wife, Janette, born in 1899. One
son, Adolph, had been born to them in 1920, Siegbert was
born 1921, Werner in 1924, Louis (who was called Lutz)
born in 1929, and the youngest was Ewald, born in 1931.
Their nephew Ernst came to live with them a year later; he
was the same age as Werner. As he ruffled through their
papers, he thought that, by Jewish standards, five sons meant
they were a prosperous family. Herman made his living
buying and selling cattle at the market, Ernst worked for a
butcher, and the three older boys worked in the carpentry
shop that the La Costa family owned.

The Wolff family soon became loyal friends with Hans
and the La Costa family, and the La Costa parents became
known to the boys as Opa and Oma. The La Costas'
carpentry shop was a good place for his three boys to learn
a trade; there they were protected, supervised, and appreciated. Herman dropped in at the shop frequently to see how
his boys were doing. Lutz was just twelve, too young to
work in the shop, but they couldn't get him to stay home.
He loved hanging around the La Costas' place where his
brothers worked and being around Tante Lut (pronounced
loot), as he called her.

Lutz was a curious and energetic boy. He had a habit of sneaking into the carpentry shop and fiddling around with the power tools, presses, and rotary saws, trying to figure out how they worked. He was a familiar sight to them by now. One day, the workers in the shop were not prepared for what happened next.

"Ouch!" Lutz cried in pain. "My finger is hot."

"Your finger is hot because you cut the end off with that saw!" Werner exclaimed as he rushed to his side. Blood was spurting from the end of the finger. "Quick! Get a clean cloth and wrap it up tightly," he said. "We'll get you to the hospital." He reached down and picked up the end of Lutz's finger that lay in the sawdust on the floor. "Well, you won't be using this anymore," he said drily as he threw it into a trash can.

"Don't throw my finger away!" Lutz protested loudly. The tears were beginning to flow as he realized what had happened to him.

"You don't need it anymore," Werner argued.

"But I want to show it to Mother," Lutz protested.

"Mother won't want to see that piece of finger!" Siegbert exclaimed emphatically.

"Yes, she will. Wrap it in my hanky. I'm taking it home," Lutz commanded. And so they did.

Tante Lut looked at the big bandage around Lutz's finger and admonished, "From now on, you are going to stay with me here in the house." She wore a big, ruffled apron tied around her waist when she was in the kitchen preparing food, and she loved to see this dark-haired boy sitting at her table chatting while she worked. More often than not, she had cookies or fresh buns ready for the growing boy, whom she treated like a son. "Now, eat your cookie," she said brusquely. "You know that equipment is dangerous. You could have hurt yourself very badly."

"Well, I have been thinking about this," Lutz replied thoughtfully. "Because I lost the end of my pointing finger, I can't shoot a gun anymore, so I won't be able to join the army."

"Phhh! The army!" she said disdainfully. "You are still a young boy; you don't need to think about shooting and the army, not for a long time yet."

"I heard that in Germany, they can join the Hitler Jugend at the age of thirteen," he offered, looking with interest into her face and waiting for her response.

"We are not like Hitler." She spat out the words passionately. "We do not send our children to war."

Lut was the one who related this all to Herman when he stopped in from work. Herman patted her on the back. "You are doing a good job with that boy, Lut. Thank you." He donned his felt hat and left the shop, whistling as he went.

The German occupation of Holland did not create undue concern for Herman Wolff. He had been awarded the Iron Cross for bravery during World War I, and he was certain that the country he had served so faithfully would not fail him now. However, when the Gestapo began rounding up Jews and sending them to concentration camps, Herman decided he may need to protect his family and asked Hans to find them a place to hide.

"But you cannot all stay together. Your family is too large," Hans objected when he heard the request.

"My friend," Herman pleaded, his eyes tinged with sadness, "If you cannot find us a place together, then we will stay in our home, where we will be a family."

Later that week, Herman appeared at the door at the La Costas' home and spoke urgently with Lut. "Would you be willing to come and pick up Lutz and give him a place to stay?"

The conversation between Herman and Lut was painful; Herman could take no more.

He took his handkerchief from his pocket and wiped his eyes, which filled with tears as he spoke. "We are planning on committing suicide together. Janette and I thought perhaps at least one of our boys could go underground in order to stay alive." When he ejected those words from his mouth, he broke down and sobbed.

Strong, rugged Herman was now forced to make bitter decisions that affected his cherished family, and it tore him up inside. As a couple, they had discussed this together in the privacy of their bedroom. What were their chances for survival? Janette's parents had been arrested and stripped of all their possessions; the SS had taken everything. Herman didn't know what had happened to his parents. They had just disappeared late one night. The neighbors had heard noises and shouting, and when they peered from their window, they saw a green SS van pull away from their door and speed into the darkness. One Jew dared not inquire with the authorities about another; that would be suicide. No one had a solution for the problem. In their naïveté they did not suspect the worst. "Resettlement" did not sound ominous;

they were willing to be resettled to another location. Wasn't that the history of the Jews?

"I believe there is a humane way to do this," Herman had consoled Janette as she sat on the edge of their bed, trying to muffle her sobs with her crumpled handkerchief.

"I don't know, Herman. I have heard so many terrible things, of people hanging themselves or taking poison. But can these hands that gave birth to my sons be the same hands that will end their lives? I cannot do it." Her shoulders heaved from sobs, and she moaned sorrowfully into her hands, which covered her face.

As he looked at Janette, he recalled their wedding day as they had stood in the sunshine in the beautiful garden under the chuppah. As the groom, he carefully covered her face with the veil as he looked into her dark eyes. Her eyes had looked at him so adoringly when he placed the ring on the forefinger of her right hand during the ceremony. His voice was strong as he read the marriage contract in Aramaic, the promise to accept marital responsibility to provide food, shelter, and clothing and to meet her emotional needs for life. Those vows now became very difficult to keep. He did not know the hard decisions that lay ahead.

His thoughts went back to the time when he had been a young soldier in World War I, laying on his belly in the cold, water-filled trenches, the sight of dead bodies all around him. He told himself that if he survived, he was sure this would be the worst thing he would ever face. He was wrong. This was worse than that.

He put his arm around his wife and spoke more softly, comforting her. "I have access to drugs because of my work with animals. These drugs could do the job fairly quickly and quite painlessly," he offered.

"All of my sons gone? I cannot bear the thought." And then it struck her—she would not be here to see that. "Could we let one son live, Herman?" She continued, "It would be easy to hide one person. Lutz spends so much time at the La Costas', and I trust her. Perhaps she would take him in?"

After Herman painstakingly divulged their plan to Lut, she responded emphatically, "You cannot take your own life; you cannot let the enemy win. There must be some answer for you. Surely there is another way. What does Hans have to say? We need to talk some more. Come over to our house tonight. We will enjoy the evening meal together, all of us."

The entire family went, as well as Hans, and as they arrived, Janette received an extra tight hug from her hostess, who whispered in her ear, "My dear, I know what you are going through." Then she exclaimed to all, "Tonight, we are going to enjoy ourselves!" Enjoy, they did! The tasty dishes were passed around many times as they ate and reminisced. *Where did Lut get all this food?* Herman wondered. It seemed as though the food multiplied every time a dish was passed around the table. They savored the meal, laughed, and delighted in one another's company, for this night, they were family.

Perhaps there was a measure of favor upon Herman Wolff's life. They were able to live in their own home for a considerable time, and they were treated humanely; many Jews were sent directly to a camp for extermination. But in December 1942, they were ordered to report to the Jewish

camp in Westerbork. This calmed them somewhat, for Westerbork was at least in Holland. Anticipating this action in
advance, they removed their wedding rings, knowing the
Nazis would strip them of everything. Was this a foolish
decision to want to spare their wedding rings? Herman
thought, *This is one piece of gold the Nazis won't get,* and
Janette confided to him, "Perhaps we will have another
wedding ceremony when we return." Wanting to preserve
this symbol of their vows, they decided to take them to
Hans for safe keeping.

*The wedding rings of Herman and Jannette Wolf,
which were brought to Hans for safe keeping.*

They arrived at Hans's door to explain their plight. Anje
was present when they arrived. "Do you know where you
are going?" she asked Herman.

"We have been told we are going to be sent to Theresienstadt," he replied, his head bowed and his hat in his hand.

"All the family?" she asked.

"Yes," he replied. "But one day when we come back, we'll get our rings from you and will live as husband and wife again."

Hans looked at them sadly, nodding in agreement. "I will keep them for you," and he tucked them into a tiny box he kept for precious items.

The family was sent to the transit camp in Westerbork and, occasionally, they saw one another; but Herman's heart ached because he could no longer protect his family, especially his lovely Janette. In 1944, they were told they were going to be sent to Theresienstadt, a large fortress that had been built in 1780 by Emperor Joseph II of Austria and named after his mother, Empress Maria Theresa. In Terezin, another name for the camp, there was a barracks for housing prisoners, and it was otherwise known as a model camp. But the journey there was a nightmare. Herman and Janette and their family were herded like cattle into a boxcar to be shipped to the camp located in northern Czechoslovakia. Herman was a family man, and he was concerned about how the lack of food and water was affecting each one of them. "God, help us!" was the loud cry that came from his parched tongue.

"Be quiet!" another man shouted. He stood beside Herman, swaying with the movement of the rail car. "There is no God!" he shouted fiercely. "If there was, he would not allow this to happen to his people."

Herman hung his head. He couldn't give up. If there was no God, there was no hope.

Werner and Siegbert contracted a contagious form of scarlet fever and were forced to remain in Westerbork until they were well. The boys wanted to leave when their parents departed, but they were not allowed.

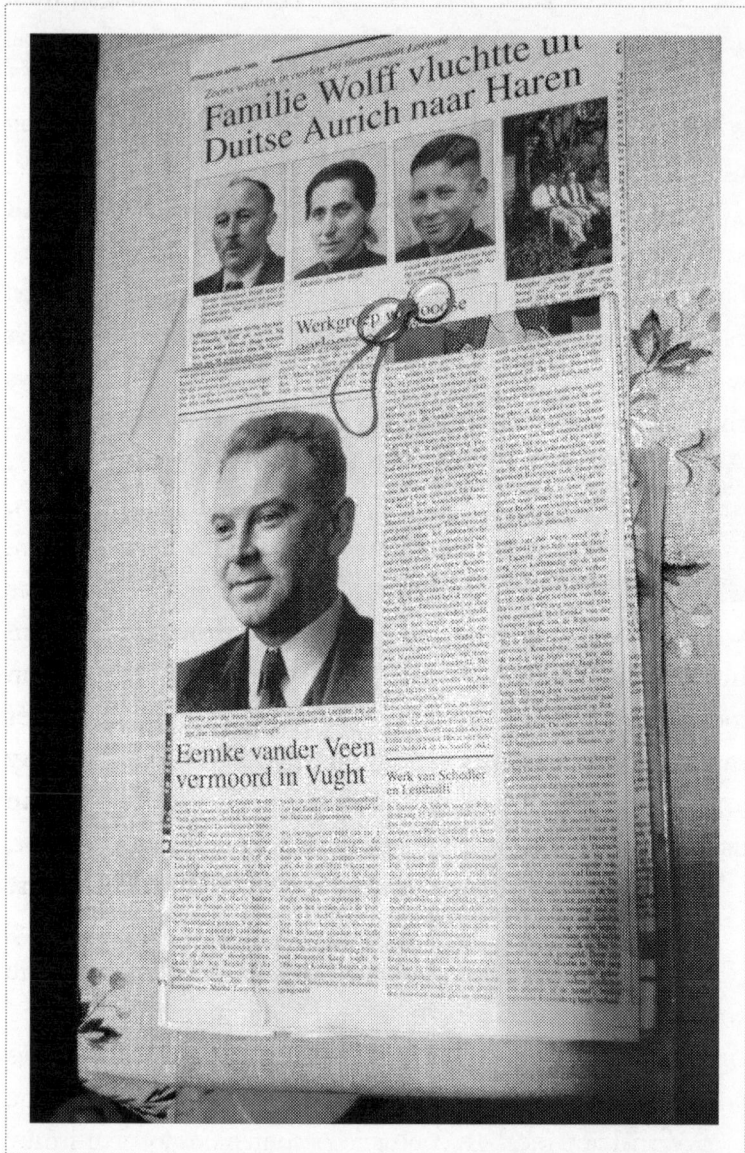

Newspaper article about "Uncle Hans" together with the Jewish family (the Wolff's).He attempted to save them from the holocaust.

"You have to be healthy and well before you go to a camp. They don't want you spreading disease," the doctor said as he monitored their health. So they waited.

When the boys recovered, they were put on a train heading eastward to Theresienstadt and then onward to Auschwitz. They were not concerned; their one goal was to be reunited with their parents.

Some of their friends happened to see Werner and Siegbert when their train stopped in Ommen, only a short distance from the La Costas'. The brothers didn't know where the rest of their family was, but at least they were not alone. Father had been adamant about their staying together. They had been shoved into a Pullman-type car with windows, and they knew they would be traveling through Ommen, their home territory. It was hot and stifling in the car. People were fainting from lack of oxygen, falling to the floor and moaning in agony, and they were stepped upon in the clamor.

Siegbert called to his brother to get over to the other side by the windows, in case they saw someone they knew. It was not easy to work their way through the tightly packed crowd of people in their compartment, but they were young and agile, and they succeeded, just as the train pulled to a stop at the station. What did they hope to accomplish? They didn't know. Could anyone save them? Crammed into this tight space, their faces pressed tightly against the coach window, they spied Kees and Gijs standing on the road beside the track. Their friends! Hope leaped inside them. They remembered the days when they had played games together as children, how they rode their bicycles on a fine summer day to their favorite swimming spot; but now, Kees and Gijs were free, and they were prisoners of the Reich. There was nothing they could do. They watched as the boys on the platform waved at them. The engine of the train whistled and began its journey eastward, with its human cargo destined for death.

Every person from the Wolff family died in the concentration camps except Ernst. Ernst was sent to Theresienstadt where he met his mother and father and another sibling, whom he had not seen in eight years. He was about 20 years old when he was sent to Auschwitz where he escaped, and returned to Theresientstadt. The family had agreed whoever survived, would return to Haren after the war. In May 1945, when he returned, he received the news that all the members of his family had perished in the gas chambers. He was the lone survivor.

A map in Dutch showing the locations of concentration camps in Europe where Netherlanders were held captive.

THE RESISTANCE

The Resistance was a well-oiled machine. Very few people knew the workings. For the most part, the Resistance consisted of small groups of people who participated in activities to help the local people. It was often referred to as the Underground.

"Hillie, I have to tell you what happened to me this week. I had a visitor," Hans declared excitedly.

Hillie and Anje huddled around to hear what Hans had to say.

"Erich and I sat in the living room of his apartment discussing the possibility of helping to free the Netherlands from the occupation and control of the Nazis." Hans pulled out a copy of an Underground newspaper, and across the top in large letters was written: "Vrij Nederland" (Free Netherlands). "He told me it's printed underground and distributed by ordinary people. We know we're not getting the truth from the Germans; they control everything. The Dutch people want some real news about the war, and so we must circulate this paper. It's the only way we can get the truth to our people. He gave me a bundle of copies to distribute and asked if I was willing to help. I told him to count me in!

"And that's not all—they have started their own organization within the Resistance, just a small group. Do you remember Edgar from Sand Dunes and Heather? He's the head of this group, and they have some things planned, some pretty big things that I can't discuss at the moment. I have a feeling that this could be more significant than we can imagine," Hans continued.

"If they need more helpers, you can count me in too, Hans," Hillie replied.

Hans was a diligent worker and activist, and his work as a secretary in the administration of the local government gave him access to strategic information. In addition to storing records, the Ausweis and other documents such as identification papers were personalized and printed, and the required officiating signature was his own, "Hans Westerkamp." Like most Dutch people, he hated the German occupation of his land, and it was an easy decision to become active in the Resistance.

After saying yes to Hans, Hillie had to stretch herself to accomplish all of her duties at the distribution office and keep a household functioning. As a result of this commitment to the Resistance, the Minnes household became like a central train station with people coming and going at all times. Each regular visitor had his or her own code doorbell ring so they knew who would be standing on the doorstep when they released the latch to open the door. Two rings were for Samuel, and three short rings identified Hans. Hans teased them when Hillie gave him his choice of rings. "It's like this," he said, as he poked his finger in the air three times to ring the bell. "Hey, it's me! That's what it stands for, in case you forget."

ies
ver-

Hillechiena
H. Minnes-Stutvoet
Koerierster LO-Haren.
Gearr. 2-7-'44 verm. door
verraad.

E

Gearr.

Hillie's photo in the Record Book of the Resistance.

The three of them laughed, but Anje knew for sure she would never forget Uncle Hans. He was such fun. He came often and always had some interesting news or surprise or gift for her; he never treated her like a child, even though she was. His love and kindness was something she had never experienced before from a man, and it was hard to explain or even understand how she felt about him. She often wanted to throw her arms around his neck and hug him, but the Dutch people in her part of the world considered outward displays of affection unseemly. *Dear Uncle Hans,* she thought as she smiled. He knew how she felt about him.

Anje was deeply engrossed in her schoolwork upstairs, but she could hear Mother and Uncle Hans speaking quietly in the back room, and as she caught snatches of their conversation, she wondered what the LO and the KP were. She knew they were engaged in underground activities, as many Dutch people were, but she didn't know exactly what they were doing. When she came down the stairs, they were sorting and counting leaflets into stacks of twenty-five.

"What are those for?" she inquired.

"They need to be delivered today," her mother replied as she continued folding. "We need to pass on information throughout the organization."

"Could I deliver them?" she asked.

"I suppose you could," Mother replied. "But for today, I will take them to their location. We need to figure out a safe way for you to carry them with you. Let's think about it."

Anje knew this was adult conversation, and she also knew Mother would have the final say in this matter, but she had overheard some of their conversation.

"I think she is too young," Uncle Hans had said. "You know there is risk involved. She is too young for that kind of responsibility."

Anje smiled when she heard that, for she thought this sounded just like what a father would say.

Mother was defending her! "I know she is young, Hans. But she is a very smart and responsible girl, and no one will suspect her because she is just twelve years old. So actually her age is her protection. I think we should let her do this; it is a relatively simple thing to do."

As Anje stood watching them, her mother spoke again after a pause. "There is one thing you must promise me if I let you do this," she said seriously, looking directly into her daughter's eyes.

"What's that?" Anje asked.

"You must never speak about this to anyone, especially not to your father."

She nodded in agreement. That wouldn't be hard to do. She rarely spoke to her father in the best of times. In fact, she rarely spoke to anyone. The only time she spoke to an adult was when she was being asked a direct question and she needed to respond. This would not be a problem. Keeping a secret sounded like fun to her. She had heard enough about the enemy and the outside world to know that the less one said, the better off one would be.

Together, Mother and Anje came up with the idea of sewing a secret courier bag. It was like a large pocket on strings that tied around her waist underneath her skirt. When Mother's grandmother had suffered from dementia in her later years, she had sewn a bag like this for herself to prevent anyone from stealing her possessions. The bag had a V-shaped slit that made it simple to slide her hand inside and retrieve something from its cozy recess. When the family had finally looked into Great-grandmother's treasure trove, they had found only bits of colored ribbon, short pieces of cotton string, and a few choice buttons. But Great-grandmother's idea was going to be so useful now.

Anje was elated as she rode along the canal on her bicycle with her precious cargo under her skirt; she had been trusted with a great responsibility, and she was determined that she would not fail. This was more exciting than anything she had tried before! Yes, she and Janny had a lot of fun together looking for excitement, but this was really important. There was risk involved, and she loved adventure! She was careful in her choice of route and adept at changing her plan if she spotted anything that looked like trouble. She was constantly thinking. Above all else, she needed to avoid a "control," where soldiers or Landwachters would demand to see her ID, search her possessions, impound anything of value that she carried, or even her take her bicycle.

She strained her eyes to read the street signs as she pedaled along her way; she was not familiar with this area, but she arrived at the house on Stalstraat where she was to deliver her goods. She slid down off her bike and looked at the street number again—#14. Yes, this was the right place. While shielding her body from view, she reached under her skirt into her pocket and removed the package she was to deliver. Her knock on the door was answered immediately by a lady who smiled, reached out her hand for the parcel, and then promptly closed the door.

There! Her job was done. It wasn't hard at all, she thought. She heaved a sigh of relief as she mounted her bicycle. She had successfully carried out her first assignment.

Anje at the age of twelve on her bicycle en route to school. She was working as a courier for the underground at the time.

The following day, when Anje arrived home from school, she went into the kitchen cupboard to find something to snack on. She found a small biscuit in the tin, and she took it. She hefted her pile of schoolbooks into one arm and began to climb the stairs to see what Mother was doing as she nibbled on her biscuit. She found her in the back room busily concentrating on sheets of paper that covered the table. She appeared to be totally focused on her project and eager to finish it.

"Anje," she called when she saw her, "we need to come up with the names of people who might be willing to take in Jews. There are so many arrests being made that the Underground has made this project most urgent. We have to find places for these fugitives to stay. Actually, let's just think of people with houses big enough to take in some extra people. Then," she continued, "we will decide exactly how we'll approach them."

Anje put down her books, realizing that her homework would have to wait. She might be working very late that night to get her science assignment finished, but she knew this had to come first.

"Well, do you have the Smidts and the Neinhuises?" she asked.

"No, but I have Mandel and Vanderboon," Mother replied.

"Do you really think those people would volunteer do this?" Anje queried. "They seem to think they are so much better than everyone else. I don't know if they would take the risk."

"Well, they certainly have big houses," Mother responded.

It was a large task to travel about and speak with people as their identity was at risk; one never knew which people were informers. They began to realize that it was not the people with the biggest homes who wanted to help; it was the people with the biggest hearts. Why wouldn't someone want to help save another person's life? Anje knew there was risk involved, but they actually risked their lives every day when they just walked down the street. It was a good thing the list they made was very long for many people said no. However, Anje was amazed because each time they needed a shelter, one appeared.

"We'll be getting new identification cards for these people," Mother said. "I took their old cards. We need to burn them. Throw them into the stove." Mother sat at the table sorting through the various documents she had in her hand and gave some to her daughter.

This is a copy from the Record Book of the Resistance, showing
that Hillie was a member of the LO (Land organization) and KP
(Knoekploeg) during the war in Holland.

Anje took the handful of well-worn cards and rifled through them casually while looking at the names. "Feingold, Epstein, Hirsch, Liebermann, Ben David—well, with names like that, they really do need new names. They are so obviously Jewish."

"But that's not the worst part," Mother continued. "So many of them cannot hide within the city with a new ID because their appearance would give them away. We need to help them get out of the country or move them underground. Those Jews who had the money and were able to get passports have already applied to emigrate to countries that will accept them. America is a favorite place to go, but I hear they're making quotas now and not everyone will be allowed to come in." Her hands were busily sorting through ID cards as she continued, "Britain has taken in so many immigrants that their doors are beginning to close. We have to find as many hiding places in Groningen as possible. They say we have about forty-five hundred Jews, and the Resistance will try to find places for them one by one; this is what the Land Organization does. Ration cards are needed so they can buy food, and that's where the KP (Knoekploeg) comes in. They are the 'strong-arm boys' who do the rough stuff."

All of this information was a bit overwhelming to Anje, but she was a thinker, and she decided to come up with as many ideas as possible. *This is a huge task,* she thought. *How do we find extra food for the Jewish families, get them new identification cards and ration coupons, and all without being detected? But I am going to find a way to do it,* she resolved.

As Mother continued sorting, she said, "Anje, did you hear what happened to Frau Veenendaal? She was buying food for some people in hiding, and she was stopped at the food market and challenged by a Home Guard. She was seen buying food the day before, and the guard noticed she was back again. They wanted to know who she was buying food for and where she got all those ration coupons. The Dutch police were called, and they went to her house and found only her family of five. It was a good thing they didn't find anything else. She was buying food for a Jewish family in hiding, and now she realizes she has to be more careful, so she is going to different places to shop so they don't recognize her. It's not easy. One must always be very careful."

The needs of people in hiding were great; the Underground was kept busy filling many requests for assistance. Anje was asked to deliver an Underground newspaper to a Jewish former business owner. The last time he went out of his apartment, he had been stopped and questioned by two SS officers. He was relieved that his false ID had not been discovered, but this close call made him reluctant to leave his dwelling.

Anje climbed the three flights of stairs of the address she had been given and walked down a dimly lit hall that led to a tiny apartment. When she knocked on the door, it was opened just a crack by an elderly Jewish lady. Her frail voice asked, "Dear, would you please get my prescription for me? I can't go to the pharmacy nearby; I have to go to the Jewish drugstore, and I can't walk that far." She coughed as she rummaged in her tattered apron pocket for money. "Here!" Her thin feeble hand was shaking as she placed the money in Anje's outstretched hand.

Anje entered the door with "Apothecary" painted on it in white lettering and pulled the prescription from the pocket of her jacket, handing it to the pharmacist. He stared at it for what seemed like hours. He raised his eyebrows, and his inquisitive blue eyes peered above his gold-rimmed glasses. "This is not for you then, is it?" he asked warily.

"No," she replied, "it's not for me."

Can't you read, you doozlehead? she thought as she watched him closely.

"Ah, yes. This will take a few minutes. Please wait," he responded. When he returned with the prescription, she placed the money in his hands.

He leaned forward and spoke to her quietly but urgently. "I filled this prescription today, but don't come back here again. I have to keep records of everything I dispense, and I don't want to be arrested. Do you understand?"

She nodded her head affirmatively. *I understand perfectly,* she thought. *You are one of those people who won't take a little risk for anybody. It's a good thing we're not all like you; otherwise, there would be no hope at all.* She thought of the frail little lady who needed her medicine. What would she do if there was no one to help her? This thought made her angry, and she slammed the door on the way out.

Brrrring! Hearing one long ring of the bell, Anje jumped up to pull the rope that opened the latch; she was expecting her contact. She briskly climbed down the steep stairs to greet the girl who delivered the goods she was to carry on to the next location.

The package was wrapped in wrinkled brown paper and tied once around the middle with a bit of frayed string.

The girl smiled, nodded her head and left, closing the door behind her. Anje had been briefed on the rules they were to follow. Don't speak to the person if possible; don't use names; if necessary, use a pseudonym; don't follow the same route each time; don't make attempts to get to know the individual. All of these orders were designed to protect their identities. The courier did not know what was in the package or its final destination; she knew she had a delivery to a certain address and it was now completed. As she left the dwelling, the lace curtains in the window across the street moved slightly as someone watched their activities with interest.

Anje looked inside the package; it was ration cards and coupons. She knew exactly where they were going. The LO needed about two hundred of them for the Jews they had in hiding. She thought they looked like postage stamps—different colors were required for different foods. When she counted randomly, she found that there were about fifteen hundred cards in her possession. Each card had about twenty coupons, and the user could tear off whatever he or she needed to make a purchase. Yellow coupons were needed for milk, red ones for bread, and one coupon bought the customer the right to buy two ounces of butter. Luxury coupons were much in demand, for with them one could obtain one hundred grams of candy or a package of twenty cigarettes, which was the ration for a whole week! Vigorous trading took place as each person attempted to get more of the items they desired to buy.

Anje knew the importance of these cards; they were a matter of life and death for the thousands of persons in hiding who needed food, for without ration cards one couldn't purchase anything. Food was in short supply; the once-full shelves in the stores were almost bare.

The Nazis had a "plant" on every block, someone loyal to the party, who observed the daily activities of the people on the street and reported anything they deemed worthy of interest to the Gestapo. Hillie and Anje were cautious of the Kaiser family living across the way. Their two daughters, Clara and Fimke, were among Anje's friends, but when Anje wanted to know more about their father's occupation, all she could extract from them was that their father was "just a painter." A painter he may have been, Anje thought, but she felt certain he was also a reporter for the Gestapo. If he truly were a painter, then he must have been a painter of pictures, for he was always at home. She was certain he worked for the Gestapo. *When does he have time to paint pictures?* she wondered. *He's always looking out the window.* She knew her gut was right. She didn't like being watched, and she decided to find a way to leave the house without being observed.

The ration cards were packed neatly into her courier bag as she and Mother made preparations to take the train to The Hague, but they were interrupted by the sound of the doorbell.

Two men stood at the door with boxes in their arms, and they quickly stepped inside after looking both ways down the street. "Do you have room for these?" they asked Hillie. As they carried the two boxes into the kitchen, Hillie pulled back the curtain on the bottom cupboard.

"Put them in here," she said as she pointed to the space where the boxes would be hidden from view. "When will they be picked up?"

"Tonight," the man with the brown cap replied.

"Good," she responded, nodding her head as they departed.

"Anje, we leave tomorrow at eight in the morning for The Hague. If Father comes home today, let's make certain he doesn't see those boxes."

Anje poked her head inside the curtain, pushed the boxes a little further back, and lifted one flap to look inside. Radios? *Well, this is an important catch,* she thought.

Radios were valuable; everyone wanted a radio. People craved knowledge of the war; they knew the news provided by the Germans was slanted and deceiving. The Germans forbid news from the outside, and radio detector vans roamed through the streets of the city at the time of broadcasts in an attempt to discover who was listening.

Anje looked out her upstairs window as she heard music coming from the street. A van with a loudspeaker on the roof was playing the national anthem, "Deutschland Ueber Alles," and when that was finished, it began extolling the wonderful attributes of the Führer. Finally, as Hitler's voice began extolling Germany and its supremacy, she closed the window. She didn't like his screaming voice and was tired of Nazi brainwashing.

On May 13, 1943, all persons were ordered to hand in their radios, and when the Nazis were not successful at banning radios, jamming stations were placed on the air to drown out the sounds from London. Since these did not cover the entire area, they decided the solution was to actively confiscate existing radios. "If people want radios," Herr Hauptmann reflected obligingly, "we will give them radios." The Germans created a central radio station and rented the receivers for a small monthly fee. Anje was amazed at how willing and eager Father was to comply with this order. He went to the station and came home with a German radio, which was a simple box with a speaker and a volume control; the listener could select from two stations. One station provided beautiful German music that the Dutch people determined they would not enjoy, and the other broadcasted news and propaganda that few individuals cared for.

THE MEETING

The small room in Erich's flat vibrated with the sounds of the animated discussion that was taking place as the five agents debated the current events. "Did you hear about the latest news?" asked the man with a hat who was sitting beside Hillie in the corner of the room. "The Underground radio station was on the air with a special report last night."

Hillie nodded.

"I heard about that too, Harry. My brother-in-law is quite expert with radio sets, and he picked up their signal late last night," another man replied. "Did you hear that five people have received the death penalty for helping downed

Allied pilots?" They all nodded. It was amazing how quickly news went through the grapevine.

"Well, boys, we know that this is not going to stop us, right?" Hans queried. He looked directly at Harry and said, "You're the printing expert, Harry. Did you bring the ID cards and the Ausweis documents we need for these four American airmen we have in hiding right now?"

Harry nodded his head affirmatively. He produced the identification cards complete with photographs, appropriately mounted on regulation paper. As Hans inspected them, he gave a low whistle. "These are really good copies, Harry. In my work, I see the real ones all the time, and after examining these, I wouldn't know they were counterfeit."

"I only have one problem," Harry said morosely. "I'm out of paper. You know that special paper with the watermark? We need more of this," he said as he waved his hands in the air as a move of desperation.

Erich perked up his countenance and replied, "No problem. We have an assignment this week, and we will obtain a large quantity of this paper for you."

Hans took the documents. "Hillie, take a look at these copies and see if you don't agree. They are just the best quality," he said as he handed them to her across the table.

She took a few documents, examined the paper closely as she held it up to the light, and nodded. "They are very good. There is one thing we need desperately, though, and that is a forger. The documents may be perfect, but the signature has to be perfect also, and I think we need to concentrate on that. Anje seems to have a great interest in learning to sign those signatures we need for our documents, and she has been practicing. I think I will encourage her to continue. A young person can learn that much more quickly than any of us. What we need to do is get good copies of the original signatures so she can learn to duplicate them."

Hans nodded. "We'll see to it that she gets them."

They all knew that perfection in documents was a must. If a person was apprehended and his documents looked good, it could be instrumental in saving his life.

For the first time that evening, Harry smiled as he settled back in his chair and lit up another cigarette.

"What are you smoking anyway, Harry?" one of the boys asked as he lifted Harry's package out of his shirt pocket. He smiled when he saw the emblem of the sailor on the package along with the name. "Players?" he said with surprise. "I haven't had one of these in ages. All I can get hold of is these awful Turkish cigarettes that smell like donkey crap." He grimaced as he made that remark. He opened the package of Players he had taken from Harry's pocket and passed it back and forth under his nostrils as he inhaled the aroma of the tobacco. "Now that's what I call a real cigarette," he said as he smiled.

Erich mused, "It doesn't look like we're suffering any. We all have a smoke in our mouths." They laughed, as by now the air was fairly blue with the haze from the smoke they were emitting. "At least we aren't so hard up that we have to make three-in-ones!"

"What's that?" Harry asked inquisitively.

"Well, this one guy I know, he takes one cigarette apart and rerolls it to make three out of it. He's real proud of himself because then he has three packs of cigarettes instead of one."

They all laughed heartily. "Well, you never know, it may come down to that yet. It could get worse before it gets better," Hans reminded them cautiously.

Shortages were everywhere, and the shortage of paper caused a great demand for Bibles. The light parchment paper was perfect for rolling cigarettes.

"Have you noticed?" Hans began. "There is more pressure being put upon the Jewish people. Do you remember last year? They required all the Jewish-owned businesses to be registered, made them get special ID cards, and then fired all the Jewish professors and civil servants and forced them to hand in all their weapons. I tell you—the signs are not good. We have to find more hiding places for Jews and ways to get them out of the country." Hans raised his eyebrows when he realized the magnitude of what he had just said. Could they actually accomplish this?

"What exactly do you mean, 'out of the country'?" Erich asked, gesturing with his hands open. "To get to Spain or Switzerland, we have to go through Belgium and France, which is also occupied, and the Swiss have military defense at their borders that forbids the entry of refugees. Italy would be a possibility since Mussolini and Hitler are friends of a sort."

He was interrupted by another spokesman. "You know, many of these people who want to leave have young children and babies. Such a trek would be impossible for them. There has to be another way, possibly across the channel?"

"We do have fisherman who are willing to use their boats to ferry people across the channel, but that is hardly suitable for young children," Hans interjected. "You know the greater problem that exists? They don't really want to leave the country. My Jewish friends tell me they want to stay in Holland until the war is over, and then they can go back to their homes and businesses and start over again."

"Some of the hiding places definitely would not be suitable if there was a baby in the picture," another volunteered.

"Yes," Hans agreed soberly as he leaned back in his chair, his hands behind his head. "There will be some hard decisions to make. Families with babies will have to be resigned to placing them in foster homes. In the meantime, we will get the LO working to find more places for fugitives."

"That's something we will definitely work on," Hillie offered, "finding people who will be willing to adopt a Jewish baby for a time. After the war, they can go back to their own parents, but in some cases it may be a permanent placement if the parents don't come back." The others nodded in agreement. These were difficult times that required difficult decisions.

"You know," Erich commented, "one family made their home right inside a haystack! It was amazing how they did that."

"That's only successful until prying eyes report them," another said drily. "My friend Johann built a cupboard with a concealed panel where he could just barely fit in, and the SS came knocking on their door one day because the neighbors reported seeing a man in the house when they looked through the windows in the daytime. Fortunately, they didn't find him. He said his heart was pounding so hard in his chest when they were banging on the walls and floor with their clubs that he was sure they would hear his heartbeat. He was so unnerved by that experience that he moved out of the house. He said it wasn't fair to his family to put them at risk like that. Now he actually lives like a mole, burrowed in a hole in the ground in a field, and his wife brings him food every day."

"The Nazis need men to work in their factories, to run their trains, and to fill all the jobs that were vacated by the men they conscripted for the Wehrmacht. They use our men from the occupied countries for the most dangerous jobs, such as working in munitions plants where they manufacture bullets and assemble bombs. Sometimes these men find they can also be useful to the cause by using their expertise to assemble the bombs incorrectly so they will not explode," Erich recalled as he scratched his head.

"And do you remember Moshe? He was the short, bald, little Jewish man who had a tailor shop on De Ruyter Boulevard. Some high-ranking Nazi officers brought him some uniforms to repair, and they liked his work so much that the colonel hired Moshe to make his dress uniform. They were so impressed with the quality of his work that they offered him a prestigious job in Germany sewing special uniforms for the military. Moshe accepted the job. The Resistance had to produce new ID documents for him, so he became Manfred Bosch. He was one lucky Jew, working for the Nazis and collecting good pay besides." Erich smiled as he remembered that episode.

Hans pushed himself up from his chair and said, "Come on, boys. Enough talk. We have work to do. Give Hillie those documents. She will be delivering them tomorrow."

"Erich, I need to talk to you before you leave," Hans commented. As Erich approached, Hans lowered his head and said softly, "It is confirmed. It will be tonight." Erich nodded his head in agreement.

THE KNOEKPLOEG GANG

It was 11:00 p.m. when five members of the Knoekploeg gang met at the railway station near Achterweg. It was not raining, but the air was so humid that the moisture clung to their skin. The weather was a benefit; it gave them anonymity in the darkness. The lights were shining at the train station, but in the fog, they merely produced a faint glow surrounded with a halo. The men who walked toward them were just shadowy figures in the mist.

"Hurry up, boys," the man in the truck called to his partners. "We don't have any time to waste. The train will soon be here."

Just then a figure emerged from the darkness and called out, "It's all ready. We set up a timed charge that will go off as the train approaches. It's just enough to derail the cars—we're not going to blow anything sky high. We can unload the cargo. It's in boxcar twenty-four, but we're not exactly certain where that car will stop. Then the boys can enter it." It was Erich. He removed his cap and scratched his head while he spoke. "This job took a lot of planning."

"Where did you get the truck from?" Hans asked.

"From the dairy," Erich replied. "Two of our boys work there."

"I didn't think you needed more than one truck to unload the cargo," Hans began, but Erich interrupted him.

"We don't, but this all has to be done very quickly, and you can't have too many bodies in the same place. It just slows everything down."

Hans was never a part of the attack. Actually, he was a pacifist by nature, but it was increasingly difficult during a war to be totally noncombatant. He liked to be on the scene to make sure everything was kept decent and to make sure no one got hurt. The fog was a bit of a hindrance since he could not see the boys up front, but it was also a help in hiding their actions.

"A guy named Franz will let them in the door at the dairy. It's a good thing it's not too far to drive," Erich offered.

"How are the goods packaged?" Hans asked.

"I don't know for certain. All I know is that they are in a crate, and I'm not sure how many kilos the crate will weigh. I hope we can handle it," Erich replied.

Just then they heard the whistle of the freight train as its headlight appeared in the mist coming around the bend.

The man nearest to Erich asked, "Who is staying up front by the engine?"

"Oh, we have two good armed KPers to handle that," Erich replied.

"Will that be enough?" he asked.

"They will whistle if they need help, I'll be their backup here just in case," Erich said as he walked away. "Now go and check on the boys by the boxcar."

Everything worked as planned. The train had already begun to slow its pace to stop at the upcoming station when suddenly the cars jangled and jerked as they crashed against one another. The wheels left the track, separated by the dynamite blast. Some boxcars crumpled as they hit the engine, but the cars at the end of the train remained on the track.

Suddenly, at the rear of the train, a flurry of activity began as the men opened boxcar twenty-four. One truck was already backed into place near the track. It didn't have enough traction to back up the slope right to the track, but it was close. Two men jumped into the railcar and began to assess the freight. They grabbed the edges of the wooden crate, which weighed one hundred pounds (forty-five kilograms), and eased it from the car to the door into the hands of two others, who gripped it and carried it onto the truck. They worked quickly and silently.

"Okay, that's enough," Hans said after they had removed twenty boxes. "We can put the rest on the other truck."

Franz was sweating as he repeatedly tried to start the other half-ton pickup. It was no use. Maybe it was too damp, but it just wouldn't start. The loaded truck was already on its way to the dairy, and when it arrived, they quickly opened the doors, unloaded it, and sent it back for the remaining cargo.

"What's in these crates anyway?" one worker said to the other as they stood beside the boxcar.

"Butter," the other said with a grin. "This boxcar is loaded with two thousand pounds of butter."

"What is the Underground going to do with that?" the other asked incredulously. "Eat it?"

"Maybe some of it," the first one replied. "But I hear that we're trading it for rifles."

"Butter for rifles?" He gave a low whistle. "Who made a deal like that?"

They heard a shot fired and some shouting.

"Darn," the first man said. "We were told to keep this robbery very quiet. We aren't supposed to attract attention."

"Derail a train without attracting attention?" another KPer said. "I don't think that's possible! Come on, let's hurry this up," he said as he lifted the end of another crate.

In the fog Hans could hear a commotion near the engine and a scurry of activity. Then he saw a hand wave and knew all was clear.

It was a successful night. The product was being doled out in the dairy warehouse. In a few hours it would all be dispersed, and the Underground would be in possession of much-needed arms.

Hans spotted a young man sitting in the corner, his head in his hands, obviously upset. He went over to him, and as he approached the young man spoke. "This is the first time I shot somebody, and I don't like that feeling I have inside," he said morosely, his eyes filling with tears.

Hans leaned over, put his hand on the young man's shoulder, and said, "You'll get over it. Maybe you didn't kill him; he may just be wounded. Don't worry about that. Someone else will take care of it. The Germans are stealing our food, and we are starving. Remember," he said, pausing, "we are in a war, and they are the enemy."

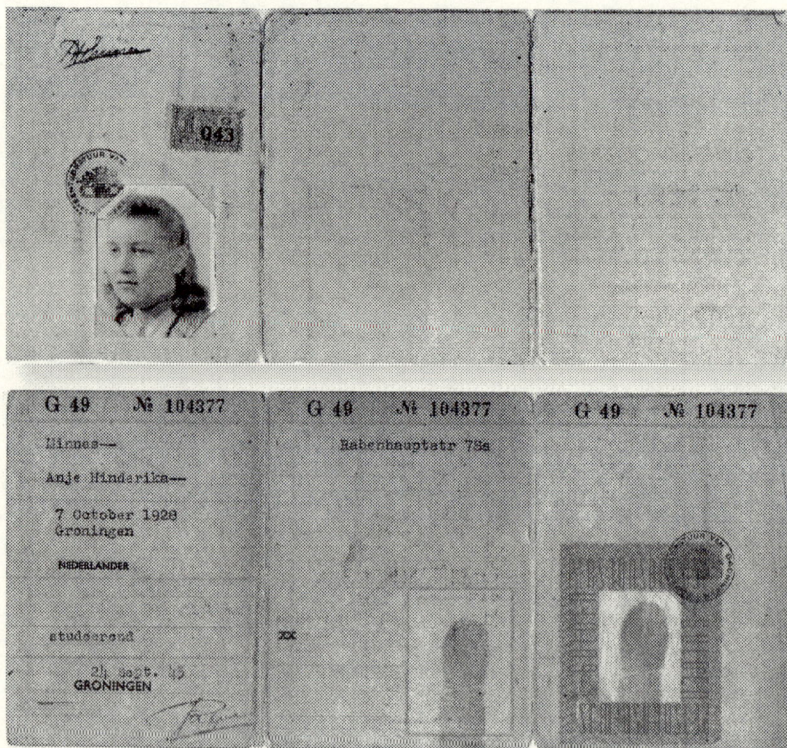

Anje's identification card (top:front/back, bottom: inside the card)

THE FORGER

Anje's mind was filled with information about documents. It seemed as though everyone needed papers delivered from one place to the next. Photos of Allied pilots were urgently required at the next destination to be perfectly positioned upon their ID cards, or an Ausweis was needed by a member of the Resistance to allow him to connect with another person. New identification papers allowed a Jew to leave the country or go underground. Occasionally Anje carried cigarettes, valued as a precious commodity. Everything required haste. She smiled at Mother as she filled her courier bag. "We have turned many Jews into Christians just by giving them new identities!"

Anje became the forger as well as the courier. The ID cards she carried in her courier bag were precut and ready to use; some were blank but some were preprinted. She could never be caught with these items on her, for the evidence would be convicting.

Every person who was in hiding required a new identity. The ID cards implemented originally by the meticulous Dutch required a photograph, two fingerprints, the signature of an official, the signature of the person holding the card, and an official stamp, all printed on special watermarked paper. The ID card was difficult to reproduce, but it was being done daily.

An Ausweis was needed by everyone who traveled or moved about after curfew. It was a short letter signed by an official and was not difficult to reproduce. Anje prepared such documents frequently, complete with signatures.

Hour after hour after school, she sat at the table in the back room practicing the signatures that had been supplied to her. She stared at them under a magnifying glass and noticed when more pressure was put on the pen; it was always in the downward move, giving a thicker stroke. She bought different colors of ink in an attempt to match the original and acquired straight pens and a fountain pen—these were her tools. She knew the signature had to be perfect. She moved her hand across the paper over and over again, learning to create the personal identification marks of certain high-ranking officials. Disgusted with the results, she threw them out, trying to come up with a system that worked. She discovered that the strokes of a signature are created in the brain; the hand could not produce something unless it had been programmed into the brain. She could not go at it slowly for the strokes of the pen were uneven and stiff. She tried tracing it and then tried looking at the signature only quickly to simulate the strokes of the original author. No, it wasn't good enough. One hundred tries—maybe a hundred more would make it perfect? It had to be good, and she knew it. Once she learned to duplicate the signature of the official whose name appeared on the identification cards, she signed it at least a thousand times.

The most difficult signature to copy was Uncle Hans's. Thousands of documents requiring his signature had been stolen by the KP from the distribution center in Haren, and they were now in her hands. His signature was so artistic that completing it was almost like drawing a picture. She felt a great deal of satisfaction when she could swirl her hand around, confidently creating the first letter of his name, and find that it actually resembled the original! *Whew! I am getting there, finally,* she thought.

She was so engrossed in her activity that she did not notice that her father had entered the room and was watching over her shoulder. She jumped when she heard the sound of his voice. "What are you doing?"

Covering her work with her hand, she slid her school-work across to cover the sheet of paper she was working on and replied casually, "I'm doing my homework."

He bent over, retrieved a scrap of paper from the floor, slipped it into his pocket, and left the room.

Would anyone suspect a shy, twelve-year-old girl of subversive activity? Maybe not, but every person was being watched by the SS every time he or she went onto the street, including her. She identified them while scooting down the streets on roller skates or pedaling her bicycle around town, and she kept a close watch on them. Some of her shadows were dressed in plain clothes (these were usually the Gestapo) and some in uniform; she even became "acquainted" with the short, stocky man in the gray tweed coat and felt hat. She knew he was Dutch for she had heard him speak. He liked to smoke a pipe and was partial to sweets, which she knew because he frequently stopped in at the candy store while he was following her. His fondness for pretty women was evident by the way he smiled and tipped his hat at them as he passed by on the street. Occasionally he changed his outer appearance to confuse her, but by now she knew his size and his gait, and she knew when he was following her.

Anje was returning from an errand when she caught sight of two "brown shirts" behind her. Being young and mischievous, she decided to have a little fun. She began by driving down one street, turning at the next corner, going up another block, and then pedaling back in the direction she had come from, traveling in a maze-like formation. Finally, she decided to head for home. She smiled to herself as she thought, *I hope you boys enjoyed that little exercise!*

She dragged her bicycle into the entrance and flounced up the stairs into the house. Upon hearing her footsteps, Mother urgently called, "Anje, there are items here for you to deliver to Haren today. Are you ready? I have a lot of confidence in you doing this job safely, but I am reminding you not to speak to strangers. I know you are a careful girl, but always remain watchful of your surroundings."

Anje nodded obediently; she always followed her mother's advice. It was a natural gift for her to be quiet and observant. She also knew that looking and acting like a schoolgirl was her best protection. She could tell from the behavior of the people around her that they did not consider her a threat. "The Underground has asked me to help plan some assignments, so I know they trust my judgment too," Anje responded. She leafed through the stack of beige-colored Underground newspapers lying on the stool and thought, *I'll need my bag for this.* She slid the papers through the side slot in the black woven bag and wrapped the apron-like strings around her waist at the back, tying them in the front. "There." She had them positioned firmly around her waist, and she smoothed down her plaid skirt with her hands, making certain that nothing could be seen beneath her dress.

She hurried over to the window and looked out onto the street. The two brown shirts were still there, propped against a light standard having a smoke. She knew that if she took her bicycle they would be right on her trail, so she decided she would walk. She reached for her navy-colored jacket, turned the collar up, tied her babushka under her chin, and peeked through a crack in the door. Since she lived close to the corner, she knew that if she could get out the door unnoticed, she could hurry down Rabenhauptstraat, turn the corner on to Achterfweg, and be hidden from their view as she walked. Just then she heard the tinkle of bells, and her heart leaped! Coming down the street was the team of horses pulling the bread wagon, just the distraction she needed. The moment the horses plodded past the soldiers, she dashed out her door, down the street, and around the corner. She kept moving at a brisk pace, not wanting to draw attention to herself but still mindful that she needed to walk the five kilometers to Haren and return before dark. She paused once, ducking into the recess in the facade of a commercial building and waiting a few moments before looking back. Her eyes scanned every detail. She was safe—no one was following her! She was elated. She had proven again that she could outwit the enemy.

She was lost in her thoughts as she walked along the street and yet still observant. *Is there a better way of doing this? Is there a shorter route?* She constantly challenged her imagination to create new ideas.

She approached Helmerstraat in Haren, looking for the row house that was to be her drop-off place. The houses all looked the same; they were narrow and tall, rising to three stories with steep roofs. Some were made of brick, but others were made of plaster or stucco with ornate wooden scrolls on the gables, all painted different hues. She counted one, two, three from the end—there it was! When she rang the doorbell that was mounted beside the heavy wooden door, she heard a dog barking inside. The door creaked when it opened, and she stepped inside. She knew she could not be seen frequently at the same location, so she often popped inside an open door to get away from prying eyes. No questions were asked—she handed her booty to the woman of the house and turned to leave. She was happy that another mission was completed, but there was still a longing on the inside of her for a little more excitement.

SACRIFICE

On June 18, 1941, a poster was displayed on the street near the grocery store: "People are required to donate all items of copper, nickel, tin, or lead, anything that could be melted down to use for war purposes." Anje and Mother read it with some dismay.

"Haven't the Dutch people given enough to this warmonger?" Hillie reacted suddenly. "Now he wants the things out of our homes too so he can make a few more bullets and bombs to use against us."

"Mother," Anje asked seriously, "do we have to do it?"

"Yes," Mother answered with finality.

Hillie wasn't in any hurry to comply with this order, but when she heard of the people who had been caught and punished, some sent to concentration camps, she wavered. The Nazis always wanted to make an example of someone to scare others into complying. She wasn't afraid for herself, but she had a daughter to protect. Eventually she decided to give in. The clatter and clang in the kitchen began as they gathered up their donation.

Hillie pulled the large copper kettle from its place inside the cupboard, and Anje asked wistfully, "Do we have to give up our small one too?"

"Yes," Hillie replied, "and the coffee pot, ashtrays, lamps, ornaments—anything else that contains those metals." They placed their belongings in two sacks and waited for the wagon to come down the street to pick it up. From there it was taken to a depot, and each item was placed in separate bins according to their metal content to be shipped to the smelter.

The following year, even church bells were sacrificed for Hitler's war purposes, and the churches in Groningen were not exempt from this decision. On November 24, 1942, laborers could be seen working on the tall church towers at this almost impossible task. Some of these magnificent bells weighed several tons, but even those were snatched from their bell towers through a complicated process of pulleys and ropes and loaded onto railway cars to await their fate at the smelter in Hamburg to be used for shell casings.

"Hitler has appointed a man named Klaus Barbie to help him rid the Netherlands of Jews," Hans declared with

THE HOUSE OF BLOOD AND TEARS

disgust to Erich, "and I hear many Jews will be shipped right here from Groningen."

As a result, riots erupted in Groningen when the people discovered that Jews were being loaded on trains in their city to be sent to concentration camps. They made attempts to stop this process at the railway stations, and the police took action, using rubber clubs and sabers. The Groningen mayor, Cort van der Linden, furiously protested to the Deutsche Ortskommandant saying, "In a country which has for many centuries been proud of its tradition to have granted the right of asylum to the oppressed, these actions are quite offensive." This decree that was proclaimed against the Jews offended the religious senses of the majority of the population, who abhorred persecution in any shape or form.

The protest was ineffective. On November 26, 1942, three mayors of the northern provinces received the same telegram, ordering them to have all Jews arrested the next day to be transported to Westerbork. The Dutch police sealed up the homes of the Jews with all of their contents and handed the keys over to the Sicherheitspolizei. Hans was among the many whose conscience was pricked. What possessed Dutch policemen to go and pick up Jews? Did they assume that service-commands had to be executed even though they were absolutely contrary to the most elementary human rights?

Eleven policemen of Grootegast refused to arrest Jews and transfer them to Groningen, and as a result, they were arrested and brought to Groningen for a hearing before the commander of the military police. Hans attended the hearing and shared the information with Hillie.

"Gentlemen," the commander said, "while I admire your stand to follow your conscience and what you believe in, there are laws to be adhered to, and my position is to see that they are carried out. I suggest you obey the command given you; otherwise, you shall go to a concentration camp, and German policemen will come and take your place, and they will do the job. Is that what you would prefer?"

When the men did not immediately respond, he continued, "I will give you one night to think it over. You can give me your answer in the morning."

The men were brought before the commander in the morning one by one and asked for their decisions. They had not changed their minds. "Unfortunately, you leave me no option," he responded as he struck his gavel on the table. "Send them to Vught."

As they boarded the train for the concentration camp, the German police officer counting them nodded. "There are eleven. *Ja, es stimmt*" (Yes, it figures).

Village constable Dirk Boonstra calmly replied, "You have made an error; there are twelve. You have forgotten God, for he goes with us always."

In Vught, those who had been arrested were tortured. Six of these men were transferred to concentration camps in Germany, and this is where Dirk Boonstra died.

Anje trudged in the direction of the library as she usually did on Saturday, her mind deep in thought. *There's a war going on, but life must go on just the same; so I am going to get some new books to read. I'll fill my mind with other things than war.*

She climbed the two short steps, pulled on the heavy wooden door until it opened, and entered the building. She loved the smell of books. Viewing the vast array of books on the shelves was such a delight. It was like being at a smorgasbord when you were really hungry. *Just imagine,* she thought, *I can pick anything I want.* Her eyes scanned the section she loved, German Romance.

Romantic novels, some of them in exotic settings and filled with the drama and excitement of faraway places, loving relationships, and even subterfuge and intrigue, sparked her vivid imagination. For a while, she could blot out all the drabness of the war, the inadequacies, and the disappointments that surrounded her and flee on a journey into her mind, into the world of books. She selected a few, placed them on the counter to be entered, and left the building.

As she turned the corner from Maeuwerdeweg, she was heading for home. She smiled as the bright sunshine warmed her rosy cheeks, and a light breeze blew by and ruffled her skirt. It was a beautiful day. Her mind was already engaged in discovering the treasure contained in her newest acquisition from the library.

Skipping up the front steps to her home, she reached her hand inside the mailbox for the key to the house and opened the door. "Mother, I am home," she called. There was no response. She ran from the entrance up the stairs into the kitchen, where she discovered a note from Mother saying she had gone out.

She was often alone as Mother went about her duties for the Resistance. *No matter,* she thought. *I'm going to spend this time reading my books.* She rummaged around in the kitchen for something to eat and found some crackers. *This will do,* she thought. The narrow wooden stairs to the attic creaked as she climbed up with her books under her arm, and she headed toward the dormer window above her bed. As she pushed the window open, the sun was beating down on the roof, and she marveled again at the unusual beauty of this sunny day. She settled herself sideways on the window ledge with her book propped up in her lap, hoping to gain a bit of tan as she began to delve into the thrilling world of adventure.

When Mother arrived home, she brought with her the news of the death of Father's brother Henry. "We are going to Uncle Henry's funeral tomorrow. I washed your blouse so you can wear it with your blue skirt."

This would be the first time they would attend a funeral for a member of Father's family. Anje and Hillie didn't have much to do with Jan's family as he kept them apart, always going to visit them alone and often staying over. The Minnes family consisted of eight boys and three girls; they were an aggressive and boisterous bunch when they were young, but Hillie was surprised at how successful some of them had become in business. The family stood reverently with their heads bowed beside the open grave as the voice of the preacher rose above the prevailing winds, "Ashes to ashes, dust to dust …"

The small group retreated after laying some flowers at the foot of the grave. Anje wondered who the flowers were for. *Are they for the dead, or are they for us?* Either way she wasn't sure it made a difference at all. She observed the mourners, walking slowly along the asphalt road toward the exit and speaking quietly amongst themselves. Father's sister Soar and her husband, Bart Reisdorf, were just ahead of them, and Father joined them as they walked along. She knew Mother was not fond of Soar; this couple staunchly supported the Nazis, and they hated Jews. When they spoke about Adolf Hitler, it was with great pride in their voices.

"I have my binoculars ready. I'll be watching the entertainment again. They will find more Jews in hiding!" Soar said with obvious glee. "Ha-ha! The 'stars' are going to be falling tonight!"

Mother looked at her with disgust, and they began to walk resolutely from the cemetery toward home. Father motioned to Mother and said quietly, "I'll be going to their place for a while. I'll see you later."

Mother nodded. She was quiet for a time as they walked, and when she spoke, she said, "Everyone has the right to their beliefs and opinions, but we have Jewish friends, and they are people just like us." She unlocked the door as they entered their home. "That's why we are doing the things we do." She reached down and untied her shoes and then scooted upstairs. They both knew morning would bring a new day.

THE SECRET EXIT

Anje wondered how she could avoid being seen every time she left her house. Being a very private person, she did not like being watched and followed. But what options were available to her? She began to explore every inch of the house in her mind. She looked out all the windows on the back side of the house that did not face the street. The bedroom windows were three stories up, so climbing out one of them would be dangerous. She checked the window from the back room, pushed up to open it, and looked outside. Since the houses were built in a row and attached, the neighbor's roof sloped down so close to that window from the back room that a small piece of roof rested just below the window like a shelf. As she observed the height, she thought, *Could I get out of that window and climb up onto the next roof? It is fairly steep; can I do that? But where would I go from there?* Her eyes followed the roof line, and a short distance away, there was a very small landing with doors that opened to the inside. She would have to slide off the roof backward down onto that second-story landing and see where those doors took her. *Should I dare try that so high above the ground? Yes, I will have to. There is no other way. When should I try that?* She thought a minute. *How about right now?* She looked at the sky. It was not raining. The slate tiles on the roof might be slippery when wet—she didn't know. She hadn't been up there before.

She pushed a chair to the window, raised the window as high as it would go, and crawled out backward. She was glad she had spent so much time training for track and field and gym because she needed agility and strength. As she pushed her legs down, her toes caught the narrow roof ledge. She was on the roof! She crouched just like a cat ready to pounce on a mouse. The roof was steep, and she didn't want to be seen above the peak. She could see the landing, and she slithered across the tiles and prepared to slide off the roof onto the landing. *I can't fall,* she thought. *I will end up on the ground, and it's a long way down!* She felt her legs slip over the edge of the roof to allow her body to slide off the ledge, waiting for the moment her toes would touch the landing. It worked! She was elated when her toes touched the firm surface. Her knees buckled slightly under her sudden weight, but she stood up, walked toward the door on the landing, and opened it. Once inside she saw a window on her left that revealed the sitting room of someone's dwelling, and to the right was a stairway that led downward. She followed it to see what she would find. It was the bakery warehouse.

Anje at the age of 18, standing in front of the door of the bakery.

This is such an interesting place! she mused as she climbed down the stairs. All the equipment needed for the delivery of goods was stored there, everything except the horses. The wagons were parked neatly in a row, and leather harnesses hung on one wall. She could smell the aroma of ground wheat and noticed barrels of flour lining one wall, while large boxes of supplies were stacked in another section. At one end of the room was a huge sliding door that rolled along a track. Just then a team of horses arrived. The door opened, and the animals were hitched to the delivery wagon that had just been loaded. There was another small door that she presumed led into the bakery. She followed the footsteps in the floury dust on the floor and opened it. The heat of the ovens hit her face as she walked in; it was almost stifling. She saw hundreds of loaves of bread on large racks, waiting to be baked. There was another small room where customers entered to be served, with a door that led out into the street. She was glowing with satisfaction and excitement inside, for now she had discovered another way to exit her home, and it was a secret!

THE CAKE BOX

It was a fine spring day in May 1942. Mother and Anje had a joint assignment that required them to travel to The Hague. Lootens Bakery next door to them was very busily engaged in their new commission of baking a variety of delectable goods for the Germans. Since all the baking was done at night, the warm fragrance of bread wafted up to the residents of the Minnes household, and early in the morning the clip-clop of horses' hooves could be heard as the bakery wagon moved down the street, preparing to deliver bread to the prison.

Anje had dreamed about this next assignment and how she could safely implement the plan. She needed to find a cake to conceal a secret, and she knew she would find it in the bakery. As she and Mother entered the bakery, the little bell tinkled to announce their arrival, and the wonderful aroma of freshly baked goods greeted their nostrils. The beautiful cake they selected from the shelf was just the right size for their project. There were no other customers in the bakery, and after they paid for their purchase, they set it on the side counter. Mother took a long knife that was sitting on the counter, cut the ends off the cake, and began to hollow out the middle. They needed enough space to fit 1,350 ration cards inside. Anje rolled up the cards, pushed them inside the cake, and then carefully positioned the ends back on the cake. Then they wrapped it up, placed it in its original box, and exited the store.

From Rabenhauptstraat, they trudged resolutely toward the train station with their Ausweis kept close at hand. This enabled them to travel to The Hague under the guise of visiting a sick aunt. Their appearance was designed not to attract undue attention. Mother wore her wool tweed coat and brown felt hat, while Anje was dressed in her knitted knee socks with her heavy wool sweater and navy plaid skirt, just like any Dutch school girl. Underneath her skirt, the courier bag was tied around her waist containing her precious cargo, and in her hand she carried a woven straw bag with handles that contained the cake.

She did not know her mother's assignment. Mother said, "It is best you do not know; that way if you are questioned, your answers will be truthful and convincing." They decided they would not sit together; it was safer. Should trouble develop, Anje was to leave the straw bag under a seat and walk away. As she sat down on the hard wooden seat, she did her best to make herself comfortable. The bag was nestled in her lap under her skirt with her hands folded over it nonchalantly.

The train wheels screeched as they slowed and stopped, allowing just enough time to allow numerous plainclothes officers from the SD (Sicherheitsdienst) to come aboard to conduct a control. The train forged ahead and gained momentum, with smoke pouring from its stack. The soldiers moved from car to car as the train swayed, lumbering across the rails, and they carefully scrutinized the documents of each passenger on board while shooting questions at them suspiciously.

Anje could taste the saliva in her mouth, and fear rose in the pit of her stomach as the soldiers came closer and closer. She stared at them fearlessly, her blue eyes keeping careful watch on Mother's brown felt hat. What exactly would she tell them if they questioned her? Of course, she was just going to visit an aunt; that would be a good reason for the cake. What would they think if they discovered she and Mother were not sitting together? She had to remain relaxed while she kept a close eye on the soldiers. Just as the officers were nearing her seat, the air vibrated with the shrill sound of an air raid siren that announced the approach of enemy aircraft. An air raid siren always meant, "Run for cover," but there was no place to run to. The planes immediately began strafing the train with bullets. The sound was deafening, and she placed her hands over her ears to protect them. Amid the roar of engines and the sharp sound of ammunition firing, she caught a glimpse of the star emblem on the side of an aircraft as it flew past her window. It was the US Air Force! Her heart leaped! *Hurrah! There is hope!*

As the guns blazed, the staccato of bullets rang out as they careened off the iron monster, some penetrating the steel while the planes flew parallel above the train. Flying in a zig-zag pattern, they attempted to seriously damage the engine to prevent the continuation of the journey. They failed. During the raid, some passengers crouched low in their seats, and others shouted as they dived to the floor, covering their heads. One mother hugged her child tightly to her breast, shielding her head with her hands. But Anje sat in her seat observing the chaos. *Why are there so many cowards in this train?* she thought. *This is exactly what we want. We want someone to come and fight those Germans so we can get back to living. We should be cheering for them, not hiding from them.* Amid all this confusion and commotion, the train screeched to a stop. The SD officers fled one by one, their feet pounding on the steps as they jumped off the train and began running for cover. Anje watched the whole scene with a huge sigh of relief, muttering quietly, "They're not so tough now. They look like rats running from a sinking ship." As she collected her thoughts, she came to the conclusion that if the US Air Force were trying to stop the train and fighting the Germans, surely this war would soon come to an end.

The train continued on to The Hague, where Mother and Anje disembarked and began searching for their delivery address amid a long row of identical houses. It was a tall structure that stood four stories high, the façade embellished with decorated gables and lattice trim; 17 Sneeuwball Straat was the destination for their goods.

CANADIAN AIRMEN

Five operatives of the Underground were huddled around a map of Europe in Edgar's small apartment; the bare bulb hanging over the table emitted a dim light. Hans, Hillie, Erich, and Walter knew they had a problem to solve—how to smuggle three Canadian airmen out of the country. Rescued by the Underground in a field the night before, they had been forced to bail out of their aircraft as it had burst into flames from enemy fire.

"Don't you think taking them through Switzerland would be our best option?" Walter suggested. "We've had some problems recently getting them all the way through Belgium and France into Spain. Switzerland is a shorter route."

"It may be a shorter route, but getting across the mountains on the French side is not going to be simple. They're not mountaineers," Erich replied. "And the Swiss don't want them."

"They don't want refugees, but wouldn't they accept Canadian Air Force personnel who are trying to get back home?" Walter asked.

"I don't know," Hans responded as he kept his gaze on the map. "I still think getting them across the channel to Britain is the best idea."

"Yes," Edgar commented, "I think so too. And it's the shortest route, but those waters are constantly being patrolled by the German Coast Guard's gunboats. That's not as simple as it sounds."

"Well," Hillie interjected, "what do you think of setting their paperwork and IDs as fishermen? We can get the proper clothing and all their other needs. But we'll have to move fast—the Germans are looking for those men."

As head of this organization, Edgar's approval was needed to proceed. He nodded his head just as Hans broke in hurriedly, "I'll contact the other organization that will bring them to the coast, and we'll do our part to get them ready."

At early Sunday morning mass in Saint Mary's Church of the Cross in Groningen, three bashful women were standing at the altar modestly dressed, with shawls covering their heads. Hans thought as he watched, *I am glad this is a weekend so I can actually be present. Anje was always so interested to know what happened to the pilots. We did a good job.* The sweet voices of the altar boys swelled through the cathedral as the airmen knelt to receive communion with the other parishioners. The priest leaned forward to place the wafer on the tongue of one as he spoke quietly in English, "Follow me into the vestry after the service." The recipient nodded his head and closed his eyes to pray and receive the blessing. *God help us* was the silent prayer he offered up that morning.

"Hurry, hurry," the priest urged as he led them through a narrow passageway, down some hewn stone stairs, and into an overgrown garden. He motioned, and a man clothed in a dark jacket and baggy pants appeared out of the dense brush that grew along the side of the building. He quietly uttered the code word "Mackenzie King" as he approached, and instantly, Hans knew they were in the hands of the Underground.

They followed the man through the thick brush into an alleyway that was covered with vines, and then, in a moment, the sunlight shone through the hedge, revealing an opening to the street. Hillie stood precisely at that spot, and as they emerged, she handed their ID documents to one of the men and quickly turned to leave.

A dark green sedan was waiting at the curb for them. The front door opened abruptly and the words, "Get in!" welcomed them. As they jumped in, the man in the dark jacket and baggy pants closed the car door and retreated to the safety of the alleyway as they sped away.

Hans seated himself beside the driver, who turned and looked at the three. His unshaven face appeared menacing with three days' growth of dark beard, but he broke into a grin and asked," Do you know Mackenzie King?"

The three broke into nervous laughter, a release from the stress of the day thus far, and replied, "He's not really a king!" The code words matched; they were on target.

"The driver here is Franz," Hans said. "He is a Frenchman. This is going to be a fast ride because we are in a stolen car. Franz here is an expert at that! We're going to take you to the next location on the southwestern coast of Holland, where we have a fishing vessel ready to set out tonight. You will be a part of their crew, weather permitting. Know anything about fishing?"

The first one who responded said, "I do. I live right near the Great Lakes in a town called Owen Sound, but Jay here is a landlubber. He comes from a place called Sas-kat-chewan."

Jay indignantly replied, "We have lakes in Saskatchewan too, but I don't live near them. Unfortunately, I get seasick."

"This crossing isn't going to be too easy on you then," Hans muttered under his breath. "The channel is kind of choppy." Then he nodded his head as he spoke sympathetically, "You know, we can give you something for seasickness."

"Yeah, a punch on the head," the Frenchman said with a grin on his face.

Just then the car suddenly lurched to the left and entered a narrow street. The driver increased speed, bouncing and hitting bottom before he quickly turned right, entering a narrow drive. As he entered the driveway, he tooted his horn and then stopped abruptly. A tall blonde woman emerged from the house, waving frantically at them. She proceeded to open the wide door of the building, and Franz drove in, shutting off the engine immediately.

The woman began to converse animatedly in Dutch with Hans and Franz while the three looked on curiously. It appeared that something was amiss. Finally, Hans came to the car and said, "You can get out and stretch your legs a bit, inside the garage. You can change your clothes now.

We'll get rid of those women's things. Give them to the lady when you are ready."

The airmen got ready to comply and began to pull the female apparel off.

"Look out," Jay called out to the other airman who was jostling him. "I don't want you to put a run in my nylons!"

"You sissy," the other replied. "You are looking real comfortable wearing that skirt."

"The only skirts I like are the ones I'm chasing," Jay laughed as he ducked to miss the shoe that was flying toward his head.

"By the way, what happened to our plan?" the first airman asked.

"We have to change plans all the time," Hans began. "Franz had a feeling we were being followed so he pulled in here to cool our trail temporarily. It seems there was an informant in church who noticed three strangers and reported it to the authorities. The SS came immediately to the church and interrogated the priest and some of the other parishioners. There are spies everywhere. We have to decide whether we will continue with our plans for you tonight or abort and wait for another day. We are not sure if this was a random act at the church or if there is an informant in our organization."

"Well," Jay said, "if we are staying, we may as well get to know each other. Anyone got a deck of cards?"

Just then they heard a loud rap on the large door of the garage. Hans's eyebrows raised, and he put his finger across his lips to indicate silence. He motioned with his hands to the three airmen to get in the car and lie down. Jay was the last one in; he dived into the vehicle and quietly closed the door. They could hear voices outside. The lady of the house was carrying on a lengthy conversation with another person.

Finally, after all was quiet, she conferred with the men. Hans and Franz retreated to a corner of the garage to deliberate.

"We have decided it's best to move on. Someone noticed our arrival, and we're going to risk the drive to the coast," Hans explained. They didn't waste another minute. Franz got behind the wheel, the large door opened, and the car pulled out. "For now stay out of sight," Hans said. "The drive will take two or three hours, depending on how slow the traffic is."

Groningen is the most northeasterly province in Netherlands; it is bordered by the cold waters of the North Sea on the north and west, Belgium to the south, and a shared 577-kilometer controlled boundary with Germany. The country's terrain, lack of wilderness, and dense population made it difficult to conceal illicit activities; there was no means of escape except by sea.

Many ears were straining to listen for the first bars of Beethoven's Fifth Symphony and the deep baritone voice of the commentator as the BBC radio broadcast began on Radio Orange. These messages in code came over the airwaves at noon, right after the Italian program. They called this commentator "The Rotterdammer," and since it was his voice that announced the news, people all over the Netherlands began to attribute the results of the news to him. As Anje listened to his marvelous voice, she was sure this Rotterdammer was a very tall, dark, handsome man.

Hans related this assignment to Hillie and Anje, and they listened to the radio with great anticipation this day for a message about these airmen. Finally, they heard these words: "Three packages arrived for Mackenzie King!" They cheered! The pilots were safely in the hands of the British. The mission had been successful.

A NEW MISSION

Anje and her mother sat at the table in the back room as Hillie began; "I have something to tell you. I am involved in many things I can't speak about, not to anyone, but I want you to know if anything happens to me, Uncle Hans will take care of you." A look of surprise flashed across her face as Mother continued, "I am working for both sides in this war. I want you to know that I would never betray our homeland, but the Underground has shown me we can be much more effective if the Germans believe I am working for them. Some of the information that I have conveyed has already been very valuable and I must do it, but it is very dangerous."

Anje's heart sank. She did not want anything to happen to Mother. She knew that what they were doing was dangerous, but what could be even more dangerous? She had seen many things. She knew how vicious the Nazis were. What would they do to Mother if they found out? What about Uncle Hans? Would he be doing the things Mother was doing? They had always worked together. She had not been worried before, but she was worried now.

Her new contact person came to her house to speak with her. His voice was very serious as he spoke. "I cannot stress enough, Anje, the importance of secrecy at all times," he said. His eyes fairly drilled into her as he spoke while looking directly into her eyes. "For the sake of security, do not discuss your job with anyone, not even your mother. Should one be picked up and interrogated, the less anyone knows about you or you about them, the better. The Nazis have ways of getting information from people. Sometimes your instructions will come from me, and sometimes from another agent." With that, he put on his cap, hopped on his bicycle, and rode away.

She thought, *I know all those things. I have been doing this long enough to know what to do. Anyway, I'm not a talker, I'm a thinker.*

Her role continued in a familiar routine. Almost every day, she delivered documents that were hidden in the saddlebag of her bicycle or placed inside her schoolbooks. She didn't know what they contained—she was a courier. Her job was to deliver them to any place required—in the city or in the country, it didn't matter to her. She knew she had to be very careful for there was harsh punishment for this crime. She didn't care. It was as Mother had said: it had to be done.

Fear was something she lived with every day. She could not show it, but it was there—fear of the unknown, fear of discovery, fear of loss. Fear was in the atmosphere. It was so tangible that one could almost cut it with a knife. It could be felt by the rush of adrenaline upon seeing German officers on the street or hearing a sudden knock at the door. The Nazi regime ruled by fear. They delighted in creating angst in the hearts of people; it gave them dominance and compliance. This philosophy ruled in the operation of the control.

It was a wonderful, sunshiny day, and she thought this would be a good day for fun. She was kept busy with her work for the Resistance and for school, but she still loved to roller skate with her friend Janny, who lived across the street. As they cruised along the sidewalk on Noordwal Straat looking for adventure, suddenly a number of army vehicles swarmed the area where they were skating. They counted two trucks with green canvas covering the rear, four passenger vans, and two army officer's cars with the swastika emblem on the side.

The soldiers swiftly cordoned off the street at both ends as four others with two black and tan shepherd dogs on leashes leaped out from the back of one of the trucks. Another officer blew his whistle and waved his gloved hand toward the men who were shouting commands to one another in German. There was pandemonium and haste. Twenty members of the German police, together with the brown shirts and four black uniformed SS officers, operated this control. Every person on the street was accosted and shoved into one of the waiting vans without any questioning, while a group of officers worked each side of the street armed with clubs and rifles and accompanied by noisy, vicious shepherd dogs.

As they observed the scene before them, Anje said quietly, "We have to get out of here before we are picked up."

"What do we do?" Janny asked hesitatingly. This was more adventure than she had wished for.

"Follow me, and do what I do," Anje replied, and she skated nonchalantly along the sidewalk toward one of the vans that blocked the street. Eyes straight ahead, she continued past the van and the guard that stood nearby, swinging her arms and moving her body rhythmically until her skates carried her right onto the next street.

Janny was a little out of breath, more from the excitement than the physical exertion. "How did we manage that? They're arresting everyone on the street, and the acted like they didn't see us."

"Maybe they didn't see us," Anje explained. "This has happened to me before. You know, they are not really interested in us. They think we're just kids."

The officers on the street began ringing doorbells and banging on the doors with their clubs to gain entry. When the door opened, they pushed their way inside, shouting loudly to the occupants, *"Heraus, mit die Juden!"* (Out with the Jews!) If there was any objection or resistance, the dog was given a command to attack, grabbing the person by the forearm and hanging on tightly while accompanying the victim toward the vans. When the victim struggled, the dog gripped tighter. There was no escape from his jaws. As the girls watched from a distance, their hearts beat fast in their chests. A scuffle took place at one of the dwellings, and finally a small man emerged, his bald head bowed low as blood streamed down his face, staining the front of his ragged shirt. The shrill sound of a whistle pierced the air, and the SS in their black uniforms came running to investigate. Their greatcoats flapped as their boots hit the pavement. Loud jubilation broke forth, and the men began patting each other on the backs. "We got one!" one of the men shouted. A thick rope was produced, and it was knotted and looped around the victim's neck. One officer tugged on this rope while leading him to the van. They were delighted. They had caught themselves a Jew!

Just then a holler was heard from the back of the house, and a brown shirt emerged with a frightened woman in tow, obviously the man's wife. Her black, curly hair was peppered with gray, and her eyes were filled with fear. Anje assumed she had been discovered while trying to escape through the backyard. Her drooping shoulders were covered with a drab brown sweater that was wrapped closely about her body, and she walked with resignation toward the van escorted by two officers.

Janny broke the silence. "They were looking for Jews, and this isn't even a Jewish neighborhood."

"That means there was an informer. That's why they came here," Anje speculated.

"And did you see? They treated him like a dog!" Janny exclaimed. It was not a good day for fun after all.

Rushing up the stairs into her house, Anje was glad that Mother was home so she could relate the whole episode of the control to her in the kitchen while she waited for Mother to fix something to eat.

"There are lots of things that we will see that we can't do anything about," Mother explained, "and we must always be careful that we remain in the background. That is what the Underground does. The plan is to help as many people as we can and still remain below the surface, unseen. The things that we do may seem small, but it is what we can do for our people. But always remember to be careful."

She gave her daughter a little hug as she carried her dish of food and placed it on the table, and they both sat down to eat. Anje was distracted for a moment; she was sure she saw the lid of the small trap door in the ceiling move. She made a mental note to check that out. When she finished eating, she went upstairs into the bedroom. Father was lying in the bed in the bedroom, but there were cigar ashes on the floor by the trap door.

MAY 1942

Boys," Hans began at a meeting of the Underground, "this news from the Underground radio is very serious. Hitler has dispatched Heinrich Himmler to the Netherlands to stop the underground activity here."

"That tells us something, Hans," replied the man who was sitting on the floor. "We have been very successful at hurting and hindering the Nazis' plans for our country. We are being effective. "

But the people were not prepared for what Himmler did next. His first act shocked them. On May 4, 1942, four hundred and sixty stalwart members of the community were taken hostage as leverage against the Resistance. The ransom for their release was the halt of all underground activity, effective immediately. Any further incidents would impose a death sentence upon these men. Members of the Resistance were taken aback. Exactly what were they to do? The lives of these men were in their hands. They decided to hold a meeting after each member diligently searched his heart.

Hans could not be present at this meeting, but his friends recounted the results to him.

"What do you think, boys, what should we do? Do we give in to them? Do we stop operating for the sake of these men?" their leader had asked.

"If we give in now, what will we be forced to do next?" one man questioned.

"One of them is my sister's husband," another cried.

"And one is my neighbor," another said drily, without emotion.

"There are consequences for each of us, for what we are doing."

Hours were spent debating the issue, and in the end the unanimous response was a resounding, "No! We cannot stop!" The men made a decision. They were risking their lives daily, hoping to accomplish something good for the people. And so, the Resistance continued.

On October 17, 1942, in a public square, the repeated cracking sound of rifles filled the air, and four hundred and sixty innocent men fell, executed by the Regime.

Bombing of Cologne

On May 30, 1942, Anje was occupied with another of her favorite novels when she began to notice the familiar drone of aircraft engines, which sounded like the wings of a thousand bumblebees beating the air. She raised her hand to shield her eyes and squinted into the distance. British aircraft were flying in formation at a high altitude, heading for Germany. They were easy to count. As she calculated, another formation would follow, appearing just like tiny matchbox images in the heavens. It was difficult to imagine that death and destruction could be caused by that battery of aircraft, which from her level, looked like little toys. She wondered, *Where are they going, and what are they about to do? Something big must be in the works.* With every battle, she hoped it would be the last.

"Mother, did you see all the airplanes?" Anje called.

Mother smiled and replied, "No, I didn't."

"They are British aircraft, and I have never seen so many of them at one time," Anje replied.

"You have your eyes on the sky much more than I do," Mother acknowledged.

Anje never tired of watching the sky. Two and a half hours later, when the mission was accomplished, the planes began heading west toward England and home. She thought the eight hundred warplanes in the skies resembled a swarm of mosquitoes rising from a slough, but by then the book in her lap needed adjusting in order to gain a little more light on the page, and she stood up.

The transmission from BBC News, London, on May 31, 1942, announced:

For the first time during this war, Britain, in an unprecedented move, launched more than 1,000 aircraft in a massive raid against Germany. Spitfire and Hurricane fighters escorted 837 Lancaster bombers, each loaded with 36,900 pounds of bombs, toward the German city of Hamburg. Due to inclement weather, the target was switched to Cologne, where enormous destruction was observed as wave after wave of bombers swept across the city releasing their payloads. Plumes of smoke could be seen shooting upward from the explosion, and fires burned intensely within the city. Crews from the bombers reported seeing sections of the Hindenburg Bridge collapse into the Rhine River broken into pieces like a toy; building joists glowed white hot in the immense fire that raged below, which rendered twenty thousand people homeless. We have inflicted a serious blow to the German Third Reich. God save the king.

However, the Cologne cathedral, the immense twin-spired structure of Gothic architecture whose construction began in the thirteenth century, remained unscathed. One of the world's largest churches, a navigational land-mark to the Allied aircraft, survived seventy hits by aerial bombs. Buildings lay in shambles all around it, but it did not collapse, still towering majestically above a smoking, demolished city.

The nation was secretly rejoicing over the enemy's loss, and the Resistance group that held their rendezvous that night toasted the campaign with their water glasses as they shouted, "To victory!"

"Finally, the Germans are getting what they deserve!" Erich exclaimed with glee.

"It was time to pay back," another chimed in as he toasted the success.

"Maybe the war will be over soon," Hillie interjected hopefully as she placed her glass upon the table.

Hans was silent. He never felt jubilation when he knew people had died as a result of another's actions.

"But for tonight, the organization still has important things to do," Edgar said firmly. "Let's get down to business."

AIRCRAFT OVERHEAD

Since Groningen was on the flight path from Britain to Germany, aircraft were constantly overhead. Their targets were often the shipyards at Bremen or the cities of Hamburg and Berlin, where the factories and power plants were located. Whenever aircraft would enter the airspace of the Netherlands, the howl of air raid sirens penetrated the air and people ran for cover. They could run, but there was nowhere to go. Very few basements or air raid shelters existed in Holland.

On the street, makeshift shelters were constructed of straw bales; one could walk down two steps and crouch behind the bales while the sirens sounded. Anje thought this seemed like a futile exercise. The shelters offered protection only from falling debris, and the one time she used one of them, she found that it smelled of urine and decided she wouldn't bother with that again. The routine was that when the safe siren sounded a single blast, each person who had huddled somewhere for shelter would proceed about their business again, picking up their bicycles and carrying on.

Sleep was often what they longed for most. Sometimes the air raid sirens sounded five times a night, forcing Mother and herself from their beds as bombs crashed around them. She lay alert in her bedroom night after night, listening and concentrating on the sounds she heard, trying to identify them. Listening had become so important; she was always listening for anything that bore the potential to harm, such as footsteps walking behind her, the creak of a door, a vehicle slowing down, the ring of the doorbell, or the sound of aircraft in the distance.

Identifying the aircraft became a game to her; she knew them by the sound of their engines. She thought the German Messerschmitt made a rattling sound that resembled rotating eggbeaters, and the RAF Lancaster engines produced an undulating sound like the rising and descending of a song, which she could readily imitate. Since the United States had only recently entered the war, she was still trying to figure out their planes. She heard about the B-17s and B-24s, and she carefully noted that the Americans flew only during the day. She found a book in the library that was all about airplanes, but it was a little out of date. Aircraft were being produced and perfected faster than the books that were written about them.

She admired the precision of the British Royal Air Force pilots, who hit their targets consistently even though their missions were flown at night. The BBC News talked a lot about the flyboys from the United States; there was a great influx of military when the US Air Force began to arrive in England in July 1942. They spent the next five months acclimatizing and training. The crews were trained for high latitude bombing using precision bombsight instruments and could achieve pinpoint accuracy in the clear blue skies of the Nevada desert in the United States, but bombing targets in Germany through dense cloud, smoke screens, and industrial haze with the Luftwaffe in close pursuit was another matter.

Walking with her dog, Jamada, was a nightly ritual that Anje had come to enjoy. Though it often seemed that there were surprises around every corner, other things were fairly routine. Every evening Mother was not home, she sat on the front steps waiting for her, straining her neck at every bicycle that approached, wondering, *Is this Mother?* She never quite adjusted to Mother's being away so much, and yet she knew Mother made every effort to be at home as much as possible. She felt lonely at times, for Uncle Hans was also busy—and Father? Well, he was rarely at home, and she never knew when he was coming or how long he was staying. He behaved more like a visitor than a father.

Another ritual she observed was the precision timing of the Allies as they began strafing the trains at 8:00 p.m. each night. She stopped to check her watch every night;

203

they were always right on time. The goal of the Allies was to stop this "raiding of the pantry," as the trains pulling boxcars laden with food and other products produced in the Netherlands were headed for the bellies of the German army.

It was a fairly dark night when she and Jamada went for their stroll before bed. The weather was a bit chilly, and she pulled her thick sweater a little more tightly around her body. Oma had knit this sweater for her, and she was glad for it as she snuggled down into the collar to keep the chill off her neck. She could hear the clatter of the wheels on the tracks as a freight train came rolling across the rails on Achterfweg heading eastward, the smoke pouring from its chimney. This was a frequent occurrence. Just then she heard the roar of engines of four Allied aircraft zooming in for the kill, their weapons blazing. Suddenly she heard a swoosh of something rushing by her in the air and felt her hair flutter in the wind. Her reflex was quick; she ducked! *Bang!* An artillery shell struck! Fragments of brick and stone showered in all directions, and some of the pieces pummeled her as the shell lodged in the wall of the building behind her, failing to explode. This all happened so fast that it was hard to grasp what had just taken place. She looked at the shell sticking out of the wall; it was about a foot long and had small wings on the tail. Her heart was pounding from the shock. "I think that one was meant for me, Jamada!" she said as she began walking toward home. "Come on! We better get out of here!"

She never got tired of sitting in her dormer window and gazing at the night sky. It was so fascinating. The dark sky exploded with energy. The antiaircraft guns on the ground were grinding and banging as metal hit metal when the huge guns discharged their ammunition, propelling large red and white cannonballs into the sky, destined for their targets. Beams from the searchlights penetrated the darkness, piercing the sky with a shaft of light and crisscrossing one another like the dancing lights in a light show as they searched for the enemy in the sky. When the outline of an aircraft appeared, the guns boomed, aiming for a hit. She was accustomed to the sound of war, and sometimes she wondered what it would be like if a bomb hit her house. Would she wake up? Or would she just die in her sleep? It was best not to think about that, she thought. Eventually she closed the window, climbed into bed, and pulled the comforter over her head to block out some of the noise so she could fall asleep.

It was partly cloudy one day in the summer of 1942 when Anje was walking home from school. She was near the Martini Tower close to the Grote Markt on Prinsenstraat when the shrill blast of air raid sirens penetrated the air. She was stubborn and getting to be rebellious; though she was only thirteen she had become hardened to all the sights and sounds of war and began to feel almost invincible. *Does it really matter if I find shelter from the airplanes?* she thought. *I don't think so. Perhaps I am being foolish, but I don't care.* As the sound of sirens continued to swell the air, she ran from house to house, huddling temporarily in the alcove of each dwelling, pressing her body against the hard red bricks. She had been frightened so many times that one day she discovered that she didn't know how to be afraid anymore. That emotion was gone.

She became aware of the scenario unfolding in the sky. Six aircraft were engaged in heavy conflict; the flak was forming small, fleecy clouds in the sky, and she could see the German Messerschmitts battling with the Americans. It looked like a fight to the end. As the aircraft appeared out of the clouds, the gunners pulled the triggers of their weapons and poofs of smoke rose from the cannons mounted behind the cockpits as the Nazis fired again and again. They whirled upward and suddenly swooped down upon the American Mustang, just like an eagle attacking its prey. The ammunition exploded, and the Germans blew the Americans out of the sky. Two planes were on fire, spiraling toward the ground as black smoke poured from the fuselage of the craft. Anje's heart was beating rapidly and her hands shaking as she watched the battle progress. A numbness was always in her heart as she had to steel herself for the inevitable—someone was going to die, and she couldn't do anything about it. Just then the crew and pilots ejected from their planes in rapid succession, their ejection seats propelling them high into the sky. Their chutes began to open one by one, and they floated toward the ground, saved by the strong wind blowing through the yards of yellow silk.

She sighed in relief, realizing the next step would involve the Underground picking up the airmen as soon as they hit the ground and sneaking them out of the country. But that relief turned to horror when a German pilot circled back, flying directly toward the Americans as they hung in the sky, helpless and unarmed. The sounds of gunfire exploded in the air, and she clamped her hand over her mouth to muffle a scream that was beginning to erupt in her throat. As she saw the limp bodies hurdle toward the earth, fierce anger exploded inside of her. "That's not fair! You killed them! They were not a threat to you. That's not fair!" she shouted to the sky. "You didn't have to kill them!" She was filled with rage, and seeds of bitterness and hatred began to grow inside her. One thing she knew for certain—she hated the Germans!

SAMUEL'S WISH

Two rings of the doorbell indicated that Samuel Troostwijck was waiting on the Minnes' doorstep. When Hillie opened the door, he stood there expectantly, some suits draped across his arm.

"Come in, Samuel," Hillie beckoned him as he entered. Anje was sitting at the table with her elbow bent, her chin resting on her arm. She was engrossed in her homework but raised her eyes to see who came up the stairs. When she saw Samuel, she came to the vestibule.

Samuel looked at Hillie questioningly and asked, "Hillie, would you keep these suits for me until I come back? I have been chosen for resettlement, and I will be away for a while." He handed her the clothing.

"Yes," Hillie assured him, "we'll keep them for you." She took them from him, preparing to hang them in the closet. The symbol of the large yellow star on the jacket blazed its message, "Jood."

"Hillie," he said as he looked at her with a tinge of sadness in his dark eyes, "would you help Esther and the boys while I am away? You know, two energetic boys can be a handful without a man around. It would be a great comfort to me knowing that my wife had someone to help her and—" he hesitated before he went on, "to watch over her."

"Yes, of course, Samuel," Anje interjected. "We would be glad to help them. Max and Bennie are my friends, and we will help them any way we can."

When Samuel left, Mother walked to the closet to put his suits away and commented to Anje, "I wonder how Father will like this arrangement. He can be funny about things like that. You know how the Minnes' family has been behaving toward the Jews recently." They were both remembering his sister's tirade at the funeral. Mother reached out and gently touched the yellow patch on Samuel's jacket. "I don't know why this Star of David is such a curse to these people, Anje," she said thoughtfully.

"Isn't there anything we can do to help them?" Anje asked for what seemed like the hundredth time.

"Yes," Mother said with a smile at her daughter. "You can go and help Esther."

When Anje opened the door to Esther and Samuel's home on Friday just before sundown, the aroma of fresh baking greeted her nostrils.

"What are you baking, Esther?" Anje asked, trying to identify the scent.

"Challah!" Esther replied as she removed it from the oven. "Challah is an egg bread that we serve for Shabbat."

Anje leaned down to inspect the braided loaf; it looked as delicious as it smelled. Esther's clean house shone, the efforts of a productive day. When Anje pulled the matches from her pocket to light the candles in the candlesticks, she noticed that the table was dressed with the finest lace tablecloth; a bottle of red wine was beside the Kiddush cup; and Esther, Max, and Bennie were dressed in their best clothes for Shabbat. After lighting the candles, Anje blew out the match and prepared to leave, turning off the lights and the gas stove. She closed the door and could hear the Jewish family reciting their prayers in Hebrew. She walked slowly toward home, wrapped up in her thoughts. What else could she do for her Jewish friends? This seemed like such a small thing when they were faced with deportation and separation from their families.

In the morning, Anje returned in time to turn on the lights and light the gas stove so Esther could make tea. This weekly Sabbath ritual was a pleasure for she was fulfilling the promise she had made to Samuel, to "take care of Esther."

THE HAGUE

Anje began packing her courier bag until it was filled with ration cards and coupons and a few other documents. She made sure that all items were safely stored inside before she tied the strings around her waist, concealing it under her skirt. Hillie smiled when they locked the door and left the house; everything appeared to be in order. She didn't offer any explanations to Anje about her role. It was best left unspoken, and Anje understood why.

Their destination once again was The Hague, and as they boarded the train, they selected separate seats. Anje sat quietly, observing the people in their coach. An elderly couple occupied a seat at the rear, a mother and her two young children were reading a storybook together, and two young lovers just ahead of her were engrossed in each other. Every so often the young man would lean over and whisper something in his love's ear, and she would smile engagingly. Their intimacy gave the impression that they were alone on this planet. As Anje continued to scan the coach, something caught her eye—it was the back of a man's head that looked so familiar to her. As she continued to puzzle over this, the man rose from his seat and began walking toward the lavatory. She recognized his gait, and her heart leaped! It was the man in the tweed coat who regularly followed her in Groningen. She was aghast! How could she be so careless? Had he been following her without her being aware of it? She needed to alert Mother, and they had to lose him before they made their delivery.

They disembarked the train and walked brusquely across the marble floor through the station's wide hall while the loud voice of the public address system echoed the arrivals and departures amid the throngs of moving people. The train tracks ran through the center of the building, so they were surrounded with people of all ages and sizes carrying their luggage to the train and buying tickets at the counter, while the military observed the movements of all. Every ticket holder was checked; this was a perfect place to pick up a fugitive or apprehend a suspect. She beckoned Mother with her eyes and a tilt of her head to follow her into the women's restroom.

"We are being followed," Anje announced. Then she paused to ask, "What do you think we should do?"

What would they do? Each time they looked out, the man was sitting on one of the long benches for the commuters watching the exit from the ladies washroom.

People were coming and going in this large restroom; there was activity in every corner as people used the facilities, washed their hands, and cast quick, approving glances in the mirror before they exited. Everything looked so normal, but how could they escape?

Light was pouring in through the windows along one side of the room, and as Anje looked up, she asked herself, *Is it possible they open?* "Mother," she said seriously, "we are going to see if that window opens, and if it does, I'm going through it." She never gave a moment's thought to what others would think. There was a war going on. At any given moment, anything could happen.

Mother responded quickly, "I will not fit through that window. I'll find some other means, but I will meet you in front of the church on Kerkstraat. Wait for me there."

Anje hesitated for a moment, but she knew she could trust Mother. "Okay," she said, "let's do it." They tugged on the handle and pushed the window upward to open it. Anje leaped onto the trash container in the room while Mother moved closer to the window so Anje could use her shoulders for more leverage. Before she knew it, Anje was out the window and gone. It was a six-foot drop to the ground, but the soil was soft and Anje was limber. She reached down, grabbed the courier bag under her skirt to make sure nothing had fallen out, quickly jumped to her feet, and began walking resolutely toward Kerkstraat.

Hillie did not hesitate. She turned her jacket inside out so that the rayon lining became the outer coat, which was now gray. She rummaged in her purse for some hairpins to fasten her hair in a bun and also found a container of loose powder, which she liberally dusted on her hair. As she scrounged in the bottom of her purse, she discovered a small pouch that contained an old pair of her mother's black spectacles. She put them on and looked in the mirror. She had aged about twenty years! As she exited the building, she shuffled along in a slow gait, favoring her left leg and always keeping her back to her pursuer. When she was about a block away, she resumed her normal pace.

Anje squinted as she watched an image coming closer. *Is this really Mother?* she asked herself. When Mother approached, she took off her spectacles and smiled. Anje wondered where she had gotten the costume. She was awed by her resourcefulness. They walked along in a carefree manner to Sneeuwball Street, and when they rang the doorbell, they were welcomed inside, as Mother needed to restore her image for the return journey.

The train ride back was uneventful. They were both lost in thought as they listened to the rumble of the wheels. Anje still had some homework to finish before school on Monday. She watched the countryside fly past and wondered, *When will this war be over? When will we have our land back to do with as we please?*

German soldiers in uniform were a common sight, their watchful eyes observing everything. When they were in view, she felt tense. Great caution was necessary for some of them could be very mean; she never knew what to expect from them. A person could be shot if he or she laughed at something or just looked at someone the wrong way—even for doing nothing. Fear was something she felt every day.

She was daydreaming as she thought of her friend Louis from school. He was just a little guy, but he was very muscular. Louis knew how to defend himself for he earned his living working as a bouncer. One day a German soldier hit him in the face, and Louis decided to bide his time until he could get even. He waited for just the right setting, and it came one starless night. Three officers were standing together visiting on the street, and Louis caught them off guard. He sprang out of the dark, beat the three of them unconscious, and then bolted unseen into the night. They never caught him. He had reasoned that those Nazis needed to be taught a lesson. They were always picking on someone, and now it was time for payback. Maybe he was right, she thought, but there were not many people like Louis. Most people just knuckled under.

When the train pulled into the station in Groningen, it came to a stop with its wheels screeching. The doors opened, and their shoes clattered as they stepped down the metal steps to the platform. Someone was waving at them, and as they came closer they saw it was Uncle Hans. He gave them both a hug and said with a smile, "I thought you would be coming back tonight. I just wanted to prepare you—there will be a special parcel arriving at your house tomorrow morning!"

"What is it?" Anje asked in anticipation, with a twinkle in her eye.

"Ah, but you will see tomorrow, sunshine girl," he said, smiling as he chucked her under the chin. The three began walking arm in arm toward Rabenhauptstraat and home.

"The organization has a meeting tonight. Will you be coming, Hillie?" he asked as he looked at her.

"I can if I'm required to be there," she said brightly.

"It would be best," he answered. "I think it may get late.

Could I plan on spending the night at your place then?" he asked.

"Yes," she responded quickly.

Anje mused, "Well, then, you may be here when the parcel arrives."

"I don't think so," he replied. "I have to leave early to be in Haren in the morning for work."

Sleep didn't come easily to Anje that night. Many thoughts rolled around in her mind, and there was still some homework to finish. She looked at her watch—it was eleven o'clock, too late to start homework. She would have to get up at five o'clock in order to be ready for class.

The day began with a light rain, and her raincoat was covered with beads of moisture. Her shoes clanged as she walked up the metal steps to cross the bridge above the railroad tracks; she could see the traffic on the road below her. The street was full of bicycles, people busily navigating their way to work. Everyone was engrossed in preparing to do what they were trained to do. As she began to walk across Herebrug near the park, she noticed the chestnut trees—they looked exceptional in the morning, so fresh in their coat of green leaves. She thought, *The Netherlands is like a big garden. Every inch of space is used to produce something.* The school had toured a cheese plant recently, and it was then that she realized that the cows ate the grass, and they produced milk, which in turn was made into cheese. She was very proud when she learned that the Netherlands was a large supplier of cheese to Europe. The tasting time had been fun. Gouda was the cheese they were most famous for, but it was not her favorite. She thought it was too hard. And now, the Nazis were stealing all these products and shipping them to Germany. It had been a very long time since she had eaten cheese, she thought wistfully. It had been a long time since she had eaten a real, proper meal like Mother used to make, with meat, potatoes, and vegetables. *I cannot think about what I cannot have,* she resolved as she kept walking.

She scanned the sky with her eyes when the familiar whirr of RAF engines began to fill the air. Not again! Those two adversaries appeared so quickly. Were they always waiting for a fight? Shooting began as planes battled with the Germans overhead. Air raid sirens began to whine, and she looked up. There was no place to hide. The canal was on one side, and the houses were too far away. Where could she seek shelter? Her brain quickly assessed the problem. She had to lie down in the ditch. *But there's no protection!* her mind screamed at her. Fear rose at the thought of debris hitting her head, so she placed her schoolbooks on her head as a shelter. When the siren stopped, she dusted herself off and continued on her way to school, just like every other day.

Her anticipation was great as she ran up the steps into the house at the end of her school day and called, "Mother, did the parcel come?"

Hillie stepped into the room smiling and holding a bundle in her arms. She replied, "Yes, it did."

"A baby?" Anje asked, her voice rising to a higher pitch. "The parcel was a baby? Can I hold her, or him?" she asked excitedly.

"Yes," Mother said, handing the bundle to her daughter.

"Her name is Lainey, she is three months old, and she is Jewish. Her parents have gone into hiding today, and they had to give her up. It is such a tragic situation, to have to give up your child for your own safety, but in this case, perhaps they will both survive. We can just keep her for the day. Someone will come and pick her up in the evening and take her to her new home. There are some Christians who are willing to help by taking a baby into their home; they are her only hope for survival."

Anje held the little girl close. She was so beautiful. This was the first time she had held such a small baby in her arms, and it almost overwhelmed her. The baby's head felt warm as Anje held her cheek against the baby's silky brown hair. "Lainey, you will survive," she said out loud, and then she added sadly, "She is so little, and already she's lost her family." Her heart was melting with love for this little one. She had seen so much tragedy, and Anje did not wish any bad things to come upon her.

Mother quickly replied, "But she is so fortunate, Anje. She is going to a good home with a new mother and father who will take good care of her. They even sent some milk along for the baby, so you can feed her a bottle in a little while," she said, "when she cries for food."

Anje couldn't take her eyes off this baby. She walked about the room rocking her gently while softly singing a little tune. Then, when her dark blue eyes closed, Anje laid her quietly on her bed upstairs. She looked at the eyelashes that swept across those chubby cheeks so perfectly shaped and said quietly, "Little Lainey, I think you are going to be just fine in your new home, and I'm so glad we can help you."

The baby awoke with a wail that could be heard all

over the house. *Now I know why you can't take a baby into hiding,* Anje thought. Lainey was sucking vigorously on her hand when Anje reached to pick her up. "My, you are hungry now, little one. I'll go and warm your milk and then you can eat."

Was that the doorbell again? she thought. She took a peek by lifting the metal latch that pulled up the little trap door in the floor in the bedroom, allowing her to see into the kitchen. Mother opened the door to allow two men from the Underground inside. They both dutifully removed their caps and asked for the goods they had come for.

Anje remembered, *Oh! It's the guys coming to pick up the box of radios!*

Mother led them to the cupboard, and they stooped down to pull out the cardboard boxes and looked inside. They nodded to each other, scooped them up in their arms, went back down the stairs, and exited the house. Anje waited until they left and then climbed down the steep, narrow steps into the kitchen to warm the milk.

Just as she finished burping the baby after her last gulps of milk, the doorbell rang again. *This must be the person who is picking her up,* Anje thought. The words of Shakespeare popped into her mind as she carried Lainey downstairs: "Parting is such sweet sorrow," she said softly as she kissed the silky brown hair one more time. The woman standing at the front door looked like a mother. She had a plaid shawl over her head and was wearing a brown coat. *Good,* Anje thought, *she looks like an ordinary person; she won't be stopped on the street.* The woman smiled and opened her arms to receive the soft bundle. A tiny pink hand reached out from the blanket, and Anje grasped it once more. "Good-bye," she said. The woman firmly held the baby against her chest, nodded, and said quietly, "Good-bye," as the door closed behind her.

Leila

While she was still enjoying the memory of having that wonderful little baby in her arms, Anje's cousin Willie arrived with a Jewish lady in tow. They could see immediately from her rebellious attitude that they were in for a battle. Leila appeared to be in her fifties, for her disheveled hair was salted with gray. Her wool skirt looked expensive, but it was wrinkled; and the dark knitted sweater that covered her shoulders was embellished with an attractive braiding on the neck and cuffs, something that would be found in a fashionable ladies wear shop. She had been in hiding at another location when the Gestapo had been tipped off to search that dwelling. Fortunately, the family had been warned by the Resistance, and she was quickly rescued from her hiding place and brought to the Minnes house for safety. She would be picked up in dark of the evening and taken to another secure Underground location.

Her dark eyes were angry. As she tossed her head and smoothed her skirt, she spewed out her distaste. "I was actually dragged out of my hiding place. Mind you, it was disgusting in this tight little closet. I don't think any of you would have liked it either." She spat the words out. "No one told me where I was going, and this horrible man actually tied my bicycle to his, so I had no option except to follow him." She glared at Willie as she spoke. She looked like a cat that had been thoroughly harassed, and all it could do was hiss and spit. "I have not had any food for two days, and I mean no food," she emphasized. "And I am hungry. I want some meat, and if you don't give me some right now, I am going to scream."

Anje looked at the woman and thought, *Lady, are you for real? What do you think we have here, a store? A mission house? We live here, and we put ourselves at risk by allowing all kinds of people to be brought here for help and contact with the Underground. This is dangerous what we are doing.*

"We would like to have some meat too," Mother explained, "but there is none. Our cupboards are empty."

"Then I am going to scream, and I will scream until you bring me some food." She looked at them daringly as she spoke, and then she began to scream loudly. Willie jumped up and clamped his hand forcefully over her mouth, his eyes glaring at her.

"Woman, you listen to me now," he said menacingly as he looked directly into her face. "Every person that has helped you until now has risked his life to save a Jew. If we are caught, we get the death penalty. Now, are you going to be quiet?"

Her eyes still burned with fury. "You are not going to be quiet? Then I will keep my hand over your mouth until you can calm down," he admonished. The afternoon wore on, and Willie was as good as his promise. He subdued his adversary with his strong right hand until she began to weaken.

Mother pulled on her sweater and left the house to go to the bakery. She was hoping to buy a loaf of bread for supper. It was still called a loaf, but the small squares of bread were only about an inch thick when cut. She brewed some weak ersatz tea by dropping the brown tablets into the teapot. When they sat down to the table to eat, Leila was asked to join them.

"You call this bread?" she said acidly as she bit on her portion.

"Yes," Hillie replied, "and we call this tea." She poured the hot brown liquid into their cups.

They were just finishing their tea when the doorbell rang, and Leila left with another operative who would take her to her destination. She gave the Minneses a disdainful look, tossing her head in the air as much as to say "So glad to be rid of you." As the door closed, Anje heaved a huge sigh of relief and prepared to climb up the stairs to her bedroom. Most of the Jews they had helped were grateful. *I guess one rotten apple in the barrel is not so bad*, she thought. *This will be a welcome sleep.* She climbed into bed, pulling the covers over her.

PRISON BREAK

A small group of people sat at the round table where the organization held their meeting in Edgar's apartment. It was a rather drab room but the only one in the center of the flat, where there could be no ears listening on an outside wall. The meeting was over. This was the first time Franz had been asked to attend a meeting for this organization. He was known as a very good driver who had nerves of steel, and since he had a very active part in this next assignment, he was asked to attend. He had done a lot of courageous things, but the stakes were even higher now. He was married, and he and his wife had just celebrated the arrival of a new baby boy. He thought he still had all those qualities inside him that made him a good agent, but he wanted to be alive to help raise his son and watch him grow up. He would resolve to be more careful, he thought, as he leaned forward in his chair to listen carefully to the plan.

Edgar went to his strongbox, removed some papers, and handed them to Hillie. "You'll have to bring the documents for these men tomorrow, Tuesday, by noon," he said as he sucked another breath of smoke from his cigarette. "And it's urgent."

She smiled and nodded. Everything was urgent. The Resistance was about to release two operatives from prison in a daring move. These two men were guilty of sabotage; they had been caught in the process of blowing up a bridge over the Amstel canal and were to be moved to the concentration camp in Vught. Their fate was sealed; they would be staring into the barrel of a rifle in the square. Franz shuddered inside. This was how the Nazis treated traitors, which is what they called members of the Resistance. He knew that if he were caught, this would be his punishment also.

The prison was a strategic place to obtain information because those who were caught were taken there first. It was a windfall for the Underground when the prison officials reported they were having trouble with their phone system and called the telephone company for a repairman. The lineman on the job that day worked for the Underground, and he described in detail to his friend Franz everything he had done. This mission had a dual purpose: he would fix the telephone problem and then make it accessible to the Resistance. Obtaining access to the telephone lines was strategic to the Resistance, as the officers in the House of Blood and Tears communicated their decisions to the prison by telephone. It took a considerable amount of time to do everything he had planned, but when he was done, the lines were totally accessible to the Resistance. They could listen to and also speak into the telephone system, which would prove invaluable to them. Several people were assigned to be listeners. It was a tedious task, but in order to be effective, the lines had to be monitored twenty-four hours a day. Their patience was rewarded when Petty Officer Robert Lehnhoff called from the House of Blood and Tears ordering two saboteurs to be picked up on Tuesday at 2:00 p.m. to be transferred to Vught for punishment. When the Resistance heard that information, they brewed an idea that had never been tried before. They were going to break someone out of prison!

For this assignment, it was decided that Franz would not be the driver. Since he spoke German fluently, he was required to sit beside the driver and appear more as the authority figure. He was one of the three agents from the Resistance dressed in German uniforms who appeared at the prison entrance driving a stolen military vehicle. Their plan was to pick up the prisoners for the transfer one hour earlier than the scheduled 2:00 p.m. As the car pulled up to the prison gate, Franz spoke with authority. "We are here to pick up two prisoners to transport to Vught." The gates opened slowly, and they were instructed to drive inside and wait as the gates closed behind them. They were now in a vulnerable position—nothing could go wrong.

The German guard returned, walked brusquely over to the car, and bowed his head as he leaned forward to speak to Franz. "There seems to be some difficulty. As yet, I have no orders for that request."

"Ja, ich verstehe!" (Yes, I understand.) Franz confidently

answered the guard. "I have the papers right here." Opening his sturdy black briefcase, he produced an official document signed by Colonel Schacht ordering the two men to be transferred to Vught. Hillie and Anje were the only two persons who knew who signed Colonel Schacht's signature.

The guard scanned the papers carefully as he walked toward the guardhouse to telephone his superiors. The men in the car sat quietly; Franz's calm exterior did not reveal the droplets of sweat that were running down his back. The minutes felt like hours as they waited for a response, and eventually a sage green army lorry pulled up in front of them and the motor was shut off.

"Uh-oh!" the driver said. "I don't like the look of this." They held their breath and maintained their composure as an officer strutted toward their vehicle. He saluted as he approached Franz, with a brisk "Heil Hitler."

Franz responded in the same manner.

"I have two prisoners here; they are scum from the Resistance. You will deliver them to Vught where they will be receiving their punishment, Ja?" he said inquisitively as he smiled.

"Indeed," Franz responded as two disheveled-looking men wearing handcuffs were pushed roughly into the back seat of his vehicle. The door was slammed shut behind them.

"Please sign my papers," Franz requested. A quick swirl of the hand created a signature, and Franz tore off a copy, handing it to the officer. He nodded his thanks as he prepared to leave.

"One moment," the guard called out as he approached the car. "Don't forget to sign my copy as well."

"Yes," Franz replied. "Excuse me!" He nodded his head

and handed him a copy of the document. He saluted with a "Heil Hitler."

The driver put his sweaty palms on the steering wheel, shifted gears, and pulled ahead. The tires crunched on the gravel as they turned the car around in the prison yard, and just then the metal gates squeaked open to allow them passage. The driver gunned the motor as he passed the barrier with the car. The clang of the prison gates closing behind them brought a huge sense of relief.

Franz turned to the two in the back seat and said quietly, "You are free. We're from the Resistance!"

The two men hugged each other jubilantly and said, "You're from the Resistance? Then we're not going to Vught? We're free?"

Franz said to himself, *And I am free also, at least for today.*

The car sped through the streets to Wijnhaven, where Hillie was waiting for them on the street corner. As the car pulled up, she handed the two prisoners a package containing new identification cards for their journey. Another group would provide a change of clothing and a place to hide until they could be taken out of the country.

However, they did not want to leave the country; Groningen was their home. They preferred to go underground. The organization applauded the success of this daring escape. They were beginning to think nothing was impossible!

IT'S FRIDAY!

It was Friday! What was special about Friday? Friday was the day that single girls were cautioned to stay off the streets because the Nazis picked up girls to be companions at their Friday night parties. There was always an abundance of wine, women, and song on Friday nights. One saying went thus: "If you have a large pickling barrel, that's where you keep your daughter on Friday night." One of Anje's friends warned her, "I was picked up one evening, Anje, and you don't want that to happen to you. The German men—some of them are very elegant and charming, but they know the effect alcohol will have on a person who is not used to drinking it. Others are very aggressive and won't take no for an answer. So they ply the young girls with hard liquor, and they can get anything they want from them. They went too far that night, and they stripped the clothes off this girl and handed her around the room on top of their hands above their heads, and anyone could feel her as she went by. This poor girl was almost unconscious from drinking, but it all came to a sudden stop when their captain entered the room. He called rank on them, and they all snapped to attention; and the poor girl fell to the floor. He said something to them in German—I couldn't understand it, but I could tell it was a tongue lashing for their behavior. You know, Anje, many girls are raped on a Friday night, so be careful." As an afterthought, she said, "But there was one bonus from that night. When I left, I stuck one of the officer's revolvers under my sweater, and nobody even noticed."

"How did that happen?" Anje asked.

Her friend laughed. "You know, the soldiers get very careless with their guns when they have been drinking. Some of them hang their gun belts over their chair, and others hang them up on the coat hooks by the door. That's how I got the one I stole."

Anje thought, I am fifteen years old, and I am not interested in guns or soldiers. And she realized that her friend didn't actually tell her what had happened to her on Friday night, and she didn't want to know.

The Germans loved to sing, and as Anje was passing by the café they loved to frequent, she could hear them singing one of their favorite marching songs, "Erika." One night an accordion player was in their midst, and they harmonized as they lustily sang while clapping their hands vigorously to imitate the sound of the drums at the end of the stanza.

"On the heath a little flower blooms and it's
called: (clap, clap, clap) Erika,
Hot from a hundred thousand little bees that
swarm over (clap, clap, clap) Erika,
Because her heart is full of sweetness, her flowery
dress gives off a delicate scent.
On the heath a little flower blooms and it's called:
(clap, clap, clap) Erika."

The air was fresh and invigorating as Anje walked resolutely along the sidewalk on Leidesestraat for Jamada's evening exercise. "Come on, puppy!" she called. Jamada lagged behind, sniffing at something he found on the street. It was early, and she observed three young girls strolling along the other side of the street, talking and laughing. Just then an army vehicle advancing toward them slowed down and then stopped at the curb near the girls, and two German soldiers climbed out of the vehicle. She could not hear their discussion, but she could tell by the gestures and the voice intonation that the meeting was friendly. One of the soldiers put his arm around the shoulders of one young girl and offered her a smoke, which she readily accepted.

I bet she doesn't even smoke, Anje thought as she watched the drama unfold, but she knew that everyone was anxious to please the oppressor. Girls, if I were you, I would get as far away from them as possible, she thought. She also knew that really was not possible in the situation. Could they say no? They could, but they dared not. She watched as the young girls climbed into the back seat of the vehicle, and the soldier slammed the door. She knew some of these girls, and she thought maybe she should warn them. They were surely going to a Friday night party, and those girls always ended up in bed. The soldier jumped onto the front seat and closed the door, and the vehicle sped away. "Come on, Jamada" she called. It was time to go home.

As she proceeded along the way, two soldiers patrolling on foot came into sight, and she hesitated slightly because everyone on the street was stopped for the purpose of checking their identification card. Experience had taught her that moving along quietly in a nonchalant manner, never hesitating, was often the best action, so she continued to walk at a steady pace. The officers were speaking to one another as they approached; their footsteps never faltered, nor did their voices change. One soldier was strutting with his right hand on the holster on his hip, and the other was cradling his rifle against his shoulder. They passed within five feet of her! Her heart skipped a few beats as she met them, but her fear turned into surprise when they kept going. But they stop everyone on the street, she thought. Yet it appeared as though they hadn't seen her! She was amazed! How could this be? They didn't acknowledge me on the street. They didn't even look in my direction. If they saw me, they would have stopped. What happened? Am I invisible?

As she laid her head on the pillow that night, she smiled as she rolled all these thoughts around in her mind and mused again, *Was I invisible?*

MAJOR STRIKE!

On Thursday, April 29, 1943, a shock wave reverberated through the Netherlands. The Wehrmachtsbefehlshaber (Supreme Commander of the Wehrmacht), General Friedrich Christiansen, announced that all Dutch soldiers were to go into captivity and become prisoners of war! This was a shock to everyone as they listened to the announcement on the radio. Hans discussed the subject with Hillie. "The Germans are hard-pressed for manpower, and they are afraid the Dutch military will be called into action if the Allies invade."

This news was a great shock, and anxiety and indignation prevailed all across the Netherlands. Half a million Dutch workers went on strike against the occupation regime; the people had made up their minds. "We won't do it! We won't go!" Why should they willingly go into prison if they hadn't done anything? This movement was far greater than anything small Resistance groups could generate. Spontaneous strikes broke out throughout the whole country. Coal miners in Limburg; Philips electronic workers in Eindhoven; agricultural workers in Friesland; and hundreds in the province of Groningen joined the strike, as did civil servants, factory and dock workers, owners of shipyards, and even farmers, who refused to supply milk. The cup of the Dutch population was filled to the brim.

The Resistance urged the people not to give in to the Germans, who were determined to quickly break the strikes. Patrolling soldiers were given the order, "Shoot to kill!" Almost a hundred people were shot in the streets, and eighty were executed after summary trials. After German patrols killed several people by firing randomly at a curious crowd that had gathered, some of the onlookers decided to go back to work when they saw the dead bodies of their friends lying in the street. Hans shook his head sadly. Was it worth it?

Resist! That word was passed down the line, and in spite of the bloody terror the Nazis were meting out, laborers at the shipyards in Hoogezand refused to go back to work, resulting in many arrests.

"You don't want to work?" screamed one of the Nazi officers who was investigating the strike at the cardboard factory of Beukema and Co. "Line them up against the wall. We'll see if you don't want to work!" Five men were rousted from the group of workers, placed against the wall, and shot. The following day, three men were executed on the grounds of the potato-flour mill where they worked. A total of thirty-two workers died as a result of the strikes, and another eight were sent to concentration camps.

The Bombing of Hamburg

The strike gave the people hope. Perhaps they could cause change to come. They were so eager for freedom, but the fighting around them and above them did not cease. The familiar sounds of hundreds of aircraft heading toward Germany interrupted Anje's reading as she lay in bed. Rushing to the window to look into the dark sky, she could see colored cannonballs shooting at planes in the sky and deafening sounds of mortars shelling, piercing her eardrums. *I wonder who is getting bombed today?* she thought as she watched. *At least it's not us.* Then she felt a twinge of remorse. Was she becoming selfish? Did it only matter if her own city was being bombed? Sometimes she couldn't even sort out her own feelings anymore. She just wished it would all stop.

The ground trembled and shook, but she knew it was not an earthquake. It was the vibrations from the mass of powerful bombs descending upon some German city not too far away. She did not know until she heard the radio that the target of destruction this day was Hamburg, which lay 230 kilometers due west of Groningen.

The BBC News was almost jubilant for the Nazis had not seen them coming. When the British developed radar in 1939, the value of this technology had been greatly under-estimated. The Germans had lost the element of surprise in the war and soon realized it. A few years later when they developed radar, the British were prepared; the skies were jammed with tinsel, which produced a thousand blips on the radar screen. This was the scene at Hamburg.

"Hamburg, the second largest city in Germany, with a population of one and a half million people, is being bombed by the Allies. This city is Germany's most important industrial center as well as the largest seaport on the European continent. The total destruction of Hamburg will have immeasurable results in reducing the industrial capacity of the enemy's war machine, and it could play a very important part in shortening and winning the war," the foreign newscaster commented. It was July 24, 1943, in the tinderbox of a summer heat wave.

Anje watched as waves and waves of Halifax bombers filled the sky day after day. Finally, the bombers took off over the North Sea, as the clouds above Hamburg reflected a red glow from the raging fires. The planes headed into a solid bank of clouds as thunderstorms erupted, and lightning streaked the skies.

With the cavernous spaces of the bomb bays empty, the planes turned back toward Britain but not in the same perfect formation as when they had left. The losses of aircraft were noted by vacant spots in the alignment.

The next morning, the city of Groningen twinkled like a Christmas tree. Strings of tinsel shimmered from light standards, power lines, and tree branches. The fences glittered in the sunshine as a reminder of the previous night's barrage from above.

"Mother, do you think this battle will win the war?" Anje inquired hopefully as she sat at the table munching on a carrot.

"Oh, I don't know, my dear," Hillie replied as she

continued to fold the clothes she had just washed. "We will just have to wait and see. Until then, there is still much for us to do." Then she smiled and added, "Maybe we'll help to win the war by what we're doing." She paused and mused, "Well, at least in the Netherlands."

"I hope so," Anje said, pondering those words.

THE RED LIGHT DISTRICT

Brrrrring! The sound of the doorbell broke Anje's train of thought. She was thinking about this lovely August day and planning what she could do to enjoy it as she clambered down the narrow stairs to answer the bell. It was not her regular contact person standing at the door but the older man who only occasionally stopped by. *Even the older people are interested in helping,* Anje thought as she looked at his wrinkled face and saw the sparse strands of white hair sticking out from the side of his cap. Most of the men wore a head covering; it helped to hide their identity. Out of courtesy he removed his hat and then reached his left hand inside his jacket to retrieve a brown paper wrapper. He thrust the package into Anje's hands and left without a word. As she inspected the paper, she noted the delivery address—Haddingestraad, the red-light district. Her habit was to get the information out of her hands as quickly as she could, so she pulled on her heavy woolen sweater, placed the package under her shirt, and buttoned up the sweater. She proceeded to drag her bicycle out of the corner under the stairs. "Mother, I'm leaving," she called as she opened the door and then disappeared down the street.

She knew her mother was waiting for a mission that would take her out of town. Whenever she went on an overnight journey, she informed Anje in advance, but she could not leave explicit notes in the event that Father would find them. He came and went as he pleased; he never shared a meal with them and only spent the night at home occasionally. Mother didn't bother asking him where he was the rest of the time.

The sky was overcast, and the streets were shiny from the moisture that had fallen as she pedaled toward the Black Cat Café. She knew the café was really a house of prostitution, but the work that Toots and a few of her girls did was valuable for the Underground.

As she pushed, the heavy café door opened, and a bell tinkled to announce her arrival. Toots strode through the split curtain in the doorway into the dining room. The small, round tables in the room were covered with blue plaid tablecloths, and a gentleman sat at a table in the middle of the room with a cigarette in one hand and a cup of coffee in the other. He raised his eyes and looked toward Anje as she entered, and then he shifted his gaze toward Toots.

Toots was about thirty-five years old. Her long, auburn

hair curled around her face. The tight sweater she wore had a low-cut neckline that revealed the curves of her body and left nothing to the imagination. She was only about five feet tall, but the spike-heeled shoes she wore made her look taller. She usually had a cigarette hanging from her red lips, but today she was blowing on her long nails as she approached.

"Fascination, a new color," she chortled to Anje as she blew on her nails to dry the polish. She nodded toward the curtain, a suggestion that Anje should follow her.

"I didn't want him to see you giving me something," she explained. "You just never know. Even though he was my customer," she grinned, "I still really don't know him."

She opened a drawer on a small beige cabinet and said, "Put it in here." Anje placed the packet inside, and Toots closed it abruptly.

Toots was always kind, and though Anje found her occupation questionable, they treated each other with respect. The items Anje brought Toots were personal letters from individuals who were hiding in the underground—people seeking news of loved ones or letters in code of others desiring information of relatives in concentration camps. Toots was providing a great service to the local population. Anje didn't know how she managed to deliver the letters, and she didn't care. That was Toots's job. Her job was to see that Toots got them. She turned to leave, and as she walked through the curtain into the dining room, she saw "The Blonde" sitting in her usual chair in the corner of the cafe, wearing her fancy fur coat and red high-heeled shoes. As she crossed her legs, her coat fell open and Anje noticed that, once again, there was nothing but bare skin underneath. She sighed as she left. *Same girl! Same coat! No clothes!* She slammed the door as she left the place. Her job was done.

The story had passed through the organization of the night a group of Nazi officers had visited the Black Cat Café, removed their leather belts and holsters, and hung them on the coat hooks on the wall. While they were occupied with the girls, someone stole their revolvers! Toots was not shy about relating this story to Anje. It just showed her own resilience and ability to deal with problems.

When the first officer returned to the dining room, he exploded when he saw the bare space on the wall where their guns had been. *"Du verfluchte schweinhund!"* he shouted, and his face turned purple with rage. The other men hustled into the room, and when Toots arrived, she was cool, calm, and unruffled as she inquired about the problem. "When they discovered their guns were missing, a great furor erupted. I thought they would wreck my place," Toots confided. "I did not want to have the police poking their noses around my café, so I needed to solve this somehow. The men had looked so dignified in their uniforms and their shiny black boots, yet they sounded like a gang of schoolboys trying to solve a problem. How would they explain this to their superiors? How could they report for duty without their guns? They could hear the rebukes from their commander—how could they be so careless? Would they be sent to the front as punishment? Losing one's weapon was a serious offense. They were all talking at the same time. My suggestion was that perhaps they could find a Luger on the black market. I assured them that someone must have come into the café and pilfered them, and I said that the next time they came, their weapons would be put in a secure place. Anje, while they were carousing, two men from the Underground had come in and retrieved the weapons, but I was the one who called them. That night, two operatives from the Underground were cycling along the canal towards Spuistraat to deliver their prize—seven Luger pistols!"

When Anje arrived home, Mother had already left. Perhaps she would be gone overnight since she had to travel by train to The Hague and then cycle twelve kilometers north to Katwijkseweg to meet some people.

"FLIGHT SCHOOL"

Hillie was confident in the safety of her assignment as she had an Ausweis that permitted her to travel. She was fortunate this could be planned for the weekend because her job at the distribution center was vital to their existence. Her boss was very lenient in allowing her to take time off when she had assignments. She had an inclination that he was aware of her other commitments to the Underground, but he never questioned her allegiances.

Precious documents were hidden next to her body under her dress; they were vital to enable the persons for whom they were destined to leave the country. Also, in her large woven straw bag, she carried numerous tins of tobacco and cigarette papers, the most sought-after prize. For most, this was not considered a luxury but a necessity. When she arrived at the train station in The Hague, the Resistance obtained a bicycle for her, delivered by a young boy. The look on his face alerted her to his dilemma.

"Is this your bicycle?" she asked.

He nodded abruptly, and his brown eyes glowed with pride.

"Don't worry," she responded. "I will bring it back to you in good condition. I should be back here by 7:00 p.m., in time to catch the evening train."

He nodded again, and this time he smiled. "Good-bye."

As she drove away, she thought about this young boy's sacrifice. The bicycle was the most prized and valuable possession he had, for without it he couldn't do anything or go anywhere. He had obviously taken good care to avoid its being snatched or having the tires stolen. *He could be about fourteen years old,* she thought. *Yes, about the same age as Anje.* Everyone becomes tough in wartime.

Her thoughts turned to the young men she was about to help liberate. Twenty-two airmen were waiting for her to arrive with their documents; they were eager to get back home. These men were the lucky ones who had survived their planes crashing in the Netherlands. They were Canadian, American, and British pilots, and they owed their lives to the Resistance. Without their help, they would never have been rescued.

It was a challenge to try to match people up with false IDs. If a person was to become French, Belgian, or Dutch, he had to look the part, right down to his clothing and his accent. She did not know the plans for all of them, but this site had a road that led down to the shore of the North Sea. Perhaps they would be taken across the channel.

She thought about some of her past experiences. Allied fugitives had been sent off in twos or threes across the countryside on foot, heading for Spain and freedom. Occasionally, an operative would accompany them and instruct them to feign deafness, drunkenness, or shell shock in order to avoid conversation when approached. The plan usually meant sleeping during the day and traveling at night in order to avoid detection. *They are all brave young men,* she thought. *I hope they make it.*

She approached the crossroad and read the sign, Katwijkseweg. Yes! She turned left, and soon the outline of a large building in the distance appeared. It looked like an abandoned barn. As she got closer, she could read an old yellow sign with the paint peeling from the wood. It was or used to be a dairy farm. She climbed off her bicycle, and two men approached her. She called out to them, "I am Sara."

They nodded and smiled. Those were the code words.

Some of the men were lying on their backs on the hay bales, while others were sitting in the main area of the barn where the floor was covered with straw and oblong bales substituted for seats and beds. Old leather harnesses hung on the wall, as well as lengths of chain and rope, and the original metal stanchions were still in place. Torn canvas fabric covered the windows. There was a large square hole where one could look up into the hayloft, where more men were lounging about. Instead of coming down the vertical wooden ladder that led to the loft, one rambunctious lad, when he saw "Sara," grabbed the thick rope to which was attached a large bale hook and swung himself down to the main floor.

"Hey, quit showing off. She's here on business!" one of his buddies called out.

The men jumped up excitedly, like eager children, anxious to see what she had brought. The leader was busy matching the IDs with the right persons while the boys were whooping and hollering as they rolled themselves cigarettes.

"Watch those matches, lads," one man with a British accent called out. "We don't want to burn this place down. It's as dry as tinder."

Some of the airmen had been there over a week awaiting documents. They were eager to travel. This place had been nicknamed "Flight School," which had become the code word for that location considering the large number of flight crews they had rescued. Flight School had a revolving door; airmen were arriving and leaving as fast as they could be processed. Four more were due to arrive—they just didn't know when.

An hour later Hillie left the barn, bidding all the men a safe journey as she jumped on the bicycle. She began pedaling toward The Hague, enjoying the remote country-side. It was lush green pastureland—no prying eyes except for the cattle that were grazing contentedly. She took her last piece of bread from her saddlebag, and as she began munching it, she could see a dust cloud forming in the distance, made by an approaching vehicle. She hesitated a little and rehearsed her reason for being there, while the dust cloud loomed larger. As it approached, she could see the sage green color of a panel truck, and as it flew past she saw the swastika on the door.

She heaved a sigh of relief, thankful that she would not have to explain her presence. She turned her head to see where the truck was going, and her heart almost stopped beating as she saw it turn down the road leading to the dairy farm. *Oh my goodness, all those men in the barn! Who tipped them off?* She was aghast for she had no way of warning them. She realized that she had leave quickly and pedaled hard toward The Hague. She was breathless when she arrived, and she found her little friend waiting patiently for his bicycle.

"Thank you!" she said to him as he turned to leave.

"You're welcome!" he replied, and he waved his felt cap in the air to signal good-bye to her.

Her thoughts were in turmoil on the train ride home. Horrific images rolled through her head. What had happened at Flight School? She contacted Hans to see if he had heard the outcome of that day. He reassured her that the message would come from the Underground. It did, through Erich.

"I wanted to tell you in person, Hillie," he began when he came to her door. "The panel truck was stolen by the Resistance, and it was bringing the last four downed pilots to Flight School. But that's not all," he continued. "Since they now had their ID cards, they were able to pile eight American pilots into the truck and give them a head start on their journey home. The Canadians and the British planned to cross the channel, but the Americans had a rendezvous planned with some guys from Intelligence. I don't know where they took them, but the goal was to go as far as possible, knowing they would have to leave the van somewhere before they were stopped at a roadblock." He paused. "Now are you happy?"

"Yes," she said as she smiled, her hazel eyes twinkling. "I am happy."

ANOTHER CHRISTMAS

Fall became winter, and though there was not much snow, it still felt bitterly cold when the north winds blew. Anje stamped her feet as she entered the house and began to remove her wet shoes before she climbed the stairs.

"Do you think we'll find a Christmas tree?" she asked Mother as she entered the kitchen.

Mother turned from the batter she was mixing and smiled. "I don't know. Everything has been chopped down for firewood, but maybe we'll find something yet."

All the neighbors on Rabenhauptstraat had to share one small Christmas tree, but everyone participated willingly. They cut off the main branches and then trimmed the secondary branches in such a fashion so they could each have a piece of this tree. The part that Anje and Mother received was a small green sprig that had two little shoots on the side. They hung it on the wall above a picture, tying two small, shiny Christmas balls on it. As they stood back to admire it, they both laughed at the little sprig. It was certainly not a Christmas tree, but it did give the house the special feeling of Christmas.

This Christmas Day in 1943 was different. The Resistance issued a death order for an informer in the police department. This was a big event for the Underground, and the members were all waiting to hear whether the mission had been accomplished. Mother and Anje sat waiting for the news, for Reint Dijkema, the operating agent, was a member of their organization. Even Jamada was restless; it seemed as though the dog knew something was amiss.

The Resistance had decided to terminate Annc James Elsinga, a thirty-five-year-old Groningen police officer, for collaborating with the Germans. Elsinga, because of his position, had extensive knowledge of events going on all around the city—including information about Jews in hiding places and names of those in the Underground—and he repeatedly passed this information on to the SS, resulting in the deaths of many people. Anje didn't feel sorry for him. He was the kind of person they feared, a Dutchman who would report the movements of the populace to the Gestapo. She was angry because some of the Jews she and Mother had helped to hide had been found and reported by Elsinga.

She hoped Reint would be successful in his mission today. The Resistance family had great loyalty toward one another.

Reint had written Elsinga a warning letter more than once, admonishing him to cease his actions or drastic measures would be taken. Elsinga paid no heed to these warnings but continued to collaborate. The Resistance decided they would not let him celebrate another Christmas and determined to do away with him when he was on his way to church on Christmas Day.

When evening came, there was a knock on the door, and a cell member brought a brief message: the plan did not go through because Elsinga had not gone to church that day. Members of the Underground discovered that he had been ill, so the date was reset for December 31, 1943, New Year's Eve.

The Underground had selected Reint and his younger brother Pete to do the job. New Year's Eve turned out to not be an ideal day for this assignment because it was pouring rain as Reint and Pete traveled by bicycle to Elsinga's house on Peizerweg. Just before nine o'clock in the morning, as the rain began to taper off, Elsinga emerged from his house, hopped on his bicycle, and began riding toward the Scholten House, the throne of the SS.

Reint and Pete each had a pistol in his pocket, and they had followed their target at a distance. Reint had been elected to do the shooting, but Pete was also prepared to do the job. As Elsinga approached the bridge, Reint moved in close with a burst of energy, firing three rapid shots. Elsinga fell to the pavement mortally wounded, and Reint and Pete escaped. The organization was elated at their success; Underground workers in broad daylight in the middle of a busy city had the audacity to attempt such a coup. This incident was called the Silbertannen Murder. Anje and Hillie read the details of the incident in the Underground newspaper.

The sheer boldness of this act of rebellion was like throwing acid in the face of the SS. They were in a murderous mood. Seven common folk from the community were killed in retaliation, and many other innocent people were imprisoned.

Anje and her mother discussed the aftermath. Had this been the right thing to do? Was it worth it? They decided it was because if Elsinga had been allowed to continue, many more people would have died. There was always a price to pay.

Ration Ticket Raid

The Groningen KPers were in the process of planning a huge operation designed to be the biggest raid of the war—the theft of a quarter million ration tickets. Ration tickets were vital to the Resistance, for without them they could not feed the thousands of people in hiding. These raids were the only means of obtaining them, and the assistance of a watchman on the inside helped the KPers accomplish their goal.

Reint and his two younger brothers planned to go to the location where the ration tickets were stored, apprehend the watchman they had procured, load their cargo into two autos, and depart. At the last moment, one of the autos broke down, and the haul had to be reduced to 131,000 tickets—still a big success. Anje was aware of the raid that was planned because these KPers were in the same organization as she, and all were alerted to the danger that existed.

Reint had received an urgent phone call that warned of a leak in information. Someone had talked, and great danger loomed ahead. He biked across the city to see if he could save the operation when he was recognized by a policeman who began to pursue him. Reint was shot in the arm just before he was apprehended and taken to the House of Blood and Tears, where he was tortured. But Reint was a brave man, and he refused to give any information to his captors. Anje heard that he shielded others from blame by claiming ownership of raids he had not participated in. Wounded and bound hand and foot, he had wrestled with the armed guard who was watching him, seized his gun, and shot him dead. Actions like this were costly. On August 22, 1944, Reint was one of the twenty Underground workers who were executed at the concentration camp at Vught.

After he was arrested, his family found a poem in his handwriting lying on top of his bureau describing the conflicting emotions and the agony of heart suffered by those who chose to serve their country in this way. Reint Dijkema was a Christian, and the body of the writing he left behind contained these words.

> "I'm only a scared soldier of God
> One who doesn't want to inflate the controversy
> And who, for fear, scoffs at the combativeness
> While he hopes without sacrifices to remain a Christian.
>
> And when His mouth says: "Die,"
> My heart may plead to live on
> A small existence without care, without struggle
> Without ever giving myself totally.
> I'm only a scared soldier of God

'One who should not exaggerate his devotion'
I know an interpretation for the hardest commandment,
But, shall I, thus, be able to remain a Christian?

Perhaps he was referring to one of the Ten Command-
ments, "Thou shall not kill." Written below were these
words: "I am only a scared soldier of God. Who out of
fear does these things. I want to remain a Christian. I
want to live in peace, without worry and fighting. I only
know one way; is this the only way? Can I live a life like
this and still remain a Christian?"

Anje received this information from Reint's brother
Pete. Reint's friends admired him for his dedication and
passion. They had lost a brave warrior. *Members of the same
organization became like family,* Anje thought. One's survival
could often depend upon the other in a given situation.
She understood that she must always be prepared for the
possibility of facing death—hers or somebody else's. That
was one of the realities of working for the Resistance. In
many cases, there was no funeral and no body to grieve over
if one was captured by the enemy. Reint was a young man,
just a little older than herself, and now he was gone. It was
true, Mother said repeatedly—we have to be very careful.

1944

Another new year—1944. Anje watched as Mother prepared to place a new calendar on the wall in the dining room. She had no idea what this year would bring. "We will just have to do the best with what we have," Mother sighed as she removed the old calendar. "We made it safely through 1943 in spite of all the challenges we faced, and we can always hope that the war will be over soon." Mother rolled up the old calendar and prepared to throw it in the trash when she observed a name scrawled on the back of one of the pages. "Oh, here is something in Father's handwriting. I must save it for him." When we heard Father's steps on the landing, she went to get the scrap of paper. "Is this something you wanted to keep?" she asked as she handed it to him.

As Father looked at the name, his face changed, and he scowled as he asked acidly, "Do you always have to snoop into my affairs? This is none of your business." He snatched the paper from her as he strode into the other room while muttering under his breath, picked up his felt hat, and then stormed out of the house.

Anje was puzzled. Mother never questioned him about his whereabouts or what he had been doing. Why was he so sensitive about a name on a piece of paper? *This is a very different home,* Anje thought. *Father is hardly ever here, and when he comes, he is in such a bad mood. Mother takes care of everything. Her paycheck from the distribution center is enough to keep things going.* There was so little they could spend their money on anyway.

Fuel became scarce; there was seldom anything to fill the potbelly stove that heated their home. Sitting in front of it was Anje's favorite place—it was comforting to sit there and read or do her homework. In better days, they had a supply of anthracite coal stored in a sack in the utility closet, and a chunk of it heated the house for a long time. People became angry when they saw long cavalcades of boxcars laden with coal from the mines in Limburg on the rails heading east to Germany to fuel the factories for the war effort. Soon, there was no more coal allotted for Holland. People hunted for pieces of coal that had fallen from the trains, or they burned "turf," which were squares of compressed straw. It felt depressing to be cold all the time. The best thing Anje could wish for was an early spring. Even with three layers of clothes on, she still felt the cold. "Cold, cold, cold," she muttered out loud as she pulled her sweater more tightly around her body. "I don't know which is worse—being cold or being hungry. Well, I am both." But she knew that no one else was more privileged than she. "We are all in this together," she sighed with resignation.

Life became more difficult each year as the war progressed. Her stomach rumbled like that of a voracious stray dog that was constantly scrounging for food. Any small offering of something edible was welcome.

"Look what I got today, Anje," Mother declared as she hauled a ten-pound bag of wheat from her bicycle carrier. "Sonjia knew a farmer who had wheat for sale, and she brought along a bag for us. It's good to chew. Try some."

Anje threw a small handful of wheat into her mouth. At first it was very hard to chew, and then as it mixed with the saliva in her mouth, it became soft. "Hmm, this is not so bad. It reminds me of chewing gum," she said.

"Yes," Hillie replied, "and much more nutritious. I'm going to put some wheat in the coffee grinder and see if I can grind some flour. Maybe we can make a few little pancakes."

Anje's attention was piqued. Pancakes sounded like heaven to her!

"Reach up to the top shelf in the cupboard, Anje, and get me that little jar with the yellow lid," Mother said. "It's baking powder."

Anje did as she was asked and thought, *I looked into that jar and smelled and even tasted it. I didn't know it was anything that we could eat.* But when it was mixed with flour, water,

and some oil, it made something quite delicious. The taste
buds in her mouth began to awaken as she and Mother
mixed their little wheat pancakes and poured round circles
of dough onto the griddle. She could hardly wait. "Mother,"
Anje said as she tasted the first bite, "these are heavenly!"
The taste of those pancakes was etched in her memory.

With the store shelves bare, they were left to their own
resources. Germany had robbed them of everything. Many
were in despair and were angry with their queen, who was
in exile in London. It was said that when she was told her
people were starving, she replied, "As long as there is grass,
they won't starve."

There was some food value in the plants or weeds growing
around them, and people foraged for whatever they could
find. The remains of sugar beets left in the field as fodder
for cattle were picked for food, as well as a sour green leaf
(sorrel) that made a nutritious soup. Those who lived in the
country walked the fields behind the harvesters and picked
any heads of wheat they could find, while others dug the
tulip bulbs growing at the nurseries. Even though they had
a foul taste, the people cooked and ate them.

The Germans were determined not to allow access to
anything of nutritional value to the Dutch. They posted
signs beside a stinging nettle plant that read, "Anyone
caught picking nettle will be shot." Anje read the sign with
disgust. She was glad she didn't see anyone picking it for
the Germans loved to follow through with their commands.
Nettle was very high in protein and was quite palatable when
boiled, but even this weed was denied as food.

A barter system was established, and the black market
thrived. Anje knew of many individuals who had hidden

their choice valuables in the Jesuit cloister for safekeeping at the beginning of the war and who came to retrieve them when their stomachs could not be filled. One fellow exchanged an expensive Persian rug for a few eggs. Hunger prevailed, and food became the item of greatest value.

One Tuesday, Mother opened the front door and was surprised to see her sister Dolly standing on her doorstep. Dolly was a fashionable lady who was known to covet beautiful things and purchase them for her home.

"Dolly, come in," Mother greeted her warmly as she hugged her sister. "Did you come by yourself?"

Dolly nodded, looking slightly uneasy, for she never came without her husband.

"I'll get us a cup of tea," Mother offered, pouring water into the kettle. "What brings you this far today? I hope there is no trouble at home?"

"No, not really. Well," she said with hesitation, "we are out of food. I was wondering if you could spare us something?" She was so uncomfortable asking for a favor that she kept wringing her hands nervously.

Mother did not indicate how little food we had in our kitchen. Without hesitation, she set down her teacup, strode over to the cupboard, and began measuring out some dry ingredients—a little sugar, some flour, and dry beans. She gave her sister half of what we had.

Mother, Anje thought, t*hey spend their money on fine furniture and things we don't have. Why should we give them our food?* But Mother didn't think about things like that. She just smiled as she continued to measure out a portion of food for her sister. Thereafter, Dolly became an infrequent visitor to their home, and many times Mother cycled across the city to deliver food to them when they were in need.

Everyone knew they couldn't exist without food, and it became much sought after. Rations were small, and anyone who knew a local farmer and was able to obtain food from him was very fortunate. Military checkpoints were everywhere, and the locals often traveled the back roads to avoid being caught with their precious "contraband." Henry, one of Anje's school friends, related his experience at trying to get some food.

"I was traveling over a deserted country road in the drizzly rain riding my old bicycle; my original rubber tires were worn, and they were bound to the rim with heavy string. My head was huddled into the collar of my coat for protection from the weather, and I was in deep thought. I had spent my last money to buy a little food for my mother and younger sister, and this made me feel good. At a curve in the road I was taken by surprise when two men dressed as ordinary citizens suddenly jumped out from behind a tree. As I stared at them, I thought, *Who are they?* The men had hunting rifles hanging around their necks on leather straps and wore tall leather boots. Their armbands told me they were Home Guards.

They demanded to know what was in my cycle bags. I was taken aback and as I dismounted, I was at a loss for words and stammered that I didn't have anything in my cycle bags. I was feeling angry at myself. I was sure that no one would be out in this rainy weather, and I was not very watchful. They commanded me in a stern voice to open up my bags, and I obeyed. The Home Guards rummaged through the contents to see for themselves. First they removed the blue enamel container filled with milk, then a small bottle of rape seed oil and a package of home-churned butter wrapped in wax paper. They looked at me triumphantly as they lifted the bottle of oil in front of my face and declared, "You call this nothing? Don't you know that it is illegal to buy food from the farmers? You are robbing your fellow countrymen." They threatened to arrest me but decided to be lenient this time and let me go. I quickly mounted my bicycle and rode off, happy that I escaped with my life. But I was not feeling good inside. How would I explain this to my mother?"

Anje knew he was barely fourteen and was acting as the head of the house since his father had gone underground to protect himself from being sent to Germany for forced labor. It was difficult in many homes without the man of the house to care for his family. Anje knew Henry had found a part-time job helping a tailor, but it didn't bring in much money. What made Anje angry was the fact that he had been robbed not by Nazis but by his fellow Dutch citizens. She could understand his regret; his loved ones went hungry while the Home Guards had eagerly consumed the food they had stolen from him. It wasn't fair, and it was the reason many people ardently helped the Underground.

Many bad things happened in the darkness of the night. Anje didn't mind the curfew that kept people off the streets at night. She was quite content to do her work during the day and be home in the evening. Everyone was aware of how the Nazis liked to terrorize people while the world was sleeping. She thought of her friend Louis the boxer—how he had used this same tactic on the enemy, hitting them at night and disappearing into the dark. She recalled Herman Wolff's recounting how his parents had just disappeared in the middle of the night, never to be seen again. Late one night the neighbors on Achterfweg were awakened as a German lorry arrived at the Troostwijck home. Esther and the boys were undoubtedly sleeping when they heard banging on the door. The neighbors heard screaming, the breaking of glass, and the sound of furniture being thrown through the windows onto the street. Finally, all they heard was the sound of a vehicle fading into the night. In the morning, nothing was left of the Troostwijck family but their furniture and belongings lying forlornly on the street. The rain pelted down on a pair of boy's skates that lay on top of the pile of the family's possessions. Esther, Max, and Bennie were gone.

FRIEND OR FOE?

On Tuesday, February 22, 1944, Mother and Anje sat on the divan, their ears straining to hear the news broadcast from the small radio. The deep voice firmly announced, "A squadron of sixteen aircraft from the US Air Force, while returning from a failed bombing mission raid on Germany due to bad weather, missed their target, releasing their bombs on Nijmegen, the oldest city in Netherlands."

These high-altitude daylight raids were specifically aimed to hit predetermined targets, but when the weather deterred them, the US bombers turned back. As the rail yards of Nijmegen came into focus through a break in the clouds, the bombers released their payloads, unaware that they were still over Holland. The inner city of Nijmegen was destroyed, taking the lives of twenty-two thousand people.

Anje got up and stomped out of the room. "Oh!" she muttered angrily. "Another mistake that we have to pay for. All we know is bombs, bombs, bombs! We get bombed by our friends, and we get bombed by our enemies. When will this ever be over? I hate this war!"

"Remember my dear," Mother called out, "there are no country borders that can be seen from the sky."

Mother always says something good about every situation, she thought. I don't care. I'm still angry that they bombed us.

The Germans used this kind of information to spew out hatred and more propaganda. "See? Who are your friends? The Americans are the ones who are bombing you."

The noisy banter in the Kroeg created some curiosity, and Hans was amongst the men who animatedly discussed the subject. Was it propaganda or reality? The desire for truth was like a balance scale weighing within each of them. Who was really bombing them? He had to find out. It was important to know the truth.

"Come on," one of the group suggested. "Bombs fell in the west end of the city last night. Let's go and dig around that place and see what we can find. Get your shovel." The three hurried off.

It was not an easy task. Jagged concrete slabs were mixed amid steel rods and splintered wooden joists that had fallen twenty feet to the soil below. They were laying helter-skelter like matchsticks. The men dug with fervor, taking turns with the spade when they hit an obstruction. All three men were down on their hands and knees digging in the dirt like dogs hunting for a favorite bone.

Bomb fragments would be unearthed as they scraped and dug, one piece of metal and then another, until a shard with an imprint appeared. As they rubbed off the dirt and held it up to the light, Hans let out a holler. "Krupp!" he shouted almost joyously. Krupp owned a leading munitions factory in Germany. They walked toward home with their shovels perched on their shoulders. They were content. Hans would have to tell Anje it was not the Allies who bombed them. The Allies were still their friends, and Germany was still their enemy.

Early in 1944, the news came that Oma had sold her house and was coming to live with them. What a delight! She and Anje were good companions. When Mother was away on her "business trips" for the Underground, Anje would not have to be alone. They decided to tear out the bed in the wall and make room for Oma. As they worked with the hammer and pry bar stripping the dark wood from the wall, Mother said, "As a bonus, we're getting some fuel for our stove." Another piece of wood broke off and clattered noisily to the floor.

The house was always cold. Jack Frost painted creative designs on the window panes, and Anje loved to analyze the swirls to see if she could find a picture in the thick frost. She wore mittens and a jacket inside, and often she and her grandmother sat huddled together around the cold stove in the front room, hoping that somehow they would get warm. But imagination did not cause any heat to radiate from the little metal stove.

"Anje," Oma said, "it is so cold this morning. Put some straw in your wooden shoes to keep your feet warm. It will help as you walk to school."

The atmosphere in school was just as frigid. The kids could see their breath in the classroom. Students left cold homes to go to frosty classrooms. As she walked home from school, Anje saw gaunt-faced people walking along the railroad tracks carrying burlap sacks in hopes of finding a few pieces of coal. Others were chopping down small trees that they would burn in their stoves. It was not uncommon to hear chopping sounds at night as folks dared to cut down even quite large trees on the boulevard and haul the limbs home in a wagon to burn as fuel to heat their homes. *Survive,* she thought. *We are all trying to survive until this war is over.*

Nighttime was the most favored time as the family snuggled down in their feather beds to keep warm. The only body part Anje left uncovered was her nose so she could draw air, and the condensation of her breath created white frost on the feather blanket. By morning, the glass of water beside the bed was covered with ice.

In the dark of the night, it was easy to allow fear to creep in. Anje's thoughts always revolved around her mother. *I wonder where she is right now. Is she safe? Was she able to avoid being followed? Did she have enough food? Did she find her address?* The constant fear of her mother's well being gnawed at her because everyone knew what the Nazis did to anyone who resisted the regime. What would she do if anything happened to her mother? She was the one who really loved her. In her nights of anguish, hot tears flowed into her pillow and she began to say the

Lord's Prayer. She did not recall where or when she had learned it, but when she opened her mouth and began to recite it, the words came pouring forth like a stream of water from a brook, and it quenched the dry, thirsty ground in her soul. Before she said amen, she laid all her problems into God's lap.

Her prayers were interrupted by the sounds of aircraft engines in the distance. Suddenly, the familiar whistle of bombs descending penetrated the air, and then all was silent. She knew the effect of bombs—the one you didn't hear was the one that killed you. These bombs were very close. She heard a noise out on the street and looked out of her bedroom window. Ba Timms had been awakened by the bombs and had grabbed his one-piece underwear in such haste that he got both his legs into one hole! He was out on the street hopping like a rabbit and calling to everyone, "Don't worry! I'll save you! I'll save you! Don't be afraid!" The effects of last night's liquor were still energizing Ba's behavior.

Another big crashing sound filled the room, and Anje shouted, "Oma!" as she threw off her covers, leaped out of bed, and hurtled down two flights of stairs. Her heart was pounding inside her chest, and the two of them huddled together in their nightclothes with their hands over their ears to protect them from the horrific noise of the impact of bombs as they crouched by the front door. One explosion was followed by another. The house shook from the vibrations of the earth until finally, all became quiet. The planes were gone.

"Oma!" she cried. "This is not good for your heart." Together, with Oma leaning on her arm for support, they slowly climbed back up the stairs, and Anje tucked Oma back into her feather bed, hoping that sleep would return.

Anje belonged to the morning group at school, and her classes were over at noon. As she trekked toward school with her books under her arm, she noticed that one block from her home, debris was strewn everywhere. Bricks, wood, broken windows, and concrete were flung askew as though they were paper. Two stories up, she could see a toilet hanging from the wreckage and a lamp dangling just above it. Thick concrete dust from the explosion was the residue from last night's bombing, and it covered everything the eye could see. As she passed by, she was flooded by a feeling of gratitude—amid all the death and destruction, she was still alive.

The teacher clapped her hands to bring the class to order the next morning. "Good morning, class. I am happy to see each one of you today, after such a dreadful night. But I am sorry to tell you that one of your class-mates did not survive. Betty Bossina and her family were killed last night when a bomb hit their home." The pupils gasped at the sad news when they realized that Betty would not be coming back. As Anje listened, she thought, *That could have been any one of us.* And the devil-may-care attitude grew stronger inside of her for she never knew if she would live to see tomorrow.

Oma was in a happy mood when Anje returned from school because she had found a treasure. As Anje untied the strings of the apron that she had worn to school, Oma smiled and lifted an unbleached cotton bag that she had discovered tucked in a small space in the cupboard.

"Look what I found today," she chirped happily. "A bag of barley!" She ran her hands across her frayed cotton apron to show her pleasure. "I boiled the water to cook the barley, but it just got hot, and then I put it in the hooikist to keep it warm." She paused. "You know, grain takes a long time to cook, and there was no more power."

"I know!" Anje exclaimed. "Let's put it in the feather bed where it'll be warm, and maybe it will cook a little more."

They took the hooikist with the cooking pot inside and tucked it deep within the feather bed, allowing the contents to sit. They knew this would take some time to cook, but Anje was so eager for this food that she wasn't able to concentrate on her homework. Every so often, the thought popped into her mind, *Is the barley cooking?* They decided to wait as long as possible. The thought of some hot food in their stomachs was beginning to cause them to drool. At one point, Anje said, "Oma, tell me a story while we are waiting."

Oma laughed as she shook the small towel she was holding in her hand and replied, "Anje, I have told you all my stories many times."

"But I never get tired of hearing them," Anje said eagerly. "Did you really work in the fields for forty-five cents a week?"

"Yes," Oma said. "Our parents were poor. We could only go to school for a few years, and then we had to go to work."

"Do you want to play a game of cards now while we wait?" Anje asked.

"Not today, Anje," Oma said with a laugh. "You always win when we play Thirty-One!"

It was evening when they decided to open the box and inspect their supper. As they lifted the box out of the bed and opened the lid, the food was still warm! That was good! As they chewed the kernels, they were soft. That was good! They carefully spooned the barley into their dishes and began to eat. Oma was in a happy mood. "We will be able to get more than one meal from that bag of barley, Anje." That thought cheered them greatly, and they agreed that Oma had found a good treasure.

Then Anje remembered her prayer, "Give us this day our daily bread." Today they had hot food for supper. And it was good!

THE EVER PRESENT ENEMY

On April 20, 1944, preparations were being made for a large celebration at Grote Markt for the Führer's birthday. Large flags and banners decorated the square which was filled with marching bands and soldiers on parade. Official speeches were delivered with great oratorical fervor expounding the greatness of the Führer, while fireworks exploded in the evening sky. Later, the German officers sang lustily, drank endlessly, and partied fervently, celebrating the success of their great leader.

Mother came through the door smiling and happy. She stored her bicycle in the entrance and proceeded to visit with her mother and daughter. "I came across a control as I was heading home, and I had to take a different route. As I came down Achterfweg, I saw four members of the SD arresting someone. It seems like no matter where you go, the enemy is there." Then she paused and added, "It's good to be home."

Oma was happy to be in this home with her daughter and granddaughter, where she was well cared for. "I have been so lonely since Opa died, Anje," Oma said, "and I am so glad I don't have to solve those problems of heat and food all by myself."

Mother was concerned about Oma's health. Her heart bothered her more, perhaps from fear and worry, and her frail body was weaker, possibly due to lack of nourishment.

Oma battled her own fears constantly, and she did not hesitate to confide in Anje. Over the years, the two had built a great bond between them. "I think your mother is working for the Resistance," she told Anje one day. "And I am afraid for her. This work is dangerous, and I do not want to see your mother come to any harm, but we do not want the Netherlands to be lost to the Nazis either. This is a job for men, but where are our men? They are hiding underground, or taken to Germany to work, or in concentration camps. And where is your father?" She hesitated a little before she said, "He is never at home. He must have some good connections, for he looks very well fed and relaxed whenever I see him. Your mother is the one who takes care of this family." She sat and rocked in the rocking chair in the back room, her eyes closed and her hands folded in her lap. Her mind rambled through the maze of her thoughts, and she slowly wiped away a tear that rolled down her cheek. "I am just an old woman. All I want is peace," she said wistfully.

It was a busy day. Hans was engaged at his desk at work when four men burst into his office brandishing weapons.

"Where are your records kept?" one shouted at him insistently.

"I don't know what you mean," he retorted. "What records?"

"The identification records that are kept in this office," came the sharp reply.

He could not resist them. They tied him to a chair and then ransacked his office, all the while shouting commands at one another as they threatened him. They were ruthless in their hunt for ration and ID cards, the most prized possessions of the war aside from guns. Ration cards and coupons would permit the purchase of food, while the identification records showed religious affiliation and were vital to hiding the identities of Jews. It was better that these records did not fall into the hands of the Nazis. When they found the metal cabinets in which these documents were stored, they began to set them on fire. One man removed the lid on a can of petrol, and another provided some matches. Hans could hear the opening and closing of file cabinet drawers as they searched for the right documents. Since the metal cabinets were fireproof, the contents of the drawers were the target. Hans could smell smoke, and when he realized they were burning the records he was sworn to protect, he screamed, "Help! Get out!" His screams alerted someone in the next office, and when help arrived, the men vanished quickly through the back door. But the damage was done. Thousands of records had been ruined and some destroyed. However, this plan was the work of the Resistance, and it was aimed to protect Hans because he was already being viewed with suspicion by the SS.

*Eemke van der Veen, known as
Hans Westerkamp to the Resistance. (Uncle Hans)*

Hans lived on the upper floor of the La Costas' three-and-one-half-story home. A busy carpentry shop was located at the rear, and there was much activity about this location. Martha, the La Costas' oldest daughter, was a friend of Hans's. She worked in the home as a seamstress and was also a fearless fighter for the Resistance.

The Nazis were masters of surprise and expert at operating the razzia. The razzia was a sudden overtaking of a person or place in which they swarmed the area with soldiers. It was designed to create fear and catch people off guard so they were not able to hide anything or warn anyone.

Martha was sitting on her large, wooden bench at her sewing machine when soldiers barged into her room. While they shouted to one another in German, she looked at them with disdain and continued to work. She never flinched or moved from her position, even when an officer whacked his club against the bench she was sitting on as he walked past. He had no clue that stored inside the bench was a shipment of guns and ammunition that Hans had overseen the delivery of the previous day.

Hans was one story above when he heard the commotion in the house below. His reflexes responded instantly, *Get out! They are coming for you!* He jumped to his feet, slid down the banister, and escaped into the rear of the house by hastily flinging open the door to the carpentry shop. His heart was beating so fast that he could hardly breathe, but he responded quickly to the situation. He spied a hammer on the bench closest to him, and he firmly gripped the handle, thinking, *This will make a good weapon.* The adrenaline that surged through him left a bitter taste in his mouth, and his brain responded with; *A good weapon against guns?* His eye caught one of the workers' caps hanging on the wall, and he reached for it, pulling it down low on his forehead. He began working with his back to the door as two soldiers entered. He whistled while he bent over the workbench; he did not want to look like a man on the run. The soldiers had their backs to him as they began to question Mr. La Costa at the front of the shop. While they were conversing, Hans slipped out the back door and into the alley unnoticed.

One of the workers had parked his bicycle against the building beside the door. "Sorry!" Hans muttered under his breath. "I have to borrow your bicycle." He turned the bicycle around, swung his leg over the seat, and quickly rode away. *Where to?* Jan and he had been best friends, but the war changed all that. They were not on the same side anymore. Hillie was his best friend and partner in the organization for the Resistance. He would go there. He knew Jan was never at home.

Hans could not resume his former life. The Nazis never left a place the way they found it. They slashed his furniture, destroyed his personal possessions, and confiscated his bicycle. On their way out, they informed Martha, "We will be watching this place. If he comes back, you must notify us."

She looked at them with disgust but remained silent.

Hans knew he must hide underground, and in March 1944, he secretly went to live in the Minnes home.

FIRST RAID ON
THE HOUSE

Razzias (raids) on homes became commonplace; one never knew who would be targeted next. On May 3, 1944, the Minnes home was raided. Mother had left to buy some food, Anje was engrossed in her schoolbooks, and Oma was taking a rest. Hans had seated himself comfortably on the divan in the back room with the newspaper when they heard the crash of the door being opened forcibly. Anje always felt safe when the door was closed and locked, but the aggressive SS officers shattered the doorjamb into pieces like matchsticks. They were under siege! Anje watched as Hans flew out of the back room and made a giant leap for the window that could take him to the roof and the secret exit. He heard the frightening sound of three pairs of men's boots stomping up the stairs into their living quarters. He didn't make it.

Anje's mind was racing. There were many unauthorized materials in their home. *Thank God,* she thought. Just last night members of the Resistance had picked up the shipment of pistols tucked under the paisley curtains of the kitchen cupboards. She had seen the word *Parabellum* stamped on the wooden boxes in large black letters. Fortunately, these pistols were now safely harbored in the capable hands of other members of the Resistance.

There was no time to think as one by one, these men quickly forced their way into their home. Three Dutch SS officers arrived first, and they were joined by four more. It was pandemonium! Seven officers were milling about every room in the house, searching for contraband—opening every door and dumping the contents from all the drawers into the middle of the room. As Anje watched, she thought, *What a mess!* All their possessions lay in shambles on the floor. Bedding, clothing, papers, kitchen utensils—anything one could imagine was in that pile.

Her eye caught sight of the blue-flowered material of the little money box that she had won at the fair where her personal treasure of seventy-five guilders was stored. This caught the eye of one of the eager soldiers, and he bent down to pick it up. He smiled when he saw the contents and decided to slip the box into his pocket. Anje was scared, but anger flared up inside her. *What right do you have to come in here, disrupt our home, and steal our possessions?* she thought. Inside she was raging, but she remained silent.

Suddenly, she heard a familiar melodic sound, and she observed one of the young Dutch officers swaying in rhythm to the music as his fingers gracefully moved across the keys of her accordion. She inhaled as she watched and thought, *Don't break that!* She loved to sit and play her accordion. Music was her consolation. She recalled when she and Uncle Hans had decided to attend music school together. He had helped her pick out this black, 120 bass accordion. And then it was silent—the officer gently placed her instrument on the floor.

One of the SS officers ordered the other, "Search under the bed." Oma's feather bed was high but the space under it was shallow, and this soldier was determined to crawl under it. Their small brown Bakelite radio was stored there in a red-and-white checkered flour bag, and a box of ration cards was stacked at the foot of the bed. Their hearts were pounding with fear as they watched him touch the checkered bag with his hand, moving it slightly to one side. He never opened it to discover the contents. He was a rather large man, and his bum was sticking out from under the bed. It was quite a humorous sight!

Oma hastily bent over, scooped up the box of ration cards, and quickly stuffed them under her housecoat. She spoke imploringly to the officer, saying, "I don't feel so good. Can I lie down?" clutching her arms around her middle.

"Yes," he said, "you can lie down."

As Anje glanced around the room, she saw the faces of two young Canadian pilots staring at her, their pictures tucked in the edge of the mirror on the mantel piece. Their passport photos had been taken as soon as the men hit the ground, and the straps of their parachutes were visible in the photos. With the help of the Underground, they were already on their way back to Canada, and Anje had kept the pictures for souvenirs. Looking around to make sure no one was watching, she removed the photos from the mantel and quickly ripped them into small pieces. But where could she put the pieces? When she discovered there was no place for them, she hurriedly stuffed them into her mouth and began to chew. Only then did she realize that the only way to get rid of them was to swallow!

The raid lasted from early afternoon until late at night. During this time, Mother returned from shopping. As she entered the room, her eyes spoke volumes for she knew what was hidden in their dwelling. Outwardly she remained calm, but her brain was evaluating all the obstacles. Anje knew she was thinking the same thoughts as she was—*the guns, the ration cards, and what other items might give us away?*

When Mother looked at Hans, there was great sadness in her eyes. Together, the three of them had occasionally discussed the dangers of working for the Underground and the consequences of being caught. Now it had happened. They were planning a future together after the war and had discussed this with Anje. Hans wanted to adopt her and be her father.

Anje's brain was on fast-forward. When a home was raided, there was usually an informer. Who was the informer? Was it possible that Father had been careless in his conversation along the way? She hoped not, but the feelings of uncertainty loomed in her heart and wouldn't go away.

Throughout the day, a few people dropped in. They were detained, scrutinized, interrogated, and then released. But one man who had arrived to visit with Uncle Hans was detained by the SS. Father, who was seldom home, arrived in time to see his house in an uproar. He sat in the back room brooding along with the others, observing all the motions of the enemy.

Finally, they were satisfied. Father, Hans, and his friend were to accompany the officers to the police station. The results of the day were surprising—no contraband or illegal materials were found in their home. Since the police knew nothing of Mother's underground activity, she was not detained. When Uncle Hans left the house, his blue eyes looked confidently at Anje, and he smiled. "Good-bye, sunshine girl," he said softly. He executed a slight wave with his left hand, which was designed to calm her fears. Sadness reflected in his eyes as he looked at Mother. He was escorted down the stairs by the black-uniformed SS officers. At the bottom of the stairs, he turned and went out the door without looking back.

This raid created turmoil in the household. Oma could not stay there, Anje had to go to school, Mother would have to hide—how would they do all this? Someone alerted Aunt Dolly and Uncle Albert of the control at her sister's place, and they arrived to take Oma to their home with the bicycle taxi. Hurrying to find her most necessary possessions in all the mess was difficult, but they finally loaded her into the taxi and were gone.

Mother looked at the clock; there were only fifteen minutes before the ten o'clock curfew! She had to hurry to get to her safe house. "Anje," she said earnestly, "we will have to be very careful from now on. This is proof that they are watching us. Stay out of sight as much as possible." She hugged and kissed her daughter good-bye and flew off into the dark on her bicycle. She pedaled furiously to arrive at her destination before ten. She parked her bicycle, climbed the stone steps, and rang the doorbell. The door was opened very cautiously, and the woman who answered offered her regrets.

"No, I'm sorry. I can't take you in," she responded tersely. "I can't afford to do this. It's too risky." The police had found someone hiding in a house down the street, and they were all taken to prison. "I have small children. I can't do that."

Mother, the one who had found so many hiding places for others, was now being refused a place of refuge. She nodded. She understood. Fear ruled; they had all suffered at the hands of the Nazis. Her bicycle clattered on the pavement as she headed toward the next address on her list. It was quite dark by then, but when the next door opened, she was greeted warmly and asked to come in and bring her bicycle into the house for safety.

At the age of fourteen, Anje was left all alone at night for the first time in her life. The SS had taken the keys to the house so the door could not be locked. The noise and activity of the pub and café just below her was daunting. Would someone come up the stairs and walk in her door? When people were drinking alcohol, anything was possible. She knew she could not go to sleep. She sat at the top of the stairs waiting and watching for something to happen. At every moment, she was listening for sounds. She had become very adept at paying attention because may times, her life had depended on it. Every sound and creak of the building frightened her. *What will I do? I have no money, no food, and no one to tell me what to do next.*

Where is everybody? Where did Mother go? Where is Uncle Hans? Who will help me? She wept bitter tears, tears of loneliness and fear. She had been abandoned.

Working for the Resistance was a very lonely life, but she had grown accustomed to that. She could never confide in anyone, but she had always had Mother to lean on. Now Mother was gone. She often talked to God silently in her head. She didn't know if he was listening or not, but someone had once told her, "When Mother and Father forsake you, then the Lord will take care of you." Was that really true?

For three days and three nights, she sat on the stairs, with no food or sleep. Her eyes spotted the familiar sight of the cover of her poezie album, and she opened it. As she began to leaf through it, she stopped at the page that said, "Groningen, 2–22–39."

> *Dear Annie,*
>> *Life is so wonderful.*
>> *It gives us time and again,*
>> *Much trouble, suffering, grief.*
>> *But yet, then again the sun also shines,*
>> *My darling, whatever your portion may be,*
>> *Grief or sunshine,*
>> *Always hold your eye focused on high.*
>> *My dearest, always remain pure.*
>> *In memory, your loving Mother.*

Another page was labeled "Haren, Sept. 4th, 1941," and the message read,

Dear Annie,
>Strew today a single flower
>On the path of a neighbour.
>From a troubled countenance,
>Smooth out a few wrinkles.
>Relieve distress and dry a tear,
>Bestow a blessing to some.
>Make them hear a word of love
>And your day is never lost.
>In memory of your loving
>Uncle Hans.

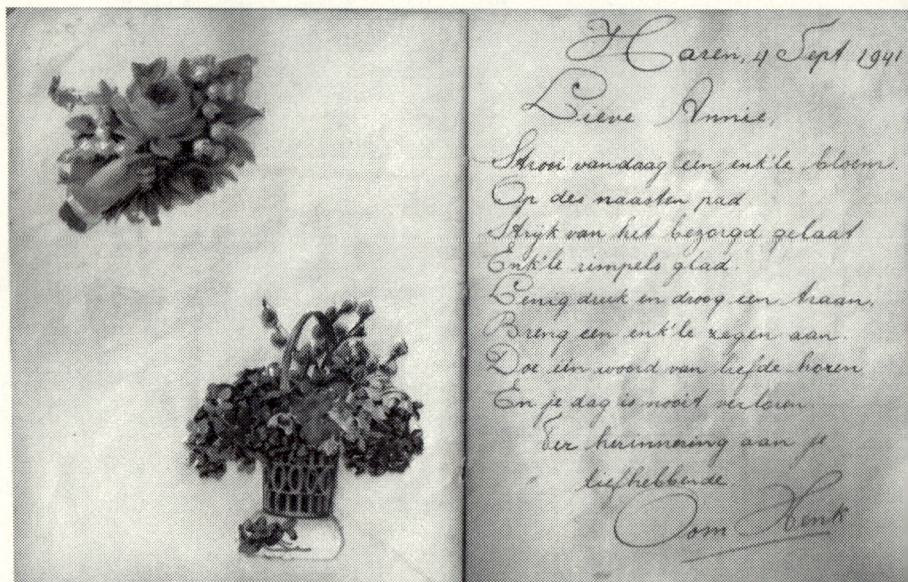

A copy of a message from Uncle Hans in Anje's autograph album.

Uncle Hans; she had spent many hours learning to duplicate his beautiful sweeping signature. He was very dear to her, the real father in her life; they had enjoyed so many good times together. *What will happen to him now? Does the Gestapo have any evidence against him?* She could not bear to think what might happen to him, or what she would do if she never saw his face again; and the sorrow settled in a little deeper. She placed her book on the step just as the doorbell rang.

She wiped away the salty tears on her cheeks as she hurried to open the door. Mr. Dykstra, Annie's Dad, was standing before her, and she was so happy to see him. Tears rushed to her eyes when he asked incredulously, "Are you still here?"

She nodded; and gratitude flooded her being. Somebody actually cared enough to come and see how she was.

"Get your things together," he said abruptly. "You can come and stay at our place." Relief swept over her as she ran to get a few things from her bedroom. She realized how fortunate she was that someone was willing to take her in!

It was beginning to get dark, and their shoes clattered as they walked brusquely down the cobblestone street past the neighboring houses. A light mist was falling. Once they were about halfway down the block, the sound of soldiers chattering in German reached their ears, and they turned to see two Nazi soldiers in gray uniforms cycling down the street. Her heart beat a little faster when she saw them stop at her house, dismount their bicycles, and walk toward the door. Suddenly the thought struck her, *What would two young German soldiers do upon arriving*

at a supposedly empty dwelling to find a young girl all alone?
She shuddered at the thought and tightly clutched her
bag of things as she hurried along. She had been rescued
just in time.

Life at the Dykstras' was just what she needed. She and
Annie were good friends, and at the end of the day, she didn't
have to be alone. She could not risk going back to school and
was careful not to be seen in public since she didn't want
to be picked up. She thought, *What would they do with me
if they did pick me up?* She was tempted to go outside, but
she remembered Mother's words: "Don't go out in public."
She thought it would be best to obey. She was restless as
she languished in their home for a week, as she was eager to
have something to do. *Perhaps the Underground doesn't know
that I am at the Dykstras', and they can't find me,* she thought.
But moments later, there was a knock at the door; someone
from the Underground delivered a package for her. When
she glanced at the address, she knew it was destined for the
hands of Toots at the Black Cat Café. She was preparing to
make her delivery when Mr. Dykstra stopped her.

"Where are you going at this time of the evening?"
he asked.

"Oh, I have to take something to Haddingestraad," she
replied as she slipped on her shoes.

He carefully removed the package from her hands
and spoke kindly as he looked into her eyes. "You can't
go there. That's not for a young girl like you. I'll deliver
that parcel for you." Inwardly, she was smiling; he didn't

know how many times she had already been there. But she appreciated his acting like a father. He was behaving just as he would to his own daughter, and it gave her a warm, comfortable feeling inside.

Once she discovered Mother's underground location, Anje visited her twice. She had to be very sure she had lost her shadow because, since the raid on the house, she was being followed everywhere she went. About a month later, Mother decided it was safe to come home. Anje was so happy to be back in her own home with Mother at her side. *What could possibly be better than this?* she asked herself. She nibbled on her piece of bread as she busily pored over her books from school. They were all used to deprivation; now the most important thing was having each other.

"I need to go out and see if I can buy a little food. There may be some fish at the market if I get in line early enough today," Mother said as she pulled her shawl over her head. "I don't know how soon I'll be back, but I will be back." She smiled as she left the room, and her footsteps could be heard on the wooden stairs as she approached the landing on the lower level.

When the winds came from the north, the air still felt cold and damp, even though it was June. Anje decided she would settle herself beside the stove in the front room, her favorite place to sit. Time flew when she was engrossed in her work, and she was startled when the doorbell rang. The surprise was even greater when she answered the door to discover two familiar-looking Dutch officers dressed in plain clothes who had been present at the raid on their house!

"What do you want?" she asked inquisitively.

"We want to ask you some questions," they replied.

"I am alone at home. No one else is here," she offered, hoping to deter them from their mission.

"That's all right," they said as they entered and began to climb the stairs to the living quarters. "We want to talk to you."

This raised her guard. She was irked by the supposition that she knew something and that she would offer them information, but she said nothing. Leading them into the front room, she gestured for them to sit on the narrow divan and seated herself in the familiar spot beside the stove.

The older man had a friendly manner and was almost coaxing to begin with.

"Do you know Hans Westerkamp?" he asked, watching her reaction.

"No," she replied, "I don't know anyone by that name." *Well, actually this is true, she said to herself. That is not his real name. The person I know is Eemke van der Veen.*

"You don't know Hans Westerkamp?" he asked incredulously as he looked directly into her eyes. He was the only one questioning; the other was listening.

"No, I don't know him," she responded.

"Are you sure?" he continued as he moved from his position.

"Yes, I'm sure."

"Well, we know he has been in this house, so you must know him," the other officer said. Now they both were engaged in this conversation.

In desperation and almost in anger, she replied, "How should I know everyone that has come to this house? I go to school, and when I come home, I go upstairs to study until eleven o'clock at night. I am busy with my homework. I am not here all the time. I say, I don't know him."

"Has he ever been at this house when you were at home?" they continued as they looked around the room, perhaps to gain a little more evidence for their query.

"Not that I know of," she replied, a little irritated. What did they think they could see anyway?

"Did he stay here, sometimes?" They observed her intently.

"Nobody has stayed at this house. We don't have room for anyone to stay here," she replied shortly.

"Do you know how old he was?" the first officer questioned.

"No, I don't know who you are talking about." Inwardly she was seething, but she did not allow that to show on her face.

"What is going on in this house? What exactly are you doing here?" he asked as he shifted his weight, moving his body forward, closer to Anje in a more aggressive position.

"We live here," she replied curtly.

"How long have you known Hans Westerkamp?"

"I told you, I don't know anyone by that name," she said.

"Has anyone else been in this house?"

"My mother, my father, and myself—we live here." She was amazed at the way the words seemed to fly out of her mouth instantly, quite without thinking. After two hours of interrogation, they decided to leave, having come up with nothing. As the door closed behind them, she was awestruck.

How was I able to lie like that? she asked herself. *I have never done that before. How did I do that?* She had been told that self-preservation was a powerful instinct during traumatic times, and she had just discovered that for herself.

It was June 13, 1944, and as Anje sat looking out her dormer window, a strange object flashed across the sky. It resembled a plane, but she knew it wasn't an airplane. This was different. It produced a quiet sound similar to that of a rotary motor. It puzzled her. What was that?

Later, Anje learned via the Underground that she had been a spectator of the launch of Germany's newest weapon, the V-1 rocket, which Hitler had named "V for Vengeance." It was launched at Drenthe just a few miles south west of Groningen. Traveling faster than the speed of sound, it took just three minutes from launch to reach its target in London. Though it produced much damage in the city of London, the British would not cave in to the demands of the Führer.

THE SANCTUARY

Church was not a regular part of her family's lifestyle, but Anje's school friends occasionally invited her to join them. *Well*, she thought, *if they like it and think it's important, maybe I should go and see how I like it.* So she went. The churches she took note of in Groningen were quite large, old, stone buildings. This one was also, but it was not a Catholic church, so the interior was not filled with statues and elaborate carvings like those she had seen on Christmas Eve. Lovely stained glass windows in the front and sides of the building had been damaged from the war and repaired with plain glass and even some with wood panels. *Everything in our land has been broken in some way and needs repair, even the people,* she thought sadly. As she looked around, she noticed that the walls were plain white but a nice background for the warm brown hue of the wooden pews. The pews were not ornate, but the oak surface shone, perhaps from all the people who slid across them on Sunday morning. She noticed that the wooden boards in the floor creaked as she walked down the aisle; it appeared they had previously been covered with a runner rug that had been removed. As they were seated, the church was very quiet, and she felt peace in that place. She noticed the morning sun beaming through the stained glass window in front of the church which clearly depicted a design of Mary and Joseph holding the Christ child lovingly in their arms. Just below, a plain wooden cross was the lone adornment on the wall. Four steps led up to the altar at the front, which was graced with a plain wooden lectern with an intricately carved panel on the front. "One of our parishioners made that lectern," her friend said quietly, "but he has since been taken away by the Gestapo."

Anje nodded. The penalty of war was felt by all.

She watched with interest as the pastor moved to the lectern to speak. The only time she had seen a pastor in a cassock was in the movies, and the cassock was always black, but this one was white. Around his neck he wore a long white stole with tassels on the end. *Very fancy*, she thought.

Because she loved music, the worship session touched her deeply. They sang with great conviction "A Mighty Fortress Is Our God." She was deep in thought. *Yes, we sure do need a fortress from our enemy, but God, how would you do that?* Listening carefully, she joined in the singing of "Love Divine," as they sang lustily, "Love divine, all loves excelling, joy of Heaven, to earth come down." *We really need love to come down to earth,* she thought. *There is so much hatred all around us. Where do we find love right now?*

As they proceeded into the third verse, some eyes filled with tears as they continued bravely, "Come Almighty to deliver, let us all Thy life receive, suddenly return, and never, never more Thy temples leave." A little shiver went up her spine. Could God really come and deliver them? She never thought about him that much, but she felt that when she was in trouble, she would call "Help!" and it seemed that he always helped her.

She fidgeted somewhat during the preacher's message as it continued for one and a half hours. She stole a glance at her friend beside her, who appeared to be listening. *But she is used to this, and I am not!* She didn't understand one bit of that religious language. The pastor might as well have been speaking Japanese. Then she noticed that people all over the sanctuary were snoring! As the minister concluded his message, soft sounds of the organ filled the church, and a deacon approached the pulpit to announce, "This is the time we give unto the Lord for all the blessings he has bestowed upon us. We will now receive the morning offering."

She watched with great interest as they took up the offering. A small velvet bag that was attached to the end of a long wooden stick was passed among the pews, and people placed their donations in it. She was amazed that people were still willing to give money to the church when it was so scarce.

Suddenly, the church doors flew open, and SS officers in full uniform marched into the sanctuary. They appeared formidable in their black tunics emblazoned with gold emblems on the collars and sleeves. The wide black belts that crossed over the shoulders also held holsters and guns, and the tall leather boots completed this display of authority. Two of the officers wore greatcoats over their uniforms, and the tallest one marched beside a pew and bent down to look closely into the face of the man who was seated on the bench at the end of the pew.

"Where is this person?" the officer demanded as he thrust a photo under his nose.

"I don't know, sir. I don't know him," the man replied shakily, gesturing with his hands.

"Liar!" shouted the SS officer as his steel-blue eyes penetrated his victim's. "We know he attends this church."

"But I don't know him," the man replied again, his frame sinking lower into his seat.

"Liar!" the officer shouted again as he raised his leather whip.

The old man ducked, an automatic reflex.

"Do you know how the SS treats liars?" he shouted as he grabbed the collar of the man's worn coat, jerking him from his seat. He hit the man so hard that he fell to the floor. "Perhaps your memory will improve. We will not tolerate insubordination!" he screamed as he addressed the rest of the congregation, his proud head held high to exhibit his authority in the situation.

"Get up! You are under arrest!" the officer shouted at the frightened man. "Perhaps a little more persuasion is needed to make you talk. Take him to SS headquarters," he commanded. The two officers observing obeyed immediately. The veins stood out on the Nazi officer's forehead as he turned sharply, stamped his leather boots loudly on the wooden floor, and began to strut down the aisle toward the vestibule. The sound resembled that of a child's temper tantrum.

Anje's heart sank. *SS headquarters? What a horrible place to take him, to the House of Torture.* She knew him. He was Annika's father, just a poor, hardworking man. *He's no threat to the Nazis. He's old. Why do they want him?* All the while, she knew that the Nazis needed no reason for anything they did. They just did it.

As the SS marched out of the sanctuary, Anje peeked when their backs were turned. She saw movement in the corner of her eye and caught a glimpse of the man in the gray tweed coat and cap as he followed the SS out of the building.

"Collaborator," she muttered under her breath disdainfully. The Nazis respect nothing, not even the house of God.

The minister raised his hand and said quietly, "Let us pray." As he began to pray, she closed her eyes tightly, attempting to shut out the evil that had entered and hoping that holiness would again prevail after the *amen* sounded.

RESISTANCE CONTINUES

Vigorous discussion was taking place as four members of the Underground sat around the table in Edgar's apartment. The Resistance was reeling from the scrutiny and the heavy clamp-down of the Nazis upon all underground activity. "Our immediate problem is obtaining food for those in hiding," Hillie said seriously, "and the black market is the only way we can get an adequate supply."

"Don't give them your little finger because they will take your whole hand," Erich admonished, referring to the black marketers. "They are like vultures when it comes to dealing. You wouldn't know they were Dutchmen. They are ruthless in their bargaining just because they know the people are starving."

"Well, Erich, we have greater problems than that to

solve," Edgar interjected. "With Hans gone and the Gestapo cracking down on our network, they are hauling people to Vught by the truckload. The hungrier people get, the more willing they are to give information. The number of available workers for the Underground has really decreased, and we still have scores of people to look after. Our job is just that much more important."

"I heard that the SS is planning to use the firing squad for punishment for the Underground instead of sending them to concentration camps. It's cheaper," Erich said drily.

Hillie recoiled at that idea. "Where did you hear that?"

Erich said vaguely, "Somewhere!"

"Hillie," Edgar said as he turned to her, "please be careful. They have come to your place once; they could come again. Make sure you have no incriminating evidence stored at your home."

She nodded. "I have to ensure that my daughter is safe. I will be careful." As she turned to leave, she added, "Erich, you need to be careful too. Things are getting pretty hot. Don't you think you should consider going underground?"

"Hillie," he said, a broad grin breaking out on his face, "I'm like a cat—I have nine lives."

"What do you think of this, Anje?" Mother queried. "We have another package coming to our house tomorrow. This time it's a boy!"

"When is he coming? In the morning or when I get out of school? Anje asked.

"He'll be coming in the morning. We have found a home

for his parents, the Levensteins. Their five-year-old will stay with them, but unfortunately they cannot keep their baby in this hiding place. It's too dangerous."

"Well, we don't need identification papers for a baby," Anje began. "Will he just stay with a Christian family, or will he become theirs? Will his parents be able to have him back after the war?"

"This is the agreement: the parents can have him back, but who knows what will happen? For now, we have a baby that needs a home and a family that wants him, so we will put them together," Mother replied quickly.

When Aaron Levenstein arrived, he cuddled right into Anje's open arms. She observed the beautiful dark eyes that looked trustingly into her face as she tried to coax a little smile from him by tickling him under the chin. He rewarded her with a big smile and "goo," with both hands waving in the air. The more she gazed at her little charge for the day, the more her thoughts centered upon helping to hide his identity. He was such a beautiful baby, but she felt his dark coloring would give him away if the courier carrying him to his destination was checked. Netherlanders in the north had fair skin, blonde hair, and blue eyes. This thought wore on her until an idea popped into her head. How could she change his identity? An adult needed papers, but a baby had only his appearance as his identification. She went to the medicine cabinet and began hunting for her bottle of hydrogen peroxide. She found the brown bottle tucked behind some toothache drops. This would do the trick! She leaned the child's head over the enamel basin and poured the liquid over his black curls. She watched with glee as she saw his dark hair begin to lose color. Thoroughly satisfied with the results, she rinsed and dried his new yellow hair with a towel. She laughed as she lifted him high to observe his new Aryan look. His blonde hair would keep him safe until he was adopted into a family.

She rocked him in her arms. How nice it would be if you lived in our home, Aaron, she thought. I could play with you all day. She thought for a moment of his mother, who had given him up in order to save his life. She will not be able to look into his dark eyes, or ruffle her fingers through his curls, or be there when he learns to walk, but she has given him life for the second time. When it was time to say good-bye to the child, she felt both happy and sad—happy for Aaron and sad for his mother. "Good-bye Aaron, my little Aryan," she said sadly. "May you always be happy, protected, and loved." She kissed this beautiful boy on the top of his head, shook his little hand, and handed him to the woman who waited with open arms to receive the precious bundle.

Hillie was enjoying the warm July day as she walked down Barestraat, her shoes clicking on the cobblestones as she hurried home from work. She was lost in her thoughts when she heard someone calling her name.

"Hillie," Sonjia called as she managed to catch up with her friend. "I was on my way to your place when I spotted you. I need to tell you, something terrible has happened to Erich."

Hillie's heartbeat almost stopped for a moment and then began beating faster. "What has happened to Erich?"

"He was caught in a control on Hofstraat, and you know Erich—he always thinks he can talk his way out of something. Well, it didn't work. One of the soldiers said to him, "You look like a Jew to me." Erich objected, but then one of the Nazis grabbed him and pulled off his pants. He fought like crazy, but what is one person against four? When they saw he was circumcised, one of the officers drew his revolver and shot him in the head. They threw his body in the back of their van," she said as she broke into sobs. "The soldier shouted, 'The only good Jew is a dead Jew!'"

Shock wasn't the right word to describe how Hillie felt. Disbelief was a better word. She had spoken to Erich such a short time ago that this didn't seem real to her. "The Nazis don't treat people like human beings," she said. "Let's go to my place. We can't talk here. You never know who's watching us."

As they walked towards Rabenhauptstraat, Sonjia began to speak slowly, "There is something I want to tell you, Hillie. I'm going back to Sweden. I've been thinking about it for quite a while. My mother is alone and getting older. I know there are problems there too, but I feel I have to go back home."

"Well, of course, Sonjia, if that's what you want. But I'm going to miss you," Hillie said as she gave Sonjia a quick hug. "Promise that you will write to me?"

"I promise," she said with a smile.

SECOND RAID ON THE HOUSE

Mother received notice that Father would be coming home on July 1, 1944. He had not been away very long, so she and Anje were surprised by the news that he had been released from the concentration camp in Amersfoort. Expecting him to come in the morning, Mother was taken aback when he appeared at the door late in the evening the night before, looking healthy and surprisingly at ease.

"Jan, you're home already?" she asked, concealing her surprise at his full head of hair. We knew that prisoners' heads were always shaved upon arrival at the concentration camp. "How has everything been going for you?"

"Oh, things could be better," he said evasively as he wandered into the back room. His eyes swept around the room, coming to rest for a moment on a piece of paper on the table. He paused momentarily and sat down on the divan as he prepared to light a cigar.

Anje was furious. *He can't fool me,* she thought. *He* wasn't in any concentration camp. *He's just trying to gain some respect and sympathy, and he doesn't deserve it because he didn't earn it. I would bet that he has been at Utrecht with his family, where he was well looked after. She watched carefully as he began removing the wrappings from an expensive cigar he pulled out of his shirt pocket. I wonder how he can afford that? We don't have enough food to eat, but he can smoke cigars!* If Jan had any explanations, it was obvious he was not going to offer them to his family.

It was very early, before the sunlight broke through the window, when Anje awoke abruptly to the sound of many footsteps and loud voices downstairs, and she hurried to pull on her clothes. What's next? How did these men get into our house? Thoughts were whirling through her head as her feet trotted down the steps into the kitchen.

Nazi soldiers were tearing the house apart room by room. *Not again!* she thought disgustedly. They pulled goods out of the cupboards and closets and never put anything back. Others trudged upstairs to the sleeping area. She hated it when they rummaged through her bedroom. It was an invasion of privacy. "What do they expect to find under my covers?" she muttered angrily under her breath. "What are they looking for anyway? We have nothing here!" She felt agitated, and her mind fluttered back to the first raid. The most devastating loss they suffered then was Uncle Hans, and they still did not know where he was being held. Some of the members of the Underground were certain that Hans had been taken to the concentration camp at Vught, where they held Gentile prisoners as well as Jews. The pain that penetrated her heart cut like a knife wound. Who will they take away from me now?

Father was standing quietly on one side of the room, and Mother moved in beside him to whisper, "How did they get in here?"

He shrugged his shoulders carelessly and said, "I must have forgotten to lock the door when I came home."

Mother raised her eyebrows, and Anje had never seen such an expression of anger on her face before. The SS officers confronted them with loud shouts of accusation. They had committed acts against the Fatherland. Working for the Dutch Resistance was treason and punishable by death.

Someone has betrayed us, Anje thought as her stomach churned. There were two things a member of the Underground feared—one was being caught, and the other was betrayal. Both had just happened. Who? We've been so careful. We don't talk to anybody. Who did this?

Her panic subsided as she observed her captors more closely. Some of the men were dressed in plain clothes; others, the brown shirts, were the enforcers; but the leaders were from the Secret Service. They appeared formidable, attired in their sharp black uniforms with the SS insignia emblazoned on their collars and the death head image mounted on the black band of the field cap. There was no way to escape; the rifles with fixed bayonets were pointed menacingly at them. One officer motioned with his gun, "Heraus!"(Get out!) he yelled and jerked his head toward the steps.

Father motioned for Anje to go ahead of him, and as she marched down the stairs, he followed, huddling behind her. As she stared into the gun barrels of the two Nazi officers standing on the landing, her fear was lessened by the contempt she felt for her father. "Coward," she muttered angrily. As she spoke that word, a new realization flooded her: It was true. Her father was nothing but a coward, and she could never respect him again.

As they marched out of their house and down the street, they knew they were going to prison. During that half-hour walk, Hillie, Jan, and Anje were in front followed by two armed men in plain clothes. Jamada ran alongside Anje with his tail wagging as he looked up at her from time to time as if to say, "What's happening here?"

Many questions were going through Anje's mind. Who was the informer? She had nagging thoughts of her father betraying them. Would he really do this to his own family? She hoped not. Would the Underground be able to help them escape? Then the reality began to set in. We are going to prison. I wonder how long we will be kept there? Her greatest fear was being separated from Mother. They might be lenient on her, but she was not so sure they would be tolerant of her mother. It was as though a knife was turning in her gut. Everything was out of her control. She was filled with many emotions, but remorse was not one of them. They both knew the consequences of being caught. They had carried out their duties to the Resistance faithfully. If the choice were offered, they would do it again. What fate awaited them? She did not know. She would have to take it one moment at a time.

PRISON

There was no trial or jury to decide whether Anje and Hillie were guilty or innocent; they were at the mercy of the Reich and the officers who were placed in charge of them. This prison was called the "Second step from the beginning without an end." They were about to find out why.

It was 7:30 a.m. when they arrived at the prison. The raid had taken all day and all night. The prison was a large, cold, stone building that had stood on this location barely used for many years, but now it was overflowing with prisoners of the Nazis. As they entered, they were escorted into a room to be interrogated by their captors and to be recorded to determine which section of the prison they would be housed in, whether it would be with the political prisoners or the black marketers.

Anje was led into a small room with a large pedestal bathtub, given some soap and a rag that used to be a towel, and ordered to have a bath. She was feeling intimidated, having to remove her clothes in this cold room in a strange place. As she stood there naked, she wondered where to put her clothes. She looked about the bare room and saw centipedes and other bugs crawling along the base of the wall on the stone floor. She shuddered and hurried to climb into the deep four footed bathtub. A woman in a gray uniform entered the room and began scrubbing her hair with a disinfectant, as a deterrent for lice. When she was finished, she picked up each article of Anje's clothing and began to examine it for lice. Anje did not feel comfortable with another person in the room, but she had no choice, so she crawled out of the tub. As she began drying herself, she wished she could shed her cares as easily as she had shed the grime in the bathtub. She only had one question in her mind: *Where is my mother?* She didn't trust the Nazis. She knew them too well. They wouldn't allow them to be together—that would be much too comfortable, and this prison was not about comfort.

Once she was dressed, the female guard led her down a long hall that seemed endless. There were doors on each side, each one opening into a cell. Finally, she could see a guard standing beside an open door, waiting to escort her into her cubicle. She entered, and the eerie metal sound that clanged when the door shut sounded so final that she had to struggle to control the fear that was rising within her. She found herself in a cramped space containing a bed, a collapsible table, and three straw mattresses. As her eyes swept around the concrete room, all she could see was filth. There was only one object of interest, a small window high above her head that was the only source of light, and it was covered with iron bars. Four other girls were housed in this tiny six-feet-by-six-feet cell. She had been detained for many hours and urgently needed to go to the toilet, which she discovered was a drab five-gallon pail covered with a heavy plank. She was shy and self-conscious but finally realized there was no choice but to squat over the pail and relieve herself. There was no room for pride; each person had to suffer the same hardships to survive.

Each spare moment was spent scrutinizing every inch of this miserable space and mulling over all possibilities of escape, analyzing every option, but there was nothing she could do to. A thick, heavy metal door was the obstacle between herself and freedom. In the door was a small, square window that opened only from the outside. The prison guards used this peephole to spy on the prisoners, and the sound of the metal latch clanging every time the window opened was a sound the prisoners hated.

The tiny space was filled, forcing the prisoners to sit uncomfortably on top of one another until their legs cramped, and it was difficult to maneuver into different positions. The boredom was broken with daydreaming, and Anje noticed that, since they were all hungry, discussions about food were at the top of their list. While others dreamed about chocolate sundaes topped with whipped cream, fresh licorice, bananas, and cream or cinnamon candy canes, Anje yearned for her sauerballen candies. Imagination was at work here, but they needed a great deal of imagination to ingest the mushy mass that was plopped into their tin cups twice a day.

"What is this?" Anje asked as she smelled the gruesome pulp in her cup the first day.

"Potatoes," the other girls replied. "Polish potatoes, with peels on."

The potatoes for the prison had begun to ferment in the storage cellar, and when needed, they were scooped up with residues of dirt still upon them, peels and all, and dumped into the huge cooking pots in the prison kitchen. Anje thought the potatoes smelled awful. They did not taste like the nice, fleshy potatoes that grew in the Netherlands.

When nighttime came, three of the girls slept on the straw mattresses, and Anje curled up in the small space left at their head, positioned just below the window. The first night she said to herself, *Lord, there is nothing I can do about this.* It had been an emotional day, and her eyes closed as she quickly sank into oblivion.

She awoke abruptly to the sound of horrific screams, and she shook Lisa, the girl who slept beside her to ask, "What was that?"

"Oh, it might be the recorded music they play for our lullaby," Lisa answered sleepily, "or it might be real. We don't know for sure. Put your hands over your ears so you can sleep." Sleep did not come easily for the rest of the night. Her neck was stiff, and her back hurt. She kept thinking about her nice pillow and comforter at home in her own bed, but that was miles away. *I have to find out where Mother is. I wonder where they've put her?* This concern was uppermost most in her mind.

Morning came too soon. She preferred the dark; at least

she could imagine she was at home. But the smell of the pail in the corner jerked her back to reality each time.

The prisoners were "aired" for fifteen minutes a day. "This is the best part of the day, Anje," Lisa whispered as the keys rattled in the door. The prisoners were escorted into a space that looked like a large cell, but the roof was constructed of iron bars, allowing fresh air to circulate in the cubicle, and Anje inhaled the pure, clean air as she walked around the circumference of the room. These fifteen minutes were like a taste of heaven after the stale, musty atmosphere of her cell, she thought. The fresh air smelled of freedom, and it kept her hopes alive.

An old, wooden bench sat at the end of the cubicle, and unknown to the prison officers, that forlorn-looking bench became the communication center. All communication was prohibited, but it was most vital to the inmates. Everyone craved news from the outside—news of their loved ones or news about the war. Someone had placed an old cotton rag on the bench, and somehow, a needle and thread found its way there also. The inmates clued her in. As Anje walked in a circle, she noticed one person drop out of line and sit on the bench, pretending to rest. This action was forbidden by the guards, but one person was appointed the watcher. The girl on the bench picked up this small piece of fabric, stitched a short message, and lay the fabric down. The next person came along and stitched something else on the fabric. Nothing missed Anje's observation. When she inquired about it, she was told that the first person had stitched the letter L, looking for a relative who had been picked up. The threads were pulled out, and the next person, who had the answer, stitched the letter V for "Vught". This indicated where their relative was being held.

Attempts to stop communication failed. The prisoners tapped on the pipes in Morse code to reveal everything they could—information on arrests, movements of prisoners who were transferred, personal family news, or situations that occurred in the cells. But Anje was dejected; there was no news about her mother. Why had that information tap dried up? Nothing was leaking out. She would keep on trying.

The emotional trauma was worse than the starvation. Every day was filled with fear. Saliva rushed into her mouth every time she heard the jingling sound of keys rattling to open a cell door or the heavy steps of boots stomping down the corridor. The most terrifying sounds were the sounds of blood-curdling screams emanating from the stairwells and shots that rang out in the middle of the night.

Their cell was on the second floor close to the metal stairs, and an interrogation room was near this location on each floor. The prisoners could hear the screams of torture that were designed to make them more cooperative, but the Germans also recorded those horrible sounds and often used them to intimidate the prisoners. Anje could not bear those sounds that pierced through her dreams at night.

Early in her imprisonment, Anje discovered the great difference between political prisoners and black marketers. The black marketers were favored because they were not a threat to the Reich; they merely shuffled goods from one person to another. And frequently, the Nazi soldiers themselves were the recipients of these goods. The black marketers were the only prisoners to enjoy the privilege of being alone in their cells and being allowed to read. The political prisoners were watched closely and given no liberties, and at this point, Anje was a political prisoner. They were required to sit straight up in the cell with their eyes forward at all times during the day. If the peephole on the door suddenly opened and they were found slouching or had their eyes closed, they were shot. Fortunately, the group in Anje's cell was young, alert, and agile, so they did not suffer those consequences.

She inquired aggressively about her mother. "Could I go and see my mother?" she asked the guards. But each time, they answered with a negative. But she could see her father. She did not want to see her father; she had nothing to say to him. She just wondered where he was and doubted that he was still captive in that prison. He seemed to have connections. He was never in trouble.

Anje's cellmate Lisa wanted to communicate with her friend in the next cell, a seventeen-year-old girl named Anke. Since the walls were thick concrete, they were not able to speak directly, but one of the girls who knew Morse code suggested they could tap some messages to Anke.

"These walls are so thick, I don't know if tapping Morse code with my metal spoon is going to be heard on the other side," Lisa commented. They waited for a time when the guard was not around, and then they tapped and listened. They could hear tapping from the other side, but it was not very clear.

"I think we have to find something that will produce a sharper sound," Anje offered. There was nothing in sight until she looked up and saw the water pipes in the space above their heads. "This would work," she suggested, "but they are so high."

"We need something to stand on!" Lisa exclaimed excitedly.

"Well," Anje said drily, "we are standing on each other all the time. Let's make a human ladder and tap on those pipes." They were shocked to discover how loud it was.

"We're going to get caught," one of the other girls said, her voice tinged with fear.

"No, we're not, because we are going to be all finished by the time they come looking," Lisa stated. She was right.

Anke was in prison because her father was a Dutch policeman, and the entire family had been arrested. For punishment, Anke was dragged out of the cell every time her father was tortured and was forced to watch as he was brutally beaten. When she returned to her cell, she was sobbing and incoherent. It was the most brutal form of torture to see her father assaulted. Lisa knew that Anke needed encouragement and comfort. The girls in her cell cradled her in their arms to support her, wary of the guards attempts to catch them. At nightfall, they prepared for sleep, huddling together to comfort one another from the brutality of their environment.

Anje's cell was small, but it was big enough to contain the hopes and fears of all the girls. When they lost hope, they began to pray, and when they needed hope, they began to sing. "Love Divine" and "A Mighty Fortress Is Our God" were the favorite songs of the prisoners. Anje was surprised when the prisoners suddenly began singing "A Mighty Fortress," until she heard the shuffling sounds of feet in the hall accompanied by the stomp of a guard's boots. One of the girls said quietly, "Someone is going to interrogation, or coming back from it. We don't know—we just want to encourage them and let them know they are not alone." The singing began in one cell, was picked up by others, and spread along the way rolling like a set of dominoes, each one triggered by the other. The SS considered this a rebellious act and attempted to stop it by running down the halls shouting, "Silence!" It failed! The sound could not be quelled. It continued to reverberate down the corridors and lodge into the hearts of the hearer, bringing hope and faith.

The prison administration was not concerned about meeting the girls' personal needs, and supplies were a scarcity. One of the girls requested some pads for her menstrual period, but no such items were available. When she persisted because the need was urgent, the guard returned with something. He didn't bother opening the door; he just pushed it between the bars of the small window that was in the door.

"What is this?" she asked. She had been given a very used piece of cloth that looked like an old tea towel folded twice, with long strings sewn on the end! She held it up, and with a quizzical look on her face asked, "What am I supposed to do with this?"

One of the girls grabbed it and said, "You could use it as a flag in a parade!" as she waved it in the air.

Another said, "If you sewed along the sides, you could use it as a purse!" Laughter ensued again.

"I once saw in a movie," Lisa said, "that professionals use cloths like this to shine shoes."

"Better yet," Anje commented, "use it as a head scarf. See, you can use these strings to tie a bow on top of your head." She demonstrated her idea.

The girls all burst into laughter and continued until tears ran down their cheeks.

The daily routine was very boring; it seemed like the clock stood still. The day began at 6:00 a.m. As soon as the lights came on, they could hear the sound of the food cart being pushed down the hall. The food was nothing to look forward to, but it eased the boredom and curbed their starvation. Once Hillie and Anje's neighbors heard of their imprisonment, they sent money to the prison for them to buy food. Anje's favorite food was the tasty fish cakes made from ground fish heads; that was a real treat. But money was scarce in the Netherlands, and when it ran out, Anje had no choice but to eat the miserable prison food. Potatoes, rotten potatoes—the choice was eat them or starve.

To pass the time, the girls talked to one another, and over the next two weeks they all shared how they came to be in this prison.

Henriette was the daughter of a barber who operated his business in their home. "We had some Jewish friends who went underground when the troubles all began. At first we hid them in our home, until we realized how dangerous this was for the whole family, and a hiding place was found for them. They had two children, ages five and seven, that they could not take into hiding, so we kept them at our place. We got documents for them and everything, but we always had to always keep them inside. Then one day the child came upstairs into my father's shop where he was cutting hair, and someone asked if this child was his, and he said yes. One of our neighbors was present, and he looked oddly at my father and said he did not recall when this child was born. We do not know who reported us, but the Gestapo came and interrogated my father and mother, and all of us in the family, and they decided that we knew they were Jewish children and removed them from our home. We heard they were sent to a concentration camp. The parents are still in hiding. We do not know where, but they have lost their children. We don't know how long we will be in prison for this. No one tells us anything. They were such lovely children," she said as she wiped her eyes.

"We helped Jews also, but my story is quite different," another girl confided. "We were just providing food for a Jewish family who are in hiding underground. We also don't know where they are hidden. The food was given to a member of the Underground. I have a sister who lives in the south, and they own a small piece of land, so they grew vegetables. She began to give me more than we could use, and I just shared it with someone who needed it. Unfortunately, someone infiltrated that organization, and when we went to take food, the Dutch police were waiting for us. And do you know what we have to do now? We have to take double that amount of food, and it is going to the Dutch police, no doubt for their own use. My mother is not in prison because she is the one that has to obtain the food and take it to them."

Ariel listened patiently to the others before offering her own. "I helped obtain ration coupons—extra ones, I mean. I had access to them, and I shared them with as many people that had a need. I was the only one of my family who knew about this, and so I am the only one who is in prison." Her story was very brief, and it was obvious she wasn't about to tell anything more.

Anje could read between the lines. Ariel had been working for the Underground, but if that fact came out, she would be in greater danger. She would not have had access to all those coupons without an organization behind her.

Lisa pursed her mouth and said to the others, "You all have done much more than I. I got caught taking food to a relative. I was on my bike, and I never thought of any danger. My aunt had been sick for a week, and my mother asked me to take her a jar of soup. She was afraid she would get too weak if she didn't eat. Then when I was stopped, the police told me it was forbidden to transport food. I am sure they ate it themselves. My aunt is getting better, so that is the good news."

Anje said stoically, "I just wonder if someone is taking care of my dog." She wanted to change the subject. She had done all of those things and more, but she was not about to divulge her story. If the Nazis knew what she knew, she would be sent to a concentration camp. She knew everything about the leaders of the Resistance—where they held their meetings, the hiding places of Jews, where they kept the ration tickets, and much more. But she was careful not to trust too much. It was something she had learned from the Resistance. She never knew who was listening or where her words would go. No, it was always best to be quiet.

The House of Blood and Tears.

THE HOUSE OF
BLOOD AND TEARS

On July 15, 1944, very early in the morning, Hillie was transferred from prison to the Scholten House, escorted by two burly prison guards This huge, magnificent home that had once been the hub of Groningen high society had become the headquarters for the SS, the SD, and the Gestapo. Many horror stories emanated from here, and people shuddered when they heard that name, which resulted in its being dubbed the House of Blood and Tears. Almost everyone knew of a friend or relative who had been tortured or killed at this place. Maurer, the husband of one of Hillie's friends, had been beaten to death there. The Gestapo had their own private cemetery where they hid the bodies of people they had murdered in their headquarters; it was in the sand dunes along the coast. When Maurer's body was found in the sand dunes, every bone in his body was broken. Tjeerd was the neighbor's friend, and he had been tortured and chained to a hot radiator on the third floor in Scholten House for nine days without food or water until he became unconscious. Large blisters had formed on his hands, and when the torture was completed, he was shipped to a concentration camp where he died.

The Gestapo believed they would extract information from prisoners if they beat them within an inch of their lives, but the Dutch people showed great resilience, strength, and loyalty. They would not implicate their friends, which often resulted in a greater degree of punishment.

Having been in the Resistance, Hillie had been informed about what to expect at this place. She knew she would be interrogated by Petty Officer Robert Lehnhoff, who was the officer in charge of this division. He was called the Butcher of Scholten House and was also known as "the murderer in patent leather shoes" because of his reputation of kicking people down the long marble staircase to their death. His dark, handsome looks were deceiving. Evil emanated from his presence, and his eyes reflected hatred.

The "workroom" where he questioned each prisoner was on the second floor at the rear of the building for privacy from the street. He worked in a diabolical manner, using intimidation as well as torture. He sat on top of his desk, one leg swinging, as he struck his thick baton into the palm of his hand while he spoke. He moved closer as he became more intense. It seemed as though poison exuded from his snake-like eyes as the words "You're lying" rolled off his lips in a surreal voice. He never hesitated to use the baton. His upper-body strength allowed him to administer heavy blows to the head, and he often jammed the end of his baton into the sternum, breaking ribs and puncturing the heart. But he did not use these tactics on Hillie. Was it because she was a woman? Was it because he had a high regard for the level of work she was engaged in? She didn't know.

Lehnhoff had been speaking on the phone to higher authorities, so he had his orders. Hillie was to be questioned, but her punishment was not to be given at the hands of Robert Lehnhoff. She would remain in prison until further instruction was received. As Hillie sat in that room, her thoughts latched onto Casper Naber, another young Dutchman who had been brought in for questioning. Afraid he might reveal something in interrogation that may harm someone else, he jumped out the third-floor window and fell to his death. He had become somewhat of a hero to the Dutch people; they saw him as a scapegoat. Hillie had a far greater objective—the protection of her daughter.

She returned to the prison at 5:30 p.m. and would not speak a word about what had happened in the eleven hours she had been detained at the House of Blood and Tears. What did she tell them? Did she make a deal with them, confessing to crimes she had never committed? Had she been able to take the focus away from her daughter? Did she convince them of Anje's innocence? No one knew.

***

Anje was being escorted down the hallway from the airing room when she thought she saw a familiar figure.

She looked again at the form and realized, *It's Mother!*
Her heart leaped! She was being escorted by two guards
as she returned from her questioning in Scholten House.
Anje could not describe her feelings at this time. The
person she had wondered and worried about so much
every day was walking down the hall beside her. It really
was Mother, but she was shocked to see that her mother's
hair had changed from dark brown to gray from morning
to evening! *Mother, what have they done to you?* her heart
cried out. *What has caused such a great change?* She didn't
understand that hair color could change under stress.
She just knew that something drastic had happened to
her mother.

As they passed each other in the corridor, Mother said
quietly, "The war is not going to last much longer. D-Day
is already past. The war is almost over."

Even now, positive words came from her mother's mouth,
words of hope. But as Anje turned to reply, the butt of the
guard's rifle in her back prodded her to move on.

Anje had been in her cell only a few minutes when footsteps echoed in the hallway and the door opened abruptly.
"You are free to go!" the guard said in a sharp tone. "But
you must report every day to SS Headquarters."

Free to go? She hesitated. She didn't want to go. It was
almost time for supper, and her stomach was yearning for
food. She should have been happy to leave this place that was
filled with terror and hatred, but she was not. When the door
on the old prison clanged shut behind her, she found herself
outside the gate. Anger rose, powerful waves of emotion
rolled over her, and rebellious thoughts gave way to furious
words. She kicked the cobblestones. "Rotten potatoes are

better than no potatoes. I have no place to sleep. Now what will I do?" In prison at least she had a roof over her head and friends to talk to. Now she had new fears to conquer. The Nazis possessed the key to her house. She had no money and no food. She was fourteen years old, completely alone, and mad at God.

In desperation she began to walk aimlessly. She needed to think. Down one street after another and as her anger subsided, she began to cry. She was all alone. A light drizzle was falling, and it made her feel forlorn. The sky was so dark that she couldn't see any stars, and since it was past curfew, there were no street lights to cast even a small glow. As she continued to amble down the dark streets, a thought emerged: *Maybe Aunt Dolly will take me in. She and Uncle Albert have always been kind. Perhaps they will have pity on me.*

It was four kilometers to their home, and since it was past curfew, she had to be cautious. In the dark, she could see the outline of destroyed buildings, now just piles of rubble. The cheese store, knitting mill, furniture store, restaurants, hotel, police office, whole blocks of businesses— all had been leveled by Allied bombs. A feeling of nostalgia settled in. She couldn't explain the devastation she felt as she realized that the familiar city was no more. Sadness began to arise as she thought of her friend Maria and her family who were killed when bombs demolished their home. Buildings could be replaced, but the people were gone, never to return. Tears ran down her cheeks as she thought of Mother and Uncle Hans. She was separated from both of them, the people she loved and who loved her. The loneliness she felt was almost unbearable. She had no one.

When she arrived at Aunt Dolly's place, she could not tell—was she happy to see her? As they chatted together at length, the evening flew by. Mother had been so kind to provide food for them; would this gain her some favor? As the cuckoo clock struck nine, Oma shuffled off to the bedroom, and finally Anje realized they were not going to ask her to stay. She knew the real enemy was fear—fear of being spied upon, fear of showing favor upon someone who was the enemy of the Gestapo. The desire for self-preservation was strong. One night of comfort and consolation was all she wanted. Perhaps by morning another solution would come to her, but that was not to be granted now. She had to go. As she rose to leave, she sensed their relief. They would not have to solve this problem. She said good-bye and walked into the darkness.

That night was a blur to her. She had been thrust out of prison so suddenly that she didn't have time to think of a solution. The Resistance called her "the thinker," but right now her brain didn't want to think. The loneliness she felt was almost overwhelming. She had never experienced this before. She just walked and walked. No one cared. No one was looking for her. It was a strange feeling. As she prowled along the silent streets, soldiers were patrolling, a Nazi vehicle roared past, and two young women strolled by, but she paid no attention to them. But when a stray dog advanced toward her, she reached down and petted him as he nuzzled her.

"Sorry, boy," she murmured, "I have nothing to give you. Are you lonely too?" She ruffled his soft fur a moment longer, and her fingers felt his ribs under the shaggy coat. *He's hungry,* she thought. *Well, we're all hungry.* As she got up to leave and continue along the paving-stone walk, the little dog followed along behind her, wagging his tail. *I wonder where Jamada is? I hope someone is feeding him,* she thought sadly.

Even though she was alone, she felt as though she was being silently guided along, and when she found herself near the home of her school friend Annie, she thought, *The Dykstra's rescued me once before. Perhaps they will take me in again.*

She rang the doorbell several times before the door was opened cautiously. A hand was extended to her, and she knew she was safe. As she lay down on the feather bed, she was filled with turbulent emotions and extreme fatigue. Her cares covered her like a blanket, and soon she was fast asleep.

The summer sun rose early, and she was awakened by a pair of doves cooing outside the tall window in the attic where she slept. She was not eager to rise, for she was filled with dread at the thought of reporting to the House of Blood and Tears every day for the next two weeks. What would she say? What would they do with her? Like all citizens, she had heard of the reputation of this place, but she sighed, threw back her covers, slid her feet over the edge of the high bed until they touched the wooden floor, and slowly began to dress.

I may as well face it, she thought. *I have to go.* It was a forty-five minute walk from Rabenhauptstraat to the Grote Markt, and the fear that gripped her was so overpowering that she could taste it in her mouth. She gazed at the majestic stone building from the distance, the sun reflecting in the tall, gabled windows facing east, and thought, *It is lovely enough to be a palace.* But appearance was deceiving. Inside, it was a chamber of evil.

She felt uneasy as she approached the building and walked up the stone steps to the landing. Tall marble pillars embossed with golden leaves stood majestically on either side of the exquisitely carved mahogany doors. She placed her hand on the ornate door handle and paused. At that second, all fear instantly left her body, and she was filled with a power and boldness she had never experienced before.

Entering by the front door, she hesitated as she looked down the long hallway. There were a series of doors along this hallway—which one should she choose? Empowered by the new boldness, she walked down the hall. She could hear people speaking behind one door and decided it best not to interrupt them. She approached another doorway with a frosted glass panel in it, and as she turned the brass doorknob, it creaked as it opened onto a landing that was surrounded with dark wooden spindles. This room had an exceedingly high ceiling, which made every footstep echo ominously as she climbed the marble stairs, emerging onto another landing. Doors were on the left and the right, and before she could decide which one to pick, a deep, booming voice commanded, "Halt!" She turned to see an SD officer standing behind her, his blue eyes glaring.

"What do you want?" he demanded of her.

"I came here to see somebody. I have to report that I have been here today," she replied.

"Komm," he said as he began to march across the landing, where he opened another door to a small anteroom to another office. Then he paused and knocked on the second door.

Prisoner's personal card of the KZ Herzogenbusch (Vught)

"Come in," a voice boomed from within.

"Corporal Schaper, this person is here to see you." Then the officer turned toward her, his eyes boring into hers, and he asked, "What did you say your name was?"

"Anje Minnes."

Corporal Schaper looked regal in his sage green uniform, with all its trimmings and badges. His cap rested beside him on the desk. He motioned for Anje to sit. She really didn't want to sit. She had a bone to pick with them, and she began boldly. "You had no right to come to our place and steal my things, and I want them back."

Corporal Schaper's face took on a look of surprise. He raised his eyebrows as he spoke to her. "Now, what is it that you want?" he asked, his blue eyes twinkling with a measure of mirth.

The words flew out of her mouth like a torrent of water rushing down a mountainside. "I don't know why you have done this to me. I am not responsible for any complaints you have against my parents. I don't know what you think they have done, but you came to our place, and you destroyed our things, and you stole my box of money, and I want it back. That was my own money that I had saved. Some of it was money I received for my birthday, and some of it I earned babysitting. There were seventy-five guilders in the box. You had no right to take that, and I want it back."

Schaper looked at her and smiled. "You know," he said, "you know where I live? I come from Hamburg. Do you know where that is?" he asked.

She nodded.

"And I have two teenage daughters just like you, at home with their mother. They are also in school, and doing quite well, I might add. Do you like school?"

She nodded.

"Good," he replied as he smiled.

He motioned to the officer who stood at the back of the room and spoke to him at length in German, while he and Anje waited.

A burly officer with a cross-looking face and a loud voice entered the room, and she recognized the blue fabric-covered box he held in his hand. As he drew closer, she saw that his face was contorted with anger as he raised his thick forefinger and shook it at her face while he almost shouted, *"Aber deine Mutter! Aber deine Mutter kommt niemals heraus!"* (But your mother is never getting out!) He thrust the box into her hands and left abruptly.

She took the box, carefully opened the lid, and mentally counted her money.

"Is all your money in there?" the corporal asked.

She nodded and got up to leave. She left the room and retraced her steps. As she passed a closed door, she heard moaning coming from within. She observed two SS officers standing and talking in the hallway, and her eyes were drawn toward their feet. One was Lehnhoff, the man with the black-lacquered shoes. His gloved hands wielded a baton, and Anje shuddered when she saw the wicked smile on his face.

As her feet hurried down the marble steps and out the front door, she noticed that the air outside smelled different—fresh and clean. She was happy, for today she had accomplished what was required. She knew that she did not have to worry when she went back tomorrow.

Her subsequent visits to the House of Blood and Tears were unusual, as each time she reported to another officer in a different setting. This house was huge, containing twenty-eight rooms, all with fifteen-foot ceilings and ten-foot windows, and every room had crystal chandeliers that hung from the ceiling. Wide marble window ledges supported simple ornaments, while on the walls hung maps of the world, portraits of Hitler, German flags, the swastika, and even a rifle. Some rooms contained a piano or a record player for the comfort of the officers, and every room had one or more desks and chairs for interrogation.

As Anje walked down the long hallways, she saw sights of horror she would not forget. Through one open doorway, she saw a man lying on the floor in a pool of blood, and as she passed the bathroom, she noted that blood stains ran down the side of the pedestal tub with claw feet. She was told that prisoners were placed in the tub during beatings so the blood could run down the drain. The officers were meticulous about keeping their elaborate headquarters clean. She drew in a sharp breath when she saw a man sitting on a chair with his hands tied behind him, unconscious from interrogation, because she recognized him as the neighbor who lived just down the block from them on Rabenhauptstraat. She knew they were giving her this tour each time she came as a warning—this could happen to you!

When she arrived on Tuesday, she saw someone sitting in that same chair with his head covered with a brown paper bag. There were other sights that she blocked from her memory, unwilling to bear the pain of recollection. She thought, *This place was correctly named by the people, the House of Blood and Tears.*

Friedrich Bellmer, the Haupt Sturm Führer (head assault commander), was the officer who lectured Anje on her last visit. He was stocky with dark hair, and his eyes penetrated her being when he spoke to her.

"You must not leave town," he said as he spoke sternly in German, looking directly into her blue eyes. "You must not go underground or be seen with known people of the Underground, or you will be picked up. We will be watching you," he continued. "In other words, you have to be a good girl."

As she left the Scholten House, she was a little offended at his words. *I am a good girl,* she thought. *The only thing I have been doing is helping other people. I don't think I'll stop doing that.*

Häftlinge dürfen nur Pakete im Gewicht zu 3 K.G.
empfangen. Schwerere Pakete werden nicht angenommen
und gehen ungeöffnet an den Absender zurück.

Berichtkarte

An

Absender:
geb. Nr.
Block

Konzentrationslager
Herzogenbusch

*A German notice sent to Anje with instructions for sending parcels
to the concentation camp.. (top:front, bottom: back)*

However, the environment had changed consider-
ably in her world. So many agents of the Underground
had been picked up and eliminated that the cells of the
organization were in disarray, and very few items were
passing through their hands. To compound the problem,

she was being followed constantly. She couldn't always see her shadow, but the eerie feeling she had in her belly when she was in public was her warning. Eyes were watching her. She knew she had to be very careful.

Several times she walked to the prison to see Mother, but she was always refused entry. Weeks went by, and finally she received something in the mail from the concentration camp in Vught. She was not happy that Mother had been sent to Vught, but she was happy to know where she was. Instructions for sending parcels to prisoners in the camp were printed on a small card: "Any parcel that weighs more than 3 kg will be returned to the sender." She began to think about what she could put in a parcel to her mother. There was very little food. The Dykstras had barely enough for themselves, but with their help, she managed to package up a small portion of prison bread they had purchased at the bakery and a very small jar of what looked like strawberry jam.

On August 5, she was excited to receive a letter in the mail from Vught. It was written on a piece of brownish colored paper, folded over and sealed. It was addressed to Anje Minnes, 15B Feithstraad, Groningen

Dear Anje,

We can receive a parcel with separate fruit package. I am good, and well. Your things arrived good. Early up and early to bed, it's not too bad. Don't worry about me. I am good and healthy, that's the best thing. Is Father home yet? I heard only Thursday that he wasn't back. If you send me a parcel and letter, the letter can't be in the parcel. Talk it over with the neighbor, if he has something to send, to put on the bread.

Everything is welcome. Darling, stay well and be strong. Greetings to all. How is Oma? Is she well? Bye darling, it will be good to hear something from you.

Love Mother.

The message from Mother was eagerly read and reread, but Anje thought, *I can't believe prison is as good as she makes it sound.* All the reports she heard about Vught were not so great, but Mother had a way of making everything sound acceptable.

On August 22, 1944, twenty-two members of different organizations from the Resistance were shot at Vught. The message announcing the executions came in code over the BBC News. When word came through the Underground that Uncle Hans was among them, Anje's world disintegrated. She had been eagerly waiting for Uncle Hans to come back; with Mother gone, she felt so alone. Now there would be no return. There was just another hole in her heart. It felt as though she was wandering aimlessly through life, just existing.

Her life was in a turmoil, and with September approaching, she needed to prepare to return to school. She was waiting for Father to return so she could go back home, and as always, hunger was gnawing at her belly.

When she returned to school, a great disappointment awaited her. She had missed so many classes due to the raids on her home, the time spent in prison, and going underground that the school would not allow her into the next grade. She would have to go back and complete the year all over again. She did not understand her own feelings. She had always loved to learn. She had been taking four languages and doing very well with them, but she refused to learn German. She didn't know when she would use Greek—and French? She just found it very hard to concentrate. The workload was too much for her. When she decided to comply with the rule and go back to the previous grade, she found the pupils so much younger than herself that it was like they were from a different generation. She had experienced so many life-or-death situations while working for the Underground that it was as though she had lived a whole lifetime during that period. Her interest for sitting in a classroom was gone. She left and did not return.

"Would you deliver a letter, Anje?" She had not acted as courier since before she was in prison, but she never refused an assignment, and so she said yes. It was a farewell letter from Hessel von Darzee to his mother. Hessel was one of the twenty-two men who had been executed at Vught. Her heart was heavy as she walked toward their home, bringing the same news that had inflicted such pain to her. As Hessel's mother wiped her tears on her large apron, she looked so frail and heartbroken. This was the very last time she would ever hear from her son. As Anje walked away, she thought, *Poor woman. I know just how she feels.*

"MAD TUESDAY"

September 5th, 1944 was called *Dolle Dinsdag*, or "Mad Tuesday." The events of that day would be forever etched in the memories of the Dutch people. Everyone in the Netherlands was longing for freedom since D-Day on June 6, 1944. They were eager for respite from hunger, cold, oppression, and fear. Thoughts of victory were in the air as the Allies swept rapidly through France and then Belgium. When the BBC News announced that Antwerp was captured on September 4, 1944, jubilation broke out. The Dutch were confident that their freedom was only days away, and they began to celebrate. Anje listened with interest. What did this mean for them? Groningen was still a long way from Antwerp.

In the towns and villages close to the Belgian border, the people watched as the shattered remains of Hitler's defeated armies streamed past their windows, together with thousands of German civilians and Dutch Nazis heading for the German border. On September 5, this frenzied exodus reached its peak. Trudging on foot in these convoys were Panzer troops, Luftwaffe men, Wehrmacht soldiers, even Waffen SS troops identified by their macabre "death head" insignia. Some of the soldiers were so disoriented that they asked for directions to the German frontier. This frantic flight had been triggered by Dutch Nazi party leaders, Reichskommissar Dr. Arthur Seyss-Inquart and Anton Mussert. They had nervously watched the fate of the Germans in France and Belgium and ordered the evacuation of German civilians to East Holland to be closer to the German border.

Queen Wilhelmina, in a BBC radio broadcast from London, carried the exciting news to her people in the Netherlands. "Liberation is at hand," she announced to her subjects. This was followed by a special message from General Dwight D. Eisenhower, Supreme Commander of the Allied Forces. "The hour of liberation the Netherlands have awaited so long is now very near," he promised. The most optimistic statement of all came from Prime Minister in exile, Pieter S. Gerbrandy: "I want all of you to bid our Allies a hearty welcome to our native soil."

Anje did not have anyone to tell her what this all meant. She listened to the news and wondered, *Where is this liberation?* She could hear of it on the news, but nothing was different in her city.

The Dutch people could not contain themselves. They were hysterical with joy as the Nazis fled for their lives.

Trains leaving for Germany were so full that huge piles of baggage were left behind on the station platform. Soldiers determined to desert begged villagers for civilian clothing. They were refused, while some unruly officers obtained horses, cars, wagons, and bicycles at gunpoint in order to flee the country.

The people were rejoicing, convinced they were seeing the collapse of the German army. Waving boldly in the streets were the horizontal red, white, and blue stripes of the Dutch flag. Trees were festooned with orange ribbons and sported on the lapels of people's coats. Stores were deluged with patrons wanting to purchase orange fabric; they could not fill all the requests. One excited young girl looked at her mother and said, "This is just like Koninginnedag, the Queen's birthday!" Many schools closed, and workers left their jobs to go into the streets to celebrate. Cheering crowds stood on the streets yelling, "Long live the Queen!" while others sang "Wilhelmus," the Dutch national anthem. One jubilant reveler phoned her sister in the north to report, "We are free! The Allies have come. We are smoking Players and eating chocolates!" The atmosphere was so charged that offices closed, and trading ceased on the stock exchange. But the people of the north had to wait over half a year before they could eat the chocolates of the liberators for the battle was not yet won.

Rumors changed every hour. The leaders of the Resistance were restless and worried. They had Underground cells in every town and village, and they knew within minutes that Gerbrandy's announcement had been premature. Using complicated circuitry, secret lines, and coded information, Resistance leaders were able to call all over the country. The

Dutch service of the BBC announced that the city of Breda, seven miles from the Belgium-Dutch border, had been liberated. But when the Resistance made a quick call to a member in Breda, they learned that no Allies had appeared as yet.

The SS leaders who had committed crimes against humanity in Camp Vught did not wait for the approaching Allied troops. Since Vught was located in the southern part of the country near the city of s'-Hertogenbosch, it would be the first camp to be liberated by Allied troops as they pushed northward. The camp commander hastily began plans to clean out the camp to erase evidence. On September 4, 1944, sixty prisoners were killed, and on September 5, 1944, more than twenty-two hundred men were transported to the Sachsenhausen camp in Germany. The following day, September 6, six hundred more males were sent to Sachsenhausen. Six hundred female prisoners destined for the death camps were shipped in cattle cars to Ravensbrück on the last train leaving the Netherlands, and Hillie was on it.

The Dutch people were excited to hear the news on the BBC that the Dutch government in exile called for a railway strike in order to hinder the Nazi troop transports from delivering soldiers into the conflict, hoping this would bring success to the Market Garden operation and cause the Nazi system to collapse. As a result, thirty thousand railway employees went into hiding, with a promise of financial support from London. Anje didn't understand what this could mean for her life.

Henk Das was the district leader of the National Organization for Aid to those in hiding, and he admitted that his group had encouraged the strike. "We were behind the railway strike, but we did think we had gone on strike too late," he said. "On September 4 and 5, the Germans were still able to deport all the prisoners of Camp Vught by train. Later we thought, 'Why didn't they begin the strike those two days?'" That action could have saved Hillie from deportation.

During this last winter of the war, resistance grew in spite of the oppression, but the strike made life difficult for all of them. Anje was not engaged with the Resistance at this time. Her life had fallen apart. There were no missions to carry out. Her mother was gone—she didn't know where—and many times she wondered if she was still alive. It was such a lonely existence without her mother's love and companionship. The Dykstras' kindness was appreciated, but she was bored. She couldn't go to school with Annie, and she detested the fact that there was nothing for her to do.

THE RETURN

Towards the end of September, word came to Anje at the Dykstras' that the neighbors had seen her father at home. She decided to go and check it out. As she walked along the street toward home, her mind was bombarded with thoughts. *How did Father get the key for the house? He must have gone to SS Headquarters. How did he dare do that when our family home had been raided? Once you're under suspicion, you're watched constantly. After all, Mother is in a concentration camp because of that raid. How did he dare go to Scholten House for the key?*

It felt strange to walk up to her own front door and ring the bell, but the door was locked, so she pressed the button. She could hear footsteps approaching, and when the door opened, her father had a surprised look on his face when he saw her standing there, but he nodded for her to come in.

She climbed up the stairs, entered the main floor into the back room, and then hurried up the next flight of steps into her bedroom. There at least she felt at home on her bed, amid her books and things. Why did she feel so uncomfortable, like a stranger in her own home? Searching her heart, she knew the answer. Mother had made this house a home. Without her, there was no love in this place. She was not accepted by her father—in fact, his reaction had made it quite obvious that he didn't want her there.

When she went downstairs, she saw Father rummaging in the closet for something as he prepared to go out. He emerged with a suit on a hanger, one of Samuel's suits, and he began to tear the threads that held the yellow star on the jacket. Anje stared at him, a look of shock on her face. Was he actually going to wear one of Samuel's suits? "Well, we know he is not coming back," Father said as he went into the bedroom. In her disgust, she walked down the stairs and went outside to sit on the step.

This reminded her of the many days she had sat there waiting for Mother. That was not so long ago, but it felt like ages. She put her head down on her arms, and a while later she felt a wet nose against her arm. Jamada! "Where have you been, Jamada?" She could tell that someone had been looking after him because he looked well fed. "How did you know I was home, boy?" He just wagged his tail and cuddled in her lap. When it was time, the two of them went inside and climbed up the stairs.

"Uncle Egbert is coming for the night," Father informed her. "He will be sleeping upstairs in that extra bed in your bedroom."

She was furious. She detested Uncle Egbert. He was rather odd in his ways, and she didn't want any man sleeping in her bedroom—single, married, or whatever.

"I am not sleeping in the same room with him," she replied tersely.

"That's ridiculous," he said. "He's coming from Utrecht, and he has nowhere else to go."

She was angry and thought, *There are other relatives in Groningen. He can go there.*

"He is not sleeping in my bedroom," she emphasized.

She knew her father. Uncle Egbert would be coming for the night anyway, in spite of her objections, and he would be sleeping in her bedroom. Anje's emotions were rising like steam on the inside of her, but she kept quiet. She would just have to find another place to sleep. She deposited her blankets and pillow on the divan in the back room, where she made herself comfortable. She had one consolation—Jamada would be sleeping beside her. Even though Father had his own way, he was miserable to her the next few days, just to show his displeasure.

The mood was about to change in the household. The next sound she heard was a clatter at the front door, and she went to see who it was. On the doorstep stood Frau Nienhuis, a spinster who lived just around the corner, and her arms were laden with pots and pans. Her ash blonde hair was fastened in a bun, and the round, gold eyeglasses she wore made her look older than she was. Her long skirt was covered with a full-length apron. It was obvious she had come here to work.

"Your father has asked me to cook for him," she explained as she entered the house. "I need to put these things in the kitchen, and then I'll go back for the rest."

While she was gone, Anje could not resist the temptation to lift the lids and check the contents of those pots. The first one contained potatoes, the second a small portion of carrots and spinach, and the third pot held some fish with rice. *Where did she get all this food?* Anje wondered.

When Frau Nienhuis returned, she wiped the oil cloth and began to set the table for one, using the glass dishes she had brought. She paid no attention to Anje; she was totally absorbed in her activity. It became clear to Anje that this food was not for her. She could see it and smell it, but she could not taste it. She decided it would be best if she went to her room and began to read one of the books she had just brought from the library. It was hard to concentrate on her book, for the smell of food kept interrupting her thoughts.

Amazing, Anje thought. *Frau Nienhuis can come and go as she pleases in this house, but I am not trusted with a key.* The more she thought about it, the angrier she got. The feelings of rejection, mistrust, and loneliness eroded her happiness. Fueled by the constant nasty remarks from her father, she decided that she didn't want to be in his presence.

When she told her friend Ineke of the abuse she suffered at home, Ineke insisted that Anje come and live at their place.

"But you know I have no ration tickets. My father keeps them all for himself, and I can't buy any food."

"That's okay," Ineke replied. "We'll manage somehow."

This generous family had come from Friesland. Ineke's father was a barber, and his barbershop was in the front room of their little home. Although there were already six children in that home, they insisted there was always room for one more and made her feel welcome. These children were delighted with Jamada and begged Anje to allow them to keep him. When she saw the joy he brought to their household, she said yes.

Ineke had volunteered for the Red Cross and worked daily at the center. "Come with me, Anje," she coaxed. "They always need more volunteers. There is lots of work to do with the many refugees coming in. Besides that, we get a good meal every day. What can be better than that?"

It didn't take much coaxing. Anje was eager to help because it would keep her mind off of things. Her mother was gone, her father had rejected her, her uncle was dead, and she had no one to care for her. She may as well keep her hands busy helping someone else.

The building bustled with activity; there were so many people with so many needs. Someone directed her toward a dishpan that had a mountain of dishes stacked beside it, and she began to wash dishes in cold water, with no soap, for three days and nights. Finally exhausted, she asked, "Where can I sleep?" And she fell into a bed in one of the rooms reserved for volunteers.

The work was never-ending. The influx of refugees every day was overwhelming. The Red Cross workers made beds in schools or any building that was available by throwing straw bales on the floor, pulling off the strings, and fluffing out the straw to make a bed for another tired group of men, women, and children. During the nights, the workers slept in shifts, while those who were awake supervised the rooms by walking through with a flashlight to make certain order was being maintained.

Food for the soup kitchen was delivered by horse and buggy. The milk cans were rolled off the cart, and the women prepared to serve the food, which contained layers of meat, vegetables, and anything else that was available. When one milk can was empty, another was rolled into place. The line of hungry people waiting to be fed was endless.

"Anje," someone called, "we need a person to find milk for one of the babies that has arrived." She left her task and began the long walk halfway across the city with a heavy baby in her arms to the location where the baby's bottle could be filled. Then she sat down and rested while the youngster wrapped his hands around the bottle, happily guzzling down the nutritious bottle of milk. As she stared down into his innocent eyes, she wondered, *What would this child do if there was no more milk?* Her reward was seeing a happy baby fast asleep as she handed him back to his mother.

The days became long, so she elected to sleep at the Red Cross rather than going back to Ineke's house. Traveling across the city at night on foot took considerable time after a busy day, and it was so dark with no streetlights. Anje and Ineke both had an Ausweis that allowed them to be on the street, but that piece of paper was no protection from aggressors for two young girls. As they walked one night, Anje felt her sixth sense warning her—she had an eerie feeling they were being watched. Managing to keep their pace, they began to hear footsteps coming closer and closer. Suddenly, Ineke screamed as a man's hands grabbed her from behind. Anje reacted like lightning, running to the nearest door. She pulled the cord that rang the copper bell mounted on the door frame, and the door opened. The man standing in the doorway was a godsend as he called out to them, "Who is there?" The attacker turned and fled down the dark street! The girls were shaken but undaunted. "Next time I'm bringing my little flashlight along," Anje insisted.

"Do you think your little flashlight would have stopped that man?" Ineke asked incredulously. They both laughed weakly and carried on walking toward home.

The Red Cross was committed to helping everyone—people who needed a place to stay, families searching for relatives they had been separated from, or those who needed a meal or two to hold them over. Hardship was something they all understood, and they were eager to help one another.

Many families wanted to emigrate to a place where the war was not as violent, but they had no documents to enable them to cross borders. Sometimes the Underground was able to help by finding a way to smuggle them across a safe border location and get them into Spain. Many of the people who wanted to travel were living under assumed names with false identification; it was not possible for them to apply for passports. Besides, obtaining a false passport was very costly and extremely complicated, so they were restricted to remaining in the violent surroundings of the war in the Netherlands.

The sky was gray and foreboding as Anje walked to work on Saturday. It was November 11, Saint Martin's day, and it certainly felt cold enough to snow. An old Czech proverb declares, "St. Martin is coming on a white horse," representing the snow that usually begins to fall in November. No one was eager to see the snow fall, for the children loved to visit neighboring houses to sing and recite poems, which earned them sweet treats from the occupants who enjoyed sharing a delectable apple, pear, or piece of candy with the little ones. She hoped that, for the children's sake, it wouldn't snow.

Anje was reminiscing as she walked along. Christmas was approaching, and the traditions that began on December 5 held so many memories for her. Saint Nicholas Day would come as usual, and the celebration would be observed, but not in her home. There would be no eager anticipation for gifts placed in her shoe, no munching on chocolate treasures, and no one with whom she could share a little happiness. She thought about her aunt, uncle, and cousins, Sophie and Willie. Their Christmas days spent together had been so much fun, and now she was shut out of their lives and shunned by most others because they knew she had worked for the Resistance.

Janny was such a good friend, and she understood Anje's loneliness. When Janny suggested that they attend Mass at the Catholic church together with some friends, Anje agreed. The two met outside on Rabenhauptsraat and chatted until they met their friends, who were waiting for them in front of the church on Gelkingestraad. Their wooden shoes clattered as they climbed the tall stone steps into the beautiful building. At that moment, Anje realized that, amid all the bareness, destruction, and loss that surrounded her, there was still a longing in the soul for beauty and majesty, and she felt comforted as she entered the church.

The celebration of Mass began at 4:00 a.m., and when the six girls arrived, every seat was full; there was standing room only. They were offered a place to stand at the rear of one of the balconies that offered a bird's-eye view of the ceremony and a closer view of the beautiful building. Anje recalled studying the styles of architecture of many old buildings in Holland. They were in Saint Joseph's Cathedral, and it had been built in the neo-Gothic style, with huge marble columns supporting the vaults of heaven, and the saints gathered in glory around the altar. The area at the front of the church was beautiful—everything seemed to reflect the light of the very tall white candles that graced the altar. The priest ministered at the altar while the strains of the magnificent organ resounded in the background, supporting the voices of the choir that seemed to echo in the sanctuary. *"Gloria, in Excelsis Deo!" Would a choir of angels sound any better that that?* she asked herself. The golden incenser held by the priest was swung back and forth in all directions, and the air became thick from the blue-gray swirls of smoke that rose up toward the vaulted ceiling.

"I liked everything about this service except the smoke," Janny whispered to Anje, stifling another cough.

Anje agreed. Their hearts were singing as they mingled amid the throng of people leaving the cathedral, and the frozen pebbles of rain that had just fallen crunched on the pavement under their feet as they walked. Anje thought, *I don't want to go home. There's nothing waiting for me at home.* The girls decided they would walk the nine kilometers to Paterwoldse Meer (lake) and enjoy the brisk fresh air this early Christmas morning. The sky was quiet. It felt as though someone had pressed a button and put the war on hold.

When they reached the frozen lake, Janny recalled a memory. "Anje, do you remember the day the Troostwijck boys chased us on skates all the way down the canals to the lake?"

"I remember," she replied. And to herself she said, *I also remember the night the Nazis came and picked them up and took them to Westerbork.* She remembered a lot of things she would like to forget.

Her mind wandered to the day she had gone sailing on the lake with some of the boys in the neighborhood. The wind had died down completely, the sailboat sat unmoving with the sails drooping, and the tide was going out. She had waited until the water receded and then decided the simplest solution was to run the eight kilometers home, right through the territory where Mother had forbidden her to go. She had not been a very obedient daughter, but it had been such fun exploring all those forbidden places. *Where is Mother now?* she thought as she walked along. This was the one thing she wanted to know.

The café at the lake was open, and the girls decided to stop for a drink and a short rest before their return journey. They stood and clinked the glasses of tart lemonade in a toast to the future. The night was now gone, and the light of day held new promise for them as they entered a new year.

RAVENSBRÜCK

Anje was restless as each day went by and she still wondered what was happening to her mother. About a week later, Mr. Dysktra handed her something that had arrived in the mail that day. A tiny scrap of brown paper that was crudely fashioned into an envelope became Anje's greatest treasure, for it was her last communication from her mother. On the front, inscribed in a lovely script was, "Anje Minnes, c/o Dykstra, Feithstraat Strad, Groningen. It was found on a station platform in Bosch." As she held the envelope, she noticed that it had been mailed from S'Hertogen. Her hands trembled as she opened it. Inside was a brownish-colored ruled paper with writing on both sides in pencil. It was obvious this came from a child's schoolbook. As she unfolded it, she read,

Dear child,

In transport. Don't know where to. Don't send anything more. Everything is all right. Lots of love.

Signed, Mother.

Beneath that, written in the same fluid script found on the address, were the words, "On transport to Germany, everybody from the camp in Vught. Found this letter on station in Bosch. Signed, the finder."

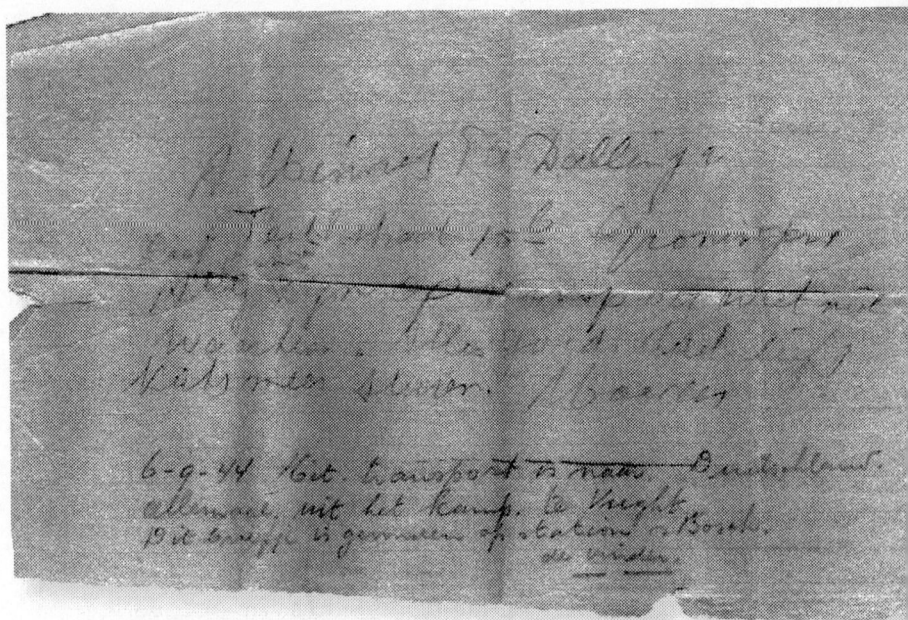

The note from Hillie which was thrown from the boxcar of the train.

Anje let out a sigh of relief—Mother was still alive! She hugged the piece of paper and held it against her cheek. She was elated to have received a message from Mother, but this was not the kind of message she hoped for.

Hillie was in Vught, and there was very little time from the moment the guards told them they were moving until they actually got to the train. She was amazed that she managed to write Anje a short note to give her the news of the move. Hillie's training with the Underground helped her to be resourceful, and she asked, "Does anyone have a paper and pencil to write a note?"

She knew she was requesting something illegal, but one woman ran to her bunk and brought out a piece of paper she had tucked in the crack between the boards of her bunk. Her son had sent his mother a page from his school notebook to show how well he was doing in penmanship. It was interesting how things got through the mail room sometimes! She handed it to Hillie. Another woman produced a short stub of a pencil. All communication was strictly forbidden, but in prison they were comrades and were eager to help one another if they could. She jotted down a quick message to Anje on the brownish colored paper. But the biggest problem was, how would she get it to her?

They marched four abreast through the prison gates and down the road toward the railroad station dressed only in their thin, striped, cotton prison garb. They were a large group. They did not know that they were being shipped to the women's prison in Ravensbrück, East Germany.

During this two kilometer march down a dusty road, they were all feeling the same emotions—turmoil, anxiety, and uncertainty. Their main aim was survival, yet all felt a sense of impending doom. Speaking was forbidden, but the guards could not be everywhere, and they managed to question one another quietly.

"How long will we be on the road?"

"Why are they moving us?"

"Where are we going?" All of these were questions that they did not have answers for.

"When do you think we'll get home?" one young girl whispered.

Hillie looked at this young blonde girl who reminded her of Anje and determined that she was going to watch out for her. "What is your name?" she asked quietly.

"My name is Janie," she replied. "Janie van Brunt."

Hillie spoke softly but directly to her. "Janie, you and I will stick together, all right? It will be better if we stay close to each other."

Janie nodded in reply. She was all alone, didn't know where her family was, and needed to be close to someone. As they marched, Janie stayed by her side. Hillie's mind was occupied with something else at the moment, though—her daughter. How would she get this message to her? She did not know in which direction they would be traveling. It had always been a comfort to Hillie knowing that Hans would take care of Anje if something happened to her, but Hans had been arrested at the raid at their home, and Anje had gone to live with the Dykstras. It was reassuring to know that someone had come to her rescue. The news of Hans's death had come to her via the Underground grapevine; he had been among the twenty-two persons who were shot at Vught, right where she had been just two weeks before. Hans's death was a great loss to Hillie. They had done so many things together; there was a strong bond of love between them. He was like a father to Anje, lavishing her with love. He had told her one day, "Hillie, I'm going to make you the beneficiary of my will." Now he was gone, and she didn't know what would happen to her; but it gave her a good feeling to know that Anje would have some financial security from Hans's will.

As they approached the station platform, they were confronted with a sea of gray, the color of Nazi uniforms, as the place was milling with armed guards accompanied by vicious German shepherd dogs. They were barking, growling, and nipping at their elbows as they passed by. It was like a zoo, and there was no means of escape. The Nazis made certain there would be no chance to flee. As the guards waved their rifles at them, they shouted loudly in German, "*Schnell! Schnell!*" (Hurry! Hurry!)

A very long row of cattle cars stretched on the track as far as they could see, and the wide doors on the sides were all open. They were herded into these cars like animals, and when the soldiers thought one was full, they pushed twenty or thirty more people in through the door as they counted. Two guards hurried to slide the door along the rail and close it, while two others forcefully pushed people inside. Clang! They could hear the sound of metal on metal. They were locked in!

An officer took his chalk and wrote on the side, "84." The number of the cargo was written on the side of each car, and as the cars passed by, the SS officer recorded it on his clipboard, added the total, and called ahead to the camp to tell them the number of prisoners that would be arriving.

This three-day journey became a nightmare. The train chugged across the countryside from Holland eastward, crossing northern Germany. Hillie knew she would have to throw her message out the window of the boxcar while they were in Holland or Anje would never get it. The only means of escape for the note was the window in the boxcar, but the window was so high that she couldn't possibly look out to see where they were. She knew the note had to be picked up in a town because if it fell in the country, it could be blown away, fall in a slough or weeds, and never be found. She was listening to the sound of the wheels along the tracks when she heard the whistle of another train, and decided she must be near a train station. She jumped up and threw the piece of brown paper into the wind saying quietly, "Please let Anje get this. Please."

In the boxcar there was standing room only, and it lacked air in some places. Hillie was fortunate to be tall; women who were shorter had difficulty breathing and jostled to get a better position. She did her best to see that Janie was safe. The weaker ones who fell to the floor among the straw were walked on; it was unavoidable due to the press of the crowd. Others helped them up, but they would only fall again. Some were weak and elderly. Worst of all, there was no toilet. Once a day, the train stopped, the officers heaved some fresh straw into the car, pails of water were supplied, and loaves of bread were tossed in. The guards seemed to enjoy the cries of hunger and thirst from the women as they screamed for a small portion of water or fought one another for a bit of stale bread. On the last day, they were particularly brutal; when the doors opened, the guards heaved water from the pail directly into the car in the same manner one would slop pigs. The women were very thirsty by then, and some of them used their tongues to lick that bit of water off their own bodies, if they were fortunate enough to get some. They all prayed this journey would soon be over.

Then the train brakes engaged, and the engine came to a screeching halt. The doors were eventually flung open, and the female prisoners staggered out onto the cinders beside the rails. The sun was too bright for them. Many were dizzy from the constant motion of the train, while others fell and couldn't get up. Hillie also fell because someone pushed her forcefully from behind, but she was strong enough to get up. At the end of the journey, the soldiers entered the car and heaved out eleven bodies of those who hadn't survived. They were flung on a pile of straw like so much dung.

The Ravensbrück concentration camp was for females only. It was located in Germany approximately fifty-five miles from Berlin. Originally intended for dissident women, the Nazis there were responsible for disposing of tens of thousands of women in the gas chambers.

Upon arriving at Ravensbrück, Hillie was surprised at how beautiful the landscape was. The waters of the picturesque lake were very blue, and a gravel roadway curved toward the entrance. Pebble stone walkways wound beneath the graceful linden trees planted neatly in rows, and the flower beds produced a blaze of color amid the tidy plots

LENORE EIDSE

of green grass. There was a huge aviary behind the watch-tower, and sounds from many species of birds could be heard, creating a park-like atmosphere. A huge wrought-iron sign above the gate read, *"Arbeit Macht Frei"* ("Work will make you free"), but the high wall and the barbed wire fence were reminders that this place was a prison.

An exerpt from the list of prisoners that arrived at Ravensbrück concentration camp. Hillie's name is misspelled Minnus.

This structure housed SS headquarters, prison cells, torture cells, a crematorium, and Jewish barracks. It may have been beautiful on the outside, but it has been said that Ravensbrück was like "looking into the mouth of

THE HOUSE OF BLOOD AND TEARS

hell." Inmates were murdered, starved, or worked to death. Children whose fathers were not alive and had nowhere else to go accompanied their mother to the camp. Many perished. Punishment for crimes against the regime were common. If the Nazis hated the Jews, they hated those who helped them even more. They were merciless in their punishment of them.

Ravensbrück was best known for its work camps nearby, which operated and thrived on slave labor. Factories here produced armaments, electrical components, and products of war. The sewing factory manufactured prison uniforms, and they remodeled the mountain of articles of clothing that were worn by the prisoners when they arrived. When the Jews were called for resettlement, they wore their best clothing for the journey or brought it in their luggage. The sewing factory fashioned the Jews' clothing into leather jackets and fur coats to be worn by the SS or Wehrmacht. Hillie had worked with clothing in Vught and did so again in the sewing factory in Ravensbrück. The textile factory wove rugs that were produced for the market, all inspired to provide funds for the regime. How they hated to be helping the Nazi regime, but it was do that or die. They all wanted to live.

The conditions under which they worked and lived were horrendous. Awakened brusquely at 2:00 a.m., they were required to stand outside barefoot in the *appelplatz* (roll call yard) wearing only thin cotton clothing, waiting to be counted. After this two-hour process, they were marched to the latrines where there were three toilets available and five hundred women waiting to use them.

367

There was no privacy; everything was done in the open with guards watching.

Their breakfast was a piece of bread, which had to be eaten quickly in order to prepare to march a few kilometers down the road to work, which began at 6:00 a.m. Everything in the camp was done by the female prisoners. They removed dead bodies, burying or cremating them; built roads, laid bricks, felled trees, and dug trenches. There was no such thing as the weaker sex in this camp. They had to be strong, as the weak ones didn't survive. Hillie constantly watched for Janie—they couldn't always be on the same detail, but they were in the same barracks.

In many ways, it was fortunate that Hillie had spent almost five years working for the Underground because she had learned many useful things. She saw things that others didn't see and was able to protect herself, figuring out ways to become almost invisible to her captors. She and the other prisoners carefully studied and observed the routine and habits of the guards, for they were very disciplined and organized. It helped them to do things behind their backs, like sneaking extra food into the barracks or passing information from the outside.

But women are generally the weaker sex and were at the mercy of their guards. Forced sterilization was practiced, so there were few pregnancies to contend with, but the guards were always looking for the opportunity to have sex. The raping of young women frequently occurred during the night. Having gray hair was an advantage; the men left these women alone.

Beginning in September 1944, when it was apparent that the Allies were winning the war, the Gestapo attempted to empty concentration camps and remove all evidence, which increased the urgency for killing prisoners. More wooden boxcars laden with prisoners arrived almost daily at Ravensbrück, and overcrowding became a great problem. Barracks that were designed to house 250 people had 1,000 in them. A bunk bed for one frequently held four women. It was fortunate that the young girl Janie shared the same bunk with Hillie. The "survival of the fittest" rule applied. Hillie knew that Janie would survive because she was young; she still had her whole life ahead of her. She became her project; she wanted to be sure that Janie would survive. When the guards came searching at night for young women, Hillie and the other women lay on top of her so she couldn't be found.

Helping Janie survive became a great benefit to her, for when she was weak and sickly, Janie took care of her. Hillie gave her last piece of bread to Janie because she was weak and bedridden, and her body didn't need much food. Her goal was to see that Janie would survive.

THE HUNGER WINTER
1945

Water in the canals was one means of transportation throughout Holland, and when the Germans decided to further tighten the noose around the necks of their captives, they controlled all transportation by closing roads, prohibiting the use of trains, and monitoring all movement. This created a virtual wall around northern and central Holland through which no humanitarian aid could enter. Food, fuel, coal, and electricity were measured out in very small amounts in what was to be a bitterly cold winter; taking a huge toll on the population. Groningen was in the northern part of the province, and Anje was among those who felt the desperation of not having enough food to eat.

Where will I find something to eat today? was the cry from Anje's tummy. She found that the hunger pangs lasted for three days, and after that it seemed the body didn't care about food. She scrounged in the house looking in every cupboard and cranny, but no food was to be found.

Families in Amsterdam became desperate and began sending their children, some as young as eight years old, on a walk 145 kilometers north to Groningen in search of food. Adults were too weak to make the journey, and the last morsels of food in the household were given to the children with the hope that they would come home with food from the northern part of the province. These hunger expeditions often resulted in death. It was a plan of desperation, for the Nazis operated the Crisis Control Service, and the SD often stood guard at bridges ready to confiscate any food carried by transients.

Anje had nowhere to go and no one to ask for help. Her father was never present when there was a problem to solve. People were trading their household goods and valuables to obtain something to eat, but Anje didn't have anything of great value to trade. She heard one wealthy woman had exchanged a valuable pearl necklace for a length of sausage. People improvised—a popular local sandwich was called "sliding sausage," as a piece of sausage was slid across a slice of bread for flavor and then repeated with the next piece of bread! Thousands were starving and suffering from diseases that were caused by malnutrition and compromised immune systems. One person resorted to eating his pet crow, and another, his pet rabbits.

The Germans set up a soup kitchen in the Grote Markt called "winter hulp," and Anje and Janny decided to go check it out one Sunday afternoon. They stood a distance away as they watched the gaunt faces of men, women, and children standing in a long line for a bowl of hot soup. Desperation and worry was etched on their faces. It was a miserable existence when people could not provide food for their own children, and no one knew when it would end.

"Isn't that your aunt and uncle over there?" Janny asked.

Soar and Bart Reisdorf were busy serving soup to the crowd. "Yes," Anje replied drily. "They are members of the Nazi party now. They think they are on the winning side. First the Nazis come and steal all our food and send it to Germany, and now they think they will be generous and feed us a bowl of soup." They watched only a short while before they left. They were hungry too, but Anje determined she was not going to eat the food of the enemy.

One family from Groningen sent a few small potatoes by post to relatives in the south for seed. These potatoes were considered so valuable that the relatives decided to eat the potatoes and save the peels in hopes they could plant them in spring. Hunting for food became the prime pastime during the Hunger Winter. People from the city left on foot with backpacks in the hope of swapping wedding rings or other jewelry for a bit of food, only to discover that the farmers had little left to sell.

The sights that Anje saw around her were depressing. The weak and elderly were most vulnerable to starvation; many fell and died right on the city streets, their bodies bloated from famine edema and dropsy. The men operating the "death wagons" were busy. This handcart on two wheels was pushed through the streets daily as the attendant searched for bodies. No wood was available for coffins; the dead were buried in a mass grave in coffins made of cardboard.

Anje heard that Aunt Lulu and Uncle Roland in Utrecht were also afflicted with swollen bellies from lack of food. It didn't matter how much money one had in his pocket because there was no food available to purchase. Father was nowhere to be found. Anje suspected that he spent this time with his relatives, and she was alone. This was a great hardship for her, enduring the loneliness and the hunger. Lacking motivation and strength, she often stayed in bed. She had no one to provide for her, and she ate anything she found whether it was edible or not. Life was difficult in a large city. There were no gardens or farmers nearby, and each person had to fend for him- or herself.

In March, two plain clothes men arrived at the Minnes' door, representing the Dutch Nazi Party. "We are here to inform you that Hillie Minnes passed away in the camp in Ravensbruck in January of this year, " they offered; "it is our responsibility to bring you this news." They left as abruptly as they came.

Anje was not shocked; she had offered up a prayer every night for her mother since her capture. In the early months of 1945, that desire gradually faded away from her, and she had an unexplainable feeling that her mother was gone. Jan came to the door in time to hear the news, and as large tears rolled down his cheeks, he reached for his handkerchief to dab his eyes and blow his nose. Anje stared at him In

THE HOUSE OF BLOOD AND TEARS

disbelief. It was so ludicrous, the man who had betrayed his wife was crying. *What did you think would happen when you reported her? Didn't you ever think about what you're actions caused? Hypocrite!* She thought as she walked away. Her tears for Hillie had been shed into her pillow every night, there were no more tears left.

THE CANADIANS

After the Battle of the Scheldt, the First Canadian Army prepared to winter. For the three months from November 8, 1944, to February 8, 1945, the Canadians were not involved in any large-scale operation. Rest was more than welcome. They had been fighting since early June, and those five months of action had had a major impact on them. Men were killed in action or wounded, and others suffering from battle exhaustion collapsed under the constant stress of dodging death, as they faced mortar shells and bullets every day. Others had been captured by the enemy, and many Canadian homes received letters that began, "Dear Mother and Dad, Just a note to let you know I'm well and a prisoner of war in Germany."

The Dutch people were well aware of the presence of the Allied Forces on their soil but had no knowledge of their movements or intentions. Anje listened frequently to the BBC News, but information of battles was not broadcast until after they happened, and she was beginning to lose hope that this war would ever be over. She had seen so many hopeful signs along the way, but those hopes had always been dashed by another battle or another harsh regulation imposed by the military. Now her attitude was just one of "wait and see what will happen next." Her time was spent reading books, which had always been her source of interest and relaxation.

After five months of campaign, Canadian soldiers were now experienced warriors, but wintering by the Maas River near Nijmegen was no party. The soldiers had to defend a bridgehead that would be used as a starting point for crossing the Rhine. They also had to keep the Germans on their toes, giving the enemy the impression that an assault was imminent so they would leave troops in that area. The Canadians donned white uniforms as camouflage in a snowy landscape, and the soldiers patrolled in an active and aggressive way, seizing every opportunity to gain a little ground or capture a prisoner.

The weather was not co-operative. Rain, snow, and sleet were common daily occurrences, and the dampness seemed to penetrate right down to their underwear. It was typical to see soldiers on duty sloshing around in mud that was a foot deep, warming themselves by a fire they had created by igniting gasoline poured into a hole they had dug in the ground. There was camaraderie in spite of teasing about their ethnic differences, for among the Canadian Corps were nine

British divisions, plus Belgian, Polish, Dutch, and American units under the command of General H.D.G. Crerar. Over one hundred thousand strong, it was the largest military force ever amassed under Canadian command.

The operation was launched on February 8, 1945, with aerial bombings and a powerful artillery offensive. The First Canadian Army left the Nijmegen area and moved toward the southeast to take over the Rhineland, a narrow strip of land between the Maas and Rhine Rivers. For the first time, fighting was to take place on German soil, and fierce opposition was expected. The Germans could rely on their excellent defense installations—antitank ditches, networks of trenches, fortified positions—as well as an inexhaustible supply of weapons and ammunition. But they were now fighting for their homeland, and this increased their determination. They fought with a fury. British and Canadian troops suffered tremendous losses from the German artillery.

As March drew to an end, the BBC News began to sound more hopeful as the Canadian troops moved northward to take Emmerich. After crossing the Rhine, the First Canadian Army was given two tasks—to liberate western Netherlands and to march through northeastern Netherlands and northern Germany up to the Weser River. Deventer was liberated in a single day by the 3rd Division with support from the Dutch Resistance fighters. In the meantime, the 2nd Infantry Division was moving along supported by airborne detachments. It reached Groningen on April 13, 1945.

"FREE THE NETHERLANDS!"

April 13, 1945, was the day the First Canadian Army set out to fulfil their commission from Field Marshall Montgomery. The order was, "Free the Netherlands!" It began as a bright, sunny spring day. The trees were budding as the first tiny, pale-green leaves were bursting forth almost magically from the brown stems that had held them captive in the winter cold.

At Lootens Bakery on Rabenhauptstraat, people went about this day as usual. The baker was preparing to bake bread for the prison in the afternoon, and his second batch of dough was rising. Anje's cousin Harlen and his fiancée Frouwke set a date to meet in the afternoon, and Frau Nienhuis was brewing some bones to make a soup broth.

By noon Anje could hear the rumbling and creaking of the tank tracks as they approached, and the boom of antitank weapons became louder.

Her curiosity got the better of her. She just had to go and see what was happening out on the street. She was two blocks from home when she noticed a Canadian Sherman tank on the bridge over the canal, and moments later, German soldiers pushed a mortar on wheels into the street. They began to fire at one another. The sound of the blasts from the tank gun were so loud that she began running down the street toward Timms Café, just below their home. One and a half blocks from home, a German Red Cross van hurried past, and a German soldier riding his bicycle down the street was suddenly struck in the head by a bullet. He fell, and his brains splattered on the wall of the building beside him.

She was rushing across Rabenhauptstraat toward the café, crouching low to avoid the bullets, when out of the corner of her eye something caught her attention. Four SD officers stood tall in the street, their legs slightly apart and their rifles raised in a stance for firing. Their identification breastplates that hung from shiny heavy chains around their necks were boldly inscribed, "Sicherheitsdienst Polizei." She was directly in their gun sights, and they were ready to shoot. She closed her eyes and thought, *This is my last day on earth.* Then she heard the *bang!* of rifles firing.

She expected to fall, but she didn't. When she turned back to look, the four SD officers lay dead in the street. She was shaking as she looked up, but she could see no one. *What happened? Where did those shots come from?* She didn't know. All she knew was that they were dead, and she was alive!

She could feel the saliva rush to her mouth, and she couldn't stop her knees from shaking as she wobbled across the street. She reached the steps of the bakery and sat down until her trembling body recovered from the terror in the street. Then she slowly stood up and went inside. The bakery had always been her place of refuge, the means of entering her home without being seen, and the location she hurried to when she needed a place to hide. It was a comfortable place, and she found the aroma of fresh bread soothing. She knew there was nothing more that she could do in this circumstance, and when she saw the wooden bench leaning against the wall, she lay down and immediately fell into a deep sleep.

When she awoke a few hours later, the shooting had not stopped, and she decided to go home. Father, as usual, was absent. She climbed up the stairs and flopped down on her bed. She wanted to open her window and watch the action, but there was so much smoke and noise that she decided it was not a good idea. A short time later, the doorbell rang, and she ran down the stairs to open the door to see Ineke standing there. She was delighted for now she had company. "Ineke," she called as she grabbed her arm, "come in quickly before you are hit with a bullet!"

"I've come to take care of you, Anje, so you won't have to be alone. Whatever is going to happen today," she said as she smiled, "at least we'll be together."

They sought sanctuary in the house as the staccato of submachine guns was interspersed with the boom of the tanks and the explosions of grenades as buildings rocked and bricks flew in all directions. Some of the Canadian soldiers had come to Europe as volunteers, and it was said that the first eighty Canadian soldiers entered Groningen secretly, capturing and holding a section of the city, were volunteers from a prison in Toronto, Canada. And they fought furiously. Two soldiers fought in the streets with artillery on wheels. "Baby tanks" rolled down the sidewalks with their guns blazing, and soldiers on rooftops took aim at the adversary below while Canadian soldiers lay in every doorway armed with antitank grenades. The tank falls (traps) that had been created to stop the Allied invasion were no problem—one tank drove into the trap, filling the gap, and the other tanks rolled right over the top.

Around two o'clock in the afternoon, Ineke and Anje decided to hide in the bakery warehouse, and they climbed down the stairs onto the landing to enter it. Many of the bakery staff had fled, wanting to hurry home to their families before the fighting escalated. Others had entered the bakery to take shelter from the barrage around them, as falling debris rained down from the buildings above. The ovens were filled with bread, but when it was ready there was no one to take it out. So the two girls began removing the loaves from the ovens and stacking it on racks to cool.

"It is doubtful the prison will receive its shipment of bread today," Anje commented as they worked.

"Well, at least it's not wasted by being burned in the oven," Ineke replied.

Anje's cousin Harlen kept his date with his fiancée, Frouwke. They thought this April 13 was just another lovely spring day and decided to sit outside on a park bench to enjoy the beautiful weather. Harlen always enjoyed teasing her, and Anje later learned from Harlen's family, that Frouwke was laughing at his joke when a grenade hit her, killing her instantly.

The sounds of the battle that raged outside were terrifying, but Anje and Ineke were young and curious, so they climbed up the landing, scurried across the roof, and slid back into the house to see what was happening. They raised the window in the front facing the street, and their heads rose just high enough so their eyes could see over the window ledge. Instantly, bullets whistled over their heads. Whew! That was close! They decided it would be smarter to lay low until the heavy fighting was over. No one dared walk down the street as chaos was everywhere. When nightfall came, they went to sleep wondering whether they would be alive in the morning.

"This is one time I am thinking of saying prayers before I go to sleep," Ineke commented as she crawled into bed. They were so exhausted from the stress and rush of adrenaline during the day that they easily fell asleep amid the noise.

That day the BBC news broadcaster reported, "At the Hague, a Dutch teenager watched the first of the Canadian tanks roll down his street. There was a big hush over all the people, and it was suddenly broken by a big scream, as if it was coming out of the earth, and the people climbed on the tank and pulled the soldier out, and they were all crying."

The second day, the air was filled with smoke and an acrid odor. The atmosphere was polluted, and the smoke settled near the ground; no one dared venture out until the shooting ended. Just before nightfall, Anje and Ineke climbed up the ladder-like stairs to the flat roof of the bakery and discovered some other people watching the battle. The neighbor and her older sister were accompanied by a Red Cross nurse whose battle-weary nerves had begun to fray as the sounds of the battle became louder. She began to shake uncontrollably, the skin on her face was pale, and her eyes radiated fear. As another shell exploded nearby, she covered her ears with her hands and was about to scream when the older sister raised her hand and slapped her across the face.

"Be quiet!" she threatened. "All of our lives are in danger. We don't want the enemy to know where we are!"

The nurse crumpled as she broke into sobs. "I'm sorry. I am just so tired. I have been working so many days without sleep. I just want this fighting to be over." The ladies wrapped their arms around her to comfort her. It was frightening for all of them, but they had to stay calm.

"Want a cigarette?" a young man asked Anje innocently. "It will settle your nerves." He pulled a cigarette out of his private pack and handed it to her. He flicked his lighter for a flame, and when it flared up, he said, "Take a puff, and draw it in real deep."

This was Anje's first experience with a cigarette, but as she followed his suggestion, her head began to spin and she immediately began to feel sick to her stomach. She spit on the ground, hoping to get the horrible taste out of her mouth. Phooey! "I'm not interested in this," she said as she threw the cigarette on the ground. But it had worked! She felt so sick that she was no longer afraid!

The group stood on the roof and watched as their city burned. They could hear the swoosh of the flamethrowers as they released their streams of deadly fire. The flames roared thirty feet across the water in the canal, and the boats on the other side instantly burst into flames. Anje's nostrils were burning from the clouds of smoke pouring from the buildings that had been set aflame by the Hitler Jugend, who were running down the narrow streets with flamethrowers resting on their shoulders. Some of these youths were as young as fifteen, and they fought with a zeal that was at times suicidal!

The rat-a-tat sounds of machine guns filled the air incessantly as the clips of bullets that were being fed into the weapons were discharged with rapid fire. As Anje watched, soldiers in foreign uniforms scurried in between buildings along the street, setting up positions for their artillery. In places, it was down to hand-to-hand combat. The Nazis wormed their ways into various properties on the street looking for a defensive position among the taller buildings.

Anje became tired of the battle—her ears were ringing and her eyes burning from the smoke—so she turned to Ineke and her other companions and announced, "I'm going home." She climbed down into the bakery. She wasn't home long when Father appeared, a worried look on his face.

"Anje, go and get Frau Nienhuis, and tell her to come to our place for safety," he ordered.

Is our house any safer than her house? she thought to herself. *Why don't you get her yourself?* But he was her father, and though she didn't want to obey him, she went. She cautiously entered the street, looking both ways to see if the coast was clear. There was still some shooting even though it was the third day of liberation. As she ran down the street, a dead soldier lay there face down, and she was forced to step over two more corpses of Nazi soldiers. She noticed the inscription on one soldier's wide belt buckle: "Gott Mit Uns" (God with us). She shook her head sadly as she passed by.

"Come quickly," she told Frau Nienhuis when she arrived. "It's not safe out there."

Frau nimbly retrieved her shawl and tied it over her head and then gathered up her cooking utensils, cradling them in her arms as she scurried down the street following Anje. They climbed up the stairs into the kitchen, and Anje headed for the back room with the window facing the front so she could watch the happenings in the street.

Anje could not believe her eyes as she watched the tanks of the Canadian Armored Division roll into Groningen amid wild cheers and shouts of jubilation from the Dutch people. Sherman tanks came into Groningen along the small dike roads and their tracks rattled along the pavement as they headed toward the city center. The extreme weight of these tanks caused many of the paving stones to crack and break as they sank into the soil, leaving high ridges on the sides of the street. No one cared. These were emotion-packed moments of victory. The liberators had come, and they were greeted with wild enthusiasm. The much feared German SS soldiers removed their uniforms, dressed in civilian clothing, and mingled with the jubilant population. But they took every opportunity to fire at Canadian soldiers of the Fifth and Sixth Infantry brigades. Retaliation was swift-- they were shot on sight.

In their euphoria, some folks were unable to contain their enthusiasm and rushed into the street to holler and wave at the military. Suddenly, the top hatch of the tank popped open and the gunner emerged halfway out, shouting urgently, "Get off the street! Get back!" He waved his arms at the people, yelling, "Get back! You'll get hurt!" The enemy was hiding in every nook and cranny, and there was still a battle ahead.

Anje was so fortunate on this day, for her own street, Rabenhauptstraat, was the first street to be liberated in Groningen, by the Cape Breton Highlanders. They completed the mission in seventy-seven hours! Soldiers, artillery, and equipment were in every respect superior to those of the lame occupying forces. The six to seven thousand German troops who occupied the city of Groningen were a real mix of army units that included veterans as old as sixty-five years, right down to the young boys of the Hitler Jugend. At the core, and in command, were fanatical German and Dutch SS troops who aimed to offer resistance as long as possible in spite of their poor armament.

Anje was curious to go out and see what was happening as the battle continued, but wounded and dying people lay in every street. The heartrending cries of young boys could be heard in German, "Mutti! Mutti!" (Mother). It was a cry that would touch any heart, Anje thought. There was a beehive of activity everywhere—sights of jeeps speeding through the streets with stretchers mounted on the side carrying the wounded, and soldiers crudely loading dead bodies of the enemy carelessly on "meat wagons" for disposal or burial. The school across the street from Anje on Rabenhauptstraat was set up as an onsite receiving center by the Red Cross, where the wounded were assessed, minor wounds treated, and the severely wounded transported by ambulance to the hospital.

Sunday, one of the last days of liberation, there was still random fighting in the streets as radical fighters from the Hitler Jugend were not willing to concede the battle. They were hiding in buildings and on rooftops, and some were holed up in the Catholic church. The crack of gunfire targeting people in the street revealed the hiding places of these fighters. The Canadians were undaunted; a big Sherman tank was positioned in the street nearby, and it began blasting holes in the church until the enemy surrendered.

There were few places in Groningen that remained untouched. Anje was sorry when she heard that the battle for the Grote Markt had ended in disaster. At seven o' clock in the evening, the Sherman tanks came into action, firing off grenades into the German nest of resistance, which resulted in the Germans igniting several properties in retaliation. Due to the ferocity of the wind, the fire passed from one building to another, and the whole north-east side of the Grote Markt became a raging inferno, with flames bellowing from the structures. Fortunately, the famous landmark, the Martini Tower, was spared. The SS, anxious to destroy documents and other evidence before they fled, set fire to the Scholten House, (that now-famous House of Blood and Tears), which ultimately resulted in a great explosion from the ammunition that was stored in the basement. This day, this notorious place mirrored its nickname, "the gateway to hell."

On the morning of Monday, April 16, 1945, the Canadians broke down the last opposition, and the German garrison commander ended the senseless battle, surrendering the city. The liberation of Groningen had taken many human lives: 106 citizens died, 209 Canadians were killed and many more were wounded, a few hundred Germans perished, and 2,500 became prisoners of war.

Is the war really over? Anje asked herself when she heard the news on the BBC radio. She didn't feel any different. The war had taken so much from her; she knew she would never be the same. Her heart still felt broken. Would that ever change?

*Canadian soldiers searched every home to make certain that no enemy was hiding and that no one was being held hostage. Anje was at the Lootens' house together with their two boys, Hank and David, when two young Canadian soldiers came down from their hunt on the roof to inspect the home. One of them spied an antique piano in the room, and he leaned his rifle against the wall and sat down. His fingers sped across the ivory keys as he began playing, "Carry Me Back to Old Virginny!" "Reminds me of home," he said as he got up from the piano bench, nodded at the boys, picked up his rifle, and continued on his way.

These soldiers are ordinary people just like us, Anje thought as she watched them leave. *They're lonesome for home, and normal life, just like us.* She remembered when she and Uncle Hans had spent hours playing the accordion, decorating the Christmas tree, playing card games, and taking fun trips to Sand Dunes and Heather. Now he was gone. She and Mother had been inseparable. Sometimes it was just the little things she missed, like making Christmas goodies together, sitting and talking, or the times they went on assignments together. There was a great bond between them that required no words. Now loneliness and despair were her constant companions, and she was sure the void would never go away.

She observed a Canadian soldier admiring a leather jacket on an eighteen-year-old Dutch lad, finally relieving him of it at gunpoint. *We have all suffered great loss due to this war,* she thought. *If you knew what we have all been through, you would not do that. This may have been the only jacket the boy owned.* Perhaps the soldier's conscience tweaked him a bit, for he decided at the last moment to give the young man a package of cigarettes in exchange for his jacket. As she walked on, she saw another soldier bend down to steal a fine gold ring from the hand of a dead German soldier. The finger was swollen, and when the ring wouldn't budge, he cut off the finger.

The Germans were also fearful and unrelenting. She heard of a young German soldier who was only sixteen years old and had enough of war. He wanted to go home and see his mother and his sister. He threw down his weapon and began removing his uniform as he walked toward the German border. He wasn't aware that he was being watched. When the soldiers shouted "Halt!" he just kept walking. He was tired of war; he just wanted to go home. He was shot in the back by his own comrades.

The streets of Groningen came alive once the enemy was under control. The people were very interested to watch the Canadian Army cooking food on their stoves right on the street. The Canadians were not aware of the extreme hunger of the Dutch and freely offered food to anyone who came by.

"Would you like a cup of tea?" one soldier said as he raised a cup toward Anje with a smile.

"Yes," she replied as she nodded, and she discovered upon her first sip of the hot liquid that it was real tea, made from tea leaves, not like the pill substitute they had, and it was delicious. He watched as she sipped her tea and then handed her a slice of white bread. She had never seen this before—this bread was so very white, not gray and doughy like theirs but soft and fluffy, almost like cake, with a very golden crust. What a treat! She ate it hungrily, but it did not take long for her to realize that her stomach could not handle this kind of food after starving for so long, and she threw it up.

The liberators were very generous. Every day as Canadian soldiers were gathered in the streets, they shared their food with others. As they observed the Dutch people watching them eat, they asked, "Are you hungry?" Every morsel of food that was offered was received gratefully, and they ate it in tiny bites, hoping to make it last longer. To many Dutch people, the very taste of liberty remained for a long time in the form of a mouthful of good bread or pastry, the taste of which they had almost forgotten. As Anje watched, one of the soldiers gave her a 5 lb. can of egg powder. She saved it until her stomach was able to handle food, but she discovered it made the most delicious scrambled eggs she had ever tasted.

Once the Canadian soldiers realized the people were very hungry, they began handing out chocolates on the street corner. *Chocolate! Real chocolate,* Anje thought, as she remembered the chocolate she had enjoyed at Christmases past. She took some, nibbling at it very slowly, savoring the delicious flavor of dark chocolate in her mouth. The pleasure was short lived, for she became violently ill shortly after.

When she was offered some canned meat, she took it but decided to save it until her stomach was conditioned to food again. Upon second thought, she decided to hide it so her father wouldn't find it.

About a week after liberation, Anje and her five friends decided to go for an evening walk. This was the very first time they were able to be out after 8:00 p.m., for there was no more curfew. They were free! There were no German soldiers on the streets, and she didn't have to get permission to go somewhere. She wasn't under surveillance anymore, and food was beginning to appear in the stores. On this beautiful evening, the full moon cast a warm glow on the landscape, and as the girls inhaled the fresh air, they marveled. It was as though they now lived in a different world. They felt so lighthearted and safe. A huge weight had been lifted off their shoulders. They continued walking toward Hauptman Park, and as they got closer, they could hear strains of music in the distance, which they recognized as the whine of bagpipes. Standing there in the moonlight, a group of young soldiers from the Cape Breton Highlanders, complete in full dress uniform, were playing their wind instruments with vigor and passion. It was a sight Anje would never forget. These young men going into a battlefield had packed their plaid uniforms along with their bagpipes in their duffle bags and hauled them across the ocean in anticipation of a victory celebration. That thought was astounding. Anje took note of the white spats on their shoes, bright argyle socks that reached to midcalf, the red and green tartan kilts with the dark green jackets. They wore special berets on their heads that looked like a small boat turned upside down with ribbons down the back! But the most unusual item of this uniform, the girls thought, was the white fur "purse" that hung in front on a belt, with some kind of ornamentation attached to it. The girls had only seen and heard of bagpipes in books or movies, and they had never seen a man wear a skirt before. They really enjoyed this "freedom concert," but wondered what was worn beneath the kilt.

Canadian soldiers on the street became a familiar sight, and as Anje approached Rabenhauptstraat on her way home one day, a lone Canadian was leaning up against the wall of a building. He called to Anje in English.

"Come here," he said as he pulled out his wallet and showed her some brightly colored Canadian money. She was very interested in this and looked at it and smiled. She tried with her limited English to understand just what he was trying to say.

Just then a very clear voice in her head said, "Anje, go home." She looked up at the soldier innocently and said, "I have to go home now," and she left. As she walked home, she kept pondering his puzzling request, and finally the light dawned: the soldiers were lonely for female companionship. He was trying to procure her services!

The liberators brought new life to the people of Holland; there was still a lack of food and rubble still lay in the streets of bombed buildings, but now there was hope. When the people accepted the reality that the war was over, jubilation erupted everywhere. People decorated their homes, banners were strung from one side of the street to the other, and victory parties were held in the streets. Anje was so delighted that she took out her camera and photographed Ba Timms wearing a cowboy outfit complete with breeches, hat, and holster—even spurs on his boots! The only thing out of character for a Canadian cowboy was the Netherlands flag he was vigorously waving. One woman was dressed as the Mad Hatter, while Herb Lootens dressed as Abraham Lincoln, with top hat and all! The revelers were waving little flags, singing and dancing and merrymaking. The tricolor flag of their homeland, which had been forbidden for five years, was flown with pride from every building. What a celebration!

The First Canadian Army had liberated the Netherlands! This was the most rewarding part of the Second World War for them. All the battles they had fought were worth the pleasure of seeing the people of the Netherlands enjoying the "sweetest of springs," free from the tyranny of the Nazis.

AFTER THE WAR

Counting the boards in the ceiling of her room upstairs while she lay in bed became the focus of Anje's day. Her motivation carried her to the bathroom and occasionally downstairs to nibble on some morsels of food, but it tasted more and more like cardboard on her tongue. Her books didn't "call out to her" to come and delve into them. She was listless and apathetic, even glad that Jamada was gone because she didn't have to walk him every day. Occasionally she looked out her window into the sky. The planes were all gone now, and she rather missed them. It was as though there was a huge void in her life. Nothing was required of her now. She had taken a great deal of interest in all the types of aircraft she had seen, where they were going, which piece of the war puzzle they fit into. It was challenging and demanding, and she thrived on it. *And we even won the war,* she thought idly, *and it didn't seem to matter.* Her life had always been black and white, and now it was just gray. When she looked down into the street, she could see the local people going about their daily business, but it didn't pique her interest at all.

Working for the Underground and being in a state of constant peril for almost five years had taken a toll on her nerves, and depression had set in. She was still listening for sounds on the street, trying to identify them, and then she realized that it didn't matter. Sometimes she wondered if she had really done all those things. Had she really been forging signatures of the leaders of the German hierarchy? Then she remembered her collection of pens. *I may as well throw them all out. I will never need them again,* she thought wryly. She had walked fearlessly past those guards on the street with contraband under her skirt and had never been questioned. Was that all real? It began to feel so far away. She just wanted to roll over in bed and pull the blankets over her head.

The constant lack of food and relentless cold had broken down her resistance. She didn't want to recall anything of the war. School wasn't an option for her anymore, the love of learning new things had always been important, but it seemed as though she had learned too much about life. She had seen and heard so many things that she now felt old, and she was just sixteen.

Loneliness was her greatest enemy now. No one cared whether she lived or died. No one cared if she had food, love, or companionship. Her father had never been a father to her, and the man whom she loved as a father had died. Her father didn't make any effort to support her. She slept in this bed in this house, but that was all. He didn't seek to engage her in conversation, and there was never a meal provided for her. She crept down to the kitchen and found small morsels of leftovers to carry her over. On one occasion she could hear a noise downstairs and went to see who was there. Father was looking in the kitchen cupboards for something, and he appeared agitated.

"What are you looking for?" she asked him.

"I was going to make myself a cup of tea," he said tersely.

"There isn't any," she replied as she draped her sweater around her and began back upstairs. *What are you thinking?* she said to herself. *There hasn't been real tea in this house for a few years. What planet have you been living on?* Then she remembered that he was spoiled. He was used to getting whatever he wanted. He cared only about himself.

Many tears of bitterness and disappointment flooded into her pillow every day. She had no family with whom she could share mutual love. Mother had been everything to her and now she was gone, and a million tears wouldn't bring her back.

Her thoughts were interrupted by the ringing of the doorbell. She didn't want to answer it. *Why isn't Father home now?* She got up from her bed and looked out of her window to gaze down into the street. Some girls were huddled around the front of the door, and they were talking and laughing. What could they possibly want with her? As she continued to gaze downward, she retreated into the background. She didn't want anyone to see her, for then she would have to answer the door. She noticed someone waving as she looked up toward Anje's window; it was her cousin Sophie! She felt a pang of guilt. Sophie had always been her friend. She shuffled reluctantly to the door.

"Anje!" Sophie exclaimed when she opened the door. "We came to see if you want to come along with us. We're going out to have a little fun!"

Fun? She didn't know the meaning of that word anymore. She couldn't remember when she had some fun. "I don't think so, Sophie," she replied. "I'm sorry. I just don't feel like it."

"Anje, you can't sit at home by yourself. It's not good for you. Come out with us for a while tonight."

There was something in her voice that compelled Anje. At least someone cared about her. She decided to go. "Wait a minute while I comb my hair and get ready."

These girls were determined to have a good time. They were laughing and talking about the new movie that was going to be showing in the theatre and about some of the handsome Canadian soldiers they had encountered. Anje felt her spirits rising; it felt good to be walking down the street with them. When she noticed they were walking down Kalverstraat, she asked, "Where are we going?"

"We're going to the hotel. I hear there's a new band playing there, and we can sit and listen to the music and have something to drink," one suggested.

The hotel was busy. People were checking in and out, the bellboy was carrying suitcases through the lobby, and among the crowd were a number of Allied soldiers still billeted in Groningen making acquaintances and having a good time. Whenever music filled the air, Anje felt at peace; it always had this effect on her. The band music was rousing, and it was playing all the favorite hit songs of the Allies, which the girls heard on the BBC broadcasts. "Auf Wiedersehen" (I'll See You Again) was playing; it was very popular with the soldiers. *Why does it have to be a German song?* Anje thought. *We're trying to forget about the Germans.* The girls began to position themselves at a round table just as the saxophone player began crooning the strains of "As Time Goes By." A few couples began dancing, and then a group of soldiers were becoming boisterous as they joined in singing the lively tune, "Don't Fence Me In," raising their glasses together. She had to admit, the music lifted her spirits, and as she sipped her drink, she thought, *Even the lemonade tasted good!* Sophie drew attention to one tall Canadian soldier in particular. He had been sitting on a tall stool at the counter, his eyes gazing intently at the group of girls who were enjoying themselves at the round table. It appeared he had something on his mind.

"He's looking at you, Anje," one of the girls chirped as she sucked on her straw and grinned. She had barely finished her sentence when the soldier walked toward their table. These soldiers all looked handsome in their uniforms, with a sharp crease in their trousers and their caps sitting jauntily at an angle on their heads. As he approached, he addressed Anje.

"Excuse me," he said politely. "I have been staring at you, and I know that's rude, but you are a dead ringer for my sister Rita back home in Alberta." He extended his hand with a smile. "My name is Brad."

They did not understand until he pulled a picture of his sister out of his pocket. It was true—Anje did resemble her. Since their English was limited, the visit was brief. He admitted he was anxious to get back to Canada, for he had been away for more than a year and was lonesome for home.

That struck a resonant chord within Anje. She thought, *I know how you feel. I'm lonesome for home too, the way it used to be.* At least he could go back to his home and family, but for her, it would never be.

"Come on, Brad," a soldier called out, motioning for him to join them.

"Look, Anje," one of the girls said. "There's the Rotterdammer."

"The Rotterdammer?" Anje said in disbelief. "Are you sure?"

"Yes, I'm sure," she replied, and just then the man spoke. That wonderful, resonant voice confirmed that this was the mystery man whose marvelous voice they heard on the BBC News, Radio Orange, and he was not tall, dark, and handsome. He was short, bald, and fat.

What a disappointment, Anje thought. Just then she noticed the Dutch police moving about the room, checking the identification of each person. *Another control,* she mused. The required age to be on the premises was eighteen, and she was only sixteen. Three of the girls were twenty-one, and one was nineteen. She decided to relax since she had been in situations like this before.

"Could I see your identification please?" the officer asked Sophie. After examining it, he continued on to the next and the next, down the row, until it was Anje's turn. He paused for a moment, his face breaking into a smile. "I don't have to see yours. You have an honest face!" She smiled slightly. If he only knew! An honest face? Perhaps this face had saved her many times for she had never been asked to show her ID even once during the war. Now she realized her honest face had been a godsend.

"Anje, if you are not going back to school, then you will have to get a job," Father had said during one of their rare conversations. Many days went by without any communication from either of them; at best, they tolerated each other.

"I want to be a nurse," she offered haltingly.

"You can go to business college and learn to be a stenographer," he said matter-of-factly, as though he hadn't heard her speak.

"I don't want to go to business school," she protested. "I want to be a nurse."

"I will make the necessary arrangements to enroll you in business college," he said curtly.

She was quiet. It was no use to object. Father always had things his way, and he would not help her become a nurse. She would have to go to business college. She didn't enjoy her training in school, but she knew she it was a requirement to find a good job. There were not many jobs available after the war because the country needed to resurrect itself from the grave. The land that had produced so abundantly needed to be reclaimed from the salt water that had flooded over it when the dikes were opened. In order for industry to flourish, rail lines need to be rebuilt for the import of raw materials, and many bridges and roads required reconstruction. Holland needed reconstruction, and, Anje realized, so did she. She completed her course with excellence. No one attended her graduation ceremony, but as she held the diploma in her hand, she left with a feeling of accomplishment.

Anje usually picked up the mail when she returned home from work, and as her hand reached into the mailbox for the house key, she found a letter inside, addressed to her. What was this? When she opened it, she discovered a letter from a lawyer that included a copy of Uncle Hans's will. She was the sole heir to his possessions, which were stored at the La Costas' and the law office. She was requested to come and identify herself to the lawyer. Father read the letter carefully, raising his eyebrows, and then he folded the letter, putting it in his pocket. "You are under age," he said. "I will have to take care of this for you."

The La Costas' business owned a large space, and they had agreed to store Hans's property that the Nazis had not destroyed until it was needed. The remainder of the goods, including a metal box, were given to Anje. Martha took her aside and whispered, "Hans wanted me to tell you that the key for that metal box is at the lawyer's office. Take care of it, for it is valuable."

The old, strong box made of a thick metal was now aged a rusty brown. It had a keyhole in front and a nicely shaped handle that required a firm grip. The six-inch by nine-inch by four-inch size was just right for carrying the important documents that had been placed inside. When she turned the key in the hole, the lid opened. Anje recognized the value of its contents—thousands of dollars of stocks and bonds that Uncle Hans had purchased. She paused and thought for a moment, and then she decided to lock the box, hanging the key on a chain around her neck. Where should she keep this box of valuables? She decided on the most common place people hid their belongings—she put it under her bed.

She was curious about the other items Uncle Hans had kept. *They must have been important to him,* she thought. *Otherwise he wouldn't have saved them.* She pulled on some chains to separate the items from each other. What was this? Dangling on this watch chain was a small, round portrait in a convex frame of Uncle Hans as a child, and when she turned it over, the other side of this tiny frame held a photo of his older brother. Hans's father had been a railroad man, and he had kept this memento of his two sons hanging on his keychain. His father's gold pocket watch hung from another set of unique chains. She flipped the back open to observe the crude engraving of his father's name, and as she snapped it shut, she wondered how many times the watch had been used to estimate the arrival of a train, or a village, while this man was on duty. Among the items was also a small, flat, metal box with a photo of the Martini Tower on the front, but the item that piqued her interest the most was a tiny, colorful box that looked like satin. She cupped it in her hands, and when she lifted the lid, she found that it contained some rings. One was a gold sapphire shaped setting that held a pink stone, and she knew it had belonged to Eva, Uncle Hans's mother; and the plain gold wedding bands belonged to Herman and Janette Wolff. When she closed her eyes, she could picture them coming to Uncle Hans, asking him to keep the rings until they returned.

The next ring of the doorbell was a surprise. Two uniformed police officers stood at attention at the door. They came as a result of a complaint against Anje Minnes.

"What kind of complaint?" she asked. They looked at each other and declared, "Prostitution!" Looking at them with a puzzled look on her face, she asked, "What is that?"

It was their turn to look puzzled. Did she really not understand the meaning of the word prostitution? They did not expect to have to explain it to her, but they did. When they continued the query, she informed them that she worked at the Bank of Rotterdam. They left, and Anje was certain they would not return. She was surprised when she received another call from them that followed a different line of questioning, and she became disgusted with the police officers. Finally she asked, "Who is making these charges against me?"

"We cannot tell you that. It's confidential," they responded in unison.

She began to see the reasoning behind this and explained, "It's my father, isn't it? He wants to get rid of me—send me to jail or to a mental institution because he wants my inheritance." After describing the situation to them in detail, they left the house, shaking their heads.

"Uncle Martijn, you'll have to help me," she exclaimed when she went to see him. She trusted Uncle Martijn; she knew her mother and siblings had been raised in a good home. Their father had been a policeman and instilled a sense of fairness and of right and wrong in them. Anje had always seen this quality in her mother. When she finished telling him her story, including the way her father had mistreated her, he was aghast.

"Anje," he said to her kindly, "in order to settle this, we will have to go to court. You don't have to come to court, though. I'll take care of it for you." And he did.

The court procedures were not long, and after the hearing, the judge removed Jan's parental rights over his daughter. He no longer had custody of her.

Anje lay on her bed, tired from thinking about the events of the day. As she rubbed her eyes, contemplating a rest, she began thinking about the strong box under her bed and reached down to retrieve it. When she grabbed the handle, to her surprise, the lid lifted. The lock had been forced open! When she looked inside, the box was empty. Her heart sank. She hung her head in disbelief. *Is this really possible? Would Father actually do this to me?* Inside her, she already knew that her father had stolen her inheritance.

She was furious, but what could she do about it? How could she prove it? Father had lied about her in court, accusing her of terrible things that she had never done, and she got to hear about it. Yes, she was tired of his dreadful ways, yet what was the solution? She didn't want to go through another emotional court experience. She didn't want to broadcast to the whole world how awful he was because she was so ashamed to call this man her father. He was a thief and a liar, and she could not trust or respect him, but he was still her father, and she had no other place to live.

When Father came home, she did not speak to him about the matter, but she brought the strong box from her bedroom and set it in plain view in the kitchen. Every time he glanced at her, she glared at him with a look that pierced right through him. Her expression said, *I know what you did.* She was glad for one thing—she was glad that Mother was not here to see how low this man would stoop for money.

She was standing in line at the store when she saw a familiar face. It was Peter, whom she knew from the Underground. Peter was one of the agents who helped in the "butter raid" as it became known. There was a still a certain camaraderie that the Resistance workers felt for each other. They would still accommodate one another if needed. After they had exchanged greetings, he nodded his head toward the door and said, "When you're all finished here, I'd like to talk to you for a minute."

She nodded.

He was waiting outside, smoking a cigarette as he leaned against the wall. His baggy pants and threadbare shoes still showed the aftermath of the war. "I was sorry to hear about your mother," he said sympathetically. "We all were. She was a great woman."

Anje knew this was an extreme compliment, one acknowledging the other's sacrifice.

"Where are you living now?" he asked as he exhaled smoke from his mouth.

"At home with my father," she replied.

"Anje, someone in the Underground told me something I think you should know."

Anje almost smiled. They were still in that mode of "someone told me," meaning if you were a Resistance worker, you never divulged names. "Continue," she said.

"This person saw your father receiving money from the Nazis for providing information to them." He looked at her with pity as he continued, "He took money from them in exchange for information about your mother. He was the betrayer."

Anje suspected this all along, but she until now she had no real proof. She nodded, "I suspected that, but now I know. Thank you for telling me." She was not surprised. This felt like old news to her. She had been quite certain Father was the betrayer, but she did not know he had been paid for his services. Now she knew for sure, and it cut like a knife inside her.

The whirlwind of emotions inside her was like a hurricane twisting out of control. She always knew Father was capable of doing evil things, but the fact that someone confirmed to her that he had betrayed his own wife for money burned a hole inside her that was so painful, it was beyond description. It did not invoke fury or anger—she was past that point—but in their place were feelings of hopelessness. Thoughts of suicide surfaced many times; she was listless, and the desperation of her situation loomed over her. She thought everything would go well when the war was over, but now she was engaged in another war—a war with her father. She was tired of fighting with him; she was tired of everything. As she walked into the house in the early evening, she made a decision: this day would be her last. *Will anyone miss me if I'm gone?* She didn't think so. She walked toward the gas stove and thought, *This will be painless. I will just fall asleep and never wake up. What will happen to me after that? I don't know. Will I go to hell if I do this? I don't care. I have already suffered so much pain that it feels like I have already been there!* When she decided to turn the switch of the gas stove on, a strong thought came into her head:

Don't do that! She stopped for a moment to think and decided to wait.

As she lay in bed that night, a thousand anguished thoughts rolled through her head. Should she, or shouldn't she? Loneliness had wrapped its tentacles around her, and they were squeezing her to death. All she felt was hopelessness. She couldn't see any way out. Her life with Father and the Frau was so unbearable that she didn't feel like getting out of bed in the morning; she didn't care if the sun was shining, she wasn't really hungry, and she didn't want to see anybody. Father had left her alone at Christmas battling hunger while he went to his relatives to enjoy himself. Big tears rolled down her cheeks as she recalled that day when everyone was celebrating with their families, and she was alone. Because she had worked for the Underground, many people, including her relatives, were afraid to associate with her, even Aunt Dolly. She thought of all the times Mother had climbed on her bicycle and rode across town to take them food during the hardest of times, but this was all forgotten in the aftermath. Now she felt shunned and neglected. The sense of loss was overwhelming. Most of her friends were gone, and Mother and Oma, who had cared for her, were no longer there to support her. Mother and Uncle Hans were dead, and Father had betrayed their family to the Gestapo. Her hatred included the Germans, for they had destroyed her happy life.

Amid the clamor of all her thoughts, a loud, audible, male voice declared to her in Dutch, **"I am the Judge!"** She sat upright in bed and looked around. Who was in her room? She saw no one, but someone was there, and that someone was invisible! A revelation flooded her being:

Someone else is going to take care of this. You don't have to worry about it anymore. All the things that cried out inside her, "It's not fair!" would be taken care of by the Righteous Judge one day. With that understanding, the cares that gripped her rolled off of her like a blanket, and she was free! She felt so light! She had forgotten what true freedom felt like. At last, she was free from bitterness, hatred, cynicism, anger, resentment, and the desire for retaliation. It was all gone! Peace settled over her being, soothing her and bringing great comfort to her soul, and she quickly fell asleep.

1946

It was an uneventful day on July 5, 1946. Her shoes clicked as she walked along the sidewalk on her way home from work. She was deeply engrossed in her own thoughts when she became aware of someone pulling along-side on his bicycle. He slowed down to match her pace, and this gregarious young man began to talk to her animatedly. He had one foot on the pedal of his bike and one foot on the sidewalk as he coasted along. "Nice day, isn't it?" he asked. She decided to ignore him, but he kept on talking. "Where are you going? Do you live around here? Where do you work?" He was an endless stream of questions, and Anje was sure that if she just ignored him, he would go away! But he didn't. Realizing that he wasn't going to get any answers from her, he began talking about himself and what he was doing while she continued to walk down Achterweg toward home. In a matter of minutes, they were travelling down Rabenhauptstraat and then were standing in front of her house. She stopped.

"Is this where you live?" he asked. She nodded. "Can I come and see you again?" She didn't commit herself, but when Saturday arrived, he was on her front doorstep.

"Come on," he said, "Let's go over to my cousin's place." As they talked, she discovered that his name was Dirk van Tongeren, he was one week away from his nineteenth birthday, he loved to tinker with cars, and he worked as a mechanic in a garage. When they arrived at his cousin's, she learned that Dirk was the operator of a movie projector. His friends, Ernie and Josephine Speelman, owned a sound system and traveled about showing films on Saturday and Sunday, providing affordable entertainment and recreation in people's homes. Often they found the entire hallway filled with wooden shoes when they arrived!

Anje decided she rather liked this young man. He was humorous, ambitious, and interesting to listen to, and he buoyed up her spirits. At five foot nine, with dark hair, hazel eyes, and a ready smile, he was quite handsome.

Anje's father disliked Dirk and considered him not good enough for his daughter because he was just a mechanic. He continually made unfavorable comments to Anje, and even Frau Nienhuis was verbal about this relationship. *You can just be quiet,* Anje thought. *You have no authority in this household.* But the Frau always seemed to be underfoot as though she was looking for something negative to relate to Jan.

Dirk loved to talk, and he told her about his own experience with the Germans. He had been one of the young men required to build tank falls (traps) in the locations the Nazis were sure the Allies would attempt to enter the Netherlands. They were also commandeered to dig trenches so the German soldiers could move from place to place without being seen, thus avoiding a sniper's bullet. The German soldier who was the overseer of the project told them he was just a farm boy and was eager to get back home. He had to teach these city boys how to dig. "He asked us to hold his rifle while he wielded the shovel," Dirk said with a smile. "We got to like him. When he told us the next day a truck would come to bring us to work in Germany, I played sick and stayed home. Later, I found out that the group on that truck had been taken to Germany to work in a munitions factory. I wouldn't be here today if I had gone."

The strong winds that blew from the cold North Sea over the land indicated that winter was on its way. Temperatures fell below freezing, turning the rain into sleet, and the streets became slippery from the icy conditions. Anje did not look forward to Christmas, for this occasion did not hold happy memories for her. In spite of that, December arrived.

One morning, she awoke with a fever and a splitting headache, She remembered that she had promised to take Dirk's little brother skating but now she realized that would not be possible. She managed to get downstairs and telephone the doctor from the telephone in the café, and when he heard her symptoms, he made a house call.

"Chicken pox," he said as he pushed his glasses up on his face. "Stay in bed and rest until the symptoms are gone."

As Anje lay in her bed, she inspected the pox that had by now had begun to appear on her body. They were the thickest in her hair. It was December 23, and her fever was not letting up. How she hated the thought of being alone again at Christmas. When Christmas Day arrived, she decided when she hopped out of bed that she was not staying home; she would go be with Dirk's family for Christmas. She pulled on her boots and went out the door into the cold, blustery weather. Dirk greeted her at the door with a hug. There was no time to be alone, but his sparkling eyes were always on her, and his arm around her shoulder showed everyone who she belonged to. It was wonderful to be loved and accepted. This was the greatest gift.

"I was here on Christmas Day to see you, and you were not at home. Where were you?" the doctor asked indignantly.

"I went to my boyfriend's place—" she began, but he interrupted her.

"You walked outside in this winter weather, across town? You could have died!"

She knew she was supposed to feel some remorse, but she didn't. The freedom and enjoyment she had at Christmas was worth the tongue-lashing.

Anje looked at the calendar on the wall in her bedroom; the year was coming to a close. What a year it had been! Her thoughts went back as she recalled New Year's Day, 1944, when Mother had changed the calendar saying, "I wonder what the New Year will bring?" Now the same thoughts rolled through her mind. *What will 1947 bring for me?*

Another surprise awaited Anje. Early in 1947, she had an unexpected visitor. Janie Van Brunt appeared at her door one day. She was about the same age as Anje, with blonde hair and blue eyes. She gave the appearance of being older than her years. *That is the effect a concentration camp has on you if you survive,* Anje thought.

"Your mother asked me to contact you when I got out," she said slowly, as though she didn't know where to begin. "We were confined together in Ravensbrück." As Janie looked at her hands with her head bowed, Anje understood her dilemma. How do you speak of something so surreal and evil in a casual conversation? They didn't. All they engaged in was small talk, and before she left, she said, "Your mother was very kind to me in prison, Anje. She even gave me her last piece of bread."

Anje nodded. That was typical of her mother.

When the concentration camp was emptied and the inmates liberated, Janie was among the group of people the Red Cross transported to Sweden. Janie married and remained in Gertaborg, Sweden.

A NEW START

In Dirk, Anje had a good friend and confidant, one with whom she could share life's problems. When Anje told him about her home life, he could not imagine that a father could treat his daughter as Jan did, and he encouraged Anje to leave her father's place and come and stay with his stepparents at the Mulder home.

Other changes came, as Sophie encouraged Anje to come and work at a sheet metal works where she was employed so they could be together. She proved to her father that she could get a job on her own.

Dirk's and Anje's work schedules often conflicted so they couldn't spend much time together, but on April 6, 1947, Dirk surprised Anje with an engagement ring. She was delighted, but the joy of that occasion was overshadowed by the knowledge that, in the Netherlands, a couple needed the parent's consent to get married until the age of thirty-one! Anje knew her father would not give consent willingly, and his signature was still required on the documents. They would have to appear before a judge to get permission to forgo the parent's signature, and they didn't want to complicate their plans. Should they go to England to get married? How would they solve this?

Jan had ignored Anje most of her life, but now he was determined to take control of the situation and exert his authority. He appeared unannounced at the Mulder home, making a great noise and fuss in demanding that Anje come home to live. His request was refused. Anje was not returning to live under her father's roof and domination; he had lost the battle at last.

Five years passed, and there still was no solution. Anje was apprehensive, Would she have to wait until she was thirty-one to be married? They needed help, and it was provided by Dirk's stepfather, who took the parental consent forms and visited Jan. After a great deal of discussion, Jan still stubbornly refused to sign the papers. In exasperation, Mr. Mulder threatened to beat him if he wouldn't cooperate! Finally, he signed.

It was 1952, and housing was extremely hard to find. Dirk and Anje kept searching for a place to live, wondering when they would be able to get married. Suddenly a house became available with a two-week possession date, and they hastily planned their wedding. Anje could hardly believe it; finally her dreams were going to come true. The long-anticipated day came on November 22, 1952. Uncle Martijn gave Anje away, and she looked lovely in her white lace wedding gown. Her father did not come. Cousin Sophie and her husband, Renus, were the only relatives from her side of the family who attended. Dirk's friends and relatives were many. Amid all the joy and celebration, Anje could not push out traces of anxiety, wondering if her father had plans to ruin this day, but her fears were unfounded. It did not happen.

With Holland recovering from the war, many young folks felt there was no future for them in the Netherlands, and Dirk and Anje were among them. They began looking for a place to emigrate to, their options being Canada, Australia, or Africa. They submitted their names and began the process by getting passports, clearing immigration and health examinations. They were relieved when they received a letter saying that Canada had an opening for them. All they needed were 60 guilders and valid Dutch passports. They were excited as they boarded the *Rijdam* steamship in Southampton, England. On October 23, 1953, they headed for a new land and a new life.

VOYAGE TO A NEW LAND

The rough seas on the eight-day journey to Canada were symbolic of the final chapters of Anje's life in Holland. This was their first ocean voyage, so they didn't know what to expect. Their cabin was in the back end of the ship in the center section, so there was no window; and the constant hum of the engines reminded them that they were right above them. It was quite an adventure for them is spite of the fact that the sea was rough most of the time. Anje loved the luxury of having restaurants, a bar, and places to play board games nearby. She and Dirk lounged about on the deck and enjoyed being served by stewards.

There were many flights of stairs for the two of them to climb in the ship to get to the dining floor. The food was excellent, but few arrived to enjoy it because so many were seasick. Even though the tables and chairs were bolted into place, there was a great clatter in the dining room from the dishes that slid off the table and smashed as the sea rolled and swelled. The waves were very high; it seemed the ship rose and fell thirty feet, and when they had enough of the heaving of the vessel, they went to the middle of the ship where it was more stable. One evening after they had retired to their cabins, Anje was a little alarmed when she heard the sound of water sloshing. "What do you think it is?" she asked Dirk. When they opened the cabin door to see where the water was coming in, they discovered shoes floating past on a stream of water! Someone had forgotten to close the storm doors, and the Americans who had placed their nice shoes outside their door at night to be polished, found them floating in the hall.

Being in the rear of the ship was kind of scary in the rough seas, and it had its surprises. One morning while Dirk was shaving, the ship lurched, and he went flying across the room! Another time Dirk had just showered and had put on clean pajamas when the ship rose suddenly. He grabbed the shower handle to steady himself and accidentally turned the water on, drenching him! He came out of the shower looking like a soaked cat in a rainstorm. He was not happy with Anje, who could not stop laughing at his misadventure.

By the time the *Rijdam* arrived in Halifax harbor, the ship was listing to one side as the luggage and cargo had shifted from the rough seas. When they disembarked and cleared customs, it was October 31, 1953, Halloween night. This was not a celebration day in Holland, and they didn't know what it represented. Seeing people walking around in strange costumes made them wonder what kind of a funny country they had come to.

A group of six travelers decided to stick together, and they found their way to the train station, their first destination being Montreal. They were so excited when they got on the train that they couldn't sleep. Others around them were trying to sleep, but Anje kept thinking about those funny costumes she had seen and the excitement of being in Canada, and she was a little giddy. The conductor came by and said, "Tickets please!" Dirk replied, "Sure," a popular English word they knew.

When they got to Montreal, they had to change trains. Some women in the train station were nursing their babies in the open with no blanket over them, and Anje was appalled. *For shame!* she thought. *We would never see a sight like this in Holland.* By then, they were very hungry, so they found a restaurant only to discover that the waitress couldn't understand them. They wanted potatoes, vegetables, and meat, but the waitress just shrugged her shoulders and walked away. A man sitting on a stool in the bar overheard this conversation, and he came over to them and asked, "Are you Dutch?"

"Yes, we are," Dirk replied.

"Just a moment," he said as he walked over to the waitress. They didn't know what he said, but her face turned red and she hurried to the kitchen to order their food.

He came back to their table and apologized. "She didn't want to serve you because she is going off duty in ten minutes," he explained. *What a strange country!* Anje thought.

The wooden benches in economy class on the train were very hard, and the passenger car was dirty with litter strewn about, but they settled in to play a game of cards. Just then the conductor came and asked them to follow him into a much nicer car, and the lady who occupied it was quite unhappy. She told him she had paid extra to have coach class, and she didn't want them there. The noise in another coach attracted their attention, and they went to check it out. Another ship had come in, and the conductor moved a group of rowdy Italians into the seats they had just vacated. They were excited to be in Canada and were friendly, but the Dutch folk couldn't understand a word that was said.

Dirk and Anje were exhausted by the time they boarded the train for Winnipeg. They had spent eight days on the ship and two days on the train, and they still another two to go. They enjoyed watching the beautiful countryside fly past the window all along the way and were impressed with the size; Canada was a big country! When they arrived in Winnipeg, they said good-bye to their friends, who continued on to Edmonton, Alberta.

When they climbed down off the train, the first person they met was a priest, who approached and asked them, "Are you Catholic?"

They shook their heads to say no.

He was gracious enough to help them anyway by putting them into a taxi and instructing the driver to take them to the immigration building on Higgins Avenue. Every time the taxi came to a corner, the driver turned and flipped the door open for them, asking, "Is this where you want to get off?" There were no street signs, and they didn't know where they were, so finally, he took them to the Immigration Hall. They were given two iron beds to sleep in, and since they never slept alone, they pushed the beds together.

In the morning, Dirk had to report to a wicket, and in his broken English, he explained to the person behind it that he wanted a job. The hall had a high ceiling, and many people were huddled around crying; it was very noisy. Many people wanted to go back home. There were no jobs because they didn't want to work outside of the city of Winnipeg. Dirk went from one booth to the next, asking for a job, and when they asked him, "Will you work outside of Winnipeg?" he said, "Sure!" That was no problem to him—a job was a job.

Olafsons owned a garage in Birtle, Manitoba, and they were looking for a mechanic, and he was asked if he wanted the job. He said, "Sure." That afternoon, he and Anje got on the bus to Birtle and told the bus driver to let them know when they got there. They drove and drove and drove. It felt like they had driven right across Holland; they weren't used to such long distances, coming from a tiny country. It was dark and there were no lights anywhere along the way. They looked at each other and asked, "Where are all the people?"

At Minnedosa, the bus stopped and everyone got out; they didn't know why. They found out it was a lunch stop, so Dirk bought a couple of chocolate bars. Finally, at 9:20 p.m., the bus dropped them off in a dark town, and nobody was there to meet them. They were very tired, but they started walking to see if they could find the garage where Dirk was supposed to work. In Europe, most people lived above their businesses, so they were surprised when they found the garage but there were no living quarters above it. Then when they saw a sign that said, "Restroom," they thought, *Good! We need a place to rest.* They were disappointed to discover it was a bathroom! Finally, they were brave enough to knock on someone's door and ask for help. A man came to the door and asked, "Can I help you?"

When Dirk mentioned the name Olafson, the man knew from their speech that they were Dutch. "Just a minute!" he said, and he put on his coat and walked them over to the Olafson's place. They were very happy to see Dirk and Anje. Their son had gone to meet the bus, but since the bus had arrived late, he had left, thinking it had already come and gone.

They sat down to talk and began to compare the cost of things in Canada and Holland. It was very confusing to Anje because all she knew were individual words she had read in the dictionary; she didn't know how to put them together in a sentence. She had a little English-Dutch dictionary with her, but she couldn't look up the words fast enough!

Olafson was Icelandic, and he spoke with a pipe hanging out the side of his mouth, making it very hard to understand what he was saying. His wife was a nurse, their oldest daughter had polio, and they had a son and a young daughter who was full of questions! They gave them an Eaton's catalog to study to help them learn the English language. They were so tired and hungry that Dirk fell asleep, but Anje forced herself to stay awake. It was after 12:30 a.m. when Mrs. Olafson got around to making some lunch for them. Anje couldn't remember what they ate, but when they were finished, she was still hungry from their journey. Finally, Mrs. Olafson drove them to a hotel, where they got a room and at last could rest.

Their hotel room was small, and there was a chain on the door for security. They were surprised when there was a knock at the door. When Anje opened it just a crack, she saw the hotel manager, who was in a tipsy state, ask, "Do you wanna drink?"

"No," Anje said. "No!" And she quickly closed the door.

Dirk and Anje were getting ready for bed when they noticed a hot air register just above their bed with heat pouring out of it. People in Holland did not heat their bedrooms; it was always cold enough for water to freeze solid! They tried to open the window, but it had a storm window on it with three tiny round holes for air. How strange! They hadn't seen anything like this before. They lay on top of the blankets all night trying to stay cool.

Dirk started work the next morning, and he only had twenty-five cents left in his pocket so he ordered coffee and two slices of toast. He ate one slice and left the other one for Anje. She didn't dare go out of the room for fear somebody would talk to her and she wouldn't be able to understand them. She was very shy. At noon, Dirk came to the hotel and brought a man with him whose name was Doug. He was going to work in Victoria, British Columbia, and his wife Lois was going to Brandon to stay with their oldest son, who was in an iron lung because he had contacted polio. They needed someone to stay at their farm, so they offered Anje and Dirk a place to live. They accepted. They stayed with them for a while and it was helpful, as they helped them to learn some English.

Anje, upon her arrival in Manitoba, Canada.

The basement in Doug and Lois's house had a furnace that burned large tree stumps, and a big pile of wood sat stacked along the fence outside. Being a city girl, Anje was scared stiff to put so much wood in the furnace. What if she burned the house down? So she waited until Dirk got home from work, and by then the fire was almost out and the house was getting cold.

Dirk was busy, so Anje decided to load the wheel-barrow with wood and began pushing it to the house through the opening in the fence. But her enemy was watching her! When she was halfway to the house, geese came after her, honking and flapping their wings. They chased her toward the fence, and boy, could they run!

So could she! She dropped the wheelbarrow and began running at top speed, just managing to jump over the fence before they caught her. They were big birds, and she had been told that they could break her arm with their strong wings. Here she was, the girl who had outsmarted the Nazis many times, but she could not outsmart those geese no matter how hard she tried.

They were always learning new things. Lois asked Dirk to pick up a dozen eggs from a farmer on his way home, and she gave him a small, oblong apple basket and twenty-five cents. Dirk was puzzled. He asked Anje how he could he get a thousand eggs into that little basket. That's when we learned that dozen in English and *thousand* in Dutch sounded very similar, at least to their ears!

One of their neighbors came over one day and told Anje to dress up in her best outfit because they were going somewhere, and it was a surprise. Eighty people had arrived at this place to throw a surprise shower for Anje and Dirk. They were overwhelmed! They received a lot of nice things. Anje's dishes had broken when traveling overseas, so she needed some. Everything she required for a kitchen was supplied, plus a lot of canned goods. She just couldn't get up and say thank you because she was too shy. But she stood beside her husband while he said it; he was never shy.

In spring Doug and Lois returned to their house, and Dirk and Anje moved into a cheap little house on the hill that had a leaky roof. It had a living room and two empty rooms for bedrooms, as well as a kitchen with no cupboards or stove. They bought a little hot plate, but it was not easy to cook meals on it. More and more people moved from

Holland, and they liked to live on farms. Somehow they all ended up at Dirk and Anje's place at some point, and she cooked for all of them on that little hot plate.

They had an outdoor toilet like most other folks, and Anje dreaded going out there in the dark by herself. She was afraid of the wolves and bears that she had heard lived in Canada. Dirk was working late one night and she needed to use the outhouse, so she took a run at it, sat down, and jumped up real fast. What a rude awakening—she had sat down on a foot of snow! When Dirk came home, she said, "That's it! We are getting an indoor toilet."

They moved into another house that they shared with Donnie and Elaine Black and became very good friends with them. Elaine taught Anje to bake pies, cake, and cookies. But Anje had a problem learning to roll out pie dough because it kept sticking to the rolling pin. One day she lost her patience with that pie dough and threw the rolling pin across the room! Eventually she learned to handle pastry and a rolling pin. In Holland, they didn't have stoves with an oven and couldn't afford to bake since ingredients were too expensive. On special occasions, they went to the fancy bakery and bought something. It was a great learning process for her to learn the names of ingredients in English; she had to identify them by smell.

She was very interested in going to church but was told a lady had to wear a hat in church. She didn't have a hat and couldn't spend grocery money to buy one, so she asked her neighbor, "Couldn't I just wear a scarf or shawl on my head like the Catholics do?"

"No," she said, "it has to be a hat." So she couldn't go to church, at least not until she could afford a hat.

She learned English from reading the comics *Blondie* and *Popeye*. Dirk had to learn all new words also because in every sentence he was using the word *bloody* until she told him that wasn't a proper English word! A bonnet became a hood, and a silencer was now called a muffler. Slowly they learned.

Every Wednesday afternoon was Dick's day off—by now everyone was calling him Dick, so it stuck. One day off, they went to the nuisance grounds to strip parts from old vehicles, and Dick began to build them a car from scratch. By the time he was finished with all the body work, they had a very jazzy four-seater, Ford Model T! Not only could they get around, but when they pulled the seats out, they could even sleep in it!

Dick's English was improving daily. He listened closely to what everyone was saying so he could learn more of the English language, and sometimes those words he heard others use were not entirely appropriate!

They moved to Rivers, Manitoba, when a new job became available. On Christmas Eve, 1956, a group of friends decided to go from house to house singing Christmas carols and wishing people a Merry Christmas and a Happy New Year. It was a lovely night, the sky was clear, and the snow crunched under their feet as they walked. They ended up at a home where they were invited to come in, and they began talking about the war. Noticing their accent, the man asked if they were Dutch and which part of Holland they were from. When Anje told him they were from Groningen, Holland, he began to cry. He had memories of the war also. As he sat at his table weeping, he haltingly told them about his buddies, who were among the twenty-two young

Canadian soldiers who had died when their tank was blown up in Groningen during liberation.

As he wiped his eyes, he asked, "What street did you live on?"

"Rabenhauptstraat," Anje replied.

She would never forget his next words.

"I was one of the Cape Breton Highlanders that liberated Rabenhauptstraat in Groningen on April 16, 1945." She was overwhelmed. Eleven years later, forty-two hundred miles from home, she was standing in the presence of her liberator!

AN ENQUIRY

The following is a letter penned by Hillie's mother,
as signed H. Stutvoet-Veentjer, a loving mother and
grandmother who wanted some clarification and
closure regarding the disappearance of her daughter.
This is the English translation.

I n response to your letter dated August 26, I am yet able
to inform you concerning the following.

My daughter, Hillechiena H. Minnes-Stutvoet, at
the time living on Rabenhaupt Str. 78A Groningen, and I
myself lived there with her, worked together with the civil
servant, the late Henk v.d. Veen from Haren, and was in
the group of P. Brons here.

The 1st SD invasion (raid) at her house took place May

2nd,'44. No evidence (single proof) fell in the hands of the SD that time. Her spouse, J. Minnes, who was not involved in any illegal activity, and the earlier mentioned Henk v.d. Veen who had temporarily gone into hiding there, were nevertheless both picked up.

Sometime later my daughter moved to an address in Haren near Groningen, after being warned by the police— just to be on the safe side.

After her husband in Amersfoort suddenly was released, she too, with her 15 years old daughter, went home to Rabenhaupt Str. for the sake of the family tie (connection) whereby she yet again was taking a great risk.

Indeed, 1 day thereafter, on July 2nd 1944, invasion (raid) no. 2 took place—without doubt its purpose was the arrest—whereby then my daughter, and also her husband and even her child were taken away. The latter two were soon set free, but I have never seen my daughter again. She was, after some time, transported (transferred) to Vught, where also the earlier mentioned Henk v.d.Veen was present. The latter executed on Aug.22nd, 1944, while my daughter, with the advancement of the Allies, on 8/9 (Sept.) 1944 was sent from Vught to Ravensbrück, after which via the S.D. here the news came of her passing away in Jan. 1945.

It still leaves me to inform you about the cause behind the arrest. This is a very thorny affair. Their family, Mr. and Mrs. Tamboer and D. Tamboer-Minnes were N.S.B.ers and pro-German, through and through, who even would have given their (Dutch) East Indian pension to see Groninger's blood flowing through the streets (I Quote!). They had a strong suspicion about my daughter's part in the resistance (movement), and also of the presence of previously mentioned Henk v/d Veen who was there in hiding. Now and again (then) they came to visit to size up the situation—the last time an altercation took place, in which the N.S.B-ster (fem.) let it slip out, "We will surely get you, and you will remember me!" Sometime later the first raid (invasion) took place, and the only chance of escape was located! (That chance unfortunately could not be used, because the daughter of the house opened too quickly the outside door after the doorbell rang.)

I have concerning all the above mentioned (events) after the liberation repeatedly tried to get into contact with the police here, but was time after time turned away with empty promises, and never is from the side of the police this concern seriously treated.

Moreoever, it should be mentioned, that this family Tamboer at several occasions their home available made to the notorious Groninger, SD.er "Keyer," who from their residence could spy on particular houses, and thus was able to seize (catch) 3 people in hiding, of which 2 never did come back. The fact that they made their home available has even been told by "Keyer" himself to a storekeeper he befriended, where also the "knokploeg" leader Jan Brons every evening came.

As last point of betrayal, I still will mention the "caving in" of the team leader (squad leader?), namely the above mentioned Jan Brons, who by a confrontation with my daughter at the notorious (ill famed) Scholten-huis has said that she should just confess everything. He too has never been punished.

Hoping that with the above, you have been informed to your satisfaction, I remain

Respectfully,

H. Stutvoet–Veentjer

P.S. Meanwhile, moved to: c/o New Boteringestraat 80C (Wid. H. Stutvoet- Veentjeer)

P.S. Due to illness, I was not able to thank you on a previous occasion for the sending of the memorial book, "Resisting (opposing) the enemy." To my address, and at this time I am doing that, requesting you to please excuse my negligence.

Would you also inform me, in due time, whether the later published book-volumes you advertised, will also be made available in cheaper (reduced) editions?

Reading carefully what I have told, the thought probably has entered your mind that there were also obscure (dark) circumstances concerning the release of her husband, who on a Friday out of Amersfoort was discharged, stayed with the family in Utrecht, and then on Monday arrived at home; while my daughter went straight home from her hiding address, and thereafter the following morning, on Tuesday July 2nd, the S.D. already turned up and proceeded to arrest them. At the same time be it noted sub rosa (under the rose: Lat. Expr.- in secret, in trust) that the executed Henk v.d.Veen had hidden between 12–15 thousand (guilders) in a canister at the house of my daughter—this was known to all of us—thus also to her husband. The content of the canister was during the imprisonment of v.d.Veen in writing earmarked for the child of my daughter, Annie

Minnes; and this written legacy (bequest) was also after the liberation declared to be legally valid; however, approx. 10,000 guilders was stolen by my son-in-law, and thereafter is the canister, with the remaining 4,000 guilders, handed over by him to a notary.

Do you still see a small chance, with reference to the enclosed information, that there still some justice (right) will come about?

This plaque is all the remains of the House of Blood and Tears.
The translation of the inscription is:

Scholtenhuis 1940-1945
Here stood the house of Nazism
Of the swastika and SS.
Here they gave Germanic lessons
In gruesome sadism.
Here those who have fought for freedom
Suffered inhumanely.

AFTERWORD

Fifty-oneyears after the war, Anje began to tell the story she had hidden inside her when she read a story by Jeris Cribbs on Auschwitz in the Elijah List magazine which said, "There comes a time where silence becomes betrayal." She began to speak at women's groups, at schools, and in a synagogue, once she discovered that she could finally talk about her life without crying.

In June 2010, Joanne van Tongeren found Ernst Wolff's son Jair on Facebook, and on June 26, 2010, this author had a response from an email to Jair saying, "My dad is indeed Ernst Wolff, he is eighty-six years old, and lives near Haifa, Israel, with his wife Rivka." Anje always knew that if she found a member of the Wolff family, she would give Herman and Janette Wolff's wedding rings to them.

In September 2010, Anje traveled to Israel with her two daughters, Joanne and Freda, in a group led by Pastor Rudy Fidel and his wife, Gina. Unknown to her, they had put the wheels into motion for her to be reunited with Ernst in Israel. The tour guide, Aharon Yahav, made contact with Ernst, making arrangements for the group to meet at his home.

An article on the Wolff family's reunion with the rings from a newspaper in Hebrew.

Ernst and Rivka live in a quaint apartment on the second floor of a senior's complex where the walls are covered with many beautiful works of art Ernst has created. It was a tearful reunion for the pair, who had the common bond of having no living family members. When Ernst commented, "And I have nothing to remember them by," Anje reached into her purse and pulled out the Wolff wedding rings. "How about these?" she said. As he held the rings of the aunt and uncle who had helped him when he escaped from Germany, he burst into tears.

Jewish Tribune article from November 24-2011

8 - The Jewish Tribune -November 24, 2011

NEWS > HOLOCAUST > FUNDRAISING >

Anje Van Tongeren had an emotional meeting with Ernst Wolf, whose family perished in the Holocaust, in Israel on a recent trip headed by Pastor Rudy Fidel of Faith Temple in Winnipeg. Anje was able to return two wedding rings that belonged to Ernst's family. She had held on to them until she was able to return them.

Righteous Christian brings wedding rings full circle

Rebeca Kuropatwa
Prairies Correspondent

WINNIPEG - Anje Van Tongeren, a Winnipegger and 'Righteous Among the Nations' candidate, was, at long last, able to return a couple's wedding rings (given to her family during the Holocaust).

Van Tongeren lived in Holland with her family during World War II. From a young age, she (and her mother) risked her life to help Jews escape the Nazis by joining the Dutch underground and forging documents for them.

"It felt very good, very right, to be able to give the Wolf Family back their rings," said Van Tongeren. "I had them, watched over them, for 70 years. Museums, Yad Vashem, B'nai Brith all wanted them, but I just couldn't do it. It was my responsibility to hold onto them until they could be returned to the Wolfs."

Van Tongeren probably saw Ernst Wolf last when he was about 17-years-old. They reunited on a recent trip to Israel.

"When I first saw Ernst, he stood there with his arms open. He was the only one of his five siblings who escaped.

"He was talking to me about how little he had to remember his family by. I had the rings with me in my wallet. I took them out and asked, 'Would you like these?' We both cried. Everyone in the room was crying."

Van Tongeren's Uncle Vin made a promise to Ernst's uncle and wife (Herman and Janet Wolf) - that he would hold onto the wedding rings for them, and would one day, when it was safe again, return them to his family.

"Everyone else had already been sent to Auschwitz," said Van Tongeren. "If they'd kept their rings on, they'd be lost forever."

Admitting she has not always been able to feel thankful, Van Toneregn said she does feel thankful today - "for being alive and being able to tell the story of the Holocaust. It makes me mad when people say it didn't happen. I was there. I know it happened.

"I always say G-d saved me for this day and age, to be able to tell people what happened - what it was like to be so hungry, to remain a good person when surrounded by evil, to survive."

Pastor Rudy Fidel of Faith Temple, along with his wife, Gina, led the trip to Israel wherein Van Tongeren and Wolf were reunited.

"Ernst Wolf lives close to Haifa, in Kiryat Bialik," said Fidel. "We had other things planned for the trip, but whatever it was, we just cancelled it. Nothing was more important than having Anje and Ernst have this time together. It was more than the highlight of the trip.

"One of the difficulties that came up was that Ernst doesn't speak English or hear well. He speaks Hebrew, Dutch and German, all interchangeably. So, while having trouble connecting with him just two weeks before we left for Israel, I called Ahron, our Israeli tour guide, and asked him to get in touch with Ernst and set up the meeting with Anje.

"It was a miracle that Anje was even able to go on this trip. A year ago she was diagnosed with thyroid cancer.... The fact that she is even able to speak - that she has a voice - is incredible.... She is a miracle.

"It's so important she's speaking to people, especially young people, so they have an image of someone real who lived through the Holocaust and is telling their story."

Reporters were present and cameras flashed as this event was covered by the *Jerusalem Post* and other newspapers. An interview of this event with Anje was aired in Canada on CBC TV in January 2011, entitled, "The Rings Came Home."

Anje visiting Israel to return the Wolff's wedding rings to Ernst in 2011.

Anje lives in Winnipeg. Her father passed away in Holland in 1996, and her husband Dick passed in November 2000. Still living in Groningen, Holland, are her cousin Henny Wjand (Sophie) and her childhood friend Janny ter Veld. Her friend Ernst Wolff still lives in Israel. A friend of Anje's, Lieselotte Oetgen (Mueller), who as a young seven-year-old girl survived the bombing of Hamburg, also lives in Winnipeg.

After the war, Martha La Costa initiated a move to have a street in Haren, in the province of Groningen, named after Eemke van der Veen, whose underground name was Hans Westerkamp.

Janny ter Veld remembers Hillie:

"During the war she was brave but also reckless. Once she was sitting in the train, and beside her was her handbag with pistols in it, which of course was very dangerous. Suddenly German soldiers came looking for illegal goods. She covered her lap with her plaid. When the soldiers demanded she open her luggage, she charmingly asked them to bring down her suitcase which was in the luggage rack. They did so, and when they inspected it, found only her underwear and things. And they left. Later she was betrayed and arrested, and sent to the concentration camp in Ravensbrück. She was very helpful to the other prisoners, but she died before the end of the war, as a courageous woman." (submitted November 22, 2012)

Janny and her husband Lammert.

Anje says, "Remembrance Day for me is still the most difficult day of the year, for I remember every day. For me it is not the remembrance of it that is difficult, but rather the forgiving and forgetting of it. The official ceremony with the lone trumpet sound and two minutes of silence just causes me to revisualize all the terror, insanity, and painful experiences. I don't want to remember; I would like to forget."

In 2009, Pastor Rudy Fidel and wife Gina of Winnipeg obtained a copy of Hillie's death certificate from Ravensbrück. Hillie Minnes died from "corpen schwachheit," or body weakness, probably due to starvation.

WORKS CITED

"Battle of Groningen," *Wikipedia*, August 30, 2011.
http://en.wikipedia.org/wiki/Battle¬_of_Groningen

Benz, Wolfgang. *The Holocaust: A German Historian Examines the Genocide.* New York: Columbia University Press, 1999.

Brome, Vincent. *The Spy.* New York, New York: Pyramid, 1961.

"Faith in Focus: The Hunger-Winter of 1944/45," The Reformed Churches of New Zealand, accessed, April 17, 2011, http://www.rcnzonline.com/fnf/a122.html

Frank, Anne. The Diary of a Young Girl. Doubleday, 1540 Broadway, New York 10036, 1967.

Gilbert, Martin. *Kristallnacht: Prelude to Destruction.* New York: HarperCollins Publishers, 2006.

Green, Gerald. Holocaust: Corgi Books, 1978.

Hartog, Kristen den and Tracy Kasaboski. *The Occupied Garden: A Family Memoir of War-Torn Holland.* New York: Thomas Dunne Books, 2008.

Haufler, Hervie. *The Spies Who Never Were: The True Story of the Nazi Spies Who Were Actually Allied Double Agents.* New York: New American Library, 2006.

"History of the Netherlands," *Wikipedia,* accessed Feb.20, 2010. http://en.wikipedia.org/wiki/history_of_the_Netherlands

"Holland, the Land of Water." Blog entry by Sandy Deden, accessed May 5, 2011. http://www.sandradeden.com/holland.htm

Jablonski, Edward. *Airwar.* New York: Doubleday, 1979.

"Jewish Groningen," *Wikipedia,* accessed 2009/12/28. http://en.wikipedia.org/wiki/Jewish_Groningen

Kidd, Margaretha. The Financing of the Resistance in the Netherlands 1940–1945. *Canadian Journal of Netherlandic Studies, XXIX(i),* 20–23. 2008.

Laqueur, Walter, and Richard Breitman. *Breaking the Silence: The German Who Exposed the Final Solution.* Waltham MA; Brandeis, 1994.

Niemeyer, Jan A. *Groningen, 1940–1945.* Groningen. Friese Pers Boekerij, 1983.

"Rotterdam Blitz," *Wikipedia,* accessed 2011/02/09. https://en.wikipedia.org/wiki/Rotterdam_Blitz

Ryan, Cornelius. *A Bridge Too Far: The Classic History of the Greatest Battle of World War II.* New York: Touchstone, 1974.

Saidel, Rochelle. *The Jewish Women of Ravensbrück Concentration Camp.* Madison: University of Wisconsin Press, 2004.

"Scholtenhuis," *Wikipedia,* last modified 2010/02/07. http://nl.wikipedia.org/wiki/scholtenhuis

Shirer, William L. *The Rise and Fall of the Third Reich: A History of Nazi Germany.* New York: Simon & Schuster, 1960.

Vance, Johnathan F. U*nlikely Soldiers: How Two Canadians Fought the Secret War Against Nazi Occupation.* Harper Collins 2008.

"War Over Holland," accessed 2011, http://www.waroverholland.nl/

"Wilhelmina of the Netherlands," *Wikipedia,* accessed 2013/10/30. http://en.wikipedia.org/wiki/Wilhelmina_of_the_Netherlands

LENORE EIDSE

Wolf, Diane L. *Beyond Anne Frank: Hidden Children and Postwar Families in Holland.* Berkeley, Los Angeles, and London: University of California Press, 2007.

World War II: The Definitive Visual History. New York: DK Publishing, 2009.

http://www.historylearningsite.co.uk/german invasion of holland.htm

http://en.wikipedia.org/wiki/Erika/song

http://www.groningerarchieven.nl/content.ph

(Photos only. Dutch script.)

Lenore Eidse has a great love of history and a thirst for knowledge. Her appetite for history was heightened by her project writing and editing *"Furrows in the Valley", 100 years of history for the Rural Municipality of Morris.* However, her writing career began earlier in the newspaper business and her feature news stories won first prize in the Canadian Weekly Newspaper Competition. *The House of Blood and Tears* is her first biographical novel. As she interviewed a close personal friend, she realized there was the potential for an amazing story; a story that needed to be told to the world, and she accepted the challenge.

Lenore and her husband live in Winnipeg, Canada. They have 4 children, 12 grandchildren, and 8 great grandchildren.

For more information
*and a **virtual tour** of*

THE HOUSE OF BLOOD
AND TEARS

go to:

HTTP://WWW.SCHOLTENHUIS.NL/

Printed in the United States
By Bookmasters